W9-CDT-884

A PUZZLE IN A PEAR TREE

ALSO BY PARNELL HALL

A Clue for the Puzzle Lady
Last Puzzle & Testament
Puzzled to Death

BANTAM BOOKS

New York Toronto

London Sydney

Auckland

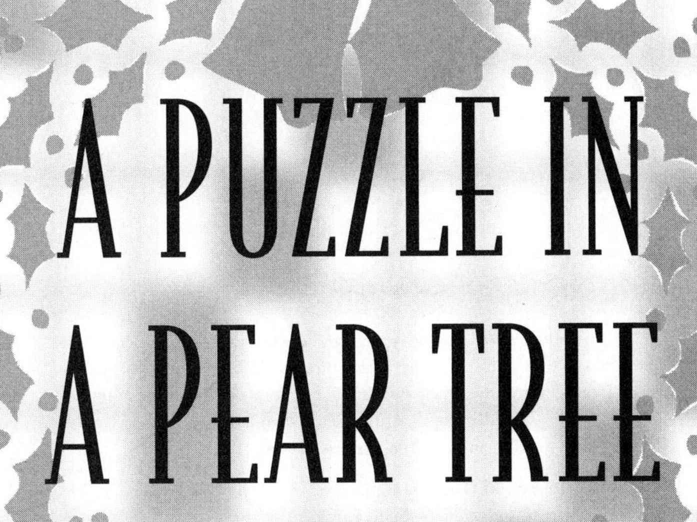

A PUZZLE IN A PEAR TREE

Parnell Hall

A PUZZLE IN A PEAR TREE

A Bantam Book / December 2002

Puzzles edited by Ellen Ripstein.

Book design by Glen Edelstein.

Library of Congress Cataloging-in-Publication Data
Hall, Parnell.
Puzzle in a pear tree / Parnell Hall.
p. cm.
ISBN 0-553-80242-9
1. Crossword puzzle makers—Fiction. 2. Women detectives—Fiction. 3. Aged
women—Fiction. 4. Acrostics—Fiction. I. Title.
PS3558.A37327 P78 2002
8123'.54—dc21 2002016423

Published simultaneously in the United States and Canada

Bantam Books are published by Bantam Books, a division of Random House, Inc. Its trademark, consisting of the words "Bantam Books" and the portrayal of a rooster, is Registered in U.S. Patent and Trademark Office and in other countries. Marca Registrada. Bantam Books, 1540 Broadway, New York, New York 10036.

PRINTED IN THE UNITED STATES OF AMERICA

BVG 10 9 8 7 6 5 4 3 2 1

For Don,
who suggested
the live Nativity.

ANOTHER KIND OF PUZZLE

An acrostic is a puzzle in which the answers to the clues are written over numbered dashes, and then the letters are transferred to correspondingly numbered squares in a grid. The filled grid forms a quotation. The first letters of the answered words spell out the name of the author and the title of the work.

Needless to say, the Puzzle Lady has never solved an acrostic, and can use all the help she can get.

A PUZZLE IN A PEAR TREE

"NO, NO, NO," RUPERT WINSTON CRIED, SILENCING THE PIANO AND vaulting up onto the stage with all the spry grace of a much younger man. Rupert tugged at his turtleneck, a habit he had when not particularly pleased. Which, in Cora Felton's humble opinion, was almost all the time. In the few rehearsals she'd had, Cora had come to detest the *"innovative and gifted"* director, as the *Bakerhaven Gazette* had termed him, who had left the *"stifling constraints of the Broadway stage"* in order to *"ply his craft in the liberating atmosphere of an enlightened village."*

Although no linguist, Cora Felton didn't have to be hit over the head with a condescending remark to recognize one. Rupert Winston had Cora's back up before she'd even met him. Being tapped to appear in Rupert's Christmas pageant was the last thing in the world Cora Felton wanted. Had she been able to think of any polite way to get out of it, Cora would have done so.

Had she known what rehearsals would be like, an impolite way would have sufficed.

"*Miss* Felton." Rupert Winston extracted his hand from his black turtleneck, entwined his long, slender fingers together, and rolled his steel-gray eyes to the heavens, as if invoking the deities to witness his tribulations in dealing with mere mortals, and inferior ones at that. "You are a *milkmaid.* A hearty, robust milkmaid, fresh from the fields, sunny and bright and imbued with a lust for life. If you are to sing the solo line, I have to *hear* the solo line. You cannot mumble it into your sleeve."

Cora Felton set down her wooden milking stool, fixed the director with an evil eye. Rupert Winston was, in Cora's humble opinion, one of those marginally famous men who affected rudeness as a sign of genius. The good citizens of Bakerhaven might be taken in, but not Cora. Particularly since Rupert invariably singled her out for abuse. Cora, who appeared in breakfast cereal commercials as the Puzzle Lady, suspected this was largely because she was on TV and he wasn't.

Cora was sorely tempted to remind Rupert that she hadn't *got* a sleeve, this *wasn't* the dress rehearsal, and her milkmaid costume had *yet* to be sewn. She stifled the impulse and glanced around the stage, where the seven other maids a-milking stood holding their stools. "You're absolutely right, Rupert," she said sweetly. "I'm totally wrong for this part. I'm sure any of the other milkmaids could do better. I understand *completely* why you'd wish to replace me."

Rupert Winston looked shocked. "Miss Felton. Did I say any such thing? Of course not. You're perfect for the part. It's just a question of pulling a performance out of you."

Cora bit back a groan. Were there any way to agree with this fool and get on with it, Cora would have done so, but she knew from experience Rupert loved to pontificate. Under the guise of giving direction, he could run through his entire Broadway résumé at the drop of a hat. Already, she could see the other actors emerging from the wings to listen. They soon filled the stage. The piece was *The Twelve Days of Christmas,* complete with pipers piping, drummers drumming, and so on. Cora could barely calculate how many actors were in the show, let alone the odds of all of them ever doing it right.

"I'm *not* perfect for the part," she protested. "I'm dead wrong for the part. I'm way too old. Just like the rest of your milkmaids—no offense, ladies—but your maids a-milking should be rosy-cheeked country girls in fetching peasant blouses."

"You're saying you can't work without your costume?"

"No, I'm saying someone else should be wearing it. It's just bad casting." Cora pointed stage left, where her niece, Sherry Carter, stood in a cluster of nine attractive young women. "Look at your ladies dancing. They're all young and pretty. *They* should be the lusty milkmaids, and we old biddies should be the refined ladies dancing."

Rupert didn't get mad. The director never got mad. Instead, he exhibited, as he always did, a tolerant amusement at the misguided views of the unenlightened.

"Yes, Miss Felton," he replied. "That is how it is usually cast. Which is precisely why I have *not* done so here. This skit is deliberately 'miscast,' as you would characterize it, for, one would hope, humorous effect. Which, as you might have gathered, is the same reason for so many entrances and exits. Which is also why rehearsal time is so crucial. I hope I don't have to spend too much of it reassuring you that you are right for your part."

"I thought you were the one telling me I *wasn't* doing it right," Cora countered.

Rupert Winston chuckled. "Well, there is a huge difference between not doing it right and not being right for it. Trust me, you're right for it."

Harvey Beerbaum stuck his oar in, as the annoying, pedantic cruciverbalist was wont to do. "Come on, Cora," he chided. "If I can be a lord a-leaping, surely you can be a maid a-milking."

That was hard to argue with. The sight of bald, portly Harvey leaping about the stage was so ridiculous, if he was willing to make a fool of himself, how could anyone else object?

"Can we get on with it?" Becky Baldwin griped. "I'm meeting a client in half an hour."

"Did you hear that?" Rupert Winston said. "Becky has only a half an hour. So this is hardly time to be worried about *our* motivation."

Cora Felton bit her lip. She hadn't said a damn thing about her motivation, but she couldn't point that out to Rupert without starting another argument, which would seem boorishly insensitive and inconsiderate, since Becky had to go.

Cora resented that too. Becky Baldwin—young, attractive, and as fashionable as ever in a scoop-neck sweater and pale blue skirt and vest—might have actually had a client, but as far as Cora was concerned, Becky's pointing it out served only to remind everyone that she was a lawyer on the one hand, and a Star on the other.

Which, in the pageant, she was. Becky had been cast as the young woman in the song, the one who receives all the season's bounty. In Rupert Winston's version of the piece, Becky started each verse alone on stage, singing *"On the whatever day of Christmas, my true love gave to me,"* and then reacting to the stampede of gifts that surrounded her. A plum role, one that Cora felt should by rights have gone to her niece. But, as always happened between Sherry and Cora, Cora was the one pushed out front.

Rupert turned to the piano, where Mr. Hodges, the high school music teacher, was dutifully waiting to play. "*You* don't have to go anywhere, do you?"

"I have a chorus rehearsal at four-thirty."

"Oh, for goodness' sakes!"

Mr. Hodges, a thin-faced, sallow man with a hawk nose, did not take kindly to the suggestion that *he* would be responsible for breaking up rehearsal. "*The Twelve Days of Christmas* is *not* the only piece in the pageant, you know," he retorted huffily. "The bulk of the show still happens to be the school choir."

"Yes," Rupert snorted. "Standing and singing. They don't *move.* What's to rehearse?"

Mr. Hodges had no desire to get into *that* argument. "We lose the gym at four-fifteen anyway for varsity practice," he pointed out acidly.

The Christmas pageant was being performed on the stage in the Bakerhaven High gymnasium, where it shared the space with the basketball team. It also shared the stage with the upcoming high school production of Anton Chekhov's *The Seagull,* so the English village square Becky Baldwin was performing in looked suspiciously like a Russian country manor. In a corner of the gym, the Bakerhaven High tech director, a wiry young man in splattered overalls and work shirt, was diligently if somewhat messily painting scenery flats to transform one into the other.

"Then we can't be wasting time now," Rupert declared virtuously, as if he hadn't been the one prolonging the squabble. "Let's take it from the twelfth day, get a look at everyone. Aaron Grant? Where's Aaron Grant?"

The young *Bakerhaven Gazette* reporter, who was standing onstage beside Sherry Carter, put up his hand and said, "Here, Rupert."

"Aaron, we're going to take it from your line, the twelve drummers drumming. Do you have your drummers ready?"

"I've got nine of them."

"Only nine?"

"That's the trouble with afternoon rehearsals," Aaron said. "People have to work."

"Well, then," Rupert said with heavy irony, "are your *nine* drummers drumming ready?"

"Yes, except we haven't got the drums yet."

"I *know* you haven't got the drums yet. This is for choreography." Having made that pronouncement, Rupert instantly contradicted it by demanding, "What props *do* we have? I know we don't have the swans and the geese, but at least we have the pear tree."

Rupert looked around and spotted Jimmy Potter, the librarian's son, sitting on the apron of the stage, listening attentively. Jimmy, a tall, gawky boy of college age who had always been a little slow, was just thrilled to death to be part of the pageant, and he had, as usual, a goofy grin on his face. However, he had nothing in his hands.

"Jimmy!" Rupert cried. "Where's your pear tree? How can you play your part without your pear tree?"

Edith Potter, the librarian and one of the maids a-milking, pushed out of the pack to defend her boy, but Jimmy wasn't upset.

"It's offstage, Mr. Rupert." Jimmy pointed stage left. "You want me to get it?"

"No, Jimmy. I just want you to have your tree for the run-through. I want you to come on carrying it, so you get used to carrying it. Okay, places, please, people. Let's take it from the top of the last verse, starting with Becky's line."

The actors took their positions in the wings.

Rupert called, "And, Miss Felton. Project, project, *pro-ject*!"

Cora, in the wings, raised her prop and muttered to Sherry, "I'd like to *pro-ject* this milking stool. Can you guess where?"

"Cora! Think of your image."

"I'm thinking of *his* image. And how I could change it with this damn stool."

"Are we ready?" Rupert Winston yelled from out front. "And . . . begin!"

The pianist played a note.

Becky Baldwin, alone on stage, rolled her eyes toward the piano. Becky was, Sherry had to admit, quite good. The expression on her face in response to that lone note was priceless. This being the twelfth day of gifts, one could scarcely wonder what her lunatic lover had sent her now. In a voice tinged with resignation and dread, Becky sang, " *'On the twelfth day of Christmas, my true love gave to me,'* " then with hands upraised, shrank back from the onslaught.

Aaron and eight other men entered from stage left, pantomiming drums.

" *'Twelve drummers drumming,'* " sang Aaron.

The drummers marched on Becky Baldwin as if she were Richmond, then turned and sang in chorus, " *'Eleven pipers piping.'* "

The pipers, eight strong without pipes, marched on from stage right, singing along with the drummers.

Ten lords a-leaping—actually eight, not leaping very high—

emerged from all sides of the stage. Had it been the tenth day of Christmas, the solo would have been sung by Harvey Beerbaum. As it was, the lords sang in chorus along with the pipers and drummers.

Nine ladies dancing, led by Sherry Carter, waltzed on from stage left.

Eight maids a-milking swooped in from stage right, sat on their stools, and had just begun to pantomime milking when the seven swans a-swimming (six men who would be carrying cardboard cutout swans, which had not yet been made), followed directly by the six geese a-laying (five in number, not laying, and without geese), sent the milkmaids diving for cover.

As always, everyone got a breather during the retarded line " *'Five golden rings.'* " The rings, presented on velvet pillows borne by liveried servants (pillows, rings, and livery yet to come), were paraded in a circle around Becky Baldwin. She broke free just in time to be confronted with four calling birds, three French hens, and two turtledoves (birds, hens, and doves to be made later).

The chorus reached a crescendo. All turned toward stage left.

" *'AND A PARTRIDGE IN A PEAR TREE!'* " everyone sang lustily.

Jimmy Potter, pleased as punch, marched onstage, carrying the pear tree. It was actually a small artificial fir tree with papier-mâché pears, but Jimmy couldn't have been prouder. He strode up to Becky Baldwin and presented her with it.

He certainly wasn't prepared for what happened next.

"Jimmy!" Rupert Winston shrieked. "Where's the partridge? Don't tell me you've lost the partridge! It's the only bird we've got!"

Jimmy, completely taken aback, gawked at the pear tree. "Gee, Mr. Winston. It was right here."

Rupert Winston leaped onto the stage. "All right!" he cried. "Who's been screwing around with our props?"

"I . . . I . . . I . . ." Jimmy Potter stuttered.

Rupert ignored him. "Jesse!" he bellowed. "Where the hell is my tech crew!"

Jesse Virdon, the paint-smeared tech director who had been

working on the flats, put down his brush. "Whaddya want?" he said, sauntering up.

"What do I want?" Rupert stormed. "You're my stage manager. Where the hell's my prop?"

Jesse shrugged. "Dunno. Been out here painting. Never went backstage."

"Well, who did?"

Alfred, a gawky teenager with black-rimmed glasses and an unfortunate nose, emerged from the wings, protesting as he came, practically stuttering in his desire to distance himself from the theft. "I didn't see anything, Mr. Winston. I was in the light booth. I never saw the tree."

Cora Felton pushed forward. "Wait a minute. What's *that*?"

There was something red among the green pine needles.

Jimmy turned the tree.

Hidden among the branches was a red envelope. It was greeting-card size. The back was facing out, and the flap had been tucked in.

Jimmy Potter blinked at it in amazement.

"What the hell is that?" Rupert scoffed. "A ransom note for the partridge?"

1 J	2 R	3 B		4 R	5 E	6 G		7 O	8 F	9 I	10 P	11 C	12 U		13 W	14 X	15 N	
16 Q	17 L	18 S		19 S	20 P	21 D	22 V	23 H	24 N	25 W	26 G		27 P	28 X	29 J	30 E		31 P
	32 S	33 H		34 J	35 N	36 C	37 P	38 A		39 L	40 X		41 W	42 S		43 K	44 O	45 G
	46 K	47 P	48 G		49 P	50 L	51 C	52 G	53 V	54 M	55 Q	56 A	57 X	58 T	59 N	60 H		61 W
62 G	63 X	64 U		65 O		66 P	67 A	68 M	69 G	70 S		71 I	72 N		73 H	74 B		75 J
76 X		77 D	78 G	79 W		80 J	81 T	82 B	83 U	84 G		85 F	86 V	87 E		88 W	89 Q	90 U
91 S	92 L	93 J		94 B	95 Q	96 M	97 J	98 C	99 I	100 Q	101 S	102 X	103 G		104 L	105 P	106 R	
107 F	108 U	109 K	110 N	111 G	112 L		113 I	114 M	115 F	116 Q		117 I	118 O	119 C	120 D	121 S	122 W	
123 C	124 G	125 H	126 J	127 K		128 K	129 H	130 T		131 C	132 D	133 B		134 S	135 E	136 D	137 M	138 H
139 V		140 M	141 A	142 F	143 X		144 T	145 N	146 X	147 U		148 C	149 T	150 I		151 A	152 H	153 X
154 C		155 T	156 V		157 T	158 A	159 B	160 M	161 E	162 C	163 P	164 I		165 V	166 R	167 F	168 T	

Clue	Answer blanks
A. Christmas stealer	38 158 67 56 151 141
B. Pressing	159 82 94 133 3 74
C. Don't cry for her, Argentina (2 wds.)	154 98 36 131 148 51 119 11 162 123
D. Bright	21 132 136 120 77
E. Fire a gun	161 135 5 87 30
F. Evil	85 8 107 115 142 167
G. "The Fall of the ___" (3 wds.)	62 111 6 84 45 78 26 48 103 69 124 52
H. "___ a home" (3 wds.)	152 23 138 73 125 60 33 129
I. Broken	71 117 113 99 9 164 150
J. Carton of sorts (2 wds.)	97 80 34 1 93 29 75 126
K. Mad	43 109 128 127 46
L. Tails counterpart (2 wds.)	112 92 50 17 104 39
M. Warming	54 160 114 140 96 137 68
N. Applause	72 59 145 15 24 35 110
O. "The ___" (Grisham novel)	7 65 44 118
P. Bullets	49 66 163 10 105 20 27 31 47 37
Q. More shipshape	100 116 89 16 55 95
R. Rooney or Griffith	2 166 106 4
S. Fought	101 42 19 91 32 134 70 18 121
T. Dancing like Chubby Checker	130 144 81 168 155 58 149 157
U. "Shake, ___, and roll"	90 108 147 64 83 12
V. Repeats exactly	53 22 86 156 165 139
W. Yelled	122 88 13 79 61 25 41
X. Naughty, naughty! (3 wds.)	57 28 63 153 102 76 146 143 40 14

Cora lifted the red envelope off the branch. She opened the flap, reached inside.

Frowned.

Sherry, at her elbow, said, "What's the matter?"

Cora pulled the contents from the envelope.
It was not a card. Just a folded piece of paper.
Cora unfolded it.
Scowled.
"Well, what is it?" Rupert demanded.
Cora turned the paper around for them to see.

2

HARVEY BEERBAUM SUCKED IN HIS BREATH. "CORA, LOOK WHAT that is."

Sherry, realizing it was entirely likely her aunt had no idea whatsoever what the puzzle was, jumped in. "Look, Cora. An acrostic. You've never created an acrostic, have you?"

"Can't say as I have," Cora said smoothly, grateful for the hint. "How about you, Harvey?"

"I've never written one, but I can certainly solve it. Let's see. . . . As I recall, the words in the grid are a quotation, and the first letters of the clues give the name of the author and the title of the work."

"First letters of the clues?" Becky Baldwin said. "What do you mean by that?"

"I mean the *solution* to the clues, of course," Harvey explained pedantically, delighted at the opportunity to do so. "For instance, clue *A* is *Christmas stealer,* and it's six letters. That would almost have to be *Grinch.* As in *How the Grinch Stole Christmas!* So you write the word *Grinch* in the blanks, then transfer the letters to the numbered squares in the grid: *G* is *38, r* is *158, i* is *67,* and so forth.

The letters in the grid will form the quote. And the first letter of the author's name will be *G.*"

Harvey positively beamed. "See what I mean? And then the first letter of the solution to clue *B* would be the second letter in the author's name. The clue is *pressing,* and it's six letters." He leaned in insinuatingly. "Care to have a go at it, Cora?"

Cora Felton winced. Lately Harvey Beerbaum had grown annoyingly suspicious of her puzzle-making expertise. Having absolutely no puzzle-making expertise, she was somewhat hard put to deal with this. "No, I wouldn't, Harvey, thank you very much. I'd be happy to work on it at home, but solving puzzles was never my talent, and I don't need the pressure of umpty-million actors watching me do it."

"Fine. Take it home and do it," Rupert Winston directed with elaborate calm. The lack of volume in his voice was positively chilling, gave him the appearance of a cobra about to strike. "Now. If you don't mind, could we go back to rehearsing our play?"

Rupert turned to the cast. "All right, let's try it again, people. And this time, drummers drumming, could we all march together, please? You start on the left foot, on *twelve.* I know you don't *have* twelve, but when you *sing* twelve." He sang to demonstrate. "It's *'Twelve drummers drumming.'* Left, right, left together, turn, as you overlap the *'Eleven pipers piping.'* Same thing, pipers, in unison, left, right, left. Joining with the drummers drumming marching in place as *'Ten lords a-leaping.'* And lords, remember, we leap on *'ten'* and we leap on *'leap.'* Think of it as *'Leap, lords a-leap.'* It's, leap, one, two, leap.

"And Mr. Beerbaum. Your leap is a half beat behind everyone else, you're on the wrong foot, and you barely get off the ground." Rupert pinched Harvey on the cheek. "I love it, you're perfect, don't change!

"Ladies dancing. Miss Carter, could we please remember, we are going here for a combination of genteel sophistication and amoral slut. So if you could add a slightly breathy quality into your line.

And, remember, it's *'Nine,'* two, three, *spin,* two, three. That's your waltz step, and your beats are *'nine'* and *'dance.'* "

Rupert turned to the maids a-milking. "Miss Felton, I heard you this time, more's the pity. Somewhat remarkable, since you were singing in chorus. Perhaps you felt *freer* to emote in the midst of other voices. This is not necessarily desirable. Let me attempt to explain. The words were assigned notes as a clear hint as to the pitch one is expected to sing. In case you need a guide, they happen to be the *same* notes sung by the ladies dancing you just heard. It would help the show *immensely* if you were to sing *those* notes, instead of inventing new ones of your own. If necessary, I could have the piano play the melody along with you, though it will stand out like a sore thumb. But not nearly as badly as if you sing it to the tune of the latest beer commercial."

Cora said, "Yes, Mr. Winston," rather contritely, but she actually looked rather smug.

Sherry caught her eye and Cora winked.

Sherry understood perfectly.

Listening to Rupert Winston might be torture, but it was a walk in the park compared with trying to solve an acrostic puzzle.

3

"WHAT'S A SIX-LETTER WORD FOR *PRESSING*?"

"I have no idea."

Cora swore. "You're a big help."

Sherry looked down at her aunt in exasperation. "*I'm* a big help? You sit there and tell me *I'm* a big help?"

Sherry was standing on a step stool stringing lights on the Christmas tree.

Cora was lounging on the couch, scowling furiously at the acrostic. "What are you so touchy about?" she retorted. "I'm the one who had the bad rehearsal."

"Uh-huh."

"You're not supposed to agree with me," Cora said indignantly. "You're supposed to point out we *all* had a bad rehearsal, and Rupert Winston picks on *everyone*."

"Almost everyone," Sherry muttered. She hopped down from the stool, moved it, climbed back up.

"Oh?" Cora said. "You're having a Becky Baldwin snit? Trust me, it's not worth it. I've had more snits in my day over some woman or other, and, believe me, they all wind up the same way. The woman always proves to be far less special than she seems."

"I'm not having a Becky Baldwin snit," Sherry said.

This was only partly true. Becky Baldwin had been Aaron Grant's childhood sweetheart. Since Becky had come back to Bakerhaven, she and Sherry had kept up a running rivalry.

"Oh?" Cora said. "Then what *are* you doing?"

"I'm trying to trim our Christmas tree. Without much help."

"Well, what do you want me to do? There's no room for me on the ladder."

"Could you hand me the silver balls?"

Cora sighed, heaved herself off the couch, and fetched the carton of ornaments from the cardboard box by the tree. She extracted a ball, passed it up to her niece.

Sherry looked at it. "Where's the hook?"

"What hook?"

"The hook you hang it with. It must be in the carton."

"Oh." Cora rummaged, held one up. "Is this it?"

"Yes, of course." Sherry accepted the hook. "Didn't you ever trim a tree?"

"My husbands always did it. Except Henry. He was Jewish." Cora frowned. "Or was it Frank?"

"Aunt Cora."

"Come on, Sherry. Help me solve the puzzle?"

"Cora, you hate puzzles."

"Yeah, I know. But this isn't a puzzle, it's a *mystery.* Someone sent us the puzzle as a clue. Don't you want to know why?"

"I'd rather trim the tree."

"What's the matter? Can't you do acrostics?"

"Of course I can do acrostics. There's nothing to it. It's just a pain, because you have to keep transferring the letters from the clue list into the grid."

"I'll transfer the letters," Cora promised. "Just tell me what they are."

"Won't it keep till I get off the ladder?"

"Hell, no. I'm racing Harvey Beerbaum," Cora protested.

"So what? Do you care if he wins?"

"Not really. But that's not the point."

"What's the point?"

"We don't know who stuck that envelope in the pear tree, but it had to be someone who has a working knowledge of puzzles."

"So?"

"So, what if it's Harvey?"

"Oh, come on."

"What's wrong with that? We know Harvey suspects me of being a fake. The old prune would like nothing better than to expose me. Why not give me a puzzle I can't solve?"

"Don't be silly. If that were his plan, he'd have the two of you working together."

"He would have, if Jimmy hadn't made copies," Cora pointed out. After rehearsal, Jimmy Potter had raced the acrostic to the high school business office and used the copy machine.

"Even so, it's a big stretch."

"Oh, really? Do you remember what he did? He took one look and said the answer to the first clue is *Grinch,* what's the answer to the second? Pretty convenient, getting the first answer just like that. Unless he wrote the puzzle."

"Nonsense," Sherry scoffed. "*Christmas stealer,* six letters, almost has to be *Grinch.* Anyone would get it."

"Is that so?" Cora countered. "I was thinking it might be *klepto.*"

"Well, *almost* anyone."

Cora handed Sherry the last ball from the carton and scooped up the puzzle again. "All right, how about *blank a home*?"

"Blank a home?"

"Yeah. *Blank a home.* Three words."

"That would be *blank, blank, blank a home.*"

"I don't care if it's *blankety-blank a home.* What is it?"

"You can't do it that way," Sherry said. "You have to look at the whole puzzle. The general setup. See where things are going to intersect. You can't pull an answer out of thin air."

"Harvey did."

"Tinsel."

"Huh?"

Sherry pointed. "Hand me the tinsel."

Cora tore open the packet, thrust the strands of tinsel at her niece. "Hey, if you don't wanna help me, fine. No skin off my nose. I thought you were the one who didn't want me to blow my image."

"I merely pointed out you'd lose your TV ads, which at the present time are paying for this house. Without that, I don't know what we'd do."

"I'd probably have to get married again." Cora sighed. "I'd really hate to. A husband can be such a nuisance."

Headlights flickered through the frosty front window.

"My God!" Cora said. "What did I tell you? It's Beerbaum, come to trip me up with the puzzle."

"Don't be silly. It's probably Aaron."

Cora darted for the window. Her mouth fell open. "It's not Aaron. It's Chief Harper! I knew it. I knew this would happen. The puzzle's connected to a crime, and the chief's gonna want me to solve it."

"Well, you're good at solving crimes."

"The *puzzle,* I mean," Cora wailed. She looked at Sherry, whose eyes were twinkling. "Oh, you can be so exasperating when you want to. The point is, the cops are gonna want me to crack the puzzle, and I can't do it."

While they were talking, the Bakerhaven chief of police got out of his cruiser, plodded through the snow toward their door.

"Here he comes. Sherry, what do I do when he asks me about the puzzle?"

"He's not going to ask you about the puzzle."

"Then what's he doing here—collecting for the policemen's ball?"

"That's a lot more likely than asking you to solve an acrostic that turned up in the Christmas pageant pear tree."

The doorbell rang.

"All right," Cora said. "Don't say I didn't warn you."

"Fine. I stand warned." Sherry marched to the door, flung it open.

Chief Harper stood on their front steps in his heavy winter coat. As an afterthought, he pulled his hat off, stamped the snow off his boots. "Oh, there you are," he said. He pushed past Sherry into the living room, stomped up to her aunt.

"So," he demanded. "You done the puzzle yet?"

4

Cora Felton smiled sweetly, tried to avoid shooting an I-told-you-so glance at her niece. "Why, Chief Harper, whatever puzzle do you mean?"

"You know what puzzle. The one you got this afternoon at the pageant rehearsal."

"Oh, that. Technically, Chief, it's not a puzzle, it's an acrostic."

Chief Harper ran his hand through his graying hair and snorted. "I don't care if it's a puzzle, a riddle, or a knock-knock joke. I need your help with it."

"Of course," Sherry interceded heartily before her aunt could respond. "We were just talking about it. Cora would have done it by now, but we were trimming the tree." Sherry took the chief's arm, guided him into the kitchen. "Sit down, have a cup of cocoa, we'll be right with you. You fill Cora in on why you're interested, I'll pencil in the answers we were just discussing."

Chief Harper shrugged off his overcoat, hung it over the back of his chair. He sat, put his hat on the table. "I don't need you to solve the puzzle. Or acrostic. Or whatever." He reached in his pocket and pulled out a folded piece of paper. "Harvey Beerbaum's already done it for me. So you can save yourself the trouble. Unless you want to double-check him."

"Oh, I'm sure Harvey's right," Cora said. She hoped her voice didn't betray how relieved she was. She slid into a chair opposite the chief. "So what do you want from me?"

1 J C	2 R A	3 B N	■	4 R Y	5 E O	6 G U	■	7 O F	8 F I	9 I G	10 P U	11 C R	12 U E	■	13 W O	14 X U	15 N T	■
16 Q T	17 L H	18 S E	■	19 S M	20 P I	21 D S	22 V C	23 H H	24 N I	25 W E	26 G F	■	27 P T	28 X H	29 J A	30 E T	■	31 P I
■	32 S A	33 H M	■	34 J G	35 N O	36 C I	37 P N	38 A G	■	39 L T	40 X O	■	41 W D	42 S O	■	43 K A	44 O R	45 G E
■	46 K Y	47 P O	48 G U	■	49 P A	50 L P	51 C P	52 G R	53 V E	54 M H	55 Q E	56 A N	57 X S	58 T I	59 N V	60 H E	■	61 W T
62 G H	63 X A	64 U T	■	65 O I	■	66 P M	67 A I	68 M G	69 G H	70 S T	■	71 I D	72 N O	■	73 H I	74 B T	■	75 J T
76 X O	■	77 D Y	78 G O	79 W U	■	80 J G	81 T I	82 B R	83 U L	84 G S	■	85 F W	86 V H	87 E O	■	88 W H	89 Q A	90 U R
91 S B	92 L O	93 J R	■	94 B G	95 Q R	96 M I	97 J E	98 C V	99 I A	100 Q N	101 S C	102 X E	103 G S	■	104 L A	105 P N	106 R D	■
107 F C	108 U A	109 K N	110 N N	111 G O	112 L T	■	113 I M	114 M A	115 F K	116 Q E	■	117 I A	118 O M	119 C E	120 D N	121 S D	122 W S	■
123 C N	124 G E	125 H V	126 J E	127 K R	■	128 K G	129 H E	130 T T	■	131 C T	132 D H	133 B E	■	134 S T	135 E H	136 D I	137 M N	138 H G
139 V S	■	140 M T	141 A H	142 F E	143 X Y	■	144 T W	145 N A	146 X N	147 U T	■	148 C A	149 T N	150 I D	■	151 A C	152 H O	153 X M
154 C E	■	155 T T	156 V O	■	157 T G	158 A R	159 B U	160 M E	161 E S	162 C O	163 P M	164 I E	■	165 V E	166 R N	167 F D	168 T S	■

A. Christmas stealer — G R I N C H (38 158 67 56 151 141)

B. Pressing — U R G E N T (159 82 94 133 3 74)

C. Don't cry for her, Argentina (2 wds.) — E V I T A P E R O N (154 98 36 131 148 51 119 11 162 123)

D. Bright — S H I N Y (21 132 136 120 77)

E. Fire a gun — S H O O T (161 135 5 87 30)

F. Evil — W I C K E D (85 8 107 115 142 167)

G. "The Fall of the ___" (3 wds.) — H O U S E O F U S H E R (62 111 6 84 45 78 26 48 103 69 124 52)

H. "___ a home" (3 wds.) — O H G I V E M E (152 23 138 73 125 60 33 129)

I. Broken — D A M A G E D (71 117 113 99 9 164 150)

J. Carton of sorts (2 wds.) — E G G C R A T E (97 80 34 1 93 29 75 126)

Clue	Answer	Numbers
K. Mad	A N G R Y	43 109 128 127 46
L. Tails counterpart (2 wds.)	T O P H A T	112 92 50 17 104 39
M. Warming	H E A T I N G	54 160 114 140 96 137 68
N. Applause	O V A T I O N	72 59 145 15 24 35 110
O. "The ___" (Grisham novel)	F I R M	7 65 44 118
P. Bullets	A M M U N I T I O N	49 66 163 10 105 20 27 31 47 37
Q. More shipshape	N E A T E R	100 116 89 16 55 95
R. Rooney or Griffith	A N D Y	2 166 106 4
S. Fought	C O M B A T T E D	101 42 19 91 32 134 70 18 121
T. Dancing like Chubby Checker	T W I S T I N G	130 144 81 168 155 58 149 157
U. "Shake, ___, and roll"	R A T T L E	90 108 147 64 83 12
V. Repeats exactly	E C H O E S	53 22 86 156 165 139
W. Yelled	S H O U T E D	122 88 13 79 61 25 41
X. Naughty, naughty! (3 wds.)	S H A M E O N Y O U	57 28 63 153 102 76 146 143 40 14

"I want your opinion. Here, take a look."

Cora took the sheet of paper with the solved acrostic, and had an instant of panic when she realized she didn't know how to read it. She squinted, saw the grid was composed of words, although that wasn't totally obvious, since some of them were broken in the middle. They all seemed to end with a black square, however. But what was the bit about author and title?

It occurred to Cora that she was taking too long and Chief Harper would notice.

He did.

"Yeah, I know," Chief Harper said. "Impossible to read, aren't they? I had Harvey write the solution out. It goes:

"Can you figure out the mischief
That I am going to do?

Are you apprehensive
That I might do it to you?

"Girls who harbor grievances
And cannot make amends
Never get the things they want
And come to gruesome ends.

"Nice, huh? The author is *Guess Who?* The title is *Death of an Actress.*"

Cora Felton sucked in her breath.

Chief Harper nodded grimly. "Yeah. You see why I came to you? There's no way to tell if this is a threat or a prank. Until I know one way or another, I've got to take this seriously."

"And you want my opinion?"

"Absolutely."

"On whether this is a real threat?"

"For starters. If so, who's at risk?"

"Oh, for goodness' sakes," Sherry said, sliding a cup of cocoa in front of the chief.

"What's the matter?" Chief Harper said.

"Don't you think you're overreacting? That poem is doggerel. It sounds like it came from a grade-B slasher movie. What reason is there to think it's anything else?"

"It could be William Butler Yeats," the chief insisted unexpectedly, "I still can't afford to ignore it. So, Cora, if you have any insights at all, I'd be happy to hear 'em."

"Well," Cora said. "The title is *Death of an Actress.* That would seem to let the men out."

"Brilliant," Chief Harper grumbled. "I'm sure glad I drove all the way over here for that."

"You want my opinion or not?"

"I want your opinion. I just didn't know it was going to be so illuminating."

"Well, *Death of an Actress* is rather vague. Now, if it had been *Death of a Director* . . ."

"Not getting along well with our *new* celebrity?"

"Are you implying that I'm jealous?"

"I gather there's some resentment."

"Heaven forbid," Cora snapped. "But I am not a singer. I am not even an actress. I get roped into this, pushed out front, and constantly ridiculed. Does that sound like your idea of a good time?"

"You're saying if Mr. Winston winds up dead, I should look no further?"

"I might even plead guilty."

Chief Harper sipped his cocoa. "Anyway, I spoke to Jimmy Potter. He never saw the envelope till he got onstage. Jimmy says Rupert was going to have a run-through, but first he had to work with the milkmaids because they weren't very good."

"Thanks a lot."

"You're a milkmaid? I should have known."

"Well, aren't you the soul of tact."

"I mean I should have known from your resentment of Rupert Winston. Anyway, first Winston worked with the milkmaids. Then he had the run-through of the whole megillah, starting with the twelve whatever. Just before the run-through he asked Jimmy where the partridge was. Jimmy ran backstage, got the tree off the props table. There was a lot of confusion with all the actors getting offstage and taking their places. He didn't notice the partridge had been swapped with the puzzle. No one noticed till he brought it onstage."

"So?"

"So, the last time Jimmy saw the bird was just before rehearsal, when he checked to see that the pear tree was there. He didn't have it when Rupert worked with the milkmaids, and he didn't have it when everyone was onstage while Rupert was giving notes. According to Jimmy, all that time the pear tree was sitting on a props table backstage right near the stage-left stairs."

"Oh."

"Which means while the actors were all onstage, anyone could have snuck up the stairs and made the substitution."

Cora nodded. "Works for me. If you want my opinion, it sounds more like a schoolgirl than a killer."

"Yes, I know. That's my opinion also. Right now we're saying, What if it isn't? What if it's a genuine death threat? What should we do then?"

"Close down the pageant?" Cora said it hopefully.

"I can't do that. Not on the basis of something that's probably a prank. What I have to do is take certain precautions. Like I said at the beginning. If this is a genuine death threat, who's at risk?"

"Any of the women in the show."

"That reasoning is not up to your usual high standard. Wouldn't you agree that the most likely person is Becky Baldwin?"

"Oh, give me a break," Sherry Carter said.

"As I understand it, Becky's the star of the show. The one who gets all the gifts. The one who sings about her true love sending to me, or however it goes."

"There's another twenty or thirty actresses in the show. Why couldn't it be any of them?"

"It could, but Becky's the star. And the puzzle in the pear tree was given to *her.* That's on the one hand. On the other, you have to figure why would anyone *want* to kill anyone in the show?"

"You think someone is jealous because Becky has the starring role?" Sherry said.

"You miss my point," Chief Harper said glumly. "Becky Baldwin is the type of woman who inspires strong feelings. You either love her or hate her. You, for example, don't particularly like her. But I can't imagine you sending her that poem, even if you were able to write puzzles."

"Thanks for your support."

"But someone else might. Plus Becky's an attorney. She hasn't been back in town long, but she's handled some high-profile cases."

"That's ridiculous," Sherry said, and immediately felt bad. What Chief Harper was saying was absolutely true. If the acrostic threat was genuine, Becky Baldwin was the most likely target.

Sherry even begrudged her that.

5

"CAN YOU BE A VIRGIN?"

Sherry Carter raised her eyebrows. "I beg your pardon?"

Aaron Grant grinned. "Can you be a virgin?"

"You know," Cora said, "in all the times I've been married, propositioned, and proposed to, I don't believe anyone's ever asked me that."

"Me either," Sherry said. "What's up, Aaron?"

"They need a Virgin Mary for the live Nativity. I figure if I can be a wise man, you can be a virgin."

"Very funny," Sherry said.

"Oh, but I'm serious," Aaron persisted. "I've already agreed to do it. Told Charlie I'd ask you."

"Who?"

"Charlie Ferric, the art teacher. Charlie's in charge of the Nativity. One of the high school girls canceled, and Charlie's one virgin short. It's just for an hour. Whaddya say, Sherry?"

"What's it entail?"

"Just posing. On the village green. In a large wooden stable."

"Posing?"

"Sure. Bakerhaven's famous for its live Nativity. Mary and Joseph are real, and the wise men and shepherds. They pose in the stable with the Baby Jesus."

"A real baby?"

"No. A baby wouldn't last an hour."

"I'm not sure I would either. You better get someone else."

"If you say so." Aaron shrugged innocently. "Becky Baldwin's doing it. . . ."

"Becky's playing the Virgin Mary?"

"Sure. She's done it before."

Sherry opened her mouth, closed it. "I'm not gonna touch that."

"So, can I put you down as a virgin?"

"Boy, talk about milking a joke," Sherry said.

"Well, why not? We got a maid a-milking right here."

"A lousy one, by all accounts," Cora grumbled. "At least according to Chief Harper's assessment of Jimmy Potter's assessment of Rupert Winston's assessment of my alleged performance."

"That's hardly fair," Aaron said. "Rupert loves it that Harvey Beerbaum's terrible."

"Now *you're* saying I'm terrible?" Cora's face reddened.

Aaron Grant put up his hands. "I came here to talk virgins, not milkmaids. I just can't seem to get a straight answer."

"When would they need me?" Sherry asked.

"The schedule's flexible. They can push the kids around to accommodate you. It's just a question of saying yes."

"Then I guess I gotta."

"Good," Aaron said, grinning. "I'll tell Charlie, you can meet with him, work it out."

"Meet with him? Why do I have to meet with him?"

"If you've never done it before, he has to show you how to pose and where to find your costume. There's two of each, the one that's being worn, and the one that's hanging in town hall, waiting for the replacement. A half hour before you go on, you go to town hall, change, and get ready to take your position in the stable at the top of the hour."

"Which hour are you doing?"

"That's not set yet."

"But you're not playing Joseph?"

"No, I am a king of Orient R."

"A what?"

"You know, *'We three kings of Orient R.'* "

"No, doofus. You *are* a king of the Orient. There's no such thing as *Orient R.*"

"Really. I've been hearing it all my life. That's what I thought it was."

"I hope you didn't use it in today's article."

Aaron had a moment of panic while he thought about it. "No, I did the pageant. The Nativity's tomorrow's piece."

A horn honked in the driveway. Cora went to the window, peered out.

The moon on the snow lit up the front lawn. A police car was parked behind Aaron Grant's Honda, and Sam Brogan clambered out. The cranky Bakerhaven officer was dressed in his winter uniform, complete with leather gloves and fur-lined hat. The hat was slightly askew, as he had been driving without it and had jammed it on his head to exit the car. Sam scowled as he stomped up the path.

Cora met him at the door. "Hi, Sam. What's up?"

"Oh, you're alive." Sam didn't sound particularly pleased. "Think you can stay that way till morning?"

"I'll certainly do my best."

"Good. Then I done my job. Lock your doors, lock your windows, if you hear anything suspicious call the police."

"You got it," Cora vowed. "Anything else?"

"Nope. Just don't get killed, or they'll be blamin' me."

"I could leave a note saying it wasn't your fault," Cora suggested.

"Yeah, that's hilarious," Sam said. "If the chief asks, just remember I was here."

"The chief told you to drive by?"

"He certainly did. So that's what I'm doin'. Drivin' by."

"And you're unhappy because you think it's stupid?"

"No, I'm unhappy because I'm makin' straight time."

Cora frowned. "What?"

"It's my shift. I'm on duty anyway. I swing by here to see you, it's part of my job. It ain't a dang thing extra. I'm workin' anyway. Protecting you on my regular watch."

"Isn't that good?"

"Yeah, great," Sam said sarcastically. "Dan Finley's out keepin' an eye on the lawyer lady. It's *not* his shift, he wouldn't be workin' now, he's gettin' time and a half for doin' it. So here's me and Dan out workin' tonight, and every time I make two bucks, he makes three."

"Dan Finley's keeping an eye on Becky Baldwin?" Sherry asked.

"At time and a half," Sam said. "I ask you, is that fair?"

"Maybe not," Cora said. "But think how angry Chief Harper will be if *she* gets killed."

"Yeah," Sam said, uncheered by the prospect. "Just remember I was here." He turned and stomped back to the car.

"Well," Sherry said, "Becky Baldwin gets a full-time bodyguard, and we just get a drive-by."

"Becky Baldwin gets a bodyguard at time and a half," Aaron corrected. "I wonder what that'll do to the town budget."

"I don't know," Cora said, "but Harper seems to be taking this thing seriously."

"And you're not?" Aaron asked.

"Oh, but I am," Cora replied. "I think the puzzle is a personal message meant for me, warning me to get out of that show. I'd be a fool not to comply."

"Oh, sure," Sherry snorted. "You think you're going to get away with that one?"

Cora sighed, but her eyes were twinkling. "I can dream, can't I?"

6

"MY, WE'VE PUT ON A LITTLE WEIGHT, HAVEN'T WE?"

Cora Felton glared down at Mabel Cunningham as the costume mistress attempted to button Cora's milkmaid skirt. A plump woman herself, Mabel seemed to take undue delight in the expanding waistlines of others.

"I haven't put on a little weight," Cora told her tartly. "I've never worn this costume before. Someone else wore it last year. Someone who was obviously shorter. If it's going to be a problem, why don't you talk to Rupert and suggest he replace me with someone the costume will fit?"

"Don't be silly," Mabel said. "I can let it out. I do that every year. Take it in, let it out. And this year, with the crazy casting, nothing seems to fit."

As if to punctuate the remark, Sherry Carter came walking up with her ladies-dancing costume hanging off her like a tent.

"Well, look at this!" Mabel cried. She fished a half dozen straight pins out of a pocket in her smock, fed them unerringly into her mouth. With a practiced hand, Mabel quickly tucked and pinned Sherry's dress. "That's good. Take it off, hang it on a hanger, make sure your hanger's marked. You're done."

As Sherry moved off, Mabel said, "There's a break. It's a lot easier to baste than let out. Though I seem to have a lot more letting out."

Cora seethed in silence. Since she'd been shanghaied into this idiotic project, her acting, her singing, her dancing, and now her weight had been called into question.

Wendy Brill, one of the high school girls who had been helping Mabel with the costumes, came running up. "Becky's here!" she announced breathlessly.

"So, give her a costume. You know where it is."

"Dan Finley's with her." Wendy's eyes were wide. "He wants to come *in*!"

"Oh," Mabel said. She glanced around the girls' dressing room, where the women's costume call was being held. Sherry Carter, now in bra and panties, was hanging her ladies-dancing gown on a rack. Other actresses were in various stages of undress. "Well, we can't have that, can we? Let me talk to Dan."

Mabel straightened, spat the remaining pins into her hand, ambled toward the door. Cora Felton, holding up her unbuttoned skirt, tagged along right behind.

Becky Baldwin and Dan Finley stood outside. The young policeman looked deeply embarrassed.

"I'm not trying to get in," he protested. "Chief Harper said not to leave her alone."

"There's only one door to the dressing room, Dan," Mabel told him. "And there's a lot of us here. I think Becky'll be safe enough with us women."

"I think so too," Dan agreed. "But I got my orders."

"You wanna come *in*?" Mabel managed to put a wealth of insinuation into a two-letter word.

Dan Finley could not have blushed more splendidly had he been caught trying to peep in the dressing room window. "Of course not. But I don't see why you couldn't bring her costume out here."

"Wonderful," Becky said. "You'd like me to dress in the hall?" She shrugged off her coat, thrust it at the beleaguered policeman. "I suppose you'd like to hold my clothes for me?"

From the look on Dan Finley's face, Becky had been torturing him all morning. "No, ma'am. But if I'm gonna deviate from my orders, I'm gonna clear it with the chief."

Becky threw up her hands. "Oh, for goodness' sakes!"

Sherry Carter, dressed in sweater and jeans and carrying her overcoat, came out the door. "What's going on?"

"Great," Becky said. "Let's get *everybody* out here, why don't we. Get everyone out here, so Dan and I can go in there together. Would you like that, Dan?"

Dan Finley had his cell phone out, was punching in a number.

"Calling for backup?" Becky teased.

"Hi, Chief. It's Dan. I'm over at the high school, Becky has a costume fitting, no one wants me in the girls' dressing room, there's a lot of women not wearing a lot of clothes. Okay to wait outside?" He listened a minute, said, "Thanks, Chief," snapped the cell phone shut. "He'll be here in two minutes."

Becky's mouth fell open. "What!?"

"I'm kidding. You can go on in."

Becky shot him a look, then sailed into the dressing room, followed by Cora, Sherry, and Mabel.

"He's only doing his job," Sherry pointed out.

Cora winced. Her niece needed to learn when to keep her mouth shut.

"Oh, is that right?" Becky replied witheringly. "You think his job is to protect me from some secret stalker? On the basis of a silly children's rhyme that has nothing to do with me? I mean, come on, give me a break."

Sherry bristled. "The poem was in the pear tree. Who gets the pear tree?"

"So *you* think there's something to it?" Becky scoffed. "As far as everyone else is concerned, *that*," she said, pointing in the direction of Dan, "is a useless precaution. But you think the threat is real, and you think it's aimed at me. What is that—wishful thinking?"

Sherry smiled sweetly. "Why, Becky Baldwin, whatever do you mean?"

Becky flushed, realizing she'd gone a little too far. An unspoken rule of their ongoing rivalry was never to openly acknowledge it.

"I mean," she answered, recovering beautifully, "that you want the puzzle to mean something so your aunt here can solve it and be the big hero."

"Heroine," Sherry corrected.

Becky frowned, then shot back archly, "You're rather preoccupied with sex, aren't you?"

"I'm not the one taunting young men in the hallways of the high school."

"Not my idea," Becky retorted. "This wouldn't have happened if your aunt hadn't convinced Chief Harper that acrostic poem meant something."

"Actually, it was Harvey Beerbaum who solved the acrostic," Cora pointed out.

"Who wrote it, then?"

"Not guilty," Cora said. "I can quite honestly say I have never written an acrostic in my life."

"Is that right?" Becky said. If Becky believed her, Cora wouldn't have known it.

Becky tossed her coat on a rack, turned to find Mabel measuring Cora's skirt. "Where's my costume?" Becky demanded.

"Skirt waist let out three and a half inches," Mabel said. She spied judiciously behind Cora's back. "Bigger all around." Over her shoulder to Becky she said, "Coat rack in the back. Dress will have your name on it. Put it on, come find me. Bring the measurement sheet pinned to it." She turned her attention back to Cora. "Did we do the blouse?"

"You mean did we make note of the fact I'm not as skinny as an anorexic fashion model? Yes, I believe we did."

"Yes, we did," Mabel said complacently, consulting her measurement sheet. She handed it to Cora. "Hang up your clothes, make sure you pin this sheet to the blouse, and you're done."

"All right, what the hell!" came a voice from the back.

All heads turned.

Becky Baldwin came striding up in her bra and panties. Her undergarments were black, lacy, and very sheer. That didn't surprise Sherry Carter any. Under ordinary circumstances, she might have cast a wouldn't-you-just-know-it glance at her aunt.

But these weren't ordinary circumstances. Becky's eyes were blazing.

There was a red envelope in her hand.

"All right, who did it?" Becky shrilled. "Whoever it was, it isn't funny."

"Where'd you get that?" Cora asked.

"As if you didn't know," Becky said. "It was pinned to my costume."

"You're kidding."

"Oh, sure. I'm really going to kid about a thing like that. You think I brought this with me, just as a joke?"

1 R	2 G	3 F		4 D	5 M	6 E		7 D	8 V	9 Q		10 F	11 S		12 A	13 P
14 K	15 R	16 V	17 Q	18 C		19 D	20 F		21 B	22 R	23 D	24 F	25 A	26 X	27 C	
28 A	29 J	30 T	31 L		32 O	33 K	34 P		35 T	36 O	37 W		38 A	39 D	40 J	
41 E	42 B		43 E	44 A		45 A	46 S		47 T	48 F	49 A	50 D	51 C	52 R	53 O	54 M
55 E	56 K	57 H		58 A	59 H	60 S	61 V		62 G	63 L	64 M		65 P	66 W	67 C	68 S
69 R	70 N		71 G	72 C	73 V	74 A	75 K	76 H		77 C	78 B	79 D	80 E		81 A	82 K
83 P	84 T	85 X		86 H		87 P	88 C	89 F	90 E	91 Q		92 A	93 T	94 C	95 I	96 G
97 H	98 R	99 D		100 J	101 E		102 C	103 B	104 P	105 J	106 E	107 W	108 U	109 N		110 A
111 C	112 E	113 M		114 I		115 B	116 U	117 W	118 N		119 M		120 A	121 C	122 D	123 J
	124 Q	125 B		126 V	127 R	128 L	129 F	130 P	131 G		132 N	133 D	134 F	135 J		136 E
137 C	138 A		139 S	140 N	141 I	142 X		143 X	144 L	145 R		146 U	147 I	148 D	149 M	150 J
	151 A	152 L	153 U	154 X	155 C	156 T	157 J		158 I	159 C	160 A	161 V				

A. First First Lady (2 wds.)
12 25 92 28 81 151 110 160 44 120
45 49 74 58 138 38

B. The ___ Bunny
103 21 115 125 78 42

C. "All I want is ___" (3 wds.)
155 88 72 137 94 27 121 67 18 77
111 159 102 51

D. Insurance option (2 wds.)
7 99 133 148 122 23 39 79 19 50
4

E. Car
112 6 136 41 106 101 55 43 80 90

F. Uninhibited
89 134 10 48 3 24 129 20

G. Neat
96 2 71 131 62

H. "___ on the Nile" (Agatha Christie)
97 57 86 76 59

I. Dolt
95 158 114 147 141

J. They're between incisors and premolars
135 157 105 40 123 150 100 29

K. Untied
56 75 33 14 82

L. Singer John
128 152 31 63 144

M. Freshen (2 wds.)
54 119 149 5 64 113

N. Elizabeth's suitor in "Pride and Prejudice"
118 140 109 132 70

O. Poison plant
36 53 32

P. 2, 3, and 4, for example
130 34 104 87 13 83 65

Q. Present
17 124 91 9

R. Uneven
69 127 22 15 52 1 98 145

S. In a fitting manner
60 68 46 139 11

T. The '60s, for example
35 84 47 30 156 93

U. Leap ___
146 108 116 153

V. Ran fast
126 16 73 61 8 161

W. The same reference
66 107 117 37

X. Rub out
142 26 143 85 154

"What's in the envelope?" Cora asked. Her eyes were sparkling.

"I haven't looked. But I know what it is. A little puzzle poem, telling me I'm gonna die."

"That's ridiculous," Cora said. "It simply makes no sense."

"Don't look at me," Becky said. "I didn't send the damn thing."

Becky ripped the envelope open. Inside was a folded piece of paper. Becky took it out, unfolded it. "Well," she said, "don't I feel foolish now."

"Why? What is it?"

Becky turned the paper around.

7

THERE WAS CHRISTMAS MUSIC IN THE POLICE STATION, BOUNCY, canned elevator music from a boom box on Dan Finley's desk. Since the young officer wasn't there, Chief Harper must have been playing it. At the moment, it was filling the station with the strains of "God Rest Ye Merry Gentlemen."

Cora Felton was neither a gentleman nor was she jolly. She glared at Chief Harper, who was drumming his fingers on his desk in a rhythm nowhere near the beat of the music. Behind him on the wall, a wreath of holly framed a wanted poster. On the table beside him sat a miniature Christmas tree, not unlike the one that had delivered the first acrostic.

Just like the one in Cora's hand.

Cora stole a look at Sherry Carter, seated next to her, then turned back to the chief. "I think you should get Harvey Beerbaum. He solved the first puzzle."

Chief Harper was having none of it. "No," he declared. "*Now.* You solve it *now.* I'm not playing games here. I'm upset. I don't care if you're as *fast* as Harvey, or as *accurate* as Harvey. I want the damn thing solved. So do it *now.*"

Cora shot Sherry a pleading glance.

"Come on, Cora," Sherry said. "I wanna know too."

Cora, utterly betrayed, gawked at her. "What?" she protested.

Sherry smiled. "Cora's embarrassed," she informed Chief Harper. "Acrostics are confusing, and she always gets mixed up transferring the letters from the clues to the grid. Come on, Cora. I'll fill in the letters for you. You just tell me what they are."

"Is that all?" Cora said.

Sherry was fishing a pen out of her purse. "Let me have the puzzle. And something to write on." She took a file folder off Chief Harper's desk, leaned the puzzle on it, scribbled a few strokes with the pen. "Let's see if this pen works."

"Oh, I gotta do it in *ink?*" Cora tried to sound like she was joking, not like it really was the last straw.

"I have infinite confidence in you." Sherry scrunched her chair next to Cora's. "Let's see."

Cora, with more chance of winning the state lottery than getting even one answer right, exhaled in helpless frustration. The music, as if to mock her, had moved on to "Rudolph, the Red-Nosed Reindeer."

Cora mentally shot herself and looked at the puzzle.

Her eyes widened.

Sherry, while testing the pen, had managed to fill in one answer. *N: Elizabeth's suitor in 'Pride and Prejudice'* was *Darcy.*

Well, better than nothing, Cora thought, even if it was merely postponing the inevitable.

"Well," Cora said, "Right off the bat, the answer to *N: Elizabeth's suitor in 'Pride and Prejudice'* has to be *Darcy.*"

"Good," Sherry said. "Okay, let me fill that in."

After *L: Singer John,* Sherry promptly wrote *Elton.*

Cora grinned as the realization struck her. Sherry had only written one clue, but that was all she needed. By filling in a new clue every time Cora gave her the answer to the old, she could keep one clue ahead of Cora until the whole puzzle was solved. A simple but brilliantly effective strategy, which Sherry had thought up on the spur of the moment. Cora never ceased to be amazed at Sherry's linguistic dexterity.

Cora began filling in words. The elevator music segued into "It Came upon a Midnight Clear." Cora could almost imagine a halo around her head.

Within minutes the puzzle had been filled in.

"Uh-oh," Sherry said.

"What is it?" Chief Harper asked.

"You're not going to like this, Chief."

"I hate it already. What's it say?"

Sherry read:

"Did you get my message?
It appears that you did not.
Or is it conceivable
That you simply forgot?

"Well, here's a brief reminder
To remember what I said.
I hope it doesn't come too late
And you're already dead!

"The author is *Me Again.* The title is *Die, Leading Lady, Die.*"

"That does it," Chief Harper said. "Before, we only suspected the threat was aimed at Becky Baldwin. This confirms it. *Die, Leading Lady, Die.* And she is the star of the show."

Sherry refrained from comment.

"Yes, she is," Cora agreed, the very picture of innocent outrage. "And this note was pinned to her costume. If I were you, I'd shut down the play."

Chief Harper frowned. "Are you really *that* bad?"

"I was thinking of Becky Baldwin's safety," Cora replied with all the dignity she could muster.

Chief Harper nodded. "Then you take this as a genuine threat?"

"Don't be silly, Chief. You gotta take *any* threat as a genuine

1 R D	2 G I	3 F D	■	4 D Y	5 M O	6 E U	■	7 D G	8 V E	9 Q T	■	10 F M	11 S Y	■	12 A M	13 P E
14 K S	15 R S	16 V A	17 Q G	18 C E	■	19 D I	20 F T	■	21 B A	22 R P	23 D P	24 F E	25 A A	26 X R	27 C S	■
28 A T	29 J H	30 T A	31 L T	■	32 O Y	33 K O	34 P U	■	35 T D	36 O I	37 W D	■	38 A N	39 D O	40 J T	■
41 E O	42 B R	■	43 E I	44 A S	■	45 A I	46 S T	■	47 T C	48 F O	49 A N	50 D C	51 C E	52 R I	53 O V	54 M A
55 E B	56 K L	57 H E	■	58 A T	59 H H	60 S A	61 V T	■	62 G Y	63 L O	64 M U	■	65 P S	66 W I	67 C M	68 S P
69 R L	70 N Y	■	71 G F	72 C O	73 V R	74 A G	75 K O	76 H T	■	77 C W	78 B E	79 D L	80 E L	■	81 A H	82 K E
83 P R	84 T E	85 X S	■	86 H A	■	87 P B	88 C R	89 F I	90 E E	91 Q F	■	92 A R	93 T E	94 C M	95 I I	96 G N
97 H D	98 R E	99 D R	■	100 J T	101 E O	■	102 C R	103 B E	104 P M	105 J E	106 E M	107 W B	108 U E	109 N R	■	110 A W
111 C H	112 E A	113 M T	■	114 I I	■	115 B S	116 U A	117 W I	118 N D	■	119 M I	■	120 A H	121 C O	122 D P	123 J E
■	124 Q I	125 B T	■	126 V D	127 R O	128 L E	129 F S	130 P N	131 G T	■	132 N C	133 D O	134 F M	135 J E	■	136 E T
137 C O	138 A O	■	139 S L	140 N A	141 I T	142 X E	■	143 X A	144 L N	145 R D	■	146 U Y	147 I O	148 D U	149 M R	150 J E
■	151 A A	152 L L	153 U R	154 X E	155 C A	156 T D	157 J Y	■	158 I D	159 C E	160 A A	161 V D	■	■	■	■

A. First First Lady (2 wds.)
M A R T H A W A S H I N G T O N
12 25 92 28 81 151 110 160 44 120 45 49 74 58 138 38

B. The ___ Bunny
E A S T E R
103 21 115 125 78 42

C. "All I want is ___" (3 wds.)
A R O O M S O M E W H E R E
155 88 72 137 94 27 121 67 18 77 111 159 102 51

D. Insurance option (2 wds.)
G R O U P P O L I C Y
7 99 133 148 122 23 39 79 19 50 4

E. Car
A U T O M O B I L E
112 6 136 41 106 101 55 43 80 90

F. Uninhibited
I M M O D E S T
89 134 10 48 3 24 129 20

G. Neat
N I F T Y
96 2 71 131 62

H. "___ on the Nile" (Agatha Christie)
D E A T H
97 57 86 76 59

I. Dolt
I D I O T
95 158 114 147 141

J. They're between incisors and premolars
E Y E T E E T H
135 157 105 40 123 150 100 29

K. Untied
L O O S E
56 75 33 14 82

L. Singer John
E L T O N
128 152 31 63 144

M. Freshen (2 wds.)
A I R O U T
54 119 149 5 64 113

Clue	Answer	Numbers
N. Elizabeth's suitor in "Pride and Prejudice"	D A R C Y	118 140 109 132 70
O. Poison plant	I V Y	36 53 32
P. 2, 3, and 4, for example	N U M B E R S	130 34 104 87 13 83 65
Q. Present	G I F T	17 124 91 9
R. Uneven	L O P S I D E D	69 127 22 15 52 1 98 145
S. In a fitting manner	A P T L Y	60 68 46 139 11
T. The '60s, for example	D E C A D E	35 84 47 30 156 93
U. Leap ___	Y E A R	146 108 116 153
V. Ran fast	D A R T E D	126 16 73 61 8 161
W. The same reference	I B I D	66 107 117 37
X. Rub out	E R A S E	142 26 143 85 154

threat. Because there's no way to tell. But I don't know what you're gonna do about it. Unless you have Dan Finley *marry* Becky Baldwin."

"I can sound him out on the subject."

"Yeah. So what's your scheme here? Short of shutting down the show, which is the only move that would be effective. *Death of an Actress. Death of a Leading Lady.* Make Becky stop acting, you thwart the killer's plan."

Chief Harper frowned, considered. "I can't do that."

"Why not?"

"I still don't know if this is a threat or a prank. On the one hand, I don't wanna close the show for a prank. On the other, if this is a genuine threat, will calling off the show really stop it? If there's a killer out there targeting Becky Baldwin, will canceling the show be effective? Or will it merely tick the killer off? The killer has promised Becky Baldwin's death. And I would say there is a ninety-nine percent chance the *reason* he wants Becky Baldwin dead is not because she got the lead in the Christmas play. So if you take away the Christmas play, that reason still remains. It screws up his poetry, big deal. Suppose he writes another poem called death of an *ex*-actress, and pins it to her body?"

"So keep Dan Finley on her."

"Indefinitely?" Chief Harper shook his head. "You see the problem here. Once the Christmas pageant goes on, it's over. Presumably, whatever our little poet intends to do will happen before then. You take away the pageant, the whole thing's open-ended. There's no telling when the killer might strike. Assuming he ever does."

Cora's eyes were brilliant with excitement and pleasure. "Oh, you sneaky devil. You and your fancy talk."

"I beg your pardon?"

"That's why you won't call off the pageant! You *want* it to happen. You have no idea who the killer is, and you figure your only way to catch him is if he makes a move on her. That's why you have Dan Finley on Becky Baldwin. Not to protect her. Becky Baldwin is bait!"

Chief Harper said nothing.

"What about opening night?" Cora persisted. "Assuming we get there. You gonna send Dan Finley out onstage with her? In period costume?"

"I'm sure she'll be safe enough onstage. And I'm sure she's safe enough now. I just want to stop this before it goes any further. If it's kids, I wanna drag them into the principal's office and let him point out why it isn't very funny."

"Sounds good to me, Chief. Just how do you plan to go about doing that?"

"Got any suggestions?"

"Have you traced the first puzzle?"

"If I had, I'd know where this one came from."

"Fair enough. Have you *tried* to trace the first puzzle?"

"That I have. As much as possible. According to the computer teacher, it wasn't done on any of the high school machines."

"The high school has a teacher to teach computer." Cora shook her head. "I am way too old."

"So no help there. And I got no grounds to start invading private homes."

"Would you have grounds if Becky got bumped off?" At Chief Harper's look, Cora said meekly, "Just asking." Suddenly, she scowled in disgust. "Oh, hell!"

From Dan Finley's boom box wafted the dulcet strains of "The Twelve Days of Christmas."

8

"IT'S A PIECE OF CAKE," CHARLIE FERRIC, THE ART TEACHER, declared to the gaggle of actors and actresses assembled in the town hall lobby. There were five Josephs, six Marys, and a couple of dozen shepherds and wise men. Two Josephs, two Marys, four shepherds, and six wise men were in costume. The rest were not.

Sherry Carter was one of the lucky ones in costume who would pose first and get to leave. Though, actually, luck had nothing to do with it. Cora Felton, who was taking Sherry to the beauty parlor, had come along and twisted Charlie Ferric's arm.

The other costumed Mary, clearly a high school girl, was having a grand time pulling the beard off one of the Josephs, who was running his hands over her blue-and-white robes in a most secular manner. This naturally involved a good deal of pinching and tickling and shrieking and giggling.

"If it's so easy, why do we have to rehearse?" one of the other Marys protested. She was feisty and argumentative, perhaps due to the fact that Cora's meddling had aced her out of a costume. Her curly brown hair, sea-green eyes, and dimpled chin made her quite attractive, in spite of her metal braces.

"We're not rehearsing, just posing," Charlie Ferric answered. "It's easy, but it's important to get it right. You, for instance, will be posing without your earrings, because the Virgin Mary did not wear earrings. Can you take off your braces?"

"Well, *duh,* of course not," she said saucily.

This wit prompted gales of laughter from the flirting Joseph and Mary.

"Then keep your mouth shut," Charlie Ferric snapped.

At the young woman's offended look, he added, "Not now, my dear. When you're posing. And that goes for the rest of you. No anachronisms. Do you know what that means?"

"Yeah, no braces," she shot back, and snuck in a tug at Joseph's beard. Mary squealed and battled her hands away. The young man, clearly the more popular Joseph, seemed to revel in this.

Charlie Ferric shook his head. "Let's ask the expert. Miss Felton, would you mind telling this young lady what an anachronism is?"

Cora, who knew perfectly well what an anachronism was, but whose mind short-circuited every time she was asked for a definition, had an instant of icy panic. Then her eyes twinkled. She shrugged. "Gee, I was going to say no braces."

The kids hooted gleefully.

Charlie Ferric bore this unexpected sabotage stoically. "It means nothing out of period," he persisted. "No watches. No eyeglasses or sunglasses. No Walkmans. Believe it or not, we had one last year. The principal came by, noticed one of the shepherds' heads kept bobbing. The principal, for goodness' sakes. That's not gonna happen this year."

Charlie Ferric put his hands on his hips, gave them his stern look. Cora Felton suppressed a smile. Charlie was tall, gawky, and plump in the middle. He reminded her of an angry ostrich.

"How come Dorrie gets a costume and not me?" the girl with braces demanded. "Just because her parents are rich?"

"Maxine!" the Mary named Dorrie exclaimed indignantly. She wrenched herself free from Joseph's grip, slipped, and almost fell before he caught her again.

"Dorrie, you're such a spaz." Maxine laughed. "Relax. Lance doesn't love you for your money, do you, Lance?"

Lance's beard made it impossible to tell if the remark bothered him, but he seemed to hug the Virgin Mary a little tighter.

"Can we get on with it?" the less popular Joseph complained. "My beard itches." From his whiny voice, Cora recognized him as the nerdy light man from the tech crew.

"Oh, knock it off, Alfred," the perky young Mary named Maxine said. "At least you got a costume." She turned back to poor Mr. Ferric. "And just why do we have to be in costume at all? We already tried it on and we know it fits."

"I want you to get used to wearing it. It's cold out there. You're going to be out there for an hour. If you're cold, you're not wearing enough underneath. Trust me, an hour's a long time."

"Yeah, fine, I promise I'll dress warm," Maxine said. "Look, Dorrie's my ride, and I don't want her finishing first and running off with Romeo. Let me go out there now, I promise I'll be good, when we get back I'll be done. Otherwise, you'll still have to deal with me, and some people think I'm a bitch."

This sally drew appreciative whoops and laughter from not only Marys and Josephs but shepherds and wise men alike. Even grumpy Alfred got a kick out of it, and Cora had to suppress a smile.

Charlie Ferric caved in with what good grace he could muster, and led the first group, consisting of two fully dressed Nativities, one extra plainclothes Mary, and one amused Puzzle Lady, out the town hall front door and down the steps.

The village green was a rectangular block bounded on three sides by the town hall, the county courthouse, and the Congregational church. All three were white, wood-framed buildings, dripping with icicles and crusted picturesquely with snow. The church boasted a steeple, the courthouse pillars, and the town hall a clock tower. The clock had not worked since 1962.

During the summer the green featured the statue of an anonymous horse and rider—or at least anonymous in that their names had long since worn off the brass plaque. In the winter, the wooden stable was placed to hide the horse. Of course, if one were to walk around, the horse and rider could be seen in the back, poised in midair, as if the stable were some gigantic steeplechase obstacle the animal was about to clear, or, more likely, as if they were a slapstick comedy horse and rider, hurling themselves directly into the wall.

The sight of the stable seemed to inspire Charlie Ferric. "You see? Isn't that something? The only problem is getting there. There should never be anything in front of the stable but the white new-fallen snow."

Maxine whispered something to Dorrie and Lance. From their reaction, Cora figured it must be something scintillating about virgin snow.

Charlie Ferric pretended not to notice. "So we always walk around the green and come up on the stable from the back."

"It's getting cold," one of the shepherds complained.

"Yes, it is," Charlie agreed placidly. "And we've only been out a couple of minutes. So dress accordingly. All right, if you're all set, then follow me."

Charlie set off around the square. The road had been plowed for cars to go by, but not enough for them to park. Parking around the green was off-limits in the Christmas season.

Charlie reached the front of the courthouse and instructed, "Try to walk in my footsteps. Aim for the tail of the horse."

That instruction prompted furious whispering and loud guffaws.

Charlie gave the troublemakers a look, then set off across the green in long, practiced strides, lifting his big feet clear of snow rather than dragging them through it. The actors, clomping along in huge rubber boots, blazed their own trail. Cora Felton brought up the rear.

They reached the horse, made their way alongside it to the back of the stable.

Charlie Ferric held up his hands. "Don't crowd. Don't push.

Stay in single file. Come up here, one at a time. Here's the latch for the back door. It swings out from left to right. Before you go in, hang up your coat, stash your boots on this little ledge, and put on your sandals or slippers or whatever you wear."

"I have bare feet," one of the shepherd boys said.

"Then we'll visit you in intensive care. One hour in bare feet isn't happening on my watch. Get some footwear or get a replacement. All right, first group, let's step up one at a time, take our places on the set. The rest of you watch through the door so I don't have to say everything twice."

Sherry Carter hung up her coat, kicked off her boots, and pulled slippers onto her feet.

"Fine," Charlie said. "Step right in, let me position you. Mary, you kneel down here behind the bale of hay. That's your makeshift crib. You're on the floor, cradling the Baby Jesus. Joseph, you stand behind her, holding her up."

Charlie placed one of the Josephs. From her kneeling position, Sherry couldn't see which one, though she assumed it was the techie, Alfred.

"Mary, the baby's lying in the hay, you have one arm under the neck, so you're not actually holding the baby, it only looks as if you are. Get your legs into a comfortable position beneath you, and lean on Joseph for support. Don't try to look up. Your head is down, gazing at the Baby Jesus. Good.

"Joseph, you're supporting her, but slightly at an angle, looking down at the mother and child. You got that? Good. Where's my wise men?"

Cora watched in amusement as the wise men were positioned. The group of boys, clearly cast to fit the costumes, consisted of one tall boy, one short boy, and one plump boy. They wore their kingly robes of purple and white, red and gold, green and blue with great dignity, except when the tall boy periodically snatched off the plump boy's hat.

On the other side of the stable, Charlie Ferric installed two shepherds, one standing, one kneeling in the straw. The kneeling one was shivering in bare feet, and would not make that mistake again.

"Excellent!" Charlie cried. "That's the pose you hit, and that's the pose you hold. Whether someone's watching you on foot, whether someone's driving by on the road, or whether there's no one there at all. Assume you're being watched, and act accordingly.

"Which means not to act at all. Which can be your biggest challenge. There's always a couple of kids think it's the height of fun to stand in front of the crèche and try to make you laugh."

"I thought no one was supposed to walk on the green," Sherry said.

"That's *just* what I don't want," Charlie said. "No one *is* supposed to walk on the green, but if they do, you can't point it out to them. All you can do is hold the pose and try not to laugh. If they throw snowballs—"

"You're kidding!"

"It's been known to happen. Don't worry, they're usually not that accurate. If they aim for you, they'll probably miss."

Cora Felton was grinning from ear to ear.

"I suppose it's too late to get out of this?" Sherry said.

"If it weren't, I wouldn't have brought the subject up. I'm kidding, of course. Don't worry, you'll be fine. No one's supposed to walk in front of the stable anyway, and—Hey! What are you doing there?"

Chief Harper clomped up to the crèche in his boots. "I'm sorry, but I have to talk to your Virgin Mary. Is she about done?"

"Oh, you messed up the snow," Charlie Ferric moaned. "Chief Harper, look what you did to the snow."

"Relax, Charlie. It's supposed to snow again tonight. Is Miss Carter done?"

"As soon as she turns in her costume. There's a lot of girls waiting for it."

"I won't be a minute. Come on. Jump down."

"Gotta get my boots," Sherry said.

"Of course," Chief Harper muttered. "It couldn't have been easy."

Sherry changed into her boots, pulled on her coat, and she and Cora joined the chief in front of the stable. "This better be good, Chief. Charlie Ferric may not bawl you out for messing up his snow, but whaddya want to bet he takes it out on me?"

"I'm sorry, but I need your help."

"With what?"

"With the puzzles."

"You need *her* help with the puzzles?" Cora said.

Sherry shot her a warning glance.

"Yeah," Chief Harper said. "You're the computer whiz. The guy at the high school said the acrostic grid was generated by a computer program, but he didn't know which one. Neither did Harvey. So, can you pinpoint the program for me?"

"I can give it a try," Sherry said.

"Thanks. I'd appreciate it."

Chief Harper turned and plodded away, cutting a brand-new trail through the snow.

"I thought you already had that program," Cora said, watching him go.

"I do," Sherry told her. "I bought it on the Internet the day you got the first puzzle."

"Why didn't you say so?"

"Force of habit," Sherry muttered irritably.

"Right," Cora agreed. "You didn't wanna admit you'd already mastered the program backwards and forwards, and probably knew as much about it as the people who created it."

A burst of giggling erupted from the crèche. Cora and Sherry looked, saw that the second Joseph, presumably Lance, was kneeling behind his girlfriend, Dorrie, *and* Dorrie's friend Maxine, supporting both Virgin Marys.

"Suppose the three of them will wind up posing together?" Cora mused.

"I wouldn't be surprised. Come on. I gotta turn in my costume."

"So what you gonna tell Chief Harper?" Cora asked Sherry as they walked back to town hall.

"I'll call him tomorrow, give him copies of the puzzle grids. I just won't mention when I printed 'em out."

"Which was slightly before he asked you?"

"Hell, I printed the first one out before the second one even arrived." Sherry shook her head. "I feel bad about misleading him."

Cora shrugged.

"What difference could it possibly make?"

9

"WE'RE LATE," SHERRY SAID IRRITABLY. "THIS IS AARON'S PARENTS. I don't want to be late."

Cora Felton eased the Toyota around a curve in the road. "We're not late. We're right on time."

"It's a quarter to seven."

"So?"

"The invitation was for six o'clock."

"Of course," Cora said. "You know who's there at six o'clock? The hosts, setting up. Assuming they're even dressed."

"Don't be silly."

"Silly? Sherry, I've thrown enough parties in my day. Believe me, I know. With Frank, all we did was throw parties. Which was good. It gave me someone to talk to besides Frank."

"Aunt Cora—"

"Trust me, if the invitation says six o'clock, you don't get there at six."

"We'll be lucky if we get there at all. Can't you go any faster?"

"Not if you want me to stay on the road. It's snowing, in case you haven't noticed."

"Do you think I'm overdressed?" Sherry asked. "I'm afraid I'm overdressed."

Under her winter coat, Sherry was wearing a blue evening dress with a scoop neck, a ruby pendant on a chain. Her glossy brown hair, fresh from the beauty parlor, featured highlights and loose curls.

"You look good."

"Is the brooch too much?"

"Not at all. If you want it to be too much, you attach it to the front of the dress so it gapes when you lean forward."

"Aunt Cora."

"I believe that is the official definition of 'too much.' I only did that when I had to get married again."

"Aunt Cora. This means a lot to me. Will you behave?"

"Don't I always?"

Sherry refrained from comment.

"There's one." Cora pointed to a house hung with colored lights and a plastic Santa and sleigh. There were not many such houses in Bakerhaven. The approved holiday decorations in Bakerhaven consisted of the understated single candle and wreath in the window. Colored lights were frowned on in Bakerhaven. Illuminated Santas simply were not done.

"Does that mean they'll be ostracized?" Sherry asked.

"Oh, absolutely. Christmas tree lights belong on Christmas trees, or hadn't you heard?"

"Oh, *now* you're an expert on Christmas trees?"

"Just because I don't trim them doesn't mean I haven't seen one." Cora fishtailed around a corner. Off to the left children were sledding on a hill. "Oh, look! Sledders."

"Watch the road."

"Aren't they precious. Do you suppose one of them will grow up to be Citizen Kane?"

Sherry took a breath. "Cora, I know you like to fancy yourself irrepressible. But this is Aaron's *parents.* I need to make a good impression."

"So I shouldn't get pie-eyed and start showing everyone your baby pictures? Never fear." Cora turned onto Maple Street, headed out of town. "Will you recognize the house?"

"In this snow I'm not sure. But it will be the one with all the cars parked around it."

"If anyone's there yet."

"Cora, it's not like New York. If they say six o'clock, it's because they expect people at six o'clock."

A couple of miles out of town they came upon a house with half a dozen cars parked out on the road. The car ahead of them pulled in and parked.

"Satisfied?" Sherry asked her aunt crisply.

"As long as we're not the first. If we're the first, it gets around, people talk, invitations start to fall off."

The Grant house had a single candle in each window.

"Fashionable," Cora commented.

"Don't be snide."

"What's snide about that?"

"Sorry, I'm just touchy."

"Hadn't noticed."

Aaron's parents met them at the front door. Mrs. Grant wore a black velvet dress and a string of pearls. Mr. Grant sported slacks and a blue blazer, a slightly more casual look than the suit and tie he customarily wore as the head of his insurance company. He seemed nice, though Sherry had never had a chance to really talk to him.

"Sherry, Cora," Mrs. Grant said, extending her hands. "Glad you could come. Here, let me take your coats. Aaron, come and take their coats."

Aaron Grant had been standing near the punch bowl, talking to one of the guests. Aaron was wearing a turtleneck and tweed jacket, and struck Sherry as a mature, handsome young man. Then his mother called him, and suddenly he was a little boy again, helping Mommy with the guests' coats. Sherry fought back the image, smiled at Aaron before he scampered up the stairs to toss their coats on the bed.

The onslaught of more guests kept the Grants busy being hosts, and Cora and Sherry found themselves ushered into the party. A Christmas tree dominated one end of the living room. It had colored lights and balls and tinsel, a star on top, and presents underneath.

The living room and dining room were separated by huge double doors. The dining room table had been pushed up against the wall to hold the buffet. A table on the opposite wall served as a bar. A third table held the punch bowls. There were two of them, tidily labeled ALCOHOLIC and NONALCOHOLIC.

Despite Cora's fears, more than a dozen guests were already there. Standing by the punch bowl was a beefy man with a jowled face, bald head, and enormous muttonchop sideburns. They were long, thick, and bushy, as might have befitted a Dickens scholar, a Dickens character, or even Dickens himself. He clutched a martini glass in a meaty hand that would have looked more fitting with a tankard of ale. He gestured with it as he talked, as if driving points home with vermouth and gin. The man had Chief Harper buttonholed, and it did not look as if there were any immediate chance of escape.

Sherry glanced around to find her aunt had rapidly bypassed the punch bowls in favor of the bar, and was already pouring some amber liquid or other over a glass of cracked ice. Sherry started across the room to add her customary word of caution, but Cora swept on to look out the patio's glass double door. As she did, Harvey Beerbaum came up behind her, spun her around, and kissed her.

Cora came up for air, blinking and sputtering in shock and surprise. "Harvey Beerbaum! Are you drunk? What in the world's got into you?"

Harvey grinned and pointed over her head. "Mistletoe. Can't buck tradition, now, can we?" He chuckled. "You'd better move away, unless you want the men forming a line."

"Well, you old rascal," Cora said. "Is this a habit with you, or am I your first victim?"

"Oh, what a nasty word." Harvey's piggy eyes twinkled. "I admit I laid in wait for you. To catch you in something for once."

Cora's heart skipped, as it always did when Harvey alluded to their respective skills. The prospect of Harvey catching her in something was a very genuine possibility. However, Harvey seemed in an exuberant mood. "I'm so glad you're here," he declared. "I've got someone who wants to meet you."

"Oh?" Cora said without enthusiasm. Harvey's contacts in the crossword puzzle world were legion. Cora wondered which cruciverbal expert she'd have to deal with now.

Harvey marched her over to the punch bowl, where the beefy, bewhiskered gentleman was still taking Chief Harper to task. "Jonathon," Harvey said, beaming all over his face. "Jonathon, here she is."

At the interruption, the man wheeled around, depositing the remains of his martini down the front of his shirt. His raised eyebrows were black and exceedingly bushy. His inquiring eyes were sky blue. His face, round with baby fat, still managed somehow to look sly. "Yes?" he said crisply.

"This is Miss Cora Felton, the woman I told you about. Cora, may I present Jonathon Doddsworth III." Harvey paused dramatically. Then, eyes twinkling, he announced, "Of Scotland Yard."

Cora's mouth fell open. "Of—"

"Scotland Yard. Yes," Jonathon Doddsworth said. "Little out of my bailiwick, aren't I? But my daughter's here. I'm home for the holidays, so to speak. Not that this is my home anymore, not to put too fine a point on it."

"You and her mother are divorced?"

"That's the ticket. Ages now, more's the pity. Yes, I'm back in Scotland Yard, and I daresay we have something in common."

"You mean crime?"

"I do indeed." Doddsworth smiled broadly. His teeth were somewhat crooked but went well with his face, gave him a warm, homey quality. His twinkling eyes made him seem friendly and attractive. "I understand you've had no little success in the matter."

Cora practically simpered. "You're too kind. Oh, this is my niece, Sherry. Sherry Carter. Absolutely invaluable in my investigations. Helps me with the computer. This Internet stuff gives me fits."

"Beastly, isn't it?" Doddsworth agreed, nodding hello to Sherry. He took a sip of his martini, was surprised to find his glass empty. "I must say, I find myself intrigued by your recent puzzles."

As usual, Cora tried to keep her face from registering alarm at the drop of the dreaded word *puzzle*. "Whatever do you mean?"

"The acrostics, of course. I was just having a bit of a jaw with Chief Harper here. In a quandary, he is, over this business. And rightfully so. Seems a children's lark, but who's to say?"

"Is that how you see it?" Cora asked.

"I haven't seen it at all." Jonathon Doddsworth set his glass on the table somewhat ruefully. Cora wasn't sure if his expression reflected the fact that it was empty or the fact that he hadn't seen the puzzles. "I'm relying on Chief Harper's recollections, which I must say seem a trifle foggy. I know the verse is not Dylan Thomas—still, one might expect it to rhyme."

"Oh, it does," Cora said. "In a maddeningly schoolgirl way."

"You wouldn't by any chance have brought it along?"

"I'm afraid not."

Aaron Grant, who had returned from taking their coats in time to hear the last exchange, said, "But Sherry could recite it. She has a fantastic memory for words."

"Could you?" Doddsworth said. "I say, that would be positively smashing."

The look Sherry shot Aaron was not kind. Showing off her linguistic prowess was the last thing in the world she wanted to do. "It's exactly as you say. They're simple children's poems. The first is:

"Can you figure out the mischief
That I am going to do?

Are you apprehensive
That I might do it to you?

"Girls who harbor grievances
And cannot make amends
Never get the things they want
And come to gruesome ends.

"The second is:

"Did you get my message?
It appears that you did not.
Or is it conceivable
That you simply forgot?

"Well, here's a brief reminder
To remember what I said.
I hope it doesn't come too late
And you're already dead!"

"Fascinating," Doddsworth murmured. "Clearly threats, but maddeningly nonspecific. I understand the titles narrowed the field. You couldn't recite them as well, now, could you, there's a clever girl?"

"The first one was *Death of an Actress* by *Guess Who?* The second one was *Die, Leading Lady, Die* by *Me Again.*"

"And this arrived in a cryptogram grid, such as might be printed in the morning daily?"

Sherry nudged Cora with her elbow.

"An acrostic," Cora supplied belatedly.

"An acrostic which had been generated from a computer program?"

"It appears so. As I say, my Sherry's the expert on computer matters."

"Yes. Miss Carter, might this perchance be a program of the sort one would be required to purchase?"

"Yes, it would."

"Well, there you are." Doddsworth nodded sagaciously. "The prankster purchased an acrostic computer program. You need only trace recent sales."

"And how would I do that?" Chief Harper asked.

"Good lord, man. You're a constable. Contact the retailer and demand the information. I can't imagine them not obliging. Though surely you could get a court directive if need be."

"Yes," Chief Harper said dryly. "But there's been no crime."

"Quite so, quite so," Doddsworth agreed amiably. "It would indeed be much more convenient were there a corpse. This actress you fancy—who would she be?"

"Becky Baldwin."

"I'm not certain having Miss Rebecca chaperoned is such a good notion. Sort of puts our fellow off, so to speak. Why not lower your guard, and let nature take its course?"

Two teenage girls came bouncing up with a young man in tow. Cora recognized one of the girls as the sassy, plainclothes Mary from the live Nativity. Tonight she was bubbly and vibrant in a royal blue sweater, a short black skirt, and her braces.

"Hi, Daddy," she said. "Enjoying the party?"

Jonathon Doddsworth's face softened into a paternal smile. He put his arms around his daughter, embarrassed her with a hug. "That I am, Max. That I am." As she wriggled free he added, "Is your mother here?"

"No, I came with Lance and Dorrie," she replied, identifying her young friends, the Mary and Joseph from the crèche.

Doddsworth's mouth fell open. "Oh, I say! Is that little *Dorrie*?" His voice grew husky. "But of course, Dorrie and Max. Same as ever. My dear girl, do you remember polo pony? I was the pony, and you and Max rode me, often at the same time. My, how you've grown."

Dorrie, who could not have looked more mortified had Doddsworth whipped out her nude baby pictures, rolled her eyes. "Puh-*leeze*!" she said, mugging in a way she undoubtedly thought was cute, but which merely underscored her youth. Without her Virgin Mary cowl, Dorrie had straight blond hair, which flew out appealingly each time she tossed her head. She had sky-blue eyes, high cheekbones, and sensitive features. Her capped teeth gleamed. Her pink sweater and white skirt were the most fashionable designer labels. Though she was gawky, awkward, and somewhat socially immature, it was clear no expense had been spared to compensate.

"Are your parents here tonight, Dorrie?" Doddsworth asked.

"No," Dorrie replied, clearly glad to have the subject changed. "Mumsy's got a cold, so Daddy didn't come."

"Oh. Pity."

"This is Lance." Maxine pushed the handsome young man forward.

Lance, who had curly brown hair and a square jaw, and who looked like a football star, was as awkward as Dorrie when it came to introductions. "Pleasetameetya," he mumbled, shaking hands.

"Likewise." Doddsworth raised his eyebrows at his daughter. "You didn't mention you had a young gentleman, Max."

"Because I don't." Maxine smiled archly. "He's *Dorrie's* young gentleman. Aren't you, Lance?"

Lance blushed splendidly, Dorrie batted at Maxine, and the three of them bounded off again in a torrent of giggles.

Becky Baldwin swept in with Dan Finley. Becky looked stunning in a strapless emerald evening gown with her hair up. Dan, in a suit and tie, seemed no more comfortable than he had in uniform. He looked like a little boy dressed up for church.

"Ah, there you are," Becky crooned. "Chief Harper, would you tell your minion he doesn't have to follow me into the john?"

Dan Finley's mouth dropped open. "Why, I never," he sputtered.

"I'm sure you didn't," Chief Harper interposed. "Becky just likes to tease."

"Becky would like to have a life," Becky Baldwin snapped. "This constant surveillance is a drag."

"You're the actress who received the threatening missives?" Jonathon Doddsworth was leaning forward with interest.

Becky glanced at him. "I remember you. You're the father of one of the girls. Went back to England, as I recall."

"Jonathon Doddsworth, of Scotland Yard."

Becky smiled. "Amazing you can say that with a straight face. Sounds right out of a PBS episode. No offense meant, of course. Listen, do you have any influence with the local cops? I'm being hounded to death, and it's putting a real damper on the yuletide season."

"I'm sorry about that," Chief Harper said. "I know you feel these are useless precautions. But I had to see if the threat was real. It would appear that it is not. So, as of tomorrow, I am discontinuing police surveillance."

"Well, that's a relief. You mean I won't have an armed guard in the stable?"

Chief Harper frowned. "I beg your pardon?"

"The live Nativity. I'm playing the Virgin Mary. There are shepherds and wise men in the tableau, but I can't recall any cops."

"When is that?"

Becky jerked her thumb at Dan Finley. "If I tell you, do you promise not to send Kojak here? It's tomorrow morning from eleven to twelve." She turned to Sherry. "You're twelve to one. Isn't that nice? You can watch me, see how it's done."

"We had a rehearsal," Sherry pointed out.

"Yes, but I wasn't there. Isn't that silly? They should have had someone show you who's done it before. Don't worry, you can take your cue from me."

Sherry smiled, then pressed her lips together tightly.

Doddsworth raised his bushy eyebrows at Chief Harper. "You believe Miss Rebecca's no longer in any peril?"

"I do."

"I wish I shared your optimism."

"I wish I had your experience. Would you care to drop by the station tomorrow, perhaps give me the benefit of your thoughts?"

"It would be my pleasure."

Cora Felton had to stifle a harrumph. *She* had not been invited to the police station. *She* had not been invited to share her thoughts. Not that she had any thoughts to share. Even so.

On the edge of the crowd, Sherry Carter sidled up to Aaron Grant. "Hi."

"Hi."

"I've hardly seen you."

"Sorry. My parents' parties are like that."

"I was hoping to get a chance to talk to them."

"Christmas parties are tough. They're pretty busy."

"So I see."

Aaron lowered his voice. "Wanna see my room?"

"I've seen your room."

"What's your point?"

Sherry looked up at Aaron. He winked roguishly.

Sherry smiled. "Okay. Show me your room."

10

"I CAN'T BELIEVE YOU'RE COMING." SHERRY WAS PILOTING THE Toyota through the freshly fallen snow.

"And miss seeing you play the Virgin M? Surely you jest."

"You can't kid me, Cora. You're on the trail of our secret stalker. You just want to see if anyone makes a move on Becky Baldwin."

"The thought never crossed my mind."

"I'll bet it didn't." Sherry glanced at the dashboard clock. It read 11:36. "I'm surprised you didn't want to come an hour early to watch Becky set up."

"Chief Harper said not to."

Sherry frowned. "What?"

"Last night. While you were upstairs with Clark Kent. He told me if I was anywhere *near* that crèche when old Becky took her place, he'd run me in for disturbing the peace."

"Why in the world would he do that?"

"You're the genius here. Why do you think?"

Sherry blinked. "You mean he *doesn't* think it's a gag? And he *hasn't* pulled his surveillance? He just said he did to set a trap?"

"Now you're cookin'. If Harper's right, you won't have to be the

Virgin Mary. By the time we get there our stalker will have made his move, Chief Harper will have him in cuffs, and the place will be a crime scene. Which would be an excellent result. I just hate to have to miss it."

"Uh-huh," Sherry said. "Does Mr. Scotland Yard have anything to do with your feelings?"

"The man is nice. And I gather he's single."

"The man lives in England," Sherry pointed out. "Were you thinking of moving?"

"I hadn't given it much thought."

"I'll bet. So that's why you came along. To check out Becky Baldwin."

"If Becky happens to be alive and well, that's hardly my fault."

"That's a nice way to put it."

Sherry drove down Main Street to the village green. There were no police cars in sight. Indeed, there were no cars of any kind.

"It would appear Becky's still alive," Sherry said.

"So it seems. Care to drive by and take a look?"

"Why?"

"You're about to play the part. Surely you should check out the tableau. You might learn something."

"I can play the part without Becky Baldwin's help." Sherry said it icily.

"Humor me."

They circled the village green. As they drove by the stable, Cora said, "Stop."

"We can't stop here. We'll block traffic."

"What traffic? We're the only car on the road."

Sherry slowed the car to a stop in front of the stable. It was on the narrowest part of the green, facing the Congregational church. The snow was undisturbed, making the stable seem a magical place, suspended in time and space, dropped in the middle of the Bakerhaven green.

The magic was lost on Cora. She snorted derisively.

"What's with you?" Sherry said.

"Look at Becky. She's kneeling over, she's got her hood down, you can't even see her face."

"Forgive me if I fail to share your disappointment."

"After your whole catfight about Becky showing you what to do, you can't even see her face, and if you pose like that, no one's gonna see your face either."

"I don't recall any catfight. And I have no intention of posing like Becky. I didn't even want to see this."

"Yeah. I did. So where's the fuzz?"

"What fuzz?"

"Exactly. If the cops are watching Becky, where are they? If Joseph's undercover, I'll cook you dinner. And no one else in the stable looks old enough."

Sherry circled the village green again, pulled into the town hall parking lot.

"The church is closer," Cora said. "How come they don't change there?"

"They used to, until they got flak from the PTA."

"Over what?"

"Associating the Nativity with organized religion."

"You've got to be kidding."

"Not at all. The PC Nativity has no religious significance, offends no one, and is famous for miles around."

"I'm way too old," Cora declared.

They went up the steps and in the front door. The town hall was empty.

"Where's the other actors?" Cora asked, looking around.

"Weren't you paying attention during rehearsal? The replacements are staggered. So as not to have the whole tableau exit at once. Virgin Marys are on the hour. Josephs are a quarter after. Either the kings or shepherds come next."

"That's confusing."

"Not if you're a Virgin."

Sherry went into the ladies' room. A blue-and-white costume hung on a hanger on the side of one of the stalls. On the floor was a large shopping bag. Sherry sat on a folding chair, took off her blue jeans and sweater, put them in the bag. Underneath she wore a bodysuit of thermal underwear.

"That looks nice and toasty," Cora observed.

"Easy for you to say. From what I hear, the actors all freeze no matter what they wear."

Sherry slipped into the Virgin Mary robes. She sat back down and pulled on her boots.

"The Virgin Mary in army boots?" Cora said.

"You got a problem with that?" Sherry put on her coat, picked up the shopping bag with her clothes.

Sherry and Cora went out. A teenage boy in parka and wool hat passed them, going up the front steps.

"Joseph?" Cora asked Sherry.

"More than likely. I haven't met them all."

"Looks too young to shave."

"They have a beard for him."

"I doubt it helps."

Cora and Sherry walked around to the back of the crèche, which was opposite the county courthouse.

"This is where we part company," Sherry said. "Unless you figured out some variation where the great-aunt shows up to toast the Christ Child."

"If it's all the same to you, I think I'll go back to trying to spot policemen."

"Probably a wise move."

While Cora continued around the green, Sherry set off through the snow. The trail was easy to follow given the number of actors who had already been over it. As Sherry walked, she glanced at her watch, saw that she was five minutes early. But that couldn't matter. It was a chilly morning. Becky would be relieved to see her.

Sherry climbed up on the back of the crèche, tugged off her boots, and put on her sandals. She stowed her clothes on the ledge, checked her watch one last time—five of twelve—before taking it off and dropping it in the bag. She shrugged off her coat, hung it on a nail on the shelf. Then she opened the back door a crack and peered out. There were no cars driving by, no one on foot, no one watching the scene. Time for the switch.

Sherry stepped out into the stable.

The Virgin Mary knelt in the hay, her arms cradling the Christ Child. She was leaning against Joseph, who was stoically holding her up, though the young face behind the long hair and beard looked distinctly pained. He'd be happy to stretch a muscle or two while they made the switch.

Sherry crept out, touched her on the shoulder. "Okay, Becky. I got it."

Becky might not have heard her. She didn't move. Didn't acknowledge Sherry in any way.

A car came into view, circling the green.

Sherry saw it and wanted to make the change before it drew alongside.

Sherry nudged Becky again, harder.

She still didn't respond. Which was odd. It seemed inconceivable that she could have fallen asleep, but she must have. It was hard to tell, as the cowl of her robe had slipped down so Sherry couldn't see her face.

Out of the corner of her eye Sherry could see the car coming their way.

"Becky!" Sherry hissed. With both hands she half lifted, half pulled her from her spot.

Carl Perkins, his wife, Nancy, and sons Randy and Jed, who had driven all the way from Greenwich to view the Bakerhaven Nativity, got far more than they had bargained for, as not one but two Virgin Marys, apparently vying for supremacy, tugged and pulled at one another, until one of the Virgin Marys spun from the other's grasp and pitched headlong from the manger, landing in a broken, lifeless heap, while the other Virgin Mary gawked in horror, then fainted dead away.

11

SHERRY CARTER OPENED HER EYES TO FIND HER AUNT LOOKING down at her.

"So, you've decided to join us," Cora said.

"What happened?" Sherry asked.

"You fainted. From shock. Perfectly normal, under the circumstances."

"Is she dead?"

"I'm afraid so."

"What killed her?"

"I don't know. And I'm dying to find out. But I had to make sure you're all right."

"Where am I?"

"Town hall. They would have taken you to the hospital, but the numbnuts doctor said you're fine."

Sherry sat up and discovered she was on a gurney in the town hall meeting room.

And dressed as the Virgin Mary.

"Where's my clothes?"

"I'm afraid they're at the crime scene."

"Oh."

On the other side of the room, Sam Brogan was questioning the actors, who were still in costume. They were all schoolkids, and seemed pretty shaken. Dorrie's boyfriend, Lance, dressed as Joseph, appeared to be taking it particularly badly.

There was no other Mary.

"Are you sure you're all right?" Cora asked. "I may have influenced the doc a little 'cause I didn't wanna have to follow you to the hospital."

"Uh-huh. Is she . . . ?"

"Is she what?"

"Dead?"

"You already asked that. Maybe I should stick around a little. But, yes, she is. Dead as a doornail."

"I guess that joker wasn't kidding. It's hard to believe."

"Yeah. Look, if you're sure you're all right, I'd like to get out to the crèche. Harper's there now, and Doddsworth's on his way."

"Go on. I'll be fine."

Left alone, Sherry realized she was still somewhat dizzy. She sat back on the gurney to catch her bearings.

On the other side of the room the interrogation of the actors continued. Sam Brogan seemed intent on his task, and no one paid the least bit of attention to her. Not that she needed it.

Still.

Sherry wished Aaron were there. Surely he'd be along soon, it being a murder.

And not just any murder.

Her murder.

Becky's murder.

Becky Baldwin.

Her rival.

Her nemesis.

The thorn in her side.

Never had Sherry been gripped with such conflicting emotions. Suddenly it seemed as if every obstacle to her happiness with Aaron

Grant had been removed. But removed in such a way as to make happiness impossible. Could she ever look at Aaron again without feeling she had won by default? That but for the hand of fate, she might not have been so lucky?

Lucky.

Sherry shuddered.

Get a grip, she scolded herself angrily. She was behaving like a child. A lovesick schoolgirl. A self-centered, self-obsessed, lovesick schoolgirl. Evaluating every action solely in terms of herself. How could she be so crass, so cruel, so—heartless? Becky was dead. Never mind what it meant to her. Becky Baldwin was dead. Murdered. Someone had killed her. As promised in the poems. The poems Sherry had dismissed as doggerel. Had ridiculed. Just as she'd ridiculed the police surveillance. Becky's bodyguard, Dan Finley. Where had he been when this happened? And what kind of trouble was he in now?

As if on cue, Dan Finley banged in the door, glanced around, then strode over to where Sam Brogan was interrogating the actors. While Sherry watched, Dan pulled Sam aside, and the two conversed in low tones.

"So where's Chief Harper?" an imperious voice demanded.

A familiar voice.

Sherry turned and looked.

Becky Baldwin stood in the doorway.

12

THE VIRGIN MARY LAY IN THE SNOW. HER COWL WAS OFF, AND her blond hair fanned out behind her like a halo. Her sky-blue eyes were open, staring. Her cheeks were frosty pale. Yet she still had that ethereal, waiflike quality.

It was heartbreaking.

Jonathon Doddsworth looked stricken. "Dorrie?" he cried incredulously. "Good God, little Dorrie!"

"Would you keep it down, sir?" Barney Nathan said snippily. The prissy medical examiner was nattily dressed in a pin-striped suit. His bow tie was red, perhaps in keeping with the season. "Hard enough, having to examine the Virgin Mary without outside interference."

"But that's my daughter's best friend!"

"Well, you can't help her now. Just let me do my job."

"Come on, now," Chief Harper said. "Come on, now." He and Cora guided Doddsworth back to the stable.

Doddsworth stumbled, climbing, had to be helped up. He rose from the straw. A tremendous sigh rumbled the features of his face. "Poor Max!"

It took Cora a second to realize he was talking about his daughter.

Doddsworth seemed overwhelmed, as though his mind refused to process the information. "And you say she wasn't supposed to be here?"

"No," Cora said. "It should have been Becky Baldwin. Somehow they must have swapped shifts."

"Good God!"

"I know it's upsetting," Harper sympathized, "but if you have any insights I'd be grateful."

"Of course, of course." Doddsworth made a visible effort to pull himself together. Cora could see him centering himself, trying to focus his attention away from poor Dorrie and onto the problem at hand. It clearly wasn't easy.

Doddsworth regarded the crime-scene ribbon stretched across the front of the stable, muttered, "Utterly ineffective, since she fell out there. Everyone and my auntie Enid's been across that snow. You've got your police, your doctor, your ambulance men, the two trolleys they pushed. Plus however many spectators were milling about."

"None. I read 'em the riot act, kept 'em on the road." Chief Harper pointed to the crowd of people avidly gathered in front of the church. "As you can see."

"Yes. But all the actors jumped down. And I understand some idiot onlookers rushed across the lawn."

Cora Felton flushed. Having been too far away to see which Virgin Mary took the plunge, she'd scampered across the green in record-breaking time. Idiot onlookers, indeed.

"So what can you tell from the tracks?" she asked judiciously, in an attempt to distance herself from the gawkers.

"Not bloody much," Doddsworth told her. "Rum show, really. Makes us dependent on the accounts of witnesses. Who, I daresay, are generally unreliable. Nonetheless, the actors here freezing their bums would surely have noticed if some bloke happened by."

"Well, they didn't," Chief Harper said sourly. "Even her boyfriend was no help."

Doddsworth's eyebrows rose. "What, her steady chap? Was he here too?"

"He was Joseph."

"Blimey." Doddsworth thought a moment. "What was the cause of death?"

"Don't know." Harper turned, called, "Hey, Barney, got anything yet?"

"I'm pronouncing her dead." The doctor jerked his thumb at the EMS unit, who were loading the body onto a gurney. "They'll run her down to the hospital, but she's beyond help. I'll finish up there."

"You got a cause of death?"

"You'll know when I do."

Dr. Nathan followed the gurney off.

"Any chance it was natural causes?" Doddsworth asked.

"Not likely," Harper told him.

"Right. Because of the childish ditties. Without the verses, it's an odds-on bet to be a natural death. With them, the reverse is true."

"Could she have been shot?" Cora suggested.

"I don't see how," Doddsworth said.

Cora pointed to the church. "High-powered rifle. Telescopic sight."

"The actors would hear the shot."

"And think it was a car backfiring," Cora pointed out.

Doddsworth shook his head. "No, we have a subtle crime here. Must have, or it wouldn't have met with success."

"As to that—" Chief Harper began.

Doddsworth cut him off, shouting at the police officer and young woman coming across the green, "See here, now! This is a crime scene! Stay in the road!"

"I want my clothes!" the police officer shouted.

Doddsworth, surprised to hear Sherry Carter's voice coming out of the officer's huge overcoat and hat, exclaimed, "What the deuce!"

"My niece," Cora explained. "She's dressed as the Virgin Mary. She came to relieve the corpse. Her clothes are part of the crime scene. She must have borrowed Dan Finley's coat."

"Is that Miss Rebecca with her?"

"Yes, it is."

"Excellent. I want a word with her. Look here," Doddsworth yelled, "you shouldn't come this way. Do go around by the actors' path."

Sherry and Becky retreated to the road and worked their way around the green to the path Sherry had taken not an hour before. They made their way to the crèche, stepped inside.

"Miss Baldwin. Miss Carter," Chief Harper said. "Just a few questions, if you don't mind. Miss Baldwin, you called me last night to tell me you were switching spots with Dorrie Taggart."

"You knew about this *last night*?" Cora said accusingly.

Chief Harper ignored her. He said to Becky Baldwin, "Why did you change your schedule?"

"I didn't change it. She did."

"Oh?"

"She called me up, said she had a shopping trip planned in the afternoon, and would I mind switching spots. I actually did mind—eleven to twelve is much more convenient than one to two—but there was no real reason why I couldn't. So I rang you up, told you I was switching spots."

"Who else did you tell?"

"No one. I assume you told Dan Finley."

"Someone might have told me," Sherry said. "I thought Becky was dead until she walked in the door."

Doddsworth regarded Sherry with interest. "So, you're the one who found her?"

"That's right."

"Do you feel up to telling us what you did?" Chief Harper asked.

"Of course," Sherry said. "I changed in town hall. I walked around the green, took the actors' path to the back of the crèche so as not to mess up the snow. I stashed my bag of clothes and coat behind the door. I'd like to get them now."

"Are they there?"

"They should be. May I have them?"

"If you don't mind us looking through them first."

"Looking for what?"

"I don't know. Perhaps a murder weapon. Perhaps a clue. Anyway, you stashed your clothes and then what?"

"I peeked out to make sure there was no one passing by. Then I crept out to relieve the girl playing Mary. I thought it was Becky. I tapped her, nudged her, got no response. I thought she'd fallen asleep. I tried to lift her. That's when I realized I was dealing with a dead weight. I lost my grip, and she fell out of the stable."

"What happened then?"

"I don't know. I'm afraid I fainted."

"So you didn't see the other actors react?"

"No. I'm sorry. You'll have to ask them."

A car skidded to a stop in front of the Congregational church. The doors slammed, and two women came pelting across the snow.

Doddsworth scowled. "Something must needs be done. I realize you have limited personnel, yet there must be some way to keep the spectators back."

Doddsworth put up his arms, started to yell at the approaching intruders. The angry words froze on his lips.

It was his wife and daughter.

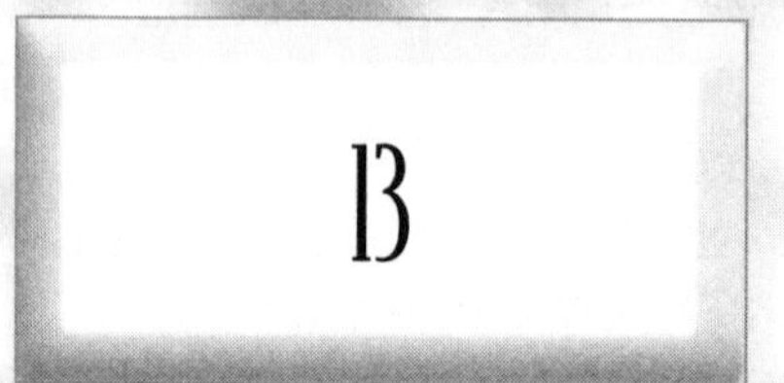

13

"DADDY!" MAXINE CRIED, DUCKING UNDER THE CRIME-SCENE ribbon and climbing up into the stable. "Is it her? Is it Dorrie? Tell me! Tell me, please!"

The inspector sighed heavily. "Yes, Max. It is."

Maxine let out a fresh wail, threw herself sobbing into her father's arms. "That can't be! It can't be! We were going shopping."

Doddsworth hugged his daughter tight, but looked up inquiringly. "When?"

His ex-wife glared at him as if this were all his fault. A slight but attractive woman with full lips and green eyes, Pamela Doddsworth resembled her daughter a great deal, yet struck Cora as an unlikely mate for the lumbering Englishman. That epiphany had evidently occurred to Pamela too. "This morning. Dorrie was going to come pick her up."

"You were at home, Max?"

"That's right. Interrogate your own daughter." Pamela pried Maxine away from Doddsworth and cradled her protectively.

"No!" Maxine cried, twisting away. "I have to know what happened."

Doddsworth shook his head apologetically. "It's too soon to tell."

"But she was fine when she came to the crèche."

Doddsworth blinked. "When she *what*?"

"She was just fine."

Cora studied the look on his face as comprehension dawned. "You mean you were the previous Mary?" Doddsworth murmured incredulously. "The one she came to relieve?"

"Yes, of course. We were going to go Christmas shopping. But she got scheduled one to two. What good was that? I was done at eleven. So she found out who was eleven to twelve, and asked her to change."

Doddsworth, overcome, could think of nothing to say.

Chief Harper stepped in. "How did she find out who was eleven to twelve?" he asked.

"I don't know. Dorrie just called me up, said it was okay, everything was going to be all right." The tears came again. "All right. How can it be all right?" she wailed. "Daddy, you have to find out who did this to Dorrie. You have to."

"It's not actually my place."

A pudgy man erupted from a Mercedes, came lumbering across the lawn. He wore a suit and tie, but no hat, coat, or boots. His black leather shoes disappeared in the snow. He slogged forward, his muscles clearly unused to any such activity. He seemed on the brink of falling down.

A woman ran after him. Thin and big-boned, she had no trouble keeping up, would have been in the lead had she not been sitting in the passenger seat and had to run around the car. She tore across the green, her blond hair streaming out behind her in the wind.

The man ducked under the crime-scene ribbon, leaned on the stable, breathing hard. His face was red. His hair, an elaborate comb-over, hung down the side of his head, leaving him virtually bald. His flesh was even flabbier than Doddsworth's, sporting double and even triple chins.

The woman scrambled up beside him.

Chief Harper, confronted with Dorrie Taggart's parents, swallowed hard. "Horace. Mindy."

"Where is she?" Mindy Taggart cried.

"Dr. Nathan took her," Chief Harper said.

"To the hospital?"

"Yes."

Mindy grabbed her husband's arm. "I told you. Come on, Horace. Let's go."

Horace Taggart had recovered his breath. "Who did this?" he growled.

"Mr. Taggart—" Chief Harper began.

"Who?"

"Horace—"

"Mindy. I have to know." Horace looked up pleadingly at the chief. "Tell me. What happened?"

"Dorrie was playing the Virgin Mary. Miss Carter here came to relieve her and found her dead."

"You did?"

From that angle Horace Taggart was a grotesque apparition. Sherry could barely meet his eyes. "Yes."

Taggart studied her from head to toe. If he found it strange that she was dressed as a policeman, he gave no sign. Cora could practically see his brain whirling, filing the information away.

"Who did Dorrie relieve?" he asked.

"Me!" Maxine Doddsworth fell to her knees. "Oh, Mr. Taggart!" she wailed. "It was *me*!"

Horace Taggart digested that fact too. His expression never changed. But Mindy Taggart looked stricken. Fresh tears streamed down her cheeks.

"Horace—" Mindy began.

Taggart put up his hand, silencing her. "Harper, I want this solved. I don't care what it takes, I don't care who gets hurt. Do you understand me?"

Chief Harper cleared his throat uncomfortably.

Doddsworth opened his mouth to say something.

"Do you understand me?" Taggart's query was like steel, cutting Doddsworth off.

Mindy Taggart seemed drowning in emotions, the loss of her daughter overcoming her natural instinct to apologize for her husband's bad manners. She looked at Doddsworth as if appealing to him for understanding.

But Doddsworth's eyes were on his weeping daughter, clasped in his ex-wife's arms.

Chief Harper exhaled heavily. "I understand you, Horace."

Horace Taggart turned and stomped back toward his Mercedes.

Mindy Taggart followed. As she went, she glanced back over her shoulder at the Doddsworths.

Cora frowned.

Mindy Taggart looked grief stricken, yes.

She also looked terrified.

14

THE CROWD IN FRONT OF THE CHURCH HAD SWELLED. THE spectacular nature of the crime, with the Virgin Mary tumbling headlong from the stable, had drawn the townspeople as well as the sightseers who had driven up to see the Nativity. Grumbling, Sam Brogan had taken on the job of keeping them back. Even so, they filled the road, making it impossible to drive around the green.

Chief Harper and his contingent from the crèche had just reached the church when a puce Volkswagen Superbeetle careened by and skidded to a stop inches from the crowd.

Rupert Winston erupted from the door. The eccentric director looked as flamboyant as ever in a full-length suede overcoat, felt hat, and six-foot-long scarf of scarlet velvet. "Is it true?" he cried, playing to the crowd, the heavens, and the last row of the balcony. "Is she dead? Is Becky really dead?"

"Not so you could notice," Becky Baldwin said.

Rupert Winston's face ran a gamut of emotions that could have served for an actor's audition piece. "Thank God!" he exclaimed. "It seemed too awful to be true, and yet! . . . And yet! . . . Thank

God you're safe!" The hollow smile on his face froze as realization dawned. The reaction was so hammy Cora couldn't tell if he really was surprised, or was simply emoting. "Then what's *wrong*?"

"One of the other girls is dead," Cora informed him.

"Oh, how awful!" he cried, though it obviously wasn't nearly as awful as if it had been Becky Baldwin. "Who is it?"

Maxine Doddsworth flung herself into the director's arms. "It's Dorrie, Mr. Winston! Dorrie's dead!"

"Oh, my God!" Rupert pried himself from her clutches, held her at arm's length. "Are you sure, Maxine? Are you sure it's her?"

"It's her," Chief Harper said. "We have a positive ID. Did you know the girl?"

"She was in my play."

Cora Felton frowned. "Really? What was she?"

"Oh, no," Rupert said. "Not the Christmas pageant. The high school play. Dorrie was in *The Seagull.*"

"So, she was an actress," Cora mused. "Interesting."

Aaron Grant pushed his way through the crowd. "What's interesting? What have we got? Murder?"

Chief Harper snorted in disgust. "This is getting out of hand. I'd like to remind you that all we've got at the present time is a potentially suspicious death. Until we know different, there's nothing to report."

"What isn't there to report on?" Aaron persisted.

Sherry grabbed him by the arm. "It's all right, Aaron. I'll fill you in."

Aaron turned at the sound of her voice, then stared. "Why are you a cop? I thought you were a virgin."

"Oh, right. I gotta get these clothes back to Dan Finley."

"Yes, you do," Chief Harper said. "And then send him out here to clear the street. There's nothing more to see, and there's nothing to report. You got that, Aaron? Let's have no irresponsible journalism here. It's almost Christmas. This is no time for another media circus." Bakerhaven had had its share of media circuses since Cora Felton moved to town.

"If it's a natural death, I'll play it down," Aaron said.

"See that you do."

As Sherry and Aaron hurried off in the direction of town hall, Sam Brogan detached himself from the crowd and ambled over.

"What's up, Sam?" Chief Harper asked.

"Dan Finley's riding herd on the witnesses. He'll be glad to get his coat back." Sam jerked his thumb. "Is that Maxine Doddsworth over there?"

"Yeah, why?"

"She's the last one. Been roundin' up anyone who was in that stable thing the same time as the victim. All kids, 'cept for Miss Carter."

"Anyone see anything?"

" 'Course not. Ask 'em yourself if you want, they're all in town hall. Best bet is the boyfriend. He was holdin' her when she took the plunge."

"Could you keep it down?" Chief Harper warned. "Miss Doddsworth was Dorrie Taggart's best friend."

"So I understand. Dorrie relieved her, which puts Maxine right in the soup. Same as Miss Carter."

"Excuse *me*," Cora Felton warned.

Sam Brogan shrugged. "I don't make the facts, I just report 'em." He flipped open his notebook. "Then there's Alfred Adams."

"Who's that?" Harper asked.

"He's the Joseph Dorrie's boyfriend relieved."

"Why's he important?"

"According to the schedule, the Marys change shifts on the hour, the Josephs at a quarter past. So Alfred Adams comes on at ten-fifteen, leaves at eleven-fifteen. He's in place at eleven o'clock when Dorrie relieves her friend Maxine. He's there for the first fifteen minutes the decedent plays Mary, until he's relieved by the boyfriend, Lance Ridgewood."

"And he saw . . . ?"

"Nothing, natch. Alfred Adams is a simpleminded lout. He's a high school senior—I guess they all are—and a member of the tech crew. He spent the mornin' hangin' lights for the Christmas pageant. Got caught up in his work and lost track of time. Was a good five minutes late for his shift."

"Anything to that?" Cora asked avidly.

Sam shook his head. "He got there ten-twenty 'stead of ten-fifteen, but it don't mean a thing 'cause Dorrie didn't get there till eleven. He was there from the time she arrived at eleven till he was relieved at eleven-fifteen. A fifteen-minute window of opportunity during which he could have killed her. If he did, I'll buy you lunch."

"Uh-huh," Harper grunted.

Sam flipped a page. "The boyfriend Lance Ridgewood's the other side of the coin. Class president, captain of the debate team. Early acceptance to Yale. If I was makin' book, my money'd be on him. If it wasn't the women."

Harper frowned.

On the far side of the crowd a car pulled to a stop, and the trim figure of Barney Nathan emerged. A few prissy, clipped *Excuse me*'s parted the crowd, and allowed him to stride up to the chief.

"I don't want you to take this as a precedent," he announced. "And don't expect me to be so fast next time."

"You have the cause of death?"

"Yes, I do, and you're not going to like it."

"What is it?" Chief Harper asked.

"Poison."

"Poison! How is that possible! She was in the stable. She didn't eat or drink anything. Are you saying she was poisoned before she posed, some slow-acting poison that didn't take effect until she was kneeling there in front of everyone?"

"I'm saying," Dr. Nathan responded dryly, "that she was killed by a quick-acting poison injected directly under the skin."

"You mean she was stuck with a hypodermic?" Chief Harper

was incredulous. "That's impossible. She was on public display in front of half a dozen witnesses."

"That's your problem, not mine," Dr. Nathan replied serenely. "But I don't think she was stuck with a hypodermic."

"And why not?" The chief sounded irritated.

"Because, unless I'm very much mistaken, I have the murder weapon right here."

Dr. Nathan reached in his coat pocket, pulled out a plastic bag, and held it up for all to see. In it was something brightly colored red and blue. At first glance it resembled the feathers of a man's hat.

Cora Felton, who was closest to the doctor, took one look and gasped.

It was a dart.

15

CORA FELTON WAS SNEAKING OUT OF TOWN HALL. IT HAD BEEN twenty minutes since the doctor had produced the dart, and Chief Harper and Jonathon Doddsworth were inside taking witness statements. Ordinarily, Cora would have loved to stay, but Doddsworth had deemed her a witness, and refused to let her listen in. Cora had deemed Doddsworth something far less flattering, and scooted out as soon as she could.

Cora came out the door to find Rick Reed, the handsome, young, ambitious, and totally clueless Channel 8 on-camera reporter, and his film crew interviewing Becky Baldwin on the steps. Seeing Cora distracted Rick, made him fluff a question. Cora smiled. The reporter was hopelessly torn. On the one hand, Cora had just come from the police and would make a better interview. On the other hand, Rick had a crush on Becky, and Cora was unlikely to give him the time of day.

Cora solved his dilemma by announcing, "No comment," and sailing on by. It occurred to her it was the nicest thing she'd ever done for him.

As Cora drew near the church, Harvey Beerbaum detached himself from the crowd and descended on her. The fastidious linguist was as agitated as she'd ever seen him. "What's going on?" he demanded. "No one knows anything, but everyone thinks they do. There are rumors going around of the most outlandish sorts. The young lady was shot with an arrow. She was poisoned with every sort of beverage from herbal tea to diet soda—decaffeinated, no less. She was stabbed, strangled, garrotted, bludgeoned, or smothered with SaranWrap."

"SaranWrap?"

"Positioned over the mouth and nose so that she could not breathe. Are any of those scenarios grounded in reality?"

"It's really not my place to discuss scenarios."

"Balderdash!"

"Balderdash?"

"Cora, it's me, Harvey. What do you know?"

"Not much more than you do, Harvey," Cora said with insincerity.

He looked around, lowered his voice confidentially. "Then tell me this. Was there a letter?"

"You mean a puzzle?"

"Yes. A puzzle poem. By rights there should be, if this is *our* killing. So was there one?"

Cora shook her head. "None was found."

"That's odd," Harvey mused. "Then maybe this was unrelated."

"Not likely," Cora told him. "The victim should have been Becky Baldwin."

Harvey scrunched up his nose. "That's a heartless thing to say."

"I mean the girl took Becky's time slot. Haven't any of the rumors alluded to that?"

"Not really. Becky was doing a there-but-for-the-grace-of-God-go-I routine, but I believed it was simply histrionics." Harvey frowned. "Well, in that case, there most certainly should be a poem. Otherwise, the setup makes no sense. Is it possible the authorities found the poem and didn't divulge it?"

"No chance. I was there when it happened. At the crime scene. Before the cops were. Trust me, there was no poem there."

"Did you look for a murder weapon?"

"I didn't find any murder weapon."

"Are you saying there was none to find?"

"You should have been a lawyer, Harvey. You have a positive gift for cross-examination."

"Not at all. I'm merely listening to what you say. It's very like solving a puzzle, really. Decoding your answers to my questions. And I don't believe you answered my last one. About the murder weapon. It seems to me I've inquired several times without getting an answer."

"Well, speaking of rumors . . ." Cora's voice trailed off invitingly.

"Yes?"

"You suppose I could tell you something without you putting it around?"

"Of course. My lips are sealed," Harvey vowed.

"The doctor found a poisoned dart in Dorrie's clothing. He thinks it's the cause of death."

"A poisoned—!"

"Could you keep your voice down? Now, assuming the killer wasn't one of the actors, a person would have to be right in front of the stable to throw a dart. Or to lean over and stick it in."

"Wouldn't the actors have seen something?"

"Yes," Cora said. "But if they had, the police would be arresting that person now. The fact the police are still questioning them is a good indication the actors don't know squat."

"Excellent point," Harvey said. Clearly, approaching the murder as a logic problem delighted him. "How is that possible?"

"Don't know. But if the actors didn't see something, maybe someone else did. You notice how the stable is set up facing the church?"

Cora pointed at a hawk-nosed man hanging out at the edge of the crowd. "Isn't that the minister over there near the bottom of the steps?"

"That's the Reverend Kimble, of course," Harvey said. "Surely you know him."

Cora, who couldn't remember the last time she'd been in a church without getting married, mumbled, "Yes, of course. Hard to tell at this distance. Listen, Harvey. The Reverend would certainly notice the Nativity. It occurs to me he might know something without being aware that he knows it. If you're on speaking terms with him, I'm wondering if you could draw him out. Ask if there was anyone who might have thrown a dart." She raised an admonitory finger. "Without tipping your hand that's what you're getting at, of course."

"Gotcha," Harvey said.

Cora had to pretend to cough in order to hide her amusement at how quickly the erudite grammarian plummeted into the vernacular at the prospect of pumping a witness. She watched as Harvey threaded his way through the crowd and engaged the Reverend in conversation. With satisfaction she noted that Harvey was directing the clergyman's attention to the stable in the center of the green.

Cora had not had long to formulate her theory of the case, but she certainly had one. If the killer was not an actor in the tableau, then the attack on Dorrie had come from the front. That left two possibilities: the killer drove by in a car, or the killer came on foot. In the latter case, the killer would have needed someplace to hide.

While Harvey Beerbaum had the Reverend's attention diverted, Cora slipped up the front steps of the Congregational church.

She entered and found herself in a small anteroom. In front of her, double doors led into the church itself. The doors were open, and Cora could see the pews for the parishioners, and the raised pulpit. Cora could imagine the Reverend Kimble in it, towering over his flock. She could also imagine him wandering through the church during the day, making it a most unattractive place to hide. Two closed doors off the foyer looked more promising. Disappointingly, both were locked with dead bolts. It occurred to Cora the Reverend Kimble had faith in both a higher power *and* modern security technology.

A narrow stairway in one corner of the foyer curved up and around. Cora tried it, found that it led to the organ loft. This was more like it. Even as she went up the stairs she could see a window in the front wall, where the killer could watch for the right time to strike. Cora checked it out. Sure enough, there was a perfect view of the stable, as well as the street below, where, she noted, Harvey Beerbaum was still chatting up the Reverend Kimble. It was the ideal vantage point, the ideal spot for a killer to lie in wait.

Cora frowned.

So what? From the road, there was a good ten or twenty yards across the snow. Out in the open. No trees for cover. No cover of any kind. Just the white, pure snow . . .

There was no way, absolutely no way, for the killer to get from the church to the stable without being seen by every actor in the tableau.

Yet somehow the killer had.

Cora sighed.

She turned from the window to check out the organ.

She froze.

The organ was the old-fashioned kind, of elaborate, carved mahogany, with ivory keys, round labeled stops, burnished brass pipes, and wooden foot pedals.

Leaning up against the side of the organ was a long stick.

Taped to the top of the stick was a bright red envelope.

Cora's heart began beating faster. She'd wanted a clue, but not this.

Not now.

Cora rushed back to the window. Apparently the Reverend Kimble hadn't had much to say, because Harvey was done with him and was now looking around, probably for her. And the Reverend was headed straight for the church.

Damn!

Cora raced back to the organ. She grabbed the envelope, ripped it open, pulled out the paper inside. Sure enough, it was another acrostic.

Cora was sweating, and it wasn't just her wool overcoat. She looked at the puzzle in her hand and muttered a comment unlikely to be found in its solution . . . and most unseemly, given her surroundings.

Cora dropped to one knee. She shoved the puzzle back in the en-

1 H	2 A		3 N	4 D	5 S	6 B	7 Q	8 C		9 T	10 E	11 J		12 H	13 D	14 R	15 E
16 V		17 U	18 P	19 G	20 Q	21 F	22 N		23 A	24 U		25 E	26 O	27 B	28 A	29 M	30 F
	31 S	32 R	33 T		34 S	35 J	36 A	37 N	38 K		39 J	40 T	41 U	42 B		43 V	44 N
45 S	46 T		47 M	48 E		49 B	50 J	51 G		52 T	53 D	54 E		55 G	56 H	57 E	
58 H	59 P	60 S		61 N	62 K	63 I	64 P	65 Q		66 M	67 S		68 Q	69 O	70 T		71 O
72 S	73 B	74 K		75 J	76 B	77 A	78 U	79 T	80 H	81 D		82 J	83 H	84 F		85 M	86 P
87 T	88 J		89 C	90 M		91 T	92 K	93 P		94 O	95 G	96 U	97 S	98 D		99 T	100 U
101 G	102 P		103 C	104 Q	105 B	106 A		107 L	108 D		109 P	110 G	111 F	112 R	113 Q		114 A
	115 N	116 T	117 H	118 I		119 I	120 O		121 D	122 R	123 L	124 S	125 F		126 B	127 G	
128 I	129 N	130 V		131 B	132 E	133 T		134 P	135 S	136 N	137 A		138 K	139 H		140 B	141 O
	142 V		143 L	144 T	145 N	146 B	147 J	148 S		149 P	150 R	151 M	152 T		153 B	154 U	155 S
156 T	157 C		158 M	159 U	160 F	161 L	162 S	163 G		164 Q	165 N	166 H		167 O	168 E	169 P	

A. Health care for the needy — 2 106 137 114 77 28 23 36

B. She picked up rice in a Beatles hit (2 wds.) — 76 105 42 6 49 126 73 27 131 146 140 153

C. Movie with Kevin Kline as President — 8 89 103 157

D. Ref's call — 53 108 4 81 13 121 98

E. Costner flick (3 wds.) — 15 10 168 25 57 48 54 132

F. Picked on — 160 84 111 125 21 30

G. Cleaning up — 19 51 110 95 55 101 127 163

H. Goddess of love — 56 117 83 166 139 12 1 58 80

I. Exclamation of alarm or surprise — 128 119 63 118

J. Card game (3 wds.) — 35 88 50 11 75 82 147 39

K. Same here — 74 62 138 38 92

L. Oath beginning (2 wds.) — 161 143 107 123

M. Sickness	85 29 90 151 66 47 158
N. Writer/director of "Sleepless in Seattle" (2 wds.)	22 165 136 3 44 61 115 145 129 37
O. "___ Night"	120 71 141 94 26 167 69
P. President's digs (2 wds.)	149 59 18 109 64 134 169 93 102 86
Q. Initially (2 wds.)	104 20 164 7 65 113 68
R. Mary's friend	112 150 32 14 122
S. Oscar-nominated Melina Mercouri film (3 wds.)	124 45 97 60 5 72 148 67 155 162 34 135 31
T. Paul Anka hit (4 wds.)	91 116 33 40 156 87 79 52 46 70 133 99 144 152 9
U. Classic Western musical	78 41 17 96 100 154 24 159
V. Southwest state	130 16 142 43

velope and flung it on the floor. She rummaged through her floppy drawstring purse and began pulling out treasures dating back as far as husband number two. A lipstick. A key chain with a key to God-knows-what. A coin purse. A gun, fully loaded, and, yes, with the safety on. A theater ticket to *Cats,* untorn—funny, she must have never gone. A paper clip. Half a roll of wintergreen Life Savers. And—

A pair of eyeglasses.

An old pair, in rather poor condition. The lenses were scratched, the wire rims bent, the left earpiece was actually gone.

Perfect.

Cora sprang to her feet, threw the glasses on the floor, and stamped on them, hard. The lenses shattered.

Cora tore off her own glasses and jammed them deep in her purse. Hastily she stuffed in her other keepsakes. When she was done, she grabbed the red envelope and the mutilated glasses, leaped to her feet, swung the purse over her shoulder, and groped her way down the stairs.

16

"COULD YOU HURRY IT ALONG?" JONATHON DODDSWORTH URGED impatiently.

Harvey Beerbaum was seated at Dan Finley's desk in the police station, working on the puzzle. Sherry, Cora, and Chief Harper were seated, watching. Doddsworth was crashing around the room like a bull in a china shop, pacing and hovering.

Harvey raised his head from the paper, gave Doddsworth a withering look. "Have you ever solved an acrostic?"

"Can't say as I have."

"Then you can't comprehend what's entailed. With Cora helping me, I could zip right through. Unfortunately, she can't."

Cora tried not to look smug. It wasn't that hard without her glasses. She squinted at Doddsworth, shrugged helplessly.

"Yes," Doddsworth muttered. "Pity." He made a gesture that from Cora's blurry vantage point might have been sticking his thumbs in the armholes of his vest, or might have been an attempt at flight. "I'm not entirely clear on the sequence, Miss Felton. You found the cryptogram, then you broke your spectacles? Or you broke your spectacles, then found the cryptogram?"

Cora, unprepared for the question, said, "Let me see . . ."

Doddsworth pounced. "*Let me see?* This requires no thought. Did you see a distinct red envelope, or a blotchy red haze?"

"Actually, I saw both. Finding the envelope startled me. I dropped my glasses and stepped on them."

Cora was quite pleased with that construction. Perfectly true statements, deliberately designed to mislead.

"The envelope was dangling from a stick?"

"That's right."

"But it wasn't *pinned* to the stick. There are no punctures in it."

"No. It was taped to the stick."

"In what manner?"

"With masking tape."

"There is no tape on the envelope. Where might it be?"

"I tore it off."

"Pardon?" Doddsworth's inflection could not have been more insinuating if Cora had just confessed to the Ripper murders.

"If I hadn't, the envelope would still be taped to the stick."

"And is that not just where it should be?" Doddsworth stroked his muttonchops and swung into lecture mode. "Tape is a jolly good source of fingerprints. Criminals never think of that. They'll cosh some bloke, wipe the bludgeon clean, then leave the victim trussed up with tape. Not masking tape, to be sure. Still, the principle is the same. Criminals neglect the fingerprints in the adhesive."

"Could you keep it down," Harvey said irritably. "I'm trying to concentrate."

"Having trouble?" Cora crooned sweetly. "I'm so sorry I can't help. . . ."

"Maybe you can. What's a seven-letter word for a *Referee's call*?"

Cora's heart skipped a beat. "I have no idea, Harvey. I'd have to *see* where it fits in."

"Which, of course, I can't show you. That's the problem with these acrostics. The answers are scattered."

"I know, Harvey." Cora sighed. "It's so *frustrating* to have a murder investigation going on and not being able to see."

Doddsworth sucked in his breath. "Miss Felton, need I point out that this murder was not committed for your personal recreation? The victim was a childhood friend of my daughter. A young girl, cut down ruthlessly in her prime. Perhaps you could endeavor not to take such pleasure in it."

Cora looked abashed.

Chief Harper, at his desk, tugged uncomfortably at his collar.

"Got it!" Harvey announced.

"You do!" the chief exclaimed. "What does it say?"

"I don't know yet. I just got that one particular clue. A *Ref's call* is *offside.*"

"Yes, yes, do get on with it," Doddsworth said, pacing.

The door banged open and Dan Finley came in. He was carrying something under his coat. "Hey, Chief. Take a look at this."

"What is it?"

Dan stopped, frowned at the number of people assembled in the office, all staring expectantly at him.

"It's all right, what is it?" Harper demanded.

Dan Finley pulled the object from under his coat. It was a bamboo pole about five feet long. A piece of masking tape dangled from the top.

"Here we are," the chief said. "Miss Felton. Is this the pole the puzzle was taped to?" Cora squinted in the general direction of the blur she assumed was Dan Finley.

"I say," Doddsworth put in. "Is this how you handle the evidence? My dear young man, please tell me you haven't *touched* the tape as well?"

"I haven't touched anything," Dan Finley retorted, indicating the handkerchief he was using to hold the pole. "I just don't have an evidence bag long enough."

"Well, there must be one here. We can get it bagged and sent to the laboratory, and—I say! Could it possibly be?"

"Be what?" Harper said.

"Here, young man, hold that up. Let me see. Is it hollow all the way through?"

Chief Harper's eyes widened. "A blowgun?"

"We have a dart. Why not a blowgun? Raise it up, young man."

Cora Felton's face fell in dismay. She couldn't bear the thought of not being able to see the murder weapon. For a moment she considered pawing through her purse and claiming she'd found a spare pair of glasses. Reluctantly, she rejected the idea. She might be able to pull it off, but Harvey Beerbaum hadn't finished the darn acrostic, and she'd be compelled to help him.

"Look!" Doddsworth exclaimed. "You can see right through it. It's a blowpipe, sure enough." He cleared his throat. "Miss Felton, did you handle this *blowpipe* in any way?"

Cora, tired of being beaten up, snapped, "I don't recall."

That was not the response to save her from further embarrassment.

"You don't recall?" Doddsworth repeated it incredulously. "In a matter of such magnitude, *you do not recall*? Do let's go over your actions again. You look. You see the envelope on what you assume to be a stick. You attach no importance to the stick, merely to the envelope, so when you attempt to remove it, you naturally grab the stick to extract the envelope, do you not?"

"It's possible," Cora conceded.

"I'll wager it is. In the event this should prove to be the murder weapon, it may have some rather misleading fingerprints. Well, let's bung it over to the laboratory. Where is the laboratory these days?"

"New Haven."

"Hard cheese. Well, do let's get it processed and get it back. We shall most likely require it."

A search of the police station turned up an evidence bag suitable to hold the blowgun, and Dan Finley was dispatched to the lab.

"Well," Doddsworth said, clearing his throat again. The sound was really beginning to irritate Cora. "What say we have another go at the actors, and see if any of them noticed anything that could have passed for a blowpipe?"

"Got it!" Harvey exclaimed.

Clue	Answer	Numbers
A. Health care for the needy	M E D I C A I D	2 106 137 114 77 28 23 36
B. She picked up rice in a Beatles hit (2 wds.)	E L E A N O R R I G B Y	76 105 42 6 49 126 73 27 131 146 140 153
C. Movie with Kevin Kline as President	D A V E	8 89 103 157
D. Ref's call	O F F S I D E	53 108 4 81 13 121 98
E. Costner flick (3 wds.)	N O W A Y O U T	15 10 168 25 57 48 54 132
F. Picked on	T E A S E D	160 84 111 125 21 30
G. Cleaning up	S W E E P I N G	19 51 110 95 55 101 127 163
H. Goddess of love	A P H R O D I T E	56 117 83 166 139 12 1 58 80
I. Exclamation of alarm or surprise	Y I P E	128 119 63 118
J. Card game (3 wds.)	I D O U B T I T	35 88 50 11 75 82 147 39
K. Same here	D I T T O	74 62 138 38 92
L. Oath beginning (2 wds.)	I V O W	161 143 107 123
M. Sickness	D I S E A S E	85 29 90 151 66 47 158
N. Writer/director of "Sleepless in Seattle" (2 wds.)	N O R A E P H R O N	22 165 136 3 44 61 115 145 129 37
O. "___ Night"	T W E L F T H	120 71 141 94 26 167 69

Clue	Answer
P. President's digs (2 wds.)	W H I T E H O U S E 149 59 18 109 64 134 169 93 102 86
Q. Initially (2 wds.)	A T F I R S T 104 20 164 7 65 113 68
R. Mary's friend	R H O D A 112 150 32 14 122
S. Oscar-nominated Melina Mercouri film (3 wds.)	N E V E R O N S U N D A Y 124 45 97 60 5 72 148 67 155 162 34 135 31
T. Paul Anka hit (4 wds.)	Y O U A R E M Y D E S T I N Y 91 116 33 40 156 87 79 52 46 70 133 99 144 152 9
U. Classic Western musical	O K L A H O M A 78 41 17 96 100 154 24 159
V. Southwest state	U T A H 130 16 142 43

"You've solved the puzzle?"

"Yes, I have. Sorry I took so long. Embarrassing, really. It's just the way these acrostics are laid out that makes them—"

"Yes, yes. But what is the solution?"

Harvey Beerbaum held up the completed puzzle.

"The author is *Me.* The title is *Don't Say I Didn't Warn You.* The poem goes:

"I'm afraid you didn't listen.
I'm afraid you didn't take heed.
So now you pay the piper
As the word becomes the deed.

"As you leave this vale of tears
I hope it dawns on you
It's hard to be a virgin
When you're eating for two."

17

BECKY BALDWIN TREMBLED WITH INDIGNATION. "ABSOLUTELY not!" She was incensed.

Chief Harper thrust his hands up placatingly. "Now, now. Please understand. *We're* not saying this. We're not saying this at all."

"Oh, no? You just did. And why are *they* here? That's what I'd like to know." Becky gestured furiously at Jonathon Doddsworth and Cora Felton seated across from her in the chief's office.

"They're helping me solve the crime," Chief Harper replied. "And they were present when the poem was read. You're lucky it's just them. Harvey Beerbaum and Sherry Carter were there too."

"Oh, good God!"

"And they're not saying a word," Chief Harper assured her. "Which actually isn't that hard. The crime has enough sensational details with the poison dart and blowgun and the first two poems to last for most entire investigations. And all in one day," he concluded glumly.

"One day? It seems like I've had a bodyguard forever!"

"I mean in terms of the crime. It's a lot of facts for the media to report. They're not going to miss one little letter."

"What if they do?"

"Then we will deal with it."

"You're saying you're not releasing the poem now, but it will probably come out?"

"Yes, of course."

"Well, there you are," Becky said bitterly. "I've already given an interview about how this girl was probably killed instead of me. You release that letter, and everyone will think it's *me* the damn killer is talking about."

"This is why it is advisable to be circumspect with the media."

"No kidding," Becky shot back sarcastically. "Tell me something. Did it occur to *you* the killer would send a note hinting I was pregnant?"

"I take it you are not?" Cora Felton inquired sweetly.

Becky's face purpled. "I'm most certainly not!" she snarled.

"Well, don't knock it till you've tried it," Cora said. "Take it from me, it's a perfectly marvelous means of getting married. Not that I've ever *been* pregnant, actually, but it never hurts to let a suitor think so."

"Thanks for the advice," Becky said icily. "I'm an attorney. I have a law practice. I live in a small town. I do *not* need unfounded rumors of this type circulating. I do *not* want people whispering behind my back."

Jonathon Doddsworth leaned in. "This rumor is unfounded?"

The look Becky gave him might have raised fear for his health. "Didn't I just say so?"

"I believe you expressed your outrage. So, how could the killer have made such an egregious mistake?"

"The killer killed the wrong person. I would think that alone would call the killer's accuracy into question."

"Quite so," the Englishman agreed placidly. "But there's a difference between mistaken identity and mistaken fact. Which, as a lawyer, you must surely know. In court, eyewitness testimony is the easiest to discredit. Whereas facts are facts."

"And misassumptions are misassumptions. The killer obviously doesn't know me. He's some sort of obsessive stalker living out a sick fantasy. Of course the details are going to be wrong because he's making them up. I should think that would be perfectly obvious."

"It would certainly appear so.... But in a homicide investigation one cannot exclude theories simply because other theories seem perfectly obvious. Surely you agree."

"I'm not in an agreeable mood," Becky grumbled. "Nor am I in the mood to debate. What about my bodyguard?"

"What about him?"

"I want him gone."

"That might be premature," Doddsworth said.

"Yeah? And then again it might not. You pretended to pull him off me, but you didn't, and look what happened. The killer killed someone else. You think it was mistaken identity, but what if it wasn't? What if the killer killed that girl because he saw the bodyguard and he knew he couldn't get to me?"

"Very unlikely," Chief Harper said.

"Whatever am I thinking?" Becky said sourly. "Because Danny Boy is the most highly skilled of undercover agents, and would never, ever be spotted," she said scathingly. "There's a pageant rehearsal tonight. Will he be going?"

"The rehearsal wasn't canceled?"

"The show must go on. At least according to Rupert Winston. Dorrie wasn't in it, so the murder's clearly unrelated."

"Except for the puzzles," Chief Harper reminded Becky. "Which appear to have been sent to you." As she opened her mouth to retort, he added placatingly, "Let's not start again. This has become a murder investigation. Dan will be used where he's best needed. Just don't concern yourself."

"That's a good one," Becky said. "Someone's trying to kill me, someone's trying to smear me with lies and vicious innuendo, but, hey, don't take it personally."

"That's the spirit," Cora applauded.

"I was being sarcastic."

"Were you?" Cora said innocently. "Well, look on the bright side."

"What's that?"

Cora smiled.

"You're not dead."

18

EVERYONE WAS SUBDUED BUT RUPERT WINSTON. JUDGING FROM Rupert, one wouldn't have known there'd *been* a tragedy. He alluded to it once in a perfunctory manner, mainly to get it out of the way. Not that he didn't emote. His voice lowered, quavered. His eyes were downcast. His body language imparted pain and loss that might have rivaled the suffering of Job.

Seconds later he could barely contain his excitement. He stood on the apron of the stage, in front of the closed curtain, and addressed his huge cast, who were seated on the basketball court in folding chairs. "Ladies and gentlemen, we are going to have a run-through to end all run-throughs. It won't, of course, we will have several more after that, but it should feel that way. So let's get started." With a flourish he cried, "Pull it, Jesse!"

With a great clanking and squeaking of metal on metal, the red velvet curtain parted in the middle. The Russian country manor from *The Seagull* was gone. In its place stood an English village square, all decked out for Christmas in wreaths and bows and jingle bells.

The tech director strode onto the stage with a theatrical *ta-da!* gesture and announced, "We have a set!"

Rupert Winston, who had clearly intended to make that announcement himself, froze with his arms in midgesture. His face clouded for an instant. Then he recovered his composure and converted his gesture to the set into one to the artist who had created it. "Thanks to our tech director, Jesse Virdon," Rupert said smoothly. "Let's give Jesse a hand, shall we?"

Jesse Virdon had an insolent arrogance born of talent. He swaggered somewhat in acknowledging the applause, and preened a bit too long before retreating back into the wings.

Rupert Winston could not be daunted. He pointed to several card tables on the side of the stage and declaimed, "We have props! We have calling birds! We have French hens! We have swans and geese! We have turtledoves! We have pipes and drums! We have golden rings!

"And," he added, gesturing to the middle table, "we have a partridge in a pear tree!"

There were ohs and ahs. Jimmy Potter grinned broadly.

"Where was it?" Cora Felton asked.

"In the props room, where it belonged." Rupert rolled his eyes in Jimmy Potter's direction. "In all probability, it never left."

Jimmy Potter frowned, processing that information. Then he realized it reflected on him. "Hey!" he protested.

"The important thing is it's back," Rupert declared, ignoring him. "We have our set. We have all our props. And we have all our actors. Do we not? Group leaders, are we all here?"

"I'm missing a drummer," Aaron Grant said.

"That's right. Dick Larson called in sick. Which, just so you know, on performance night you do not do. There is a tradition in the Theater. The show must go on. If you have measles, wear makeup. If you have fever, bundle up and try not to breathe on your neighbor. If you are coughing, gargle a full bottle of cough suppressant, and clamp your mouth closed. But be here." Rupert raised his head, yelled, "Jesse!"

Jesse Virdon emerged once again from the stage-right wings. "Yeah?"

"For this rehearsal, you are a drummer drumming."

"All right!" Jesse raised his arms in self-congratulation. The young tech director was in his midtwenties and still rather boyish.

"Jesse is our man for all seasons," Rupert explained. "In addition to being our tech director, set designer, scene painter, and stage manager, Jesse is also our understudy. In the event there is someone who cannot walk, crawl, or be carried to the theater on the night of performance, Jesse will fill in."

"For the men," Jesse corrected.

"For anyone but Becky Baldwin," Rupert declared. "Did you know in Shakespeare's day there were no women in the theater? Men played all the roles. If I need you as a maid a-milking, Jesse, I'm sure you'll be fine."

Jesse was clearly appalled by the prospect. He dropped his macho bravado, crinkled up his nose. "I don't think I can be an understudy."

"Why not?"

"I'm the stage manager. I got too much to do."

"Yes. And filling in for the actors is one of your duties."

Jesse shook his head stubbornly. "I got too much to do."

Rupert frowned. Jesse Virdon was a teacher, not a student. And the pageant was not a high school production, so, actually, Jesse was a volunteer. If Rupert pushed him too hard, he'd quit. And the trim on the set still needed painting.

"Alfred!" Rupert bellowed, improvising.

"Sir?"

"Out! Here!"

Alfred Adams scurried from the stage-left wings. "Yes, Mr. Winston?"

"You're a drummer drumming."

Alfred's mouth fell open. "But I'm the light man. . . ."

"I know that. Just fill in for now."

"But . . ."

Cora nudged Sherry, whispered, "He's the first Joseph. The one in the stable when Dorrie took her place."

Becky Baldwin, seated between Aaron Grant and Dan Finley, leaned in. "That's Dorrie's boyfriend? You've gotta be kidding."

"No, no," Cora hissed. "Dorrie's boyfriend was the *second* Joseph. The one holding her when she took the dive. *This* guy is the one Dorrie's boyfriend, Lance, relieved."

"Doesn't look like a killer, does he?"

"So you know him?" Cora asked.

"Miss Felton," Rupert reproved from the stage. "I'm sure you believe what I'm saying applies to everyone *but* you, but in point of fact, it does not. If there is anyone here who could benefit from rehearsal, it is most certainly you. So, please, try to pay attention. . . . Now then, I am going to call your groups one at a time, to find your props and take your places backstage. We'll count down, starting with the twelve drummers drumming. Will the drummers come up here, please?"

Aaron got up from his seat next to Sherry and made his way onstage, where he, ten drummers, and Alfred Adams hung toy drums around their necks.

"All right? Do all the drummers have drums?" Rupert demanded.

Alfred Adams raised his hand. "I'm missing a drumstick."

"Make a note of it."

"Yes, Mr. Winston." Alfred started offstage.

"Where are you going?"

"To write a note."

"Not now! You're a drummer drumming. Write a note when you're done drumming."

"Yes, Mr. Winston."

"All right. Pipers piping, come get your pipes."

"There better not be a puzzle attached to any of those props," Cora whispered.

There wasn't. No red envelope appeared. The actors all took their places without incident. At the piano, Mr. Hodges played the opening strains.

Becky Baldwin wandered out onstage. As it was the first day of Christmas, her face was cherubic, anticipating her lover's gift. She sang sweetly, " '*On the first day of Christmas, my true love gave to me . . .*' "

A sandbag whizzed from the rafters, missing her by inches.

19

Chief Harper was fit to be tied. "You were supposed to be watching out for her!"

"I *was* watching out for her," Dan Finley protested wretchedly.

"Then how did this happen?"

"I was watching for an attack from the ground, not from above."

"If someone killed her from *above* that didn't count? And what about you?" the chief raged at Cora Felton. "I would have thought you might have kept your eyes open."

"Right, Chief. I should have been climbing around in the rafters looking for faulty ropes."

Rupert Winston stuck his nose in. "It's too bad the sandbag fell, but it didn't hit anyone. Can't we leave it at that?"

"You're not concerned? It nearly squashed your star."

"Yes, but it didn't. And I've got a play to rehearse."

"Maybe, maybe not. I would find it understandable if Ms. Baldwin was too upset to go on."

"Ms. Baldwin is fine." Becky strode up and struck a pose. Having gotten over the initial shock, she seemed to relish playing plucky and courageous. "There is no reason to call off rehearsal just because a sandbag fell."

"Sandbags don't fall," Chief Harper pointed out grimly. "Sandbags get *dropped.*"

"They can fall if they're tied off wrong," Rupert Winston suggested.

The sandbag in question was attached to rope and was part of a counterweight system used for flying flats. It was a round, ten-pound affair, which would have crushed Becky Baldwin to a pancake had she had been standing two steps farther stage left. Now it lay in the middle of the stage along with the length of rope, which had fallen after it.

"Where was the rope tied off?" Chief Harper asked.

Rupert pointed. "The rope went up into the flies over a pulley, then stage right over another pulley, then down the side wall where it's tied off to the pinrail. Just like all the other ropes."

"Looks like someone did a sloppy job. And who would that be?"

Alfred Adams, still carrying his drum and one drumstick, opened his mouth to protest, but Rupert interposed smoothly, "It could have been anyone on the tech crew."

"Were they here today?"

"Oh, now, look—" Alfred protested.

"I take it *you* were here?"

"Alfred was in here this morning. Before he had to be in the stable."

"Right," Harper said grimly. "You were Joseph," he told Alfred. "As I recall, you realized you were late for your turn, and had to run out. What were you working on before you left here?"

"I was hanging lights."

"On a ladder?"

"No. Onstage."

Chief Harper looked puzzled.

"The lights in the flies are hung on bars," Rupert Winston explained. "The bars are lowered to stage level and lights are hung. Then they're hoisted back up into the flies and aimed."

"Hoisted how?"

"They're hoisted by ropes, and tied off to the pinrail."

"The same pinrail where that sandbag was tied off?"

"Yes, as a matter of fact, it is."

Chief Harper eyed Alfred Adams critically. "Any chance you could have untied one rope when you thought you were tying another?"

"No way!"

"Hmm. Let's see the pinrail."

Drummers, pipers, lords, and ladies gave way as Rupert Winston led Chief Harper into the stage-right wings, with Cora Felton tagging close behind.

On the side wall, about waist high, was a long, black pipe, about six inches in diameter, with sturdy black pegs sticking straight up and straight down about a foot apart. Ropes were twined around each pair a few times and tied off with a half hitch.

Flats, door frames, and furniture, piled up against the wall, obscured over half the pipe.

"What's all this?" Harper asked.

"Oh, that's the *Seagull* set." Rupert was getting impatient. "It's the high school play I'm directing. We had to move the set out of the way for the Christmas pageant."

"Well, the set is blocking your pinrail. When was it moved?"

Rupert's eyes widened as the significance of the question dawned on him. "Just this afternoon, but I assure you—"

"Who moved it?"

"I did," Jesse Virdon answered defiantly. The young tech director was wearing his headset, even though it wasn't connected to anything. He stuck his chin out, as if daring anyone to find fault. "I took down the old set and put up the new one. All by myself. I worked all afternoon. And no one helped."

Harper sized him up. The quarrelsome young man was thin but muscular. The chief could imagine him schlepping the whole set by himself. Harper pointed to the pipe. "You untie any of these ropes?"

"I untied four ropes connected to the set I took down. And I tied off the same four ropes when I connected them to the set I put up."

"Where was the sandbag tied off?"

"How the hell should I know?"

Harper turned to the director. "How about it, Mr. Winston?"

"I have no idea. You see the free spaces on the pinrail? It could have been any one of them."

Chief Harper inspected the rail. "What is this rope here?"

The rope had been wound around the bottom and top pegs a couple of times, but had not been tied off.

"I don't know. Let me see."

Rupert took hold of the rope, pulled on it.

Everyone looked up.

In the flies, a long pole with several stage lights attached to it rose slightly.

"My God," Rupert said. "It's the light pole. I thought you tied that off."

"I *did* tie it off!" Alfred protested.

"It's not tied now. And neither was that sandbag. You mind telling me how that happened?"

Alfred, picked on, looked betrayed. "I have *no idea* how it happened. *I* tied everything off."

Jesse Virdon folded his arms and jutted out his chin. "*I* didn't untie it."

"Well, tie it off now," Harper said, "and let's make sure everything else is tied."

Everything was.

"Satisfied?" Rupert Winston asked, somewhat querulously. "Now, could I go on with my rehearsal?"

Harvey Beerbaum stuck his oar in. "How about a red envelope? Shouldn't we be looking for another puzzle?"

Cora Felton ground her teeth, but, uncharacteristically, held her tongue.

"Yes, yes, we'll *certainly* be on the lookout for that," Rupert Winston told Beerbaum impatiently. "Now, if we could *please* get on with it—"

But before they could, Jonathon Doddsworth burst in. "I just heard! Is everyone all right?"

Rupert Winston clapped his hands to his head. "God save me!"

"Everyone's fine," Harper informed the inspector. "A sandbag just fell."

"Great Scott! Where?"

"On the stage."

"It didn't cosh anyone?"

"No, it didn't."

"Did it come close?"

"It just missed Miss Baldwin."

"By a mile," Becky corrected. "I'm fine. Everyone's fine. Let's rehearse."

"Steady on," Doddsworth insisted. "Did you conduct a search?"

"No. We didn't."

"Really?" Doddsworth's eyebrows formed perfect arches. "And yet the first puzzle was discovered right here onstage. And the second in the girls' dressing room. Which would be downstairs, would it not?"

"Yes, it would be."

"I should think a search was warranted."

"Well, go ahead and conduct one," Rupert Winston said, "but would you mind doing it to music?"

Doddsworth stared him down. "A girl has met her death. Perhaps you appreciate the importance of an investigation?"

Rupert never blinked. "I certainly do." He gestured to the actors. "And these people do too. If they don't get out of here until after midnight, I'm sure they'll understand who is responsible."

Doddsworth's nose twitched. "So be it. You go about your business and I shall go about mine. This is not a dress rehearsal?"

"No."

"Then you shan't be using the changing rooms?"

"No, we won't."

"Splendid. I'll begin with them. How might I get there?"

"The stairs in the backstage corner."

"Which corner?"

"Either. There's two stairs."

"Really? Fascinating." Doddsworth pushed his way into the wings.

Rupert rolled his eyes and clapped his hands together. "Now then, people, if you wouldn't mind, let's take it from the top."

It was deadly quiet as Becky Baldwin stepped out onstage. No one moved, but everyone watched. Chief Harper and Dan Finley watched from the wings.

Becky Baldwin, despite her bravado, seemed almost hesitant. But there was a proud defiance to her carriage. She kept her chin high, glided to the exact spot where she had been when the sandbag came crashing down.

Chief Harper kept an eye on the pinrail.

Dan Finley watched the flies.

The music trilled.

Becky smiled and began, " *'On the first day of Christmas, my true love gave to me.'* "

Jimmy Potter marched proudly on from stage left, singing in a clear tenor, " *'A partridge in a pear tree.'* "

Jimmy thrust the partridge and pear tree at Becky, who oohed and ahed and fussed over them while the music vamped. Then, quick as a wink, Jimmy and his present were gone from the stage, as Becky began again, " *'On the second day of Christmas, my true love gave to me.'* "

Mary Cushman, the plump owner of Cushman's Bake Shop, accompanied by an even plumper woman Cora did not know, entered the stage holding large papier-mâché birds. Mrs. Cushman sang the solo line, " *'Two turtledoves.'* " Then, as Jimmy Potter came marching back onstage, he and the two women sang, " *'And a partridge in a pear tree.'* "

Cora, backstage with her pail and milking stool, mentally calculated the odds of Rupert Winston stopping the run-through before he got to the maids a-milking. She figured them to be pretty high. Of course, her calculation might have been influenced somewhat by the glimpse of Jonathon Doddsworth disappearing down the stage-right stairwell with the stated intent of searching the dressing rooms.

This, Cora knew, was a fool's errand. Surely there was nothing of import in the dressing rooms.

Even so.

Cora bristled at the thought of Jonathon Doddsworth searching them.

What if he found something?

Onstage, Becky Baldwin began musing about the third day of Christmas.

Rupert Winston cried, "Wait! Wait! You've jumped the gun! You must leave time for everyone to get off. Take it from the exit."

The interruption tipped the scale.

Cora Felton set her pail and milk stool along the back wall, and slipped quietly down the stairs.

The hallway was empty. Cora, who'd never entered it from backstage, had to take a moment to orient herself. The costume and props rooms would be on her left. The girls' and boys' dressing rooms would be down the corridor to the right.

A light was on in the costume room. Cora peeked in, but there was no one there. Just dress dummies, sewing machines, full-length mirrors, and racks and racks of costumes. It occurred to Cora, if Doddsworth chose to search it, it would take him some time.

Cora left the costume room, crept down the hall.

Light spilled out under the girls' dressing room door. If Doddsworth was in there, he had closed the door behind him so as not to be disturbed. Well, wasn't that just like him. Tough luck, Sherlock.

Cora turned the knob, pushed open the door.

Inspector Doddsworth stood at the far end of the room, inspecting the costumes hanging from the rack. He spun around at the sound of the door.

Cora's heart skipped a beat.

In Doddsworth's hand was a red envelope.

20

"WHERE'D YOU GET THAT?" CORA BLUSTERED. SHE WASN'T EXACTLY sure what she was going to do about another puzzle, but she managed to put up a brave front.

Doddsworth seemed reluctant to tell her. After a pause he said, "I found it in a costume."

"Pinned to it?"

"No. Propped up."

"Becky Baldwin's costume?"

"I wouldn't know. Which one would be Miss Baldwin's costume?"

"I'm not sure it's even here. These are just the finished costumes. The ones the wardrobe lady is still working on are in the costume shop. That's where mine is. I saw it when I peeked in just now," Cora blathered. Would Doddsworth notice she was prattling on nervously, desperately trying to figure out what she was going to do when he opened the envelope? "Let's see, this is a ladies dancing. That's a ladies dancing. That's a maid a-milking, but it's not mine. Ah, here we are." She stabbed a finger at a pale pink dress with an attractive embroidered lace trim. "That's Becky's dress."

Doddsworth nodded. "That's the one. The envelope was wedged in the neck hole."

"Interesting," Cora said. "The first one was pinned."

"Well, this one was not." Doddsworth held the envelope up. "Not a puncture in it, now, is there?"

"I can see that."

Doddsworth was holding the envelope by the corner with his handkerchief. He whipped a crumpled plastic bag from his coat pocket, shook it out, stuck the letter in. "Not that I expect any prints. The first three envelopes were clean. But as to the contents . . ."

Cora's eyes flicked. "Yes. The contents."

"If this should be another puzzle, your presence is fortuitous."

Cora was trying to think of a comeback when from above there came a bellow as thunderous as a foghorn. "WHERE THE HELL IS MY MAID A-MILKING?"

The unmistakable bellow of Rupert Winston rattled the rafters. Luckily, no more sandbags fell.

"Oh, my God, I missed my cue!" Cora grabbed Doddsworth by his coat sleeve. "Come on! Come on! You gotta show them what we found—all right, *you* found—but I need a diversion or I'm gonna be hung out to dry!"

"I'm not sure everyone should see this—"

"Fine. Take it away with you," Cora suggested, desperately dragging him toward the stairs. "Grab Chief Harper and get out of here. Just make enough noise doing it so Rupert has someone else to yell at. I'll owe you one."

"If it's a puzzle we'll need your help," Doddsworth pointed out.

"Take Harvey. Rupert won't care. If you take me, he'll freak."

They had reached the top of the stairs, where dozens of actors hissed, "Come on, come on, where are you! Get out there!"

Cora walked out onstage, where Rupert stood motionless. The director looked like a time bomb primed to explode.

"Miss Felton. How thoughtful of you to join us."

Astonishingly, Doddsworth came to Cora's rescue. That was

how it looked to everyone in the theater. The inspector strode out onstage, his overcoat flapping behind him, and stepped between Cora Felton and the director, actually shielding her behind his arm. "Mr. Winston. I regret that a situation has arisen which requires Miss Felton's attention. I fully appreciate your need to rehearse, and I promise I shall return Miss Felton with all due speed. But at the moment, the game's afoot. So do carry on in our absence, there's a good chap."

"Now, see here," Rupert Winston sputtered. "You can't do that."

"I can and I will," Doddsworth told him. "I happen to need Miss Felton's assistance with this." He reached into his coat and pulled out the plastic bag with the red envelope. The gesture would have been more dramatic had he not dropped the evidence bag on the floor. Even so, its production was greeted with oohs and ahs.

Rupert Winston's mouth fell open. For once the director could think of nothing to say.

"So," Doddsworth went on airily. "Perhaps we can clear up this little matter of someone bombarding your actress. Chief Harper, if you would accompany us. Miss Felton, where's your wrap?"

Cora cast a pleading glance stage left, where Sherry Carter stood amid the ladies dancing. Sherry shrugged helplessly. Under the circumstances, what could she do?

"Sure you don't want Harvey?" Cora whispered desperately as Doddsworth spirited her away.

"From the expression on your director's face, it would be prudent to remove you from the line of fire."

On any other occasion Cora might have been grateful.

As they drove to the police station, Doddsworth filled Chief Harper in on the discovery of the fourth envelope. Cora barely heard. She was too busy trying to think of a way out.

Cora was trapped, and she knew it. Any minute now she was going to be confronted with a puzzle that she could not solve. This time there was no escape. Sherry wasn't there to slip her the answers. Harvey wasn't there to do the puzzle for her. She could hardly smash her glasses again. Maybe she could drop them, lose them in the snow. It was coming down harder now, covering the road. Maybe Chief Harper would skid and have an accident.

It occurred to Cora how desperate she was.

And how short the trip was from the high school into town.

Chief Harper cruised down Main Street and pulled up before the police station, a white building with green shutters that could have passed for any of the other shops on the picturesque street, and had once actually been one. He ushered Cora and Doddsworth up the steps and fitted the key in the door. A native New Yorker, Cora could never get used to the concept of a police station that was locked because no one was there.

Chief Harper flipped on the lights, stamped the snow off his boots, and led the way into his inner office.

"Let's not stand on ceremony," he said. "Where's the new clue?"

Doddsworth fished the plastic bag out of his pocket, then put on thin rubber gloves. "Useless precaution. Our poet doesn't leave prints, but even so. Have you a letter opener, Chief?"

The chief did. Doddsworth inserted it into the flap, slit the envelope. He pulled out a folded piece of paper and opened it.

Cora Felton sucked in her breath.

"Well?" Chief Harper demanded. "Is it another puzzle?"

Doddsworth looked up from the paper at Chief Harper, then looked at Cora, then down at the paper again.

He turned the paper around for them to see.

On it was written:

WRONG GIRL.

21

THE BAKERHAVEN MALL WAS LIT UP LIKE A CHRISTMAS TREE, WITH enormous plastic Santas blazing bright on every lamp pole. There were also angels, stars, bells, and wreaths, but they were discreet wire sculptures outlined in tiny white lights, actually rather artistic and tasteful, if one could see them through the commercial Christmas haze.

Not that any such reminder to shop was necessary. The parking lot was jammed, and cars were hungrily circling.

"Good lord," Cora griped as she piloted the Toyota through the rows. "What kind of shopping mall is this? No parking spaces?"

"It's almost Christmas."

"Exactly. Which is why we need to shop."

"I still feel funny about it. I mean, that young girl just got killed."

"Sherry. Life goes on. You wanna get something for Aaron?"

"Of course I do. I just can't think of anything. Come on, help me out. What do you think he'd like?"

"I *know* what he'd like."

"Aunt Cora."

"You wanna make Aaron happy, give *yourself* something from Victoria's Secret."

"You're not helping."

"Not that I ever did that. Though I wouldn't even wanna tell you some of the things Melvin used to give me."

Taillights gleamed as a car backed out down the row. Gunning the engine, Cora skidded toward it, but a man in a sports utility vehicle rounded the corner and screeched into the spot.

Cora voiced her opinion on men, malls, Christmas, SUVs, men, shopping, husbands, and men.

Sherry was lucky to keep her from leaping out of the car.

Cora eventually drove off, but not before treating the other driver to a rather unseemly gesture.

"Boy, what a shock finding that new clue," Sherry said, largely to distract Cora, who was driving angrily, and a little too fast. "You should have seen the look on Rupert Winston's face. I swear he thought you left it yourself just to get out of rehearsal."

"I didn't, but what a great idea." Cora skidded around a corner, tore down another row of solidly parked cars. "I wonder where I could get some red envelopes. . . ."

"Cora! Don't you dare!"

"Killjoy."

"So what do you make of the case?"

Cora grimaced. "It doesn't make sense. That's the most striking thing about it. Everything's a contradiction. The girl was killed in a stable. Aside from you, the only ones who could have killed her there are her boyfriend, her best friend, and Alfred the One Drumstick Wonder Nerd. Which makes perfectly good sense, except, drat it, she was the wrong girl. Everything points to the fact Becky Baldwin was the target. The poems were delivered to Becky Baldwin. Becky Baldwin was supposed to be in the stable, not Dorrie. As soon as it becomes clear that the murdered girl was not Becky, there is another attempt on Becky's life. And, just in case there is any doubt, the killer leaves a message stating that he—or she—blew it."

"Assuming the message was from the killer."

"It was in a red envelope."

"Yes, but it wasn't a puzzle."

"Of course not. Those first three puzzles were prepared in advance. Then the wrong girl gets bumped off. Oops. Slight miscalculation. Becky Baldwin still needs to be dispatched. A sandbag on her head will suffice, but a note needs to be found, informing us *this* was the real crime. This time, the killer doesn't have time to write a poem and stick it in a puzzle. But this time, the killer doesn't have to. All the killer needs is a short, blunt message, getting the point across."

Cora, seeing a snub-nosed minivan snag a parking space, muttered a short, blunt message herself, getting the point across.

"And who was the killer?" Sherry asked. "Who planted this message?"

"I have no idea. Except for one thing. When I saw Doddsworth in the girls' dressing room with that envelope, it occurred to me he might be the one who put it there."

"Come on."

"Correct me if I'm wrong, but didn't all this start, the puzzle in the pear tree and all that, didn't that start *after* that Brit got here?"

"The policeman is the killer?" Sherry arched her eyebrow. "Isn't that a popular plot twist in some of those books you read?"

Cora ignored the remark. "He wasn't there when the sandbag fell. He came right after, claiming he'd just driven up. Well, maybe he did. Or maybe he was at the top of the backstage stairs—the ones he pretended he didn't know where they were—and maybe he was there with a rope dropping a sandbag on Becky Baldwin's head, sneaking out the back door, walking around the high school, and walking into the gym as if he'd just arrived. Now, wouldn't that work?"

"Perfectly," Sherry said. "He comes over from England to murder his daughter's best friend. Someone he used to play with when she was a little girl. I can't think of a thing wrong with that."

"Well, when you put it that way."

A car turned the corner, coming their way. Cora skidded sideways to let it go by. Instead, it slammed to a stop in front of them, forcing them to stop too.

This time, Cora was out of the driver's seat while the Toyota was still rocking. She came pelting around the front of her car to accost the other driver, who was climbing out of his.

It was Chief Harper.

Cora was still steamed. "What the hell do you think you're doing?" she raged.

"Looking for you. Aaron Grant thought you two might be here."

"I told him we were going shopping." Sherry got out of the car too. "What's up, Chief?"

"I assume you've been discussing the crime?"

"That's a brilliant assumption," Cora said irritably.

"What's your opinion of it?"

"It's a bummer."

"Yes, it is. Unfortunately, as police chief, I have to be slightly more specific."

"That's tough, Chief. Would you mind moving your car? I'm trying to get a space here."

"Oh, I'll be going. I just wanted to make sure you have as bad a night as I do."

"I *beg* your pardon?" Cora snapped.

"Barney Nathan just weighed in with his autopsy."

Cora's eyes widened. "And . . . ?"

"Dorrie Taggart was two months pregnant."

22

It was a typical teenage room. Crumpled clothes on the floor. A poster of what appeared to be terrorists but was probably just a rock group on the wall. A boom box by the bed blaring some incomprehensible noise, perhaps the terrorists' latest hit.

Lance Ridgewood lay in bed. He was unshaven. He wore ratty jeans and a dirty T-shirt. Cora decided that was a costume, part of his image. It occurred to her Lance was a handsome young man, would clean up pretty well.

She slammed the door to attract his attention and said, "Hi, Lance. Mind if I ask you a few questions?"

He raised his head, looked at her. "Cops already did."

"Yeah, your mom told me. I thought maybe I could help."

"Don't need help."

Cora walked over to the boom box, switched it off.

"Hey!" Lance threw his legs over the side of the bed and sat up. "What you doin', lady?"

"Your girlfriend just got killed. I know you're in shock, but you can't hide behind a wall of sound forever. The cops were here last night?"

"If you talked to my mom, you already know that."

"I know what she said. I'd like to hear what you have to say."

"Yeah, the cops were here. During the Knicks game, for Christ's sake."

"Dorrie *was* your girlfriend?" There was just the hint of a sarcastic edge to Cora's voice.

"We'd been going out. Yes, I'm upset, but why hassle me? I already told them everything I know."

"That was before they found out she was pregnant."

"Boy, was that a shock. I don't know how that happened."

"You and your father never had a little talk?"

"That's not funny."

"No, it isn't. Come on, Lance, give me a break. I don't think you murdered Dorrie, and I'm going to find who did. How about helping me out?"

"What do you mean, you don't think *I* killed her?"

"I thought you got into Yale. You were holding her when she died. You were her boyfriend. And she was pregnant. A scandal that would freak out your parents and might scare off your college. If you were taking an SAT test, and the question was *Who had the best murder motive,* you think you might be leaning toward *A, The boyfriend* as the most likely answer?"

"I didn't do it," Lance grumbled.

"No, I don't think you did. Unfortunately, proving it is going to take more than just your say-so. First off, was that your kid?"

"No way."

"Well, that's mighty strange. Dorrie was playing the Virgin Mary. Another immaculate conception is just too much coincidence, even in Bakerhaven. What's the matter, weren't you using birth control?"

"I can't talk to you about this. You're a . . . woman."

Cora smiled. "You started to say *old woman,* didn't you? Thought you might offend me. That wouldn't offend me nearly as much as if you lie to me. So, try again. Was the kid yours?"

Lance glared at her for a moment. Then his lip quivered. "I don't think so."

"Why not?"

"If it was, she would have told me."

"And she didn't?"

"No." Lance snuffled and looked up. His eyes were wet. "You gotta understand. Dorrie wasn't like that. Yeah, she was a bit of a klutz. It would be just like her to screw up her birth control and get pregnant. But not with someone else. She wouldn't do that. And there's no way she wouldn't tell me."

"So how do you account for it?"

"The doctor must be wrong."

Cora's silence was eloquent.

Lance's face hardened. "Look, lady. You didn't know Dorrie. I did. And you're way off base."

A fresh tear formed in Lance's eye, started down his cheek.

Cora thought about it, then sighed. "Hey, buck up, kid. Maybe I'm doing you a disservice. You pushed my buttons griping about the Knicks game. If Dorrie really meant something to you, help me get her killer. Okay?"

"How?"

"Tell me about Dorrie. What was she like?"

"Dorrie was fun. That's what makes this so hard to believe. She had real spirit, you know. Threw herself into everything."

"Like what?"

"I dunno. Whatever. Lately it was skiing. We went to Catamount just last week."

"Dorrie was a good skier?"

"No." Lance smiled fondly at the memory. "She'd fall down a lot. Real klutz, you know. But she never got frustrated. She knew how to laugh at herself. Had more fun than anyone."

"She tease people?"

"Oh, sure. But not in a mean way. Everybody liked Dorrie. Everybody."

"So who would want to kill her?"

Lance shook his head. "That's the thing. No one would. It's gotta be a mistake."

"Uh-huh," Cora said, without enthusiasm. "So help me understand what happened. You were in the manger holding Dorrie. . . ."

Lance shuddered. "Yeah."

"Did you know it was her?"

"Sure."

"You saw her face?"

"No."

"How come?"

"Her whatchamacallit was down. You know, the thing over her head."

"Her cowl."

"Yeah. The hood of her costume."

"So how did you know?"

"I saw her in town hall. Before. That's where the costumes are. I was going in to change just as she was coming out."

"Did she say anything?"

"She said, 'See you out there.' "

"That's all?"

Lance flushed. "She said, 'See you out there, hot stuff,' if it really matters."

"What did you say?"

"I asked her what she was doing. She told me she'd swapped spots."

"What happened then?"

"She said, 'Gotta go,' and ran off." He exhaled irritably. "If you must know, she said, 'Gotta go, Joey babe.' She called me Joey babe and I called her Mary kid. When we did the Nativity."

"So what did you do?"

"Went and changed."

"The next time you saw her was in the manger?"

"That's right."

"Did you speak to her then?"

"No, I didn't."

"Why not?"

"No talking, no kidding around, no personal contact. Those were the rules. I expected her to break them. But if she didn't, I certainly wasn't going to."

"When you got there, where was she?"

"On the floor, holding the Baby Jesus, leaning against Joseph."

"Who was Joseph?"

"I don't know. Some dweeb."

"Alfred Adams?"

"Yeah. I don't know him. I only know 'cause it was on the schedule sheet."

"You talk to Alfred?"

"No way. I did just what I was supposed to. Crept up behind him, tapped him on the shoulder, slid into his place. And he slipped out the door."

"You took Alfred's place holding Dorrie up? Was she dead?"

He cringed, young and vulnerable. "I don't know. That's what the cops asked me, and I don't know. I mean, how could I? I was just grateful Dorrie wasn't trying to crack me up. You don't screw around with the Nativity. Mr. Ferric would tell the principal, and there'd be hell to pay. But Dorrie didn't always follow rules."

"What do you mean by that?"

"Like I said. Dorrie liked to kid around. And sometimes she'd crack *herself* up doin' something stupid, and once she started giggling, you couldn't stop her." He nodded. "Dorrie was a gas."

"I see."

"Anyway, she didn't, and I was glad. That's what I was feeling then. I was just glad she was taking it seriously."

"She stayed like that for how long?"

"Until the next Mary relieved her. That would be your niece, right? Is that why you're so interested?"

"A Yale man after all. My third husband was a Yalie. Yes, I confess to having a personal interest. Though I doubt if anyone seriously suspects Sherry. Anyway, you were holding Dorrie when Sherry came. What happened then?"

"They wrestled around, and Dorrie fell out of the stable."

"You saw her fall?"

"Sure. I thought she just tripped. Like I said, Dorrie could be a real klutz. But she didn't get up. I jumped down to help her. I rolled her over, raised her head. But . . . But . . ." His eyes filled with tears again.

"Tell me something," Cora said. "Before it happened. When you were posing in the crèche. Did anyone come close?"

"You mean in front of the stable?"

"In front of the stable. Behind the stable. *In* the stable. Did anyone come close to you and Dorrie?"

"No." After a pause he added, "Just your niece."

Cora grimaced. "Right." She plodded on determinedly. "How about on your way to the stable? Did you see anyone?"

"Of course I saw Maxine."

"Why do you say 'of course'?"

"Because she was playing Mary. Dorrie relieved her."

"And you passed Maxine on the path. How would that happen? Wouldn't that make Maxine late leaving, or you early?"

"I didn't pass Maxine on the path. I met her in town hall. She came in while I was getting ready to go outside."

"What did she say?"

" 'Boring, boring, boring.' She said her first Joseph hadn't dressed warm enough and kept shivering. But he was a dream compared to the second Joseph, who stood like a stone statue and didn't relate to her at all. Which is the problem with women. They expect guys to pay attention to them at all times under all circumstances." At Cora's look, Lance mumbled, "Sorry. I mean some women."

"I know what you mean," Cora told him. "So Maxine Doddsworth was one of those women?"

"I didn't mean to say that. That's not really fair. I guess I'm just biased on the subject of Maxine."

"Why is that?"

Lance shrugged the hair off his forehead and answered casually, as if everyone in Bakerhaven were aware of what he was about to say.

" 'Cuz Maxine used to be my girlfriend."

23

MAXINE DODDSWORTH'S ROOM WAS NOT MUCH DIFFERENT FROM Lance's, except the terrorists on her poster were cleaner cut.

Maxine lay facedown on her bed, her head buried in a pillow. Even in that position her designer jeans looked stylish, her pink cable-knit sweater lush.

"Maxine," Cora said.

"Go 'way."

"Maxine, we have to talk."

"I said go 'way."

"I just talked to Lance. Would you like to know what he said?"

Maxine didn't answer, but she didn't say *go 'way* either.

"He said you two used to date. Go out. Go steady. Be his girl. Whatever you kids call it these days. Anyway, you were his girlfriend before Dorrie."

Maxine's head turned sideways on the pillow. One bleary eye glared up at Cora. "So?"

"The police are looking for someone with a motive to murder Dorrie. Stealing your boyfriend sounds like a good motive."

Maxine sat up in bed. "That is *so* lame. That is *so* bogus. Dorrie was my best friend!"

"Did you know she was pregnant?"

"I can't believe it! That is *so* not Dorrie."

"It happens," Cora said.

"No. It can't be true. Dorrie would have told me. Except . . ."

"Except what?"

"Nothing."

"You were going to say except if it was Lance. Dorrie might not be so eager to tell you if Lance was the father of her baby. Isn't that it?"

Maxine's mouth twisted in despair, and her metal braces gleamed. Cora wondered vaguely if a boy might dump a girl with braces for one without. She knew from bitter experience, men were capable of anything. Cora sighed. "Tell me about you and Dorrie."

"Why?"

"Because I intend to get whoever did this. If anyone can help me, it's you. I take it you and Dorrie were real close."

"Absolutely. We did everything together. *Everything.*"

"That's how she met Lance?"

"That wasn't her fault!"

"No, I suppose not. Never mind Lance. Tell me about Dorrie."

"Like I say, we did everything together. She went horseback riding, I went horseback riding. I went skating, she went skating."

"You go skiing last week?"

"Sure. With Lance and Dorrie. What about it?"

"Who'd she ride the lift with, you or Lance?"

Maxine's mouth fell open. "What are you getting at? What difference does that make?"

"Probably none. What about it?"

"We took turns. I rode with Dorrie. Dorrie rode with Lance. Lance rode with me."

"Dorrie didn't mind?"

"Hell, no. You are *so* off the wall. Dorrie and I were like *that.*" Maxine held her thumb and first finger together defiantly. "Just like *that.*"

"How about in school?"

"We took the same classes. The same activities and sports. We were both in the school play."

"Was that your idea?"

"Hell, no. I'm no actress. But she had a passion for it."

"How about the Virgin Mary? Was doing that her idea?"

"Well, it sure wasn't mine. Bundle up and stand in the cold? But she wanted to, so I did."

Cora approached it tentatively. "And changing hours?"

"We wanted to go Christmas shopping, that's all."

"Whose idea was it to switch?"

"Both of ours."

"Yes, but someone must have brought it up."

"I think Dorrie did. I don't remember."

"Tell me about being Mary."

"I relieved the first girl. She crept away. I took her place. It wasn't that bad. Joseph put his hands on my shoulders, I could lean against him."

"Did you talk?"

"Not at all. That's strictly forbidden."

"Even so. You're high school kids."

"We probably would have if we'd had a good group. But I checked the schedule. The first Joseph was Mr. Virdon, the tech director. He's young, but he's a *teacher.*" Maxine imbued the word with the same *oooh-gross* expression as if she'd said *"slimy worm."* "The one who relieved him was that geek Alfred, who would have run straight to Mr. Winston. So I kept my mouth shut."

"What about when Dorrie relieved you? Did she say anything?"

"She squeezed my shoulders, whispered, 'Move it, buster.' "

"Did Joseph hear?"

"If he did, he didn't let on. So I doubt it. Alfred's the type who would have told, trust me. A real geek."

"So what did you do when Dorrie relieved you?"

"Went and got my coat. It was cold out there."

"Your coat was in back of the stable?"

"That's right. And you know what? A coat that's been hanging outside for an hour isn't that warm."

"So you got your coat and boots, and went back over the actors' path. Did you meet anyone?"

"On the path? No. No one."

"How about when you got to town hall?"

"Lance was there. Dressed like Joseph."

"You could tell it was Lance? Even with the long hair and beard?"

Maxine shrugged. "Lance is Lance. Anyway, we talked."

"What did you say?"

"Nothing much. Just told him it was freezing and real boring."

"What did he say?"

"He said, 'Great.' "

"That was your whole conversation?"

"I told you, I was freezing."

"But you knew right away it was him? Lance?"

"Sure I did. I'd seen the schedule. I knew it was his turn."

"So when Dorrie switched spots with Becky Baldwin, you knew she'd be working with Lance?"

"It didn't bother me."

"But you knew?"

"Sure. That's when I saw the schedule. When we looked to see who Dorrie could swap with."

"Where did you see the schedule?"

"It's posted in town hall."

"I know. And that's where you saw it?"

"Yes. We drove over to check it. Dorrie's got a car, of course." Her eyes faltered. "*Had* a car, of course. Anyway, we checked the schedule and saw that Becky Baldwin had the slot. So Dorrie called her, asked her to switch places. And Becky did."

"Did that surprise you? That Becky agreed?"

"Not at all. Dorrie always gets—got what she wanted."

"Why was that?"

"You know. She has rich parents." Under her breath, Maxine muttered something Cora couldn't quite catch.

"What was that?"

"Nothing," Maxine said.

Cora let it go. But she had the distinct impression what Maxine had murmured was, "Two of 'em."

24

Pamela Doddsworth was waiting for Cora at the foot of the stairs. Her face was drawn and pale, in stark contrast to the bright and festive striped candy canes, silver tinsel, and colored balls and lights on the Christmas tree behind her. Pamela seemed every bit as upset as her daughter, Maxine. Perhaps more so.

She also *looked* like Maxine. The resemblance Cora had noticed at the crèche seemed even more pronounced today. Besides the green eyes, curly brown hair, and turned-up nose, Pamela Doddsworth was also dressed like Maxine, in slacks and cable-knit sweater. Neither was as stylish as Maxine's, however. That, coupled with Pamela's age, gave her the appearance of a knock-off copy of her daughter.

"How is she?" Pamela demanded. "She won't talk to me. Just lies there. I feel so helpless. Did she talk to you?"

"A little."

"She won't talk to me at all. And I'm her mother."

"That's *why* she won't talk to you."

"Do you have children?"

"No. But I used to *be* one. When you're a teenager, parents are a real drag."

"She talked to her father." Pamela didn't bother to keep the bitterness out of her voice. "Jonathon was here this morning. Went on up, stayed about a half an hour. Said she was upset, but she'd be okay."

"That's probably about right," Cora said.

"Oh, is it?" Pamela said. "The man's been gone for years, then he waltzes in and takes charge. My daughter will speak to him, but she won't speak to me. Of course not. All I've done is raise her. Care for her, give her what she wants. While he's off in England playing cops and robbers. Just a little boy who never grew up. Then he comes back and she acts like he's never been away."

"Absence makes the heart grow fonder. Or it doesn't. It could make a person miss him or hate him. Apparently, in her case, she missed him."

"And I'm wrong to resent him? How'd you like to marry a man and have him leave you?"

Cora frowned. "I would have to stop and count the number of times that's happened. But the alimony helps."

"Yeah, well the alimony's damn small, considering I have a girl to raise. Although I suppose Jonathon feels the pittance he pays gives him paternal rights."

"You say he was here?" Cora prompted, in an effort to steer the conversation away from Pamela Doddsworth's litany of grievances.

"Yes, he was. He showed up yesterday, large as life, as if he owned the place. Let himself in the front door. I'm sitting in my living room, the key turns in the lock. And in he walks, just as if he never left."

"He kept his key?"

"Yes, he did. All these years. Just to annoy me."

"Did you ask for it back?"

"Soon as he came in the door. And he wouldn't give it to me. How do you like that? Wouldn't give it up. I told him a thing or two. At least today he rang the bell."

"He was here yesterday and today?"

"Yes, of course. And she talked to him both times."

"She *had* asked him to solve the crime," Cora ventured.

"And what did he do? He just galloped in like some white knight to save the young damsel in distress."

"So what did he tell you?"

"I should be asking you. I'm sure he tells you more than he tells me. I might be invisible for all he cares. Comes in, uses the computer, uses the phone, raids the refrigerator, and off he goes, without so much as a by-your-leave."

"That was yesterday?"

"That was today. Right after he talked to Maxine. I tried to draw him out. At least see if she was okay. And he was so rude, like you wouldn't believe. 'Woman, I have work.' That's what he said. As if I were the hired help. He marches into the office, sits down at my desk as if he owns the place, and picks up my phone. Before he dials he looks at me, and says, 'Out.' "

"Is there an extension in the house?"

Pamela's eyes faltered. "I tried that once. When we were still married. He didn't like it."

"You didn't try today?"

"I let him alone. Anything I did would only make it worse. And Maxine would be blaming me."

"You talk to him when he was done?"

"Not at all. He bolted out of the office and drove off as if he'd just cracked the case. Which he didn't, of course. He never solved a case that quickly in his life. Not his way. Bumbling. Plodding. Methodical. That's Jonathon Doddsworth. He lulls his prey by acting like he couldn't find his couch in the living room. Then bores them to death through dogged persistence."

A regular Columbo, Cora thought. "Why did he run out?"

"Probably to avoid me." Pamela's lip curled up, revealing straight, pearly white teeth, the only clear edge she had on her daughter. Maxine evidently had her father to thank for her braces. That, too, probably was on Pamela's list of grievances.

Pamela sighed, then leaned in confidentially. "If you could do me a big favor."

"What's that?"

"Beat him. Solve the crime first. You're clever. You figure things out. Figure it out before Jonathon. If he solves the case, I'll never hear the end of it. He'll be a goddamn hero in my daughter's eyes. Then he'll go back to England and leave me here. And Maxine will go off to college, and I'll be the wicked, unsympathetic mother, and she'll never come home again. Except for money. And that will be that."

"You paint too gloomy a picture," Cora said. But she feared it was true.

"Will you help me?"

"I intend to solve this murder. I don't know if that will help you."

Pamela looked at her sharply. "Why do you say that?"

"I'm not doing it to hurt your husband. And I wouldn't arrange things to see that happen."

"I'm not asking you to. Just make sure he doesn't solve it first."

"That may be the thing I can't arrange."

Cora left the Doddsworths' with an uneasy feeling. Jonathon Doddsworth might be methodical and plodding, but he was certainly making quick work of it. What had he learned from his phone calls that had lit such a fire under him?

And what was he up to now?

25

SHERRY CARTER OPENED THE DOOR TO FIND JONATHON DODDS-worth all bundled up in a fur-lined overcoat, wool scarf, and tweed hat. "I'm sorry," she said. "My aunt isn't in."

Doddsworth smiled, a most disarming smile. "Actually, I came to see you."

"Me?"

"Yes. Might I come in? It's rather nippy out here. And, as you can see, it's beginning to snow again."

"Well, ah, yes, of course. Come in," Sherry said.

Doddsworth stamped the snow off his boots, stepped inside. "Am I interrupting something?"

"Not at all." In point of fact, Sherry had been constructing a crossword puzzle column, but she wasn't going to tell him that. "You must be frozen. Come in the kitchen. I'll make some coffee."

"That would be civil of you. But I don't drink it. Now, if you had some tea . . ."

"Of course."

Sherry sat Doddsworth down and put the kettle on. The *Baker-*

haven Gazette lay on the kitchen table. VIRGIN MARY ICED screamed from the front page.

Doddsworth shuddered.

Sherry flushed and moved the paper. Aaron Grant had already called to apologize for the headline, even though it was none of his doing.

Doddsworth unwound his scarf, shrugged off his overcoat, put his hat on the table. His head was bald on top, and his bristly muttonchops were flecked with gray. But his eyes were hard.

Sherry sat down opposite him. "So, is this your first time back? Since you moved to England, I mean."

"I was back shortly after the move. To see if my family might follow me. No luck, alas."

"Where are you staying?"

"A motor inn just out of town."

"Not a bed-and-breakfast?"

"I don't need some old biddy fussing over me. Plus I get cable telly. A far cry from the BBC. Still, I fancy the news." His eyes drifted to the *Gazette.*

"Did you see my aunt?"

Doddsworth frowned. "What, this morning?"

"No, on television. Aunt Cora does commercials."

"Go *on*! I say, that's a lark." Doddsworth allowed himself a brief smile, which swiftly faded. "I wonder if we might examine your statement a little."

"Feel free. But I've told you all I know."

"You have made a full, frank, and open disclosure to the authorities?"

"Yes, I have."

"Then you should have no difficulty doing so again. If I might just ask a few questions to illuminate certain matters . . ."

"Fire away."

"When you arrived to relieve the Virgin Mary you had no notion it was Dorrie Taggart?"

"I thought it was Becky Baldwin."

"When did you learn of your error?"

"Not until Becky came walking into town hall. Everyone assumed I knew, so no one told me differently. Up until then, I thought it was Becky who was dead."

"I see. And what can you tell me about Aaron Grant?"

"I beg your pardon?"

"I understand you two have been stepping out."

The kettle whistled.

"There's your tea!" Sherry exclaimed. She leaped up, took the kettle off the stove. "Sleepytime, Earl Grey, or Red Zinger?"

"Earl Grey would be splendid, thank you."

Sherry poured the tea, set the cup and saucer on the table. "Milk? Sugar? Lemon?"

"Milk and sugar, if you please."

Sherry produced them. Doddsworth sloshed in milk, added three heaping spoonfuls of sugar, stirred the mixture around. Before he was done, his saucer held nearly as much tea as his cup.

"Had time to think of an answer yet?" he asked.

"I beg your pardon?"

"About dating Aaron Grant."

"It's no secret I've been seeing Aaron Grant."

"Is this a serious relationship?"

She considered telling Doddsworth that was none of his business. Decided not to. "I would say so."

Doddsworth nodded gravely. "And what would young Mr. Grant say?"

Sherry bristled. She restrained herself with an effort. "You'll have to ask Aaron."

"I certainly intend to. I was wondering what you imagined he might say."

"Is this part of your *police* investigation?"

"Oh, absolutely. Relationships are at the heart of any crime. Far more material than eyewitness testimony. Which is often inaccurate and apt to be wrong. The only way to comprehend a crime is to comprehend the people involved. At the moment I'm attempting to ascertain the relationship between you and Aaron Grant. In analyzing that relationship, I am naturally taking into account the degree of cooperation encountered when posing the question. Your constant avoidance is in itself quite telling. As is your indignation." Doddsworth smiled thinly. "But, please, let's be friends. Let's move the conversation to less delicate terrain. You were at the rehearsal last night?"

"Yes."

"Were you there when the sandbag fell?"

"Yes, I was."

"I have heard varying accounts of how close it came to striking Miss Baldwin. Can you tell me the margin by which it missed her?"

"I'm afraid I didn't actually see it fall."

"And why is that?"

"I was in the wings at the time."

"Who was onstage?"

"Just Becky."

"The other actors were all in the wings?"

"Yes, they were."

"Who was in the audience?"

"I have no idea."

"Well, who would logically be? The director?"

"Rupert would either be in the audience or onstage leaning against the proscenium."

"In either case, he would have been watching Becky Baldwin?"

"He would."

"What about the accompanist? The piano player. Would he have seen where the sandbag fell?"

"You've got me. I don't play the piano. If I did, I'd look at the keys. A musician probably doesn't have to."

"And the technical director—where would he be?"

"Most likely in the wings. In performance he'd be on the prompt book giving the light cues. In rehearsal I don't know."

"What about the light man? Wouldn't he be watching?"

"He would, but he'd just been assigned a drum set. He was offstage with the drummers drumming."

"Ah, yes," Doddsworth said. "And I gather the other tech students were not there."

"Then you know more than I do," Sherry replied. "In fact, you know the answers to all these questions, don't you? So why are you asking them?"

"To put you at your ease. To make you comfortable answering. So we can return to the questions that are bothering you."

"Nothing's bothering me."

"Oh, but it is. You take offense even at the suggestion that you take offense. Clearly there is something about your relationship with Mr. Grant that you do not wish to discuss."

"You're dead wrong," Sherry countered. "I do not wish to discuss my relationship with Aaron because it is nobody's business but my own, and has nothing to do with the crime. I have been dating Aaron Grant. There is nothing particularly special about the relationship. Certainly nothing worthy of your attention."

"I see." Doddsworth sipped his tea. "And did this same Aaron Grant not at one time have a relationship with Miss Becky Baldwin?"

"I believe they knew each other in high school," Sherry said evenly.

"You believe so?"

"That is my understanding. I didn't live here at the time."

"So you're a more recent arrival. You moved to Bakerhaven, met Aaron Grant, began a relationship. At that time Miss Baldwin herself lived elsewhere, didn't she?"

Sherry said nothing.

"She then returned to town, took up residence, renewed her old acquaintance with the young Mr. Grant. Her work drove them together. She's a solicitor, is she not? And you, I believe, are a substitute preschool teacher."

The phrase, delivered with clipped, British tones, hung insinuatingly in the air.

Doddsworth smiled at her over his teacup. "Would you take an EPT?"

That startled her. "What?"

"An early pregnancy test. Will you take one?"

"I most certainly will not! What in the world do you think you're doing?"

"My job," Doddsworth answered implacably. "With regard to the third poem. The one that's not yet public. But of which you are doubtless aware. Have you heard the poem?"

"Yes, of course."

"It refers to the difficulty of being a virgin while in the family way. Assuming the line does not suggest immaculate conception, one can conclude our Longfellow here is alluding to the inappropriateness of the actress playing a virgin."

"Yes, of course," Sherry said. "Dorrie Taggart was two months pregnant."

"Yes, but did the killer know that? According to the postmortem, Dorrie was in the first trimester. She may not have been certain herself, let alone our killer. One must ask oneself, what if it is *not* Dorrie Taggart the killer is referring to? Who else might apply? Is there any other Mary who might find it hard to be a virgin?" Doddsworth steepled his fingers. "You, I believe," he intoned, "are a divorcée."

Sherry glowered.

"So," Doddsworth mused, "if you were with child, what a sticky wicket that would be. You move to Bakerhaven, strike up a promising match with a young reporter chap. You are happy. Then his childhood sweetheart returns to town. She assumes a position of power, and proceeds to command more and more of his time. You find yourself with child, but instead of joy you are filled with apprehension. You are afraid to even broach the subject of your condition with the young man. Would you not agree that under such circumstances Miss Baldwin might be considered the chief obstacle to all your happiness? Would you not wish her dead?"

"I don't believe this!"

"Will you consent to a pregnancy test?"

"Absolutely not!"

Doddsworth nodded serenely. "Your refusal is noted. I confess I find it intriguing." He pushed back his cup and saucer, got to his feet. "Thanks for the tea."

Sherry remained seated, said nothing.

Doddsworth slipped on his coat and hat, wound the scarf twice around his neck. He smiled down at Sherry quite paternally, then let himself out the front door.

26

CORA FELTON WAS SURPRISED TO SEE CHIEF HARPER'S CRUISER parked in front of the school gym. Of course, the gym was where the sandbag had been dropped. But that was only an *attempted* murder. With an *actual* murder to investigate, Chief Harper had many things that were much more pressing. Why did he have to be *there*?

Cora didn't want Chief Harper there because she was about to suffer the ultimate indignity—a private rehearsal with Rupert Winston. To work on her solo. Since Cora's solo consisted of a total of four words (and that only if one counted *maids a-milking* as three), a private rehearsal seemed like overkill. Between Cora's singing and Rupert Winston's scathing direction, it would certainly be humiliating, and Cora didn't need Chief Harper around to witness her humiliation.

Cora was in a foul mood as she stomped up to the gym.

There was a sign taped to the door. It read: REHEARSAL MOVED TO MUSIC ROOM, ROOM 127—USE MAIN ENTRANCE!!!

Cora's first thought was, *What a relief.* Chief Harper wouldn't hear her sing after all.

Her second was, *Why is he here?*

Cora pulled the gym door open, slipped inside.

Dan Finley stood in the center of the basketball court. The young policeman was in his stocking feet, having removed his boots and overcoat. He was holding the blowgun in his right hand with one end on the floor, like a native posing with a spear. The blowgun was nearly as tall as he was. As Cora watched, Chief Harper walked up to him, handed him what appeared to be a dart. Dan did not look happy.

"Okay, try again," Harper told him.

"It's not that I'm not trying," Dan Finley said.

"I know you are. You're just not very good."

"You wanna try it, Chief?"

Finley fed the dart into the blowgun, raised it to his lips. Aimed at the far end of the court, where a four-by-eight-foot piece of Sheetrock had been set up. The silhouette of a man had been crudely drawn on it with Magic Marker.

"A little higher," Chief Harper corrected. "It has to arc."

"I can't aim that way."

"Never mind accuracy. I want distance."

Dan Finley filled his lungs with air. Wound up, and blew.

The dart flew from the end of the blowgun, arced through the air, and imbedded itself in the court, well short of the target. It didn't even reach the foul line.

"Damn it," Harper said. "Get that out of the floor. Is it going to show? The principal will kill me." As Cora started forward, he wheeled with a guilty look. "Oh, it's you! What are you doing here?"

"I have rehearsal."

"Rehearsal's moved. Didn't you see the sign on the door?"

"No, and I didn't see that hole in the floor, either. You mind telling me what you're doing here, Chief?"

"We got the blowgun back from the lab. The technicians were all excited that they got such clear prints. I didn't disillusion them, so they're going to be puzzled when I don't make an arrest. And guess whose prints they were?"

"You were telling me what you were doing here, Chief."

Chief Harper pointed to a fifty-foot measuring tape laid out on the gym floor. "At the nearest point it's thirty-six feet from the road to the crèche. I'm trying to see if this blowgun can shoot a dart thirty-six feet."

"Is that the same dart?"

"It's an exact duplicate. Considering Dan's accuracy, I decided against his shooting a poison dart."

"When you say exact duplicate . . . ?"

"It's close enough. We're not talking mathematical certainty here, we're looking for possibility. Is it possible for a dart to go thirty-six feet? So far, it would appear it isn't," he concluded glumly, glaring at his young officer.

"Not to knock young Dan, here," Cora said, "but how much experience as a dart blower does he have?"

"None. Which in itself is telling. There's every indication it would take an expert. Assuming it can be done at all."

Cora examined the setup. "You're talking laterally, Chief."

"I beg your pardon?"

"You're assuming the shooter is standing on the ground. The blowgun was found in the organ loft in the church. The window in the loft—you could open that, shoot from a greater height."

"And from a greater distance," Chief Harper pointed out darkly. "You'd lose more than you gained."

"Maybe. I just mention it because this doesn't seem to be working."

"Well, *that* wouldn't either."

The back door clanged open and Rupert Winston sashayed in and immediately struck a pose. "Oh, there you are. Why am I not surprised? Do you have a timepiece, Miss Felton?"

"Why, is one missing?"

That stopped him in midsneer. "You're joking. And an old joke at that. At least it's a sign of life. If only you could channel some of that into your performance . . . You happen to be late for rehearsal."

"Yeah. Chief Harper here was just telling me it's been changed to the music room."

"Is the sign on the door down? That will never do! I have more rehearsals this afternoon." Rupert strode to the outer door, wrenched it open. "No, it's right here. Apparently, Miss Felton, you are a double threat, who can neither sing nor read." He turned to the policemen. "Gentlemen, please, go on with your game. I'm sorry we interrupted you. Miss Felton, this way."

Room 127 turned out to be a minuscule music practice room with a piano and a couple of school desks. Mr. Hodges, the music teacher, sat at the piano. "Ah, you've captured her," he said. "Good. I don't have all afternoon. And how many more after her?"

"Just two. But they, at least, can keep a tune. I'm not sure what you're going to do here."

Mr. Hodges made a deprecating gesture, as if assuring Cora he was not the one impugning her talents. "Not a problem, not a problem. We just need the time to work. Miss Felton, I'm going to have you reproduce some tones for me. I'll play the note, you hum the note. Are you ready? Here we go."

Mr. Hodges played middle C. When Cora looked at him, he hummed, "Hmmm."

"Hmmm," Cora tried.

"A little higher."

"Hmmm."

"Little higher."

"Hmmm."

"That's it. Again."

"Hmmm."

"Good. Try this." He played another note.

"Hmmm."

"A little higher."

"Hmmm."

"Excellent. Again."

"Hmmm."

They hit a few more notes. Then Mr. Hodges said, "Now, Miss Felton. The note you're humming. You're going to hum it again, then you're going to sing on the exact same note, hmmm, *eight,* hmmm, *eight,* hmmm, *eight.* Now you try it."

"Hmmm, *eight.*"

"You're drifting."

"Hmmm, *eight.*"

"You've lost the note now. Start again."

It was beyond humiliating. Mr. Hodges put her through the musical equivalent of *See Spot run,* while Rupert Winston's face ran the gamut of incredulous, scathing, pained expressions. Nonetheless, at the end of fifteen minutes Cora Felton warbled, " *'Eight maids a-milking.'* "

Mr. Hodges said, "Perfect!" Granted, he'd been playing the melody note for note along with her; still, it was an accomplishment.

Cora escaped from the practice room with an incredible sense of relief.

Harvey Beerbaum sat in the hallway, waiting his turn.

"Et tu, Harvey?" Cora said. "I thought Rupert was happy with your performance."

"He'd still like me to hit the notes." Harvey lowered his voice, whispered eagerly: "You got anything new on the crime?"

"I'm kind of out of the loop, with Doddsworth in town."

Harvey couldn't hide his disappointment. He nodded glumly, went in the door of the practice room with no more enthusiasm than Cora had shown.

Before leaving the high school, however, Cora detoured back by the gym.

Dan Finley was up on a twelve-foot ladder, trying to aim the blowgun. He was not having much luck. The ladder was wobbly, and most of his energies seemed directed toward maintaining his perilous balance.

Chief Harper wasn't helping him. The chief was off in the corner, talking to Jonathon Doddsworth. Cora spotted them, started over.

Chief Harper saw her, yelled, "Hey!" He flushed slightly and added, almost apologetically, "No shoes."

Cora bristled. Doddsworth was wearing shoes.

Cora was wearing fur-lined slip-on boots. She stopped, yanked them off, padded across the gym in her stocking feet. "I notice you're still poking holes in the gym floor," she observed. "Does the height make any difference?"

"Not for Dan. It might if we had an expert."

"Well, there you are," Cora said. "Have a dart-blowing contest, and arrest the winner."

"Most amusing, Miss Felton," Doddsworth said. "Have you any suggestions of a practical nature?"

"I'd advise shutting down the Christmas pageant."

"Because of the attack on Miss Baldwin?"

"For one thing."

Doddsworth looked puzzled. Cora waited for Chief Harper to pick up his cue on her get-me-out-of-this-pageant jest, but he didn't. Cora wondered what was wrong. "Any developments?" she asked.

"Nothing we don't already know," Harper answered. "No one remembers tying that sandbag off. No surprise there. Which leaves a lot of candidates. If it was done during rehearsal, it leaves half the cast. If it was done before rehearsal, it leaves all of them. And anyone else, for that matter."

"Then how could the drop be timed?"

"Very easily, if it was someone in the wings. They just stand with their back to the pinrail, untie the rope, wait for the right moment, and let go.

"If it was anyone else, they couldn't be backstage. They'd untie the rope, run it over a back beam, tie it off near the top of the back stairs. Then, during rehearsal they'd creep up the stairs, untie the rope, and let it drop. Which would fit in with the clue, *Wrong girl,* being found in the girls' dressing room."

"That's not facts, just speculation," Cora pointed out. "I could have told you that myself. Come on, you got anything *new*?"

A dart whizzed by, stuck into the floor by Chief Harper's big toe.

"Jesus H. Christ! Dan, are you trying to kill us?"

"Sorry. That one got away."

"Where were you aiming?"

"I was aiming at the target."

"How could you miss by that much?"

"I was trying to get some distance. By swinging the blowgun like a whip."

"Well, it didn't work."

"It went farther."

"Farther *from* the target. This only helps if it's accurate."

"You think Sam might have better luck?"

The thought of cranky Officer Brogan wielding the blowgun did not cheer Chief Harper. "No," he said glumly. "Keep trying."

"I need a dart."

Chief Harper tugged the dart from the floor and walked over to the ladder, leaving Cora alone with Jonathon Doddsworth.

Their eyes met.

Cora tried to size him up. A superb poker player, Cora was used to sizing up opponents. Sensing their strengths and weaknesses. Looking for an edge.

Doddsworth she couldn't read. Oh, he was arrogant, overbearing, and self-important, as well as plodding, methodical, and slow—everything she already knew. But what lay behind his facade she couldn't tell. She sensed the ruthlessness, the dogged determination his ex-wife had alluded to. But something else too.

Fear.

The fear she sometimes sensed in a card player, the fear that someone might call a bluff.

Was Doddsworth bluffing? Or did he really *have* substantial leads? Had Doddsworth known she'd question his daughter, and run out of the house as if he'd discovered something, just so his wife would report that fact? Was he that clever? That devious?

Or was he just that *good*?

Was he going about his business without a thought to what she was doing? And was this all in her mind?

It occurred to Cora that if she were playing poker with Doddsworth, she wouldn't know whether to call, raise, or fold.

27

Cora got home to find Sherry working on the computer.

"Hi," Cora said. "How's your day?"

"I'm trying to finish the Puzzle Lady column. I keep getting interrupted."

"Sorry about that."

"No, not you. Aaron took me to lunch."

"You could have refused."

"Don't be silly. I was hungry."

"That hardly counts as an interruption."

"Then Doddsworth came by."

"What did he want?"

"To know if I was pregnant."

"Glad I asked."

Sherry filled Cora in on Jonathon Doddsworth's visit.

"What did you say?" Cora asked her.

"I told him to go to hell."

"Probably not the most tactful answer."

"Well, not exactly in those words. But I told him I sure as heck wasn't taking any test."

"Oh, dear."

"Did I do the wrong thing?"

"No. But it's a no-win situation. You either let him force you into taking the test, or you refuse and let him insinuate you have something to hide."

"I know."

"You're not preggers, are you?"

"No, I'm not."

"Are you sure?"

"Yes, I'm sure."

"Maybe you should take the test just to throw it back in his face."

"I will not take the test. It's a matter of principle."

"Maybe you get your own home pregnancy test and do it by yourself. Quietly, without telling anyone. Just to make sure you pass. I remember when I was dating Henry—"

"Aunt *Cora*! I am not in the mood!"

"Well, you better be prepared. Doddsworth's planning something. He and Chief Harper have their heads together, and, frankly, I don't like it."

"Where did you see 'em?"

"At my music lesson."

"What?"

Cora told Sherry about the experiments in the gym.

"Granted, it's not conclusive," she said, "but it's a good indication the blowgun had nothing to do with the dart."

"Then why was it there?"

"As a red herring. To make it look like that's how Dorrie was bumped off. When actually the killer placed the dart by hand."

"That's your deduction?"

"That's how it looks. Now, without ruling out the possibility one of the wise men threw it, the only ones who could have done it are Maxine Doddsworth; Lance, the boyfriend; that tech geek, Alfred something; or you."

"Or her," Sherry said.

"Huh?"

"Or *her.* Dorrie Taggart. She could have done it herself. Knelt in position and stuck the dart in her neck."

"Why on earth would she do that?"

"How should I know? We're talking possible here. It would have been possible for her to do it."

"Good for you," Cora said. "Living with me is finally starting to rub off. Yes, she absolutely could. If I use that, I'll be sure to give you credit."

"When has *that* ever been an issue?" Sherry said dryly.

A car came up the driveway, closely followed by another.

"Looks like we're throwing a party," Cora said.

Chief Harper and Jonathon Doddsworth got out of the first car. Dan Finley got out of the second.

"It's the cops. I hope they have some news." Cora opened the front door. "Come in, gentlemen. You'll forgive us if we're not prepared to entertain, but you might have called first. What's this all about?"

Chief Harper didn't answer. He avoided her eyes, walked in, tugged off his overcoat, and stood, fidgeting.

Doddsworth, by contrast, seemed utterly at home. The inspector stepped in, smiled a condescending smile, and gestured to Dan Finley as if he were the MC of some gala event. "Officer?"

Dan Finley looked as uncomfortable as Chief Harper, only more so. His face was pink with embarrassment. He had not removed his coat, and he was already starting to sweat. He reached in his pocket, pulled out a piece of paper. "Miss Felton. Miss Harper. I have a warrant, issued by Judge Hobbs, to search these premises for evidence pertaining to the homicide of one Doris Taggart. This warrant was issued on this day pursuant to allegation and belief of Chief Harper of the Bakerhaven police force. The order is legal and binding, and mandates a search of these premises. Please do not interfere."

"You have *got* to be kidding!" Sherry exclaimed. Cora, on the other hand, looked fascinated.

"He's not," Doddsworth said. "We clearly have probable cause. Or, rather, *they* have probable cause. Chief Harper and his minion will be conducting the search. I, of course, have no authority here. But I certainly have a right to advise. Young man, I would start with the computer."

Dan Finley gulped. "Yes, sir, I know." He reluctantly plodded off toward Sherry's office.

"Would you care to have a go, Chief?" Doddsworth said. "The longer you delay, the longer this will take."

Chief Harper took a breath. "And where would you suggest that I look?"

Doddsworth considered the question as if it had been serious. "I'd begin here, move toward the bedrooms. There's no call to disturb the ladies' private items unless we really must."

"Private items?" Cora cocked her head. "You're going through my undies?"

"Not if we can help it," Doddsworth assured her.

"Well, that's a fine how-do-you-do. Judge Hobbs did this to me? Remind me to cross him off my eligible bachelors list."

Dan Finley emerged from the office with a small black rectangle in his hand. "Got the computer disk," he reported miserably.

"Did you search the office?" Doddsworth asked.

"No, sir. Just got the disk."

"Well, chop-chop, lad, move your bum."

Dan gave Doddsworth an agonized look, shrugged helplessly, and walked back down the hall.

"You're taking my computer disk?" Sherry said.

"Oh, that's not your disk. It's his." Doddsworth's smile was smug. "The young chap just copied some data."

Sherry's face darkened. "If he messed up that computer—"

Sherry hurried down the hallway to the office, where Dan Finley was going through her desk drawers. "What did you do to my computer?" she demanded.

Dan looked up guiltily. "I didn't do anything, Miss Carter. I just downloaded files."

"What files?"

"The acrostic files."

"Why?"

Before Dan could answer, Cora swept into the room. "All right, you. Would you mind telling me what you're looking for?"

"Proof you wrote the poems."

Cora's mouth fell open. For once she was speechless.

"Not you. Her." Dan pointed to Sherry. "The theory is *she* wrote them, and then *you* worked them into puzzles for her. That's assuming she wasn't able to do it herself."

"You've got to be kidding."

"I wish I were. Doddsworth has this theory, and he did some detective work and forced Chief Harper's hand. Judge Hobbs bought it, and here we are."

"Are you going to search the whole house?"

"We are if you're innocent. We have to search till we find something. If you're not guilty, we won't find it."

There came a triumphant "Aha!" from the living room. Moments later, an exultant Doddsworth strode in the door.

Chief Harper trailed in after. He looked sick. In his hand was a stack of red envelopes.

"Miss Carter," Doddsworth prompted. "I believe Chief Harper has something to say to you."

Chief Harper shuffled his booted feet. He seemed to deflate under Doddsworth's piercing gaze. He cleared his throat twice. "Sherry Carter. You're under arrest for the murder of Dorrie Taggart."

28

SHERRY CARTER GLARED AT CHIEF HARPER ACROSS THE TABLE IN the tiny interrogation room, an adjunct of the police station's twin holding cells. Dan Finley sat beside the table with a steno book and pencil. Jonathon Doddsworth stood by observing and radiating smugness.

"Miss Carter," Chief Harper began. "You understand you don't have to talk to us. You have the right to remain silent. But should you give up the right to remain silent, anything you say can be taken down and used against you in a court of law. You have the right to an attorney. If you cannot afford an attorney, an attorney can be appointed for you. Do you understand these rights as I have just read them to you?"

"I don't believe this."

"Miss Carter. Could you please signify that you understand your rights?"

"I understand my rights."

"Sir, you're going a little fast," Dan Finley protested. "I'm not so good at this."

"She hasn't said anything yet," Chief Harper said irritably.

"I didn't get all her words."

"Just make sure you get the part where she says she understands her rights."

"Yes, sir."

"Miss Harper, I hand you a stack of envelopes and ask you if you recognize them."

"Recognize them?"

"Yes. What are they?"

"Red envelopes."

"Where did you get those red envelopes?"

"You just gave them to me."

Chief Harper flushed. "That's not what I mean, and you know it. These envelopes were found in your house. How did they get there?"

"I haven't a clue."

"You claim you never saw these envelopes before?"

"I saw them when you found them at my house."

"I mean before that."

"I never saw them before that."

"I'm way behind," Dan groaned.

"Damn it, Finley."

"I'm doing the best I can, Chief."

"Might I suggest you proceed," Doddsworth put in. "The evidentiary value of this interrogation pales beside its practical worth. I seriously doubt a suspect as astute as Miss Carter would say anything to implicate herself."

If Chief Harper appreciated the suggestion, he didn't show it. "Miss Carter. I want to impress upon you, you are in very serious trouble here. If you have any explanation for the facts, now would be a real good time to produce it. These envelopes were found in your house. How did they get there?"

"I haven't the faintest notion."

"That's a less than satisfactory answer."

"It's the only one I have. Since I have no knowledge whatsoever of the envelopes you speak of. Where exactly did you find them?"

"You needn't tell her that," Doddsworth interjected. "If the envelopes are hers, she knows."

"Well, they're not, and I don't," Sherry stated. "If you don't wish to tell me, I will continue not to know. Which is certainly an unsatisfactory situation from my viewpoint. How does it look from yours?"

Chief Harper scowled. "This is getting us nowhere."

"Of course not," Doddsworth said. "Never mind the allegations you *can't* prove. Concentrate on the ones you *can*."

"Such as?"

"The computer program."

Chief Harper took a breath. "Miss Carter, do you own a computer program called Enigmacross?"

"Yes, I do."

"When did you purchase the program?"

"A few days ago."

"How many days?"

"I don't recall."

"Let me ask you this: When did you purchase it with relation to the encrypted poems that were discovered in the high school theater?"

"It was right after that."

"After the poems were discovered?"

"Yes."

"Miss Carter, do you recall a conversation you had with me after the second poem was found pinned to Miss Baldwin's costume? After your aunt had translated that poem for me? Do you recall a conversation on the village green? When I asked you if you would look into what kind of computer program could generate such a puzzle? And you assured me you would. Do you recall that conversation?"

"Yes, I do."

"And that was *after* the second puzzle was found?"

Sherry said nothing.

"Miss Carter, a check of your credit card records shows that you actually purchased the program the day *before* that conversation, the day the *first* puzzle poem was found. Do you have any explanation for that?"

The door flew open and Cora Felton burst in. "Well, well, the old third degree," she declared heartily. "What, no rubber hose?"

Doddsworth's face darkened. "Miss Felton, you have no right to be here."

"And you *do*? You seem to be somewhat confused. Let me clear it up for you. Connecticut is in *New* England. You probably heard the word *England* and got all excited. It's not really your jurisdiction. See, there was this little thing called the War of Independence a while back. I don't recall all the details, but the upshot is we don't have to listen to you Brits anymore. So, if you could just hold your water, I'm talking to Chief Harper. He, I believe, is an American."

"Damn it, Cora," Chief Harper said. "You're only making this worse."

"Well, that's a neat trick. You've arrested Sherry for murder. Would you mind telling me how it could be worse?" Cora put up her hand. "Please, don't bother. The point is, Sherry's got rights, and, just because she's a friend of yours, there's no reason for her to give them up. Particularly when your friendship is so tenuous as to include a murder accusation."

Jonathon Doddsworth had recovered his composure. "Miss Felton, must I remind you that you are not an attorney?"

"Oh, don't worry," Cora replied. She smiled, radiating sweetness. "I've *got* an attorney."

Becky Baldwin came walking in.

29

Becky Baldwin looked like a million bucks. Maybe two million. Becky always looked good, but today in particular. Her makeup was invisible, so carefully applied as to be impossible to detect. Her matching silver earrings and necklace were exquisitely understated, discreet. Her blue Armani sheath might have been a business dress but could have passed as evening wear. Sherry got the impression that when Becky had heard who the client was, she'd rushed right home and changed.

Becky shooed everyone out of the interrogation room, sat at the table across from Sherry.

"All right," Becky said. "You wanna tell me what happened?"

"I'd rather be shot dead."

Becky grinned. "I understand the sentiment. However, this is a murder case. In a murder case, it's advisable to talk to your lawyer."

"You're not my lawyer."

"Oh, but I am. Your aunt gave me a ten-thousand-dollar retainer."

"Ten thousand dollars! Good God, she'll have to get married again."

"I'd hate to be the cause of that. Still, ten thousand is almost nominal in a murder case."

"This is absurd."

"Isn't it? You wanna fill me in? Your aunt only had time to hit the highlights."

"Exactly what highlights did Aunt Cora hit?"

"The police found the envelopes to the puzzle poems hidden in your house." Becky made a face. "It is generally considered a bad move to hang on to such incriminating evidence."

"Funny. What else did Cora say?"

"That's not enough? It convinced me you need a lawyer."

"I wouldn't imagine accepting ten thousand dollars takes much convincing."

"Let's not make this about money. It becomes so tawdry when it's about money."

"You could always refuse the case."

"I could, but you'd have to pay *some* lawyer. Clearly you need one."

"Is that all Cora told you?"

Becky's eyes twinkled mischievously. "You mean did she mention the pregnancy test? Don't worry, she didn't say a word. You're not pregnant, are you?"

Sherry sighed. "This isn't going to work."

"Oh, but it is. And very nicely too. You're charged with killing the Virgin Mary. Do you know what the media's going to do with that?"

"What a nightmare."

"Actually, it's not bad. I got Mr. Channel Eight wrapped around my finger. He'll do practically anything I want." Becky raised her eyebrows archly. "Now, if we just had an in at the *Bakerhaven Gazette* . . ."

"Ha-ha," Sherry said. "And the MTV movie award for cattiest defense attorney goes to . . ."

Becky raised her hand as if acknowledging thunderous applause. "Thank you. I'd just like to say that I could not have won this award without the help of the defendant, Sherry Carter. Thank you, Sherry." She picked up a pen and poised it over her legal pad. "Okay. You done sparring? You got anything useful you'd like to tell me?"

"For instance?"

"You have any priors? A criminal record they'll be able to throw in my face?"

"Sorry to disappoint you. I had all my prostitution convictions expunged from my record because I was underage at the time."

"Good. I'll be able to push for bail. How much do you make?"

"I beg your pardon?"

"You're a substitute teacher, aren't you? How much do you earn?"

"What's that got to do with it?"

"Setting bail. The judge is gonna wanna know what your ties are to the community, whether you pose a flight risk. A lucrative job is an inducement to stay."

"Then I haven't got one. The work is part-time. The salary is negligible."

"Really? What do you live on? Alimony?"

"No."

"You couldn't get alimony?"

"Are you enjoying this as much as you appear to be?"

"If I have to put you on the stand, the prosecutor is going to throw questions like this at you. I have to know how you're going to answer."

"I don't have alimony because I didn't want it, and didn't ask for it. I found myself in a relationship with an abusive drunk. I didn't want his money: All I wanted was out."

"You won your divorce?"

"It wasn't that hard. He'd been arrested twice for beating me up."

"Twice?"

"I didn't go back to him. He came after me."

"I see."

"You sound as if you don't believe me."

"I'm a lawyer. I could argue his side of the case at the drop of a retainer. Right now I'm prepared to argue yours."

"Oh, really," Sherry said. "What are you prepared to argue? You haven't even asked me anything. Except about my personal life."

"What would you like me to ask you?"

"How about those envelopes found in my house. How come you haven't asked about them?"

"I assume they're not yours."

"Of course they're not mine!"

"So what do you want me to ask about them?"

"How about who put them there?"

"Do you know who put them there?"

"Of course not."

"I didn't think so. If you did, you'd have told me. So what's the use asking?"

"We could discuss who *might* have put them there."

"That we could. Tell me, were you and Cora both out of the house at any time today?"

"Cora was gone all morning. Aaron took me to lunch."

"When did Cora get back?"

"After I did."

"There you are," Becky said. "The house was unoccupied during lunch. Anyone could have planted those envelopes."

"Exactly," Sherry said. "You have to find out who."

Becky winced. "Oh, dear."

"What's the matter?"

"You've been watching too much Perry Mason. My job is *not* to find out who did it. My job is to prove it wasn't *you.* And I use the word *prove* in a legal sense, as in *prove beyond all reasonable doubt.* It doesn't matter if all twelve jurors think you did it, as long as they don't have grounds to vote for a conviction. If I can arrange for that happenstance, I've done my job."

"Wouldn't *suggesting* who might have done it tend to help?"

"Yes, of course. If there are any likely suspects, trot them out. Was anyone at your house today?"

"Just Doddsworth."

"What did he want?"

Sherry's eyes shifted.

"Right." Becky nodded. "The pregnancy test. Did he have any chance to plant the envelopes?"

"You suspect *Doddsworth*?"

"No, but it doesn't matter. If he had the opportunity, I can *suggest* that he might have. Could he have done it?"

"No. I'd have seen him."

"Are you sure?"

"He was never out of my sight. I let him in, let him out. Watched him drive off."

"You didn't leave him in the living room just to get him a drink?"

"I brought him into the kitchen."

"Did he precede you into the living room on his way out?"

"No."

Becky shrugged. "Oh, well. I can still raise the implication. The prosecution would have to prove different. But we're better off on the lunch angle. How long were you gone?"

"About an hour and a half."

Becky nodded. "Aaron takes nice lunch breaks. So, there was plenty of time for anyone to have planted the envelopes. The problem is, why on earth would anyone want to frame *you*? Can you think of anyone who has it in for you?"

"Present company excepted? No, I can't. Clearly it is a case of the killer attempting to pass the buck to get off the hook."

"So it would seem. We still can't rule out the possibility it was done specifically to get you." Becky exhaled. "Okay, let's go get you arraigned for murder."

30

JUDGE HOBBS SURVEYED HIS COURTROOM WITH DISPLEASURE. IT was packed, which was unprecedented for a simple arraignment. But the venerable jurist understood the situation perfectly. The defendant was an attractive young woman. The defense attorney was an attractive young woman. And the crime was sensational. How often does the Virgin Mary get bumped off? The TV guy had even tried to bring his camera into court. Judge Hobbs had put an end to that. Even so, the TV crew was doubtless hanging out on the front steps waiting to shoot interviews.

Judge Hobbs scowled, picked up his gavel, banged the courtroom quiet.

"Thank you, ladies and gentlemen. Somewhat against my better judgment I have allowed spectators for whom there are no seats. This privilege in not irrevocable. If you can't be quiet, you can leave. I would imagine most of you are here because you expect a show. Well, you're not going to get one. I'm sorry to be a killjoy, but this is not fun. A girl has been murdered. A young woman has been charged. This is an arraignment for the purpose of binding her over for trial."

Becky Baldwin rose to her feet. "I object to that, Your Honor."

Judge Hobbs froze with his mouth open and his finger raised, midpontification. He turned to the defense table in surprise. "Excuse me?"

"Excuse *me*, Your Honor," Becky Baldwin rejoined. "But I object to Your Honor making statements as to the outcome of these proceedings. Surely the defendant has some rights."

"And I assure you none of them will be violated," Judge Hobbs said dryly. "Now, if you will allow me to proceed . . ."

"Certainly," Becky said, and sat down.

Judge Hobbs scowled, nettled. He turned to the prosecution table, where Henry Firth sat fumbling with his papers. "Mr. Prosecutor, what have we here?"

A little man with a thin mustache and a twitchy nose, Henry Firth had always reminded Cora of a rat. He located the document he wanted, looked up, and said, "Your Honor, this is the case of the *People versus Sherry Carter* with regard to the death of Doris Taggart. We ask that the defendant be bound over on the charge of murder in the first degree and attempted murder in the first degree."

Becky shot to her feet. "Make up your mind," she said. "Is it murder or attempted murder?"

Judge Hobbs banged the gavel. "Young lady, I will thank you to address the court and not opposing counsel."

"Your Honor, I will thank you to address me as *Ms.* Baldwin rather than by a pejorative sexist term."

"Then you're outta luck," Judge Hobbs informed her. "If you were a male attorney your age, I'd address you as *young man.* If you want equal footing, you can't have it both ways. Now, then, *Miss* Baldwin, what is your problem?"

"Speaking of having it both ways, Your Honor, the prosecutor is charging the defendant with murder *and* attempted murder. Any crime that is committed is also attempted. Not that my client did either. Still, this would seem like a case of the prosecutor gratuitously piling up the charges."

Judge Hobbs cocked his head. "Mr. Firth?"

Henry Firth's smile was a smirk. "That is not true, Your Honor. What we have here is a case of mistaken identity. The defendant killed one woman under the belief that she was another. In order to cover all bases, we are charging the defendant with murder in the case of the decedent, and attempted murder in the case of her intended victim."

"How about jaywalking, in case neither of those charges sticks?" Becky Baldwin suggested.

Judge Hobbs scowled. "Young lady, if I call you Ms. Baldwin will you show me some respect? The prosecutor has a legitimate point. That doesn't mean I'm going to recognize it, but it's certainly legitimate."

"Oh, really? And just whom, may I ask, is the defendant accused of attempting to murder?"

"That would seem a reasonable question, Mr. Prosecutor."

"She's accused of attempting to murder Miss Rebecca Baldwin."

There was a rumble of voices in the court. Judge Hobbs silenced it furiously with the gavel.

Becky Baldwin smiled. "You see why I wanted you to address me by name, Your Honor? The prosecutor is accusing my client of attempting to murder *me.* The absurdity of such a claim goes to the heart of their case, which is equally absurd."

Judge Hobbs frowned. "This is a simple arraignment, and I intend to keep it that way. Mr. Prosecutor, I ask that you drop this attempted murder charge, which can always be reinstated at another time, and arraign the defendant solely on the murder of Doris Taggart. Is that acceptable to you?"

"Yes, Your Honor."

"Very well. The defendant is hereby charged with the murder of Doris Taggart. Does the defendant wish to enter a plea?"

"The defendant does not," Becky Baldwin said.

Judge Hobbs blinked. "I beg your pardon?"

"The defendant does not wish to respond to any such charges. Such charges are absolutely without merit, and I ask that they be dismissed."

"Miss Baldwin, this is not a probable cause hearing, this is a simple arraignment."

"Your Honor keeps using the word *simple*. There is nothing *simple* about it. Why should this young woman be forced to endure a stigma on her good name just because the prosecutor has chosen to accuse her on a frivolous whim? We demand to know on what grounds he asks that Ms. Carter be arraigned."

"Mr. Firth?"

"I'm not prepared to put on evidence at this time. If Your Honor would schedule a probable cause hearing—"

"Ms. Baldwin. Is it acceptable to you that the defendant be arraigned on murder and released on her own recognizance pending a probable cause hearing?"

"Absolutely not, Your Honor. Unless the prosecution can explain on what evidence Ms. Carter is being arraigned."

"I said I wasn't prepared to put on proof," Henry Firth shot back irritably.

"I'm not asking you to put on proof. I'm asking you if you have grounds."

"Of course I have grounds."

"What are they?"

Judge Hobbs banged the gavel. "We'll have no more banter between counsel. Mr. Prosecutor, could you state briefly on what grounds you're asking the defendant be bound over?"

"Certainly, Your Honor. As a result of the search warrant issued by you, red envelopes matching the ones used to send the threatening puzzle poems were found secreted in Miss Carter's house."

Becky's eyes widened in mock surprise. "The defendant had *red* envelopes? Why didn't you say so? I understand completely your charging her with murder. I of course withdraw all my objections."

"That will do!" Judge Hobbs snapped. "Young lady, any more sarcasm out of you and I will take you at your word. Mr. Prosecutor, what else are you prepared to show?"

"I'm prepared to show that the defendant had the most opportunity to kill the decedent. Both were playing the Virgin Mary in

Bakerhaven's live Nativity. The defendant relieved the decedent. Miss Carter bent down and took hold of Miss Taggart, whereupon the decedent fell dead."

"You're prepared to show this by competent witnesses?"

"I will be, Your Honor."

Judge Hobbs nodded. "Miss Baldwin, nice try. I find there is sufficient reason to believe the prosecution would prevail in a probable cause hearing. The defendant is hereby arraigned on a charge of murder and released on her own recognizance."

31

RUPERT WINSTON POPPED TWO PURPLE TABLETS INTO HIS MOUTH and washed them down with Evian water. Rupert frequently popped pills during rehearsal. Whether they were medicinal, recreational, or merely a sugar candy prop to further his image was the subject of much speculation. His abrupt mood swings merely fed the fire.

Tonight, with one of his actresses charged with murder, it was clear the man was going for high drama. He jammed his plastic pillbox back in his briefcase, leaped onto the apron of the stage, and addressed the cast of the Christmas pageant as if he were Henry the V and they were his British troops. "Nothing has changed," he declaimed. "I have told you the show must go on. Now I tell you it must go on with us *all.* We must rally round Miss Carter. It is clear she has been unjustly accused. We support her, we embrace her, she is a valued member of our cast. This accusation is patently false; we must put it from our minds and pay it no heed. I'm sure all the ladies dancing will do the same.

"As for Miss Baldwin, she has informed me that she will not be intimidated and intends to go on with the play."

This declaration was delivered in a way that under other circumstances might have prompted applause. As things were, Winston's audience regarded him with mute skepticism. Becky, proud and defiant, sat beside Dan Finley. If she resented the young policeman's continued presence, she gave no sign.

"All right, people," Rupert continued. "We're gettin' down to crunch time. We're on in three days. This will be a stop-and-go run-through, with attention to detail. If there are any kinks, now is the time to iron them out. I want to warn you, this will be slow going. That is why we have chairs in the audience. I want no one backstage except the actors about to enter, and I will tell you when to go there. When I do, please have your props ready, and take your positions quickly without talking. We have an enormous amount of work to do.

"All right. Places, please. That's Becky Baldwin onstage, Jimmy Potter offstage left with the pear tree."

Becky Baldwin detached herself from Dan Finley and made her way onstage. To her credit, she strode right out, with no apparent trepidation about falling objects.

Jimmy Potter took his position stage left.

Rupert Winston gestured to the music director, who played a trill.

Becky Baldwin sang sweetly, " *'On the first day of Christmas, my true love gave to me.'* "

Jonathon Doddsworth barged in the side door. " *'A partridge in a pear tree,'* " the inspector declared tonelessly, preempting Jimmy Potter. "Sorry to intrude. Police business. Mr. Winston, I need a copy of the schedule. Of the Nativity actors. I understand you drew it up."

"Why do you want that?" Rupert demanded irritably.

"As a witness list. Do you have it?"

"It's probably at home."

"Ah. Then let's fetch it, shall we?"

Rupert blinked. "I beg your pardon?"

"I need the list. My rental's outside. I'll run you round."

"Now?" Rupert said incredulously. "I have rehearsal—"

"Have you back in a jiff." Doddsworth put his arm on the director's shoulder. "Come, now, there's a good chap."

Rupert twisted away furiously. He glared at Doddsworth. The two men stood toe to toe. The lithe, slender director and the hulking British policeman.

Dan Finley slipped between them like a referee breaking up a prizefight. "Now, now, boys. Mr. Winston, we gotta have that schedule. Whaddya say we speed things along?"

Grudgingly, Rupert gave ground. "Maybe I have one here," he muttered. He went over to his briefcase, pawed through it, pulled out a paper.

"Ah, good show," Doddsworth murmured, as if the production of the schedule had been completely voluntary. "Carry on. Sorry to intrude."

Doddsworth practically bowed his way out the door.

"All right." Rupert Winston rolled his eyes to let one and all see that he was carrying the weight of the theatrical world on his shoulders. "If we could *try* the opening again . . ."

The music trilled, Becky sang her line, and Jimmy Potter came marching out with plastic bush and paper bird, singing, " *'A partridge in a pear tree.'* "

In Cora Felton's opinion, Jimmy did it very well, but Rupert Winston immediately sprang up onstage to give Jimmy a litany of directions. Cora could practically see poor Jimmy's brain churning, trying to follow the nuances Rupert Winston was attempting to convey.

While this was going on, the gym lights went out. The stage lighting, which had been pink, faded into blue, and a spot came up on Becky Baldwin.

"That light's not flattering Becky any," Sherry whispered.

"That's because she's wearing street makeup instead of stage makeup," Cora whispered back. "Even so, it's pretty harsh."

As if in response to Cora's comment, the light on Becky dimmed a bit.

"That's better," Sherry said.

Dan Finley stood up in the audience. "Hey. Is someone up there aiming lights?"

"Oh, could we have one *more* interruption!" Rupert raged. "No. No one is aiming lights. Just replugging the board. Cast members! Pay no attention to the lights. If they don't seem right for your scene, it's because they *aren't.* Alfred is merely working on the board." He turned to the stage-left wings. "Alfred, do what you've gotta do, just don't plunge us into total darkness. And *try* not to upset the policeman."

From the wings came a reedy reply. "Yes, Mr. Winston."

Aaron Grant slid into the seat next to Sherry. He shrugged off his drum, set it on the floor.

"Hey, shouldn't you be with the drummers drumming?" Sherry whispered. "You'll get into trouble."

"Oh, now you're an expert on trouble?" Aaron whispered back.

Cora Felton put her finger to her lips. "You kids do what you want. Just don't get *me* into hot water."

Cora slipped out of her chair, made her way to the far end of the basketball court. She looked back, saw that Rupert Winston was deeply engaged in metaphysical speculation on the nature of Christmas gifts. Cora quietly eased the door open a crack and squeezed through.

She found herself in a long hallway lined with metal lockers. She wondered vaguely if any of them might hold a clue. If so, she wondered what type of court order it would take to open them. Or if a credit card might do the trick.

Cora looked around, tried to get her bearings. The music practice room was down the hall. If she remembered correctly, there was a stairwell next to it.

There was. Cora pushed the door open, descended the stairs, found herself in another hallway. She made her way back toward the stage, passing the girls' dressing room, where Doddsworth had found the clue *Wrong girl,* and climbed the stage-left stairs.

The work lights were out, the wings were dark. Onstage, Rupert Winston was still discoursing on the right and wrong methods of presenting a pear tree.

The stage-left wing was piled high with Russian drawing room furniture from the act 4 set of *The Seagull.* Cora picked her way around it, careful not to make a sound.

A wooden ladder attached to the front wall near the proscenium led to the lighting booth.

Cora climbed the ladder, peered inside.

A pair of battered work boots and paint-smeared jeans protruded from the booth. Alfred Adams, the nerdy tech assistant and erstwhile drummer drumming, lay half in and half out of the booth as he groped behind the dimmer panel to plug in a cable. Alfred's face was contorted, and he was fumbling and mumbling, so engrossed in his task that he did not notice Cora. With a grunt of triumph, he straightened, spotted her, and jumped a mile.

"Easy!" Cora hissed. "I'm an old lady, and I don't land well."

"What the heck are you doing here?"

"Can you keep your voice down? Rupert won't like it."

The name of his director seemed to alarm Alfred. "I got work to do," he pointed out defensively.

"Yes, I know. I'm going to get out of here and let you do it. I just have one or two questions first."

"I don't want to talk to you."

"Why not?"

"Just don't. Get out of here. Go away. Now."

Alfred seemed unduly agitated. Cora perched thoughtfully on the edge of the loft, wrapped her arm around a beam, mindful of the fact a good quick push could send her tumbling fifteen feet to the stage. "Why don't you wanna talk to me, Alfred? What is it you know?"

"Don't know anything."

"Then why don't you wanna talk?"

"You kidding me? You're the Puzzle Lady. When there's a crime, you talk to people. Then they wind up dead. I don't know anything, but if I talk to you, people will *think* I do."

"Hey, you keep your voice down, no one will know you talked to me. Tell me what I wanna know, and I'll get out of here."

Alfred regarded her miserably, then sighed. "Whaddya wanna know?"

"About you playing Joseph."

"I already told the police."

"Tell me."

"What?"

"Did you see anybody while you were posing?"

"Sure."

"In cars or on foot?"

"Both."

"Close enough to have thrown a dart?"

"Sure, but they couldn't have done it."

"Why not?"

"Dorrie wasn't there. She didn't come on till eleven. I got relieved at eleven-fifteen, so I was hardly with her at all."

"But you were there when Dorrie relieved Maxine Doddsworth?"

Alfred sighed again. "Yes, I was." He looked like he was going to weep.

"And what did you see?"

"Nothing. Dorrie taps Maxine on the shoulder. Slides in as she slides out. Their backs are to me. I can't see them. And they're not paying any attention to me. I could be a statue, for all those girls care."

"Isn't that what they're supposed to do?"

"Yeah, sure. If it was Lance Bigshot, they'd find an excuse to turn around."

"But they didn't?"

"No."

"When Maxine slid out, did she ever put her hand on Dorrie's neck?"

"Don't know."

"Weren't you watching?"

"Not for that. She might have, and she might not have."

"Are you saying that because you're afraid?"

"No. I just didn't notice."

"How come?"

"I was real cold. I was hassled. I had all this work to do."

"What work?"

Alfred pointed. "Hanging lights. That's what I should have been doing instead of playing Joseph. I tried to get out of it. Mr. Winston wouldn't let me."

"How come?"

"He'd had enough hassles about the schedule. Mr. Ferric—that's the art teacher—Mr. Ferric made up the schedule. Mr. Winston made him change it."

"Why?"

"For rehearsal. Mr. Ferric had actors scheduled for the Nativity when Mr. Winston wanted to rehearse. So Mr. Ferric told him to make his own schedule."

"So?"

"So, after making such a stink about it, Mr. Winston wasn't going to change it for anybody."

"He changed it for Dorrie Taggart."

Alfred shook his head stubbornly. "Dorrie didn't ask him. She and Miss Baldwin did it themselves. That's where I made my mistake. I should have just changed with somebody. But I didn't know who to ask."

Cora could imagine that. Alfred Adams, too much of a stickler to change the rules himself, appealing to the one who'd made them. "So you had to play Joseph *and* do the lights?"

"Right. And it's a big job. The lights, I mean." Alfred leaned in confidentially, gave the impression of lowering his voice, even though they'd been whispering to begin with. "Mr. Winston is a perfectionist. Everything's gotta be done just right. I don't just have to hang the lights. I gotta take 'em apart, wash and dry the lenses, put 'em back together again too. I mean, yes, they're old and filthy, but, come on, give me a break. Here I am, fighting to get everything done before I gotta be Joseph."

"And you didn't get everything done?"

"No. Time just flew. Before you know it, Mr. Winston's tapping me on the shoulder saying, 'Shouldn't you be outta here?' And I look at my watch and it's already ten o'clock. I got fifteen minutes to get to town hall, change, and get in position."

"But you were only five minutes late. How'd you get there so fast?"

"Mr. Winston drove me."

"That was nice of him," Cora admitted grudgingly.

"Oh, yeah? Mr. Winston didn't do it for me. He just didn't want Mr. Ferric to know his schedule screwed up." Alfred winced. "Sorry. I shouldn't say 'screwed up.' "

"I've heard worse," Cora assured him.

"Pssst!" came an angry whisper from below.

Cora and Alfred looked over the edge of the loft.

Glaring up at them from the shadows was the paint-smeared face of tech director Jesse Virdon. He had a headset jammed on his head. A thin cord ran from the earpiece to a power pack on his belt. "Alfred, for Chrissake!" Jesse hissed. "Where's your headset?"

"There's no cues," Alfred protested. "I took it off."

"Yeah, well, Rupert wants you to kill the lights that are aimed at the audience. It would have been nice if you heard me on the headset. If it doesn't happen *right now*, he'll be up to tell you himself."

Alfred gulped and dived back into the booth. Cora was amazed at the speed and dexterity with which, given the proper motivation, he could manipulate the dimmers. Within seconds, the offending lights had been extinguished, leaving the rest of the stage lights on.

Alfred whirled from the dimmer board, breathing hard. His face was pale. "Now see what you've done?" he moaned. "You got me in trouble. And Mr. Virdon *saw* you up here. Lady, you're bad news."

"You're not in any danger," Cora told him.

"Oh, yeah?" Alfred shot back. "Are you sure of that? You promise you won't get me killed?"

"Absolutely. I one hundred percent guarantee it."

Alfred gawked at her. "How can you do that?"

Cora smiled, her trademark Puzzle Lady smile.

"If I'm wrong, you won't know."

32

Cora Felton sat bolt upright in bed. Something was wrong. She could sense it. That is, something was wrong beyond the fact that her niece was being framed for murder. Something was wrong with the facts as she knew them. Something simply wasn't right.

Cora had the terrible feeling it had to do with Alfred Adams. What was it about him?

Alfred Adams was a geeky techie, socially gauche, but probably very bright. Quite possibly a computer nerd.

Capable of composing puzzles.

Could Alfred have been jealous of his more popular peers? Resented in particular a wealthy, attractive girl who had spurned him, perhaps ridiculed him for some ill-conceived, bumbling advance?

Could it be Alfred?

And if so, why hadn't she suspected him before?

Cora sat in bed, crunching the facts, knowing from bitter experience she would not be able to sleep until she had the answer.

All right, she's in the light booth. She's questioning Alfred. Rupert is working with Becky onstage. Everyone else is out on the gym floor.

And she's effectively written Alfred off. Even though he was one of two Josephs who handled the victim and could have planted the dart.

Now, why has she written him off?

Why couldn't she think straight?

Cora fumbled on the night table, switched on the bedside lamp. Her drawstring purse was on the floor next to the bed. She reached inside, fished out her cigarettes, fired one up, and took a greedy drag.

There. That was better. Now she could think.

Her first thought was what a hell of a time to be awake.

The front door clicked shut.

Cora stiffened.

Good God! That was what had woken her up. Not the nerdy tech geek. An intruder.

Cora snubbed out the cigarette, grabbed her purse again, reached inside. She pulled out her gun, slipped the safety off. Her fifth husband, Melvin, had once told her, "Never shoot anyone with the safety on." It was the only thing about Melvin she remembered fondly.

Cora slid out of bed, pushed the door open, crept down the hall. She eased around the corner, leveled the gun at—

"Sherry! What the hell are you doing?"

Sherry Carter blushed red in the moonlight. "I'm a little late. What's the big deal?"

"A *little* late? It's two in the morning!"

"I know what time it is."

"Yes, of course you do. I'm sorry, I'm just an old fogy. I was young once. I've never been busted for murder, though."

"You will be if you're not careful. You mind putting that thing down?"

"Oops. Sorry." Cora lowered the gun, snapped the safety on.

"I'm sorry you're up. I was trying not to wake you."

"I was up already."

"How come?"

"Lemme get my smokes. I just got one lit when you came bursting in."

"You left it lit?"

"I stubbed it out. At least I think I did."

"Check," Sherry said.

The cigarette was out. Cora grabbed her purse, plodded into the kitchen. Switched on the light, took the bottle of Cutty Sark out of the cabinet, poured a shot, and slugged it down. She lit a cigarette, took a drag. "Okay. I'm wide awake. Help me think."

"Think of what?"

"Are you kidding? Ways for you to beat a murder rap."

"I thought you already knew how. Hire Becky Baldwin as my lawyer."

"That was a smart move."

"Strategically, maybe. In terms of my mental health . . ." Sherry held up her hand, palm down, waggled it back and forth.

"What do you think it will do for your mental health if you get convicted of murder?"

"I need some coffee."

"At two in the morning? You'll never get to sleep."

"I'll make decaf."

"Big deal. Regular coffee's ninety-seven percent decaffeinated, decaf's ninety-nine percent. It's nearly the same thing."

"Is that true?"

"No, I made it up. Sounds good, though."

Sherry filled the automatic-drip coffeemaker, switched it on.

"So where were you, over at Aaron's?"

"Uh-huh."

"Did his parents know? They didn't, did they? He snuck you in. You must feel like a teenager."

Sherry sighed. "I know you're just trying to be amusing, but frankly I feel like the whole world's picking on me."

Cora put her arm around Sherry's shoulders, chucked her under the chin. "Come on, help me solve this thing. I gotta think it out."

"Whaddya got so far?"

"The obvious scenario is Doddsworth's daughter, insanely jealous of her best friend Dorrie's wealth and social position, bumps her off. Doddsworth, realizing his daughter Maxine is the killer, panics and frames you."

"You believe that?"

"It's the obvious solution. He called on you this morning so he could plant the envelopes."

Sherry shook her head stubbornly. "I was watching him all the time. He couldn't have done it."

"Uh-huh," Cora said. If she was convinced, Sherry wouldn't have known it. "You ever see a magician work up close?"

"Doddsworth's not a magician."

"Granted. I said that was the obvious solution. It doesn't mean I'm going for it. The next obvious solution is the boyfriend bumped her off." Cora waggled her cigarette. "The problem with obvious solutions is they're obvious. That's why I get hung up on the what-if-it-isn't-obvious."

"What do you mean?"

"The techie. Alfred Adams. I talked to him tonight and I'm not happy."

"What's wrong with his story?"

"Nothing. There was everything right with it. But he didn't want to talk to me."

"Your feelings are hurt? Or you think he has something to hide?"

"I don't know what I think. But that kid was squirming. He figured talking to me would make him a target. At least that's what he said."

"You don't believe him?"

"I think he thought it was true, but I don't know why."

Sherry poured the coffee. "Well, if you wanna ask him, I think he's still up. I just went by the high school and the lights are on in the theater."

"Maybe they just left the gym lights on."

Sherry shook her head. "The gym lights are out. The stage lights are on."

Cora Felton frowned. She pushed back her untasted coffee and stood up. "I'm going over there."

"Now? I was only kidding."

"I don't like it." Cora marched to the hall closet, took out her overcoat.

"You gonna talk to him in your nightgown?"

"I hope so. I'm worried about his health."

Cora pulled on her boots, grabbed her purse, wrenched open the front door.

"Wait for me," Sherry said.

"You wanna come, come. I'm not waiting."

Cora hurried down the path. The night was very cold and crisp. The moon was three-quarters full, reflecting off the snow and lighting up the yard. The Toyota was at the top of the driveway in the space the neighbor boy had plowed for twenty bucks that afternoon while she was out.

Hiring a lawyer for her niece.

Cora hopped into the car, gunned the motor.

Sherry slid into the passenger seat.

"You coming?" Cora said. "You don't think I'm being silly?"

"You also have a habit of being right."

Cora backed the car around, skidded out of the driveway, headed for town.

"What's the idea?" Sherry asked.

"When I questioned the kid, he claimed he was bustin' his hump trying to get the lights hung before he had to play Joseph. That's why he wound up late."

"So?"

"If he was nearly done then, why is he still working now?"

"That was *hanging* the lights. During rehearsal he was *plugging* the lights. After rehearsal he'd be *aiming* the lights."

"Until two in the morning?"

"That's not the point. The point is, what bothered you was the fact that he was almost done. When actually he had more work to do."

"I hope you're right."

"Why are you so upset?"

"I promised the kid he wouldn't get bumped off."

"Huh?!"

"It was a joke. He was scared I was putting him in danger. I swore I wasn't. Told him he'd be fine."

"How could you do that?"

"What was I gonna do? Tell him to write his will? How was I to know he was gonna stay late and aim lights?"

"Come on. It's two A.M. Don't you think his parents would have freaked out if he wasn't home?"

"Did Aaron's parents know you were there tonight? Till all hours, I mean?"

"What's that got to do with it?"

"Normal people go to bed. They don't sit up till the crack of dawn."

"Even if their son's out?"

"He's probably done tech before. Comes in quietly, doesn't wake them up."

"You're talking yourself into a nervous breakdown."

"I'm not talking myself into anything. It's happening on its own. I got you charged with murder. I got Sherlock Holmes Doddsworth running around messing things up. And now this kid." Cora shook her head, gunned the motor again.

Sherry knew better than to push the subject. She gritted her teeth, braced herself on the curves.

Within minutes the high school appeared on the right. It was dark except for the gym, where the glow of pink and blue stage lights flickered.

Cora swerved into the driveway, headed for the gym. "Same lights you saw?" she asked grimly.

"I think so."

"I don't like it."

Cora slammed the car to a stop, tore out the door before the motor even died. She ran up to the gym door, grabbed the handle, and yanked.

It was locked.

Cora banged on the door, yelled, "Hey! Open up in there!"

There was no answer.

"Looks like no one's here," Sherry said.

"Yeah." Cora marched to the car, took out a flashlight, switched it on, started around the end of the building.

"Where you going?"

"I'm going in."

"How?"

"Any way I can."

The backstage door was locked. So was the door to the cafeteria. But a window in the hallway was unlatched. Cora reached up, pulled it open. "Hey, give me a boost."

"Cora, you can't go climbing through windows."

"We've gotta get in there."

"So let me go."

"I can't boost you. I'm a little old lady."

"Little?"

"Hey, watch it."

"Aunt Cora—"

"I'm goin' in. You wanna help me, or should I drag a box from somewhere?"

Sherry laced her fingers together, boosted her aunt up. Cora pulled herself over the sill, flopped on the floor in a heap. She got to her feet and retrieved the flashlight. "Okay, go around to the gym door. I'll let you in."

Cora shone the flashlight ahead of her, hurried down the corridor, pushed her way through the doors into the gym.

The stage lights were on, but they were aimed helter-skelter, that is to say they had not been aimed at all. Several were focused not on the stage but on the gym floor. One blue-gelled spot was right in Cora's eyes. She blinked, held up her hand so as not to trip on the folding chairs left set up from rehearsal as she picked her way across the gym floor. Cora pushed her way through the double doors to the gym entrance and let Sherry Carter in.

"Anyone here?" Sherry asked.

"Doesn't look like it."

"Lights are cockeyed."

"Yeah. Someone didn't aim 'em. Let's find out why."

Cora and Sherry started for the stage. As they made their way up the stage-right stairs, Sherry suddenly gasped and grabbed Cora's arm. "Look!"

Cora, following Sherry's gaze, let out a small, anguished cry.

Hanging in the flies, upstage center, in the pink light of a misaimed spot, a pair of feet dangled from behind the teaser curtain, swaying gently in the still air of the gym.

The feet wore combat boots.

Cora pelted up the steps, rushed upstage to get a better view.

He hung in the flies, a rope around his neck, his face contorted, his tongue lolling out, a grotesque spectacle in the eerie light.

Cora stared at the dangling figure in horror. Her eyes widened.

Sherry, at her elbow, gasped, "Is it . . . is it Alfred?"

Cora blinked in amazement.

"No," she whispered.

33

"THIS CAN'T BE HAPPENING," RUPERT WINSTON PROTESTED. FOR once the dapper director's hair was uncombed, and his hastily thrown-on outfit did not match. He looked up at Chief Harper and Jonathon Doddsworth as if prevailing upon them, as rational men, to reconsider and let him go home.

Their silence was eloquent.

The three men were standing on the basketball court. Sherry Carter and Cora Felton sat on folding chairs off to the side. In the background, a weary EMS crew was loading the body of the hanged young man onto a gurney in preparation for removing it from the stage.

Rupert sighed. "All right, all right, it *is* happening. I just can't imagine why."

"Well, perhaps you can help us with how," Chief Harper retorted. "You had a rehearsal this evening?"

"That's right."

"During rehearsal your tech crew was plugging lights."

"One of them was. Alfred Adams."

"Who is not the young man there?"

"No."

"And that would be?"

"That's my tech director. Jesse Virdon."

"Why was he here?"

"I assume he was touching up the paint on the set."

"He was here when you left?"

"That's right."

"Was anyone else here?"

"Alfred Adams. He had to finish plugging lights."

Doddsworth raised his eyebrows. "Rather late for a school lad. Why didn't you stay and help him?"

Rupert Winston looked at him coldly. "I can't do everything. I'm teaching class. I'm rehearsing the Christmas pageant. I'm directing a play. I'm putting on *The Seagull,* and I just happen to have lost a key actress. You have no idea what it will entail working another girl into the role."

"I assure you I don't," Doddsworth said. "Nor can I fathom how you could be thinking about that now."

"I'm *not* thinking about that *now,*" Rupert snapped. "I was responding to your irrelevant and insensitive question as to why I wasn't working tonight. I *was* working, just not on lights."

"I think we get the picture," Chief Harper interposed, to forestall any further sparring between the two men. "Now, why would anyone want to kill your tech director?"

"You've got me."

"Was he a witness to the murder of Dorrie Taggart?"

"I have no idea. Didn't you take statements?"

"Yes, we did. I don't recall his."

Rupert shrugged. "Then I guess he wasn't."

"Was he part of the live Nativity?"

"I think so." Rupert pointed to Doddsworth. "You have my schedule."

"Yes, I do. According to which, Mr. Virdon portrayed Joseph from nine-fifteen to ten-fifteen in the A.M."

"That sounds right, but I really wouldn't know."

"Uh-huh," Chief Harper said. "And what can you tell us about the means of death?"

"What can *you* tell *me*?"

"The body was hanged from a rope, the rope was tied off at the pinrail."

A warning cough from Doddsworth cut off this exchange. "We know what *you* know, Chief. Let's have a listen what the *witness* has to say, shall we?"

"I fail to see how I'm a witness," Rupert protested.

"You needn't see," Doddsworth said shortly. "Tell us about the rope."

Rupert Winston looked up at the stage, where a single rope now hung from the flies to the floor. "That's the rope you mean?"

"But of course. Pray illuminate us. What might it be?"

"It's similar to the rope that dropped the sandbag. Except that was downstage center, this is upstage center. And I gather there was no sandbag attached. A noose?"

"No. Just a knotted rope," Harper told him grimly. "A poor knot, but good enough to hold. It did the job."

"Any chance it was a suicide?"

"None." Chief Harper jerked his thumb at the grid. "There's no place to jump from. Whoever did this tied the rope around his neck and hauled him up."

"Chief *Harper*," Doddsworth said in his most pained voice. "Mr. Winston pled a busy schedule. Perhaps we should allow him some sleep."

"I appreciate it," Rupert said. "This is a *terrible* tragedy. Still, the show must go on."

"I'll be the judge of that," Chief Harper said.

Rupert looked stricken to the very soul. "You can't shut down my show."

"He's the chief of police," Doddsworth pointed out. "He can do anything he wants."

"Except speak for himself," Cora muttered under her breath.

Sherry nudged her in the ribs.

The two sat quietly and were good while the director was ushered out. Then Doddsworth instantly turned his attention to them. "So. This is what comes of an anemic judicial system where we release suspects on their own recognizance, then scratch our heads in bewilderment when another murder results."

Cora Felton's eyes blazed. "Are you accusing my niece of this crime?"

"Merely making a general observation. But that certainly is a most intriguing notion. Chief Harper, would you mind terribly if I posed a question or two in order to clarify the situation?"

Chief Harper looked like he minded a great deal but couldn't think of an easy way to say so. "Be my guest," he muttered.

"Miss Carter," Doddsworth said. "Do tell us how you happened to find the body."

Cora bristled. "Just a minute. Let's not lose sight of the fact Sherry's been charged with murder. Before she answers any questions, she should have her lawyer present."

"That's not necessary," Sherry said.

"Sherry, honey, you haven't a clue what's necessary. So I suggest you either clam up or you pick up the phone and call Becky Baldwin. I don't imagine she'll be real pleased about it, but she'll be a lot happier than waking up tomorrow morning and finding out you spilled your guts."

"Whaddya think?" Sherry asked Doddsworth. "Should I call my lawyer?"

"Perhaps we may try another tack. Miss Felton, I don't fancy you've been charged with anything, now, have you? Do you need a solicitor before *you* speak?"

Doddsworth was practically daring Cora, egging her on, goading her into speech. Surely the best way to thwart him was to keep quiet. But to refuse to answer? To claim *she* needed a lawyer . . .

Cora hesitated. Glared at him.

He was smiling at her, a smug, taunting smile. His crooked teeth ruined the effect. So did his dress shirt, which in his haste he had buttoned wrong. The uneven collar was ridiculous. What could she possibly have to fear from such a man? After all, she had done nothing wrong.

Cora stuck out her chin. "What do you want to know?"

"Nothing to fret about." Doddsworth practically purred. "Merely finding the body."

"What about it?"

"The door to the gymnasium was secured?" Doddsworth said, slipping right into interrogation mode.

"That's right."

"You tried the door and couldn't open it?"

"That's how I knew it was locked."

"So how did you gain entrance?"

"I found a back window that was open."

"And how did you get through this back window?"

"I climbed."

"Was that easy?"

"Not particularly."

"But you had help?"

Cora pressed her lips together.

"This is not a big admission, Miss Felton. You and your niece came here together. I assume Miss Carter assisted you through the window. At any rate, you entered the gymnasium and saw immediately that something was wrong."

"I wouldn't say wrong."

"What would you say?"

"I saw that the lights were aimed incorrectly. Some were aimed out over the audience instead of at the stage. One was actually aimed at me in the door."

"So you investigated these misaimed lights and spotted the young man hanging over the stage."

"I saw his boots."

"Of course. You knew at once who it was?"

"Actually, I thought it was the techie. Alfred Adams. He had the same boots."

"And what made you think it would be young Adams?"

"I had talked to him earlier in the evening. About playing Joseph in the Nativity."

"So, when you saw the boots hanging there you imagined your inquiries had come to a most dreadful fruition."

"I was afraid I'd stirred something up, yes."

"And in fact, you hadn't. The dead man in question, this Jesse Virdon, you don't know at all. Is that correct?"

"I knew he was the tech director."

"But you never conversed with him?"

"I was there when he bawled Alfred Adams out for not wearing his headset."

"When was that?"

"Tonight. During rehearsal. He came by while I was talking to Alfred."

"And just where was this?"

"In the light booth."

Doddsworth raised his eyebrows. "Jesse Virdon observed you and Alfred Adams having tea and crumpets in the light booth? Fascinating."

Cora stuck her chin in the air, said nothing.

"You weren't concerned for Mr. Virdon's welfare?"

"No, I wasn't."

"But you *were* concerned for the welfare of young Mr. Adams, whom you spoke to earlier tonight?"

"I said I was."

"And that is why you came by the theater. To make sure everything was all right with Mr. Adams?"

"Yes, it is."

"At two in the A.M. Rather late to be checking up."

"It's a good thing I did. Or you wouldn't have found the body until tomorrow."

"Granted," Doddsworth agreed. "I'm merely wondering *why* you did. Particularly with regard to these misaimed lights. Did you perchance check on the theater because the lights were on?"

"What if I did?"

Doddsworth smiled. "Well, then, my next query would be, how did you *know* the lights were on? Who *told* you the lights were on? Who aroused your curiosity to such a degree as to send you out at two in the A.M.? It is a thorny dilemma, indeed. Particularly in light of the fact you are in your nightdress and your niece is fully clothed. Is it a fair inference, Miss Felton, that your niece motored by the gymnasium, spotted the lights on, drove home, told you about it, and the two of you ventured out to investigate?"

Cora pressed her lips tighter and said nothing.

"You see my problem," Doddsworth mused. "Here's a young woman, charged with homicide. Her solicitor gets her released. That very night she visits the site of an attempted murder, and, lo and behold, another murder occurs. This is a trifle much. She can't report it to the authorities without falling under suspicion. She needs someone else to find the body for her. It was your niece who informed you of the lights in the theater, was it not?"

Cora sat mute.

"Well," Doddsworth concluded smugly. "For once the prosecuting attorney will know what questions to ask."

34

Aaron Grant burst into the gym, rushed up to Sherry, grabbed her shoulders. "Sherry! Are you all right?"

"Relax, Aaron. I'm fine."

"Oh, yeah? Have they charged you with this one yet?"

"Not yet," Sherry answered. "I think they may be having a little trouble with the motive."

"Oh, no problem there," Doddsworth said blandly. "Clearly the poor bloke was killed to cover up the first murder."

"I'm glad that's clear to you," Cora said. "I'd be tickled pink to have it pointed out to me."

Chief Harper had had enough. "Well, I wouldn't. This case is not going to be argued in the press. Aaron, you can't stay. The morning paper's already printed. You'll get everything you need for your story tomorrow. So get on home. And do me a favor: Take Miss Carter with you. She's had enough excitement for one day. If you could drive her home, I'd be very grateful."

"Why can't Miss Felton take her?" Doddsworth asked.

"I need Miss Felton here." Chief Harper shooed Aaron and Sherry out. "Go on. Get."

Aaron reluctantly walked Sherry out.

Doddsworth watched them go, then cocked a bushy eyebrow at Chief Harper. "Do you really think having Miss Felton here is wise?"

"I don't know, and I don't care. But I'm not having any more people murdered in my town. So I'm talking to you, I'm talking to her, I'm talking to anyone I can. You may not like each other, but you happen to be the best minds I got. So bury the hatchet and help me out."

"Very well." Doddsworth said it grudgingly.

"Can you do that, Miss Felton?"

"Of course," Cora said unconvincingly. She and Doddsworth eyed each other like two dogs contesting a chunk of meat.

"Fine," Chief Harper said. "Now, let's forget for the moment we're on different sides and solve this damn thing." He gestured to Doddsworth. "You say this murder was done to cover up the first crime. How do you figure?"

"It's the only thing that makes sense. The tech director is not important in and of himself. A lonely man painting scenery, who could really care? With a previous crime, there must be a link."

"That's your only reason to think so?" Cora said. "The fact you have no other theory?"

Doddsworth bristled. "Have *you* another theory?"

"I don't even have the facts. Though my theory's sure to differ from yours, since you are so confused as to who committed the other crime."

"Hang on," Chief Harper interposed irritably. "Now, that's just what I don't want. Stick with issues, please. If this Jesse Virdon is killed to cover up the first murder, how is that possible? When did he play Joseph?"

"From nine-fifteen to ten-fifteen."

"And when did Dorrie play Mary?"

"From eleven to twelve."

"See? It doesn't work. When the crime happened, Virdon wasn't even there."

"How do you know?" Cora asked. "Maybe he hung around."

"Couldn't have done," Doddsworth said. "He had to go change. To leave his costume for the next Joseph. They were only rotating two, as you recall."

"You're arguing against your own theory?" Cora observed.

"Not at all. I'm merely pointing out what must have happened. When relieved, Jesse Virdon must have changed. Leaving his costume in the town hall. Where it was worn at eleven-fifteen by Lance Ridgewood. But that doesn't mean Virdon left. He could have been there in street clothes when Dorrie Taggart came on at eleven."

"Big deal," Cora snorted. "Suppose Jesse Virdon *was* hanging around the Nativity. What could he have possibly seen?"

"How about the killer putting his hand on Dorrie Taggart's neck?" Chief Harper suggested.

"Then why doesn't he tell the police?" Cora said. "If he had such direct evidence, he surely would."

"I quite agree," Doddsworth said.

"Then how do you support your theory?"

"The young man didn't know what he'd seen. Or didn't understand its importance."

"Interesting," Cora said.

"It follows that Virdon went to the killer purely out of curiosity, with no notion the killer might *be* the killer," Doddsworth said. "The poor chap had merely observed something he wished explained. Something he thought could easily *be* explained."

"That's obvious."

"It's also obvious the killer was someone he never would have expected. Someone he would have felt totally comfortable with. The techie Alfred Adams fits the mold. He relieved him playing Joseph. He was in the crèche when Dorrie took her place."

Cora nodded. "He seemed unduly nervous when I talked to him."

"He'll be questioned," Harper assured them. "Now, how about this. So far we've found no clue. No puzzle poem. Do you think we will?"

"No," Cora and Doddsworth said together.

"Interesting," Chief Harper said. "And why is that?"

"Because we took Miss Carter's envelopes," Doddsworth said, "leaving her with none."

"Because the envelopes were planted in her house," Cora corrected, "leaving the killer with none."

"Assuming the availability of envelopes, would you or would you not expect a puzzle poem?"

"Difficult to say," Doddsworth mused. "But I would lean toward no. The other rhymes were devised in advance. They were used in connection with a well-laid scheme culminating in death. The killer had no poems planned beyond the first murder, because the killer did not anticipate making a mistake. This crime, being improvisational, off-the-cuff, and committed for the sole purpose of covering up the other, would involve no puzzle. First, because no such puzzle would be ready. Second, because the elimination of such a one would involve no vitriolic verse."

"Is that your opinion also?" Chief Harper asked Cora.

"I'll go along with the fact the killer's not prepared. But he still might leave an uncoded message, just like the Becky Baldwin one."

"How about that?" Harper asked.

Doddsworth shook his head. "Miss Baldwin is without question part of the original equation. Part of the killer's plan. As such, she must needs be explained. Gloated over, even. But this young fellow has nothing to do with anything. No one cares about him. He is merely an inconvenience to be removed. Not worth tuppence."

"You expect no clue at all?"

"That's the ticket."

"Then I guess we're going to have a pretty bad night."

"What do you mean?"

Harper shrugged. "Looking for something that isn't there."

35

BECKY BALDWIN'S OFFICE WAS A MODEST, ONE-ROOM AFFAIR JUST off Main Street over the pizza parlor. It boasted an ancient oak desk, a half-filled bookcase, a four-drawer metal file cabinet, and two straight-backed client's chairs. Apparently any third-party actions were out of luck. Becky seemed embarrassed by the office. If so, it was the first time Sherry could recall ever seeing her embarrassed.

"You should have woken me up," Becky said huffily.

"There was nothing you could do."

"How do you know? At least I could have kept you from making damaging statements."

"I didn't make any statements."

"You told them about finding the body."

"Actually, Cora told them."

"I could have shut her up."

"You could have tried."

"This is not a game. This is not a joke. You know what they teach you in law school? Crime statistics. Wanna hear one? *Most crimes aren't solved.* You tell yourself you're not guilty, and when everything gets sorted out everyone will realize that and you'll be free. All you have to do is sit back and wait for them to catch the killer. Well, guess what? Doesn't happen. So you have to ask yourself, what if they don't catch this killer? What if no killer emerges? What if all they're left with is *you*?"

"I understand the concept."

"Do you? I don't think so. If you did, you'd have called me last night. *Before* you called the police."

"Chief Harper doesn't think I'm guilty."

"No, but he has to act on the evidence, and the evidence is bad. Even without you running around finding bodies."

Sherry took a breath. "Becky, this isn't going to work. I've had about three hours' sleep, and I don't feel like being used as a punching bag. You have any practical advice, fine. If you just wanna get off on telling me what a bad girl I am, I think our relationship is over."

"Point taken," Becky said. "Tell me how you found the body."

"Actually, Cora and I found it together."

"What made you look?"

"Driving by the high school I noticed the lights were on."

"Were you with your aunt at the time?"

"No, I was alone."

"Where were you going?"

"Home."

"Where had you been?"

"What difference does that make?"

"The police will ask these questions, so I need to know your answers. Where were you coming from?"

"I was over at Aaron's."

"Oh." Becky raised an eyebrow. "He still have his varsity letters on the wall?"

Sherry bristled. "Don't you know?"

"No," Becky said. After a pause she added, "I have my own place. I don't live with my aunt."

"Gee, that's grand. You can have that brainy TV reporter over any time you want."

Becky formed a T with her hands. "Time out. I admit I needled you just now because you were coy about where you'd been. Let's start over. You were coming back from Aaron's, you saw the stage lights in the gym. What time was that?"

Sherry hesitated a moment, then said rather defiantly, "One-thirty."

Becky smiled slightly.

Sherry glared at her.

Becky returned her gaze.

They stared each other down.

The corners of Sherry's mouth twitched.

Both women burst out laughing.

"All right," Becky said, when the laughter finally subsided. "Let's try this again. You were driving home from Aaron's at one-thirty A.M. and you saw lights in the theater. You went home and told your aunt. Did you wake her up to tell her?"

"No. She was awake. She was worried and couldn't sleep."

"Did you tell her first thing? 'Hey, I think there's something wrong in the theater'? "

"Let me think. Let's see, I came in, Cora was up, I asked her why, she asked me where I'd been, yadda yadda, then we started talking about the crime."

Becky raised her eyebrows. " '*Yadda yadda*'?"

"Don't start. Cora told me about talking to Alfred Adams and how he seemed nervous, and I told her he was probably still up, because the stage lights were on."

"So you went over looking for Alfred and found the tech director hanging from a rope?"

"That's right."

"Over a pulley and tied to the pinrail?"

"Yeah. Just like the sandbag. If you'd been out there singing, someone could have dropped him on you."

"Charming," Becky muttered. "So, what's the police theory of the case?"

Sherry gave Becky a rundown of what Cora had told her.

"Interesting," Becky said. "So he was part of the Nativity?"

"Yes. Not during the crucial time. But he might have seen something."

"Maybe that's the wrong track."

"What do you mean?"

"I would say it's far more likely he knew something about that sandbag."

"Like what?"

"Like who dropped it. Only we get into moron territory. How could someone possibly know that much and not talk?"

"True," Sherry said. "But there are other possibilities."

"Such as?"

"The puzzle poems. Maybe he saw someone leaving a puzzle poem. Or happened to know who had a bunch of red envelopes."

"Sure," Becky said. "Or maybe he knew who was blowgun champ. We got so many bizarre elements to these crimes you can almost take your pick."

"So what are we going to do?" Sherry asked.

"I can tell you what *you're* gonna do. You're gonna smile and say 'No comment' every time someone shoves a microphone in your face."

"That's gonna make for great public opinion."

"Just tell 'em your lawyer's making all statements for you."

"You must love that," Sherry told her.

"Don't be silly," Becky said. Her eyes were wide. "Believe me, I don't like this at all."

Sherry didn't believe her for one minute.

36

CORA FELTON DREAMED SHE WAS BEING ARRESTED. IT WAS A STRANGE dream, because while Cora could think of many things she might be arrested for, it wasn't for any of them. Instead, she was being arrested for shoplifting, something she had never done, and never would do. But that didn't matter. The police were there, and they had a warrant, and the warrant was for shoplifting.

Cora was charged with stealing a blowgun. Stealing it, and then hanging it from a sandbag onstage. A sandbag with lights focused on it. Pink- and blue-gelled lights, aimed in all directions, but somehow focused on the same place. The place where she was.

Swiping a blowgun.

Getting arrested.

Cora opened her eyes to find Chief Harper standing over her. Good God, she *was* being arrested.

Cora blinked. Her mouth fell open as it dawned on her where she was.

"Excuse *me*!" she exclaimed. "What the devil are you doing in my bedroom?"

"Sorry," Chief Harper said. "It's eleven o'clock. I thought you'd be up."

"You thought wrong. I was up all night. I'm sleeping now. And—" Cora broke off angrily. "What difference does that make? Get the hell out of my bedroom!"

"Of course, of course. I'll meet you in the kitchen."

"I don't *want* to meet you in the kitchen," she retorted, but Chief Harper had clomped out.

Cora snorted in disgust. She didn't want to give Chief Harper the satisfaction of talking to him, but she was too wide awake now to go back to sleep, and she really wanted to hear what he had to say.

Grousing mightily, Cora heaved herself out of bed and put on her clothes. As a gesture of defiance she pulled on her Wicked Witch of the West dress, a comfortable but tattered smock that sported cigarette burns and a liquor stain or two, and wasn't meant for company. Which suited her just fine. Chief Harper wasn't company.

Cora freshened up in the bathroom and went in the kitchen to meet the chief. She found him pouring a cup of coffee.

"You made coffee?" she said skeptically.

"Your niece must have. It's still warm. Want some?"

Being offered coffee in her own kitchen after being rousted out of a nightmare seemed the ultimate insult. "No," she said curtly. She marched to the refrigerator, took out tomato juice, mixed herself a Bloody Mary. She did not offer one to the chief. He would not have drunk on duty, and Cora knew that.

Cora sat at the table, lit a cigarette, and said, "This better be good."

"It gets worse by the moment. I don't know what to do."

"You think my niece committed murder?"

"No, I don't."

"You arrested her for it."

"You have to admit I had no choice."

"I have to admit nothing of the sort. I know she didn't do it. You know she didn't do it. What the hell is going on? Ever since this thing happened, you've been acting like a stranger. You let this refugee from a BBC crime show walk all over you. What gives?"

Harper sipped his coffee, observed, "A little cold."

"Zap it fifteen seconds in the microwave, medium high. That should give you time to think of an answer."

Chief Harper put the coffee in the microwave, said, "How do you start this thing?"

"Oh, for goodness' sakes! Even *I* can use a microwave." Cora elbowed him aside ruthlessly, punched in the code, and hit START. "Are you always so helpless?"

Harper winced.

Cora sat at the table, took a drag on her cigarette, picked up her drink, and pondered its scarlet depths glumly.

The microwave bleeped.

Chief Harper picked up the coffee, sat down again. "I'm in a bad position. Worse than usual. Usually, I'm just being pushed by the prosecutor. This time, it's money."

Cora frowned. "Excuse me?"

"The Taggarts have money. The Taggarts have clout. You know how many facilities in Bakerhaven have the Taggart name on them? The new rec hall. The visitors center. The elementary school playground. The high school science lab. Hell, even the town hall renovations."

"You're telling me the Taggarts have enough dough to railroad Sherry into jail for killing Dorrie?"

"They've got enough money to make life unpleasant. And the fact is, Taggart and Doddsworth were great buddies way back when. Played golf together. Hung out. Daughters were inseparable. Threw them together."

"So tell me something I don't know."

"When Doddsworth went back to England, he wanted to take his wife and daughter with him. His wife wouldn't come."

"Because they'd had a fight. I know that too."

"You know what they fought about?"

"No, but don't judge me too harshly. I got here ten years after the fact."

"Rumor has it they had an affair."

"They? Who's *they*?"

"Taggart and Doddsworth's wife."

Cora's eyes widened. "You don't say."

"That was the rumor at the time. Now, I know you women are better at rumors than we are—better at details, I mean—but the way I understand it, when Doddsworth found out, he didn't want to stay. It's a small town, everybody knew, Taggart was his best friend. It was just too soap operaish for him, and he didn't like the role he was playing. He felt he had to leave."

"And that's why he dumped his wife?"

"No. He wanted her to come. She wouldn't."

"She wanted to stay with Taggart?"

"No, she just wanted to stay. She wasn't going to be pushed around."

Cora considered that. She recalled Pamela Doddsworth's fury at her ex-husband invading her home, ordering her about.

"So Doddsworth comes back to see his daughter after all those years. Walks into an atmosphere that's supercharged to begin with, and bumps into a murder. And who does the victim turn out to be? The teenage daughter of the man who cuckolded him. And his own daughter's best friend." Harper spread his hands. "Who stole his daughter's boyfriend. Duplicating the whole sorry situation. A Taggart stealing a Doddsworth's lover away."

"Oh, good lord," Cora murmured. There were cigarette ashes all over her dress.

"Exactly. Doddsworth did nothing to strike back, but was his daughter made of sterner stuff? Did his daughter avenge herself on the Taggarts?"

"Sterner stuff?"

"Sorry. The situation lends itself to clichés."

"Glad to hear it. You've known all this from the start? Couldn't you have let me in on it?"

"At what juncture? The girl gets killed. Doddsworth's daughter asks him to investigate. And when we start interrogating the witnesses, I get my marching orders before you even find the blowpipe."

"Orders from whom?"

"From the county prosecutor. But he's just preaching the gospel according to Taggart. And Mr. Taggart has requested Jonathon Doddsworth go along for the ride."

"Why?"

"Claims he wants his daughter's murder solved. And he doesn't trust me to do it."

"Sorry I asked."

"That's just what he *said.* Frankly, I don't buy it. It may be perfectly true, but I don't think it's the reason. I think Taggart looked at the evidence and saw exactly what I saw. A motive for Maxine to kill Dorrie. Assigning Doddsworth is saying, 'I think your daughter killed my daughter. Disprove it if you can. Otherwise I want to rub your nose in it by making you dig out the facts that convict her."

"You think Taggart's that vindictive?"

"He just lost his daughter. His only child. I can't conceive how vindictive he might be."

"Granted." Cora nodded. "But if you'll pardon a real stupid question, if all the evidence points to Doddsworth's daughter, why have you arrested my niece?"

"Because more evidence points to her." As Cora started to protest, Chief Harper said firmly, "Please. Don't try to sell me on her innocence. The thing is, with all this public scrutiny, and outside pressure from Taggart via the selectmen and the prosecutor, I can't fail to act on the evidence, even if it points in a direction I don't like."

"Suppose it pointed at Maxine Doddsworth?"

"I would have to arrest Maxine Doddsworth."

"Of course you would. Suppose someone was manipulating the evidence so it pointed *away* from Maxine Doddsworth?"

Chief Harper scowled, did not answer.

Cora sighed through a haze of cigarette smoke. "So, where do we stand?"

"Nowhere. The second murder, rather than simplifying the situation, complicates it. Plus it's the wrong victim again. By rights, the victim should have been Alfred Adams, the techie. But, no, it's gotta be the guy who had nothing to do with anything."

"Did you find a letter saying *'Wrong guy'*?"

"You know we didn't. You were there when we didn't find it."

"I mean since. You didn't find a puzzle poem?"

"If we had, I'd have asked you to solve it."

Cora thanked her lucky stars that hadn't happened. "What does the techie say?"

"Alfred finished plugging lights and went home just before midnight."

"Leaving the lights on?"

"He says he turned 'em off."

"What about Jesse Virdon?"

"He says Virdon wasn't there. Alfred turned off the lights and locked up."

"How'd Virdon get in?"

"He had keys." Chief Harper snorted. "After all, he *taught* technical theater."

"Why do you say it like that?"

"A background check on the late Mr. Virdon shows he drifted into town this fall, got a teaching job at the high school with glowing references. Ten minutes on the phone was enough to prove almost all of them were forged. The late Jesse Virdon may have had artistic talent, but he was actually a product of the Pennsylvania social services system, who spent most of his life in juvenile correctional facilities for offenses ranging from petty theft to attempted rape."

Cora's mouth fell open. "Rape?"

"Attempted rape. Hell of a nice guy to have hanging around the high school. With his record, he should be the killer, not the victim."

"Suppose he was the killer? And he hung himself in remorse."

Harper nodded. "Wouldn't that solve all our problems? But no such luck. Barney Nathan says Virdon was hit over the head, most likely with a two-by-four, then strung up over the stage."

"Interesting."

"Yeah." The chief sounded glum.

"You got anything else?"

"Not much. Guess where the blowpipe came from."

"Am I supposed to tell you and give myself away?"

Chief Harper snapped his fingers in mock disgust. "Darn. Outsmarted me there. Blowgun came from an antiques shop. Larry Fishman's place."

"Who bought it?"

"He did."

"Huh?"

Harper grinned. "Sorry. Couldn't resist. Larry died last spring. Shop's been closed ever since."

"Then how'd you trace the blowgun?"

"Dan Finley recalled seeing it in the window. So did I, after he mentioned it. Not part of a display. Just lying there, with a bunch of other items. Real hodgepodge. Right there in the window. Larry wasn't much of an antiques dealer."

"How'd the killer get it?"

"Wasn't that hard. Jimmied a side window. Just the sort of stunt you'd pull."

"So now you think I'm the killer?"

"No, but you did find the blowgun in the church. Doddsworth thinks you might have put it there to take the heat off your niece, make it look like someone else could have committed the murder from a distance."

"What about the dart?"

Harper shrugged. "No one recalls seeing a dart in the window. With the blowgun, that is. So maybe it came from the antiques shop, maybe it didn't. The theory that it didn't ties in with the theory that you stole the blowgun. However, the dart fits the blowgun, and there's every indication they go together."

"Thank goodness for small favors. How about the poison? Is it the arrow poison of the South American Indians?"

"Would you expect anything less?"

"I was joking."

"I could tell."

"So what's the poison?"

"Curare. The arrow poison of the South American Indians."

"Give me a break!"

"It's not that unusual. Curare is also used in surgery. Most likely it was stolen from a hospital."

"And the dart was dipped in it?"

"There were traces on the dart."

"You got your murder weapon. Why don't you look happy? What's wrong with the evidence?"

Harper grimaced, sipped his coffee, grimaced again. "The curare used in surgery is not for the purpose of killing the patient. The amount that would cling to a dart would hardly be a lethal dose."

"How do you explain that?"

"I don't. I try to *keep* from having to explain that. I try to keep people from asking me that. In particular, I would appreciate it if your niece's pushy lawyer would refrain from popping the question."

"So Sherry can go to jail? That's asking a bit much."

"If this goes to court, all bets are off. I mean *now.* I would not like to be asked those questions *now.* Particularly by any newspaper or TV guy."

"Why are you telling me this, Chief? What makes you think these questions will come up?"

Chief Harper scowled into his coffee. "Because Taggart's going to make a statement."

37

THE MULTIMILLIONAIRE'S PUDGY FACE HAD AGED CRUELLY SINCE his daughter's murder. His cheeks were sunken, his eyelids sagged, and his skin was chalky. Taggart had evidently rejected makeup as inappropriate for the occasion, although his hair was plastered in place. He stood alone in front of Bakerhaven High School. The TV reporter was not in the shot. Instead, Taggart clutched the microphone himself, hung on to it for dear life, as if it were a lifeline that could pull him back into a more pleasant reality. Indeed, he might have resembled a doomed fish on a hook waiting to be reeled in were it not for his eyes.

His eyes were hard.

"My daughter is dead. And I don't know why. There are an abundance of theories. One theory is that she was killed by accident, that she was tragically mistaken for someone else. That seems too grotesque to imagine. And yet it may be true. On the basis of that theory, the police have made an arrest.

"I have been asked not to comment on the police case, and so I will not do so at this time. Chief Harper may be right, he may be wrong. I simply do not know. But I assure you, I intend to find out. I assure you, I will not rest until I know what happened here.

"But that is not what I came to say. My beautiful Dorrie, my only child, the sum of all my hopes and dreams, is gone. My loss is overwhelming, impossible to comprehend, and yet, for my Dorrie's sake, I must put my grief behind me and do something for her now.

"My Dorrie was a young woman of many passions, but perhaps none greater than her love for the theater. In two short years she had come so far. From walk-ons to leads. This year, she was to have starred as Nina in Anton Chekhov's *The Seagull.*" His ice-chip eyes glittered with tears. "She took her script everywhere, was always working on her lines. She would have loved to play that part."

Taggart snuffled, then pulled himself together. "And that is why I am here today. To announce that, with the approval of the selectmen and the board of education, I am hereby making a donation of nine million dollars for the establishment of the Dorrie Taggart Memorial Fund, in preparation for the groundbreaking this spring for the Dorrie Taggart Memorial Theater here at Bakerhaven High School."

Taggart paused, cleared his throat. "With the proviso, of course, that the case is solved. And my sweet daughter's murderer is revealed as the monster he or she is. I thank you."

Cora clicked the TV on mute. "Well, at least he didn't come right out and accuse you of murder."

"Thank goodness for small favors," Sherry said.

"Oh, I don't think it's a small favor," Becky Baldwin said. "Taggart was extremely careful *not* to accuse you of murder. 'As the monster he *or* she is.' There's nothing in his speech that could be considered actionable. I'll bet you a nickel it was vetted by his attorney." Becky took a bite of the risotto. "This is good."

"You sound surprised."

"Sherry," Cora said. "Accept the compliment. We got work to do."

Becky Baldwin was dining with Cora and Sherry in the living room in front of their TV. This unique social occasion had been prompted by Chief Harper's tip that Taggart would be making a public statement. Becky had already heard about it from Rick Reed, so she was not entirely floored by the invitation.

"So, what do you think?" Cora asked with her mouth full. "Aside from not being libelous, what does this do to these murders?"

"Nothing directly," Becky said. "How do you see it?"

Cora poked absently at a piece of asparagus. "It's a squeeze play, and we're smack in the middle. Taggart's pressuring Doddsworth to crack this case. The more things implicate Doddsworth's daughter, the more eager he will be to hang the crime on Sherry."

"And that's okay with Taggart?"

"Not at all. He's counting on us to be slippery enough to wriggle out of it. He wants Doddsworth left on the hook."

"Do you really think he planned all that?" Sherry asked.

Cora and Becky looked at each other. "Entirely too naive," Cora told Becky.

Becky nodded. "I gathered that."

"Hey," Sherry protested. "The situation's bad enough. You guys start double-teaming me, all bets are off."

"Right," Becky said. "Cora, lay off my client."

Cora's eyes widened. "Me? Well, I like that."

"Say, what is this?" Becky was poking the chicken and vegetables.

"Just a mishmash," Sherry told her.

"Yeah, but what's the recipe?"

"No recipe. I just threw it together."

"You can do that?"

"Girls," Cora said. "I hate to interrupt, but we have these murders. . . ."

"Of course." Becky straightened up, wagged her finger in reproof. "Listen up, now, Sherry. Go on, Cora, we'll be good."

Sherry smiled in spite of herself.

"You get anything else out of ~~Doddsworth's~~ TAGGART'S statement?" Cora asked.

"No. He just seemed to be extolling the virtues of his daughter."

"I notice he didn't mention she was knocked up."

"Aunt Cora!"

"Well, he didn't. And it happens to be a fact. One worth considering. Particularly with a hunky boyfriend headed for the Ivy League."

"Who hardly seems the type to write that kind of poem," Sherry reminded her.

"True. But if old Lancelot had an *ex*-girlfriend helping him . . ."

"You're back to Maxine Doddsworth." Becky was frowning.

"Everything leads back to Maxine Doddsworth," Cora insisted.

"Suppose she is guilty," Sherry said.

"Then her father will move heaven and earth to convict *you*," Cora told her.

Becky speared some chicken. "Just *why* does Maxine Doddsworth do in her best friend?"

"Jealous," Cora said promptly. "Dorrie stole Maxine's boyfriend."

"That was some time ago. And Maxine didn't even seem to care."

"But now Dorrie's gotten herself preggers."

Becky shook her head. "If Dorrie was in trouble, Maxine wouldn't be jealous, she'd be gloating."

Sherry and Cora exchanged glances.

"Or so I understand," Becky amended.

"Suppose it wasn't that," Cora said. "Suppose Maxine's jealous of the fact Dorrie is a spoiled little rich brat who always gets everything she wants. Suppose Maxine doesn't even know about the baby? If she did, she'd be gloating, and she'd let it live, to prolong Dorrie's public humiliation. But she doesn't know Dorrie's knocked up, so she puts her carefully designed plan in motion."

"Carefully designed because of the poems?"

"Exactly." Cora's eyes gleamed as she worked it out. "So this crime could date back to the theft of the boyfriend. Or it could be something else. . . ."

"Such as?"

"What did Taggart say on TV? About Dorrie being a star in the school play—what was it—*The Seagull*? Suppose Maxine's in *The Seagull* too. With Dorrie's death, would she get the star part?"

"That's absurd," Becky said.

"Is it? Someone tried to drop a sandbag on your head. Could it be someone who wanted *your* part?"

"Not Maxine Doddsworth. She isn't even *in* the Christmas pageant."

"Forget Maxine. How about anybody else?"

"It doesn't work," Sherry objected. "There's no high school girls in *The Twelve Days of Christmas.* And there won't be grown-ups in the high school play."

"I don't mean both," Cora insisted. "I mean either."

"*Either* makes absolutely no sense," Becky argued. "In terms of a motive. If someone wants my part in the Christmas pageant, why knock off Dorrie?"

"Because they thought she was you," Cora said. "Unfortunately, the only one who fits that criteria is Sherry. You wouldn't kill to get a bigger part, would you?"

"Cora—"

"I, on the other hand, would *kill* to get a *smaller* part." Cora cocked her head at Becky. "You know why Doddsworth left town?"

"Sure. His wife had an affair with Taggart."

"You knew that?"

"*Everybody* knew that."

"You must have been pretty young at the time."

"His daughter was pretty young at the time. I was old enough."

"Hmm." Cora's eyes narrowed.

"What are you thinking?" Sherry asked her.

"What if that was the whole point in killing Dorrie? What if someone wanted *Taggart* to suffer?"

"You mean Maxine?"

"Or her father."

"That's ridiculous," Sherry said.

"Why is it ridiculous?"

"Why would Doddsworth kill Dorrie and implicate his own daughter?"

"He's not trying to implicate his daughter. He's trying to implicate *you.*"

"But he killed Dorrie in a manner in which his daughter would be likely to be implicated. Never mind that. *How* did he kill her? Unless he's some super blowgun champ who could hit a bee at fifty paces."

"A bee?"

"The point is, Doddsworth couldn't have done it. Neither could Taggart. Basically, the only ones who could have done it are Maxine, the boyfriend Lance, and the wrong techie guy."

"Wrong techie guy?" Becky said.

"Well, the one who's still alive. Alfred. If the dead tech director is important, what could he have possibly known?"

"We're going around in circles," Becky said.

"That's because there's nothing to come up with." Sherry sighed. "We listened to Taggart's statement, and it didn't tell us a thing."

"I wouldn't go that far." Cora's eyes were suspiciously bright. "We know he's got nine million bucks to build a theater."

"That's no big news," Becky said. "The Taggarts have always been filthy rich."

"He also mentioned Dorrie was his only kid," Cora pointed out. "As such, she stood to inherit his dough. Now that she's dead, who gets it?"

"I would assume his wife," Becky said.

"So would I. I wonder if that's true."

"Now you're suggesting her *mother* killed her?" Sherry said it skeptically.

"Someone did. Who profits from her death? *Cherchez le dough,* I always say."

Sherry frowned. "That motive only works if Taggart dies too."

"Well, why not?" Cora said. "We've had two killings already. And an attempt at a third. Whoever's behind this ain't exactly respectful of human life."

"That's for sure," Becky agreed. "But from a monetary standpoint, the only one likely to gain *is* Mrs. Taggart."

Cora wrinkled her nose. "Yes and no. Remember, Taggart and Mrs. Doddsworth bumped their uglies. Suppose Mrs. D's still got the hots for Mr. T. Mr. T digs her too, but Mr. T and his wife have stuck together for the sake of the kid. Well, that obstacle to their romance just got removed. The big winner could be Mrs. Pammy Doddsworth."

"Good God, you have a devious mind!" Becky exclaimed enthusiastically. "So, your theory is Pamela Doddsworth kills her daughter's best friend with a poison dart to give herself a shot at her daughter's best friend's wealthy father?"

Cora disentangled that sentence, then shrugged. "Some people are basically not nice. Those who kill tend to fall into the not-nice category."

"Uh-huh," Becky said. "And those are the only suspects you can come up with who gain financially?"

"Not at all. You've got my favorite director, Rupert Winston, who gets nine million bucks towards a new theater."

"Winston couldn't have known that would happen."

"He might have surmised it. And he's so obsessive about his, quote, art, unquote, I wouldn't put it past him."

"You just don't like him because of the Christmas pageant."

"Well, do you hear how he talks to me? How he talks to everybody, for that matter. Everybody except you."

"Oh, yeah?" Becky said. "Then you haven't been listening lately. According to Rupert, I haven't done a thing right since someone dropped that damn sandbag. Thank God there's no rehearsal tonight."

"Yeah, well, don't thank Rupert. He'd have had one if the theater wasn't a crime scene."

"Of course he would," Sherry said. "The show's in only two days."

Cora made a small noise. "Two days?"

"Well, when did you think it was? It's the *Christmas* pageant. They're usually *before* Christmas."

"With everything that's happened, I just lost track of time. Two days?"

"If there *is* a Christmas pageant," Becky reminded her. "Maybe they won't have one, in light of the killings."

"From your lips to God's ear," Cora said fervently. "But that will never happen. People don't sit and brood. Not in Bakerhaven. Life goes on," she added glumly. "Don't worry, you'll get your chance to be a star."

"That's not what I meant," Becky protested.

"Yeah, right."

Aaron Grant arrived, swiftly took in the situation, and did a heroic job of hiding his shock at seeing the three women together. If anything, he was a bit too casual about it.

"Hi, girls," Aaron said. "You see Taggart's statement?"

"I just came for the food," Becky replied. "My client is an amazing cook."

"Yes, I know. So what did you think?"

"The asparagus risotto was to die for. The chicken mishmash isn't bad either."

"I meant about Taggart's statement."

"Frankly, we're plum out of insights," Cora said. "You got anything helpful?"

"No, but you may get another statement on the late news."

"Oh? How come?"

"I was just over at the Country Kitchen. Inspector Doddsworth is having dinner with Rick Reed."

"Really?" Cora said, perking up. "They been there long?"

"I doubt it. They were just ordering when I left."

"Were they, now?" Cora shoved back her plate, got up from the coffee table. "You kids carry on without me. I have other fish to fry."

"Cora," Sherry warned. "You're not going to bust in on Jonathon Doddsworth's dinner. Promise me you're not."

Cora's smile was angelic.

"I wouldn't dream of it."

38

JERRY LYNCH, THE PROPRIETOR OF THE SURF & SUN MOTEL, WAS impressed. "You're the Puzzle Lady in the ads. On TV."

"Yes, I am."

"That's amazing."

Cora blushed, as usual, embarrassed by her fame. "Oh, it's nothing."

"No, it's amazing. The Puzzle Lady in my motel. Don't you live in town?"

"Yes, of course."

"Then why do you want a room?"

Cora grimaced. She had to get the one proprietor in America who had to know why before he rented a room.

"It's my niece." Cora leaned her head in confidentially. "She's entertaining a young gentleman, and she doesn't need her aunt underfoot." Cora hoped she'd be forgiven for destroying what little remained of Sherry's tattered reputation.

"Uh-huh," Jerry Lynch said. Cora wasn't sure if he bought it or not. Still, he reached under the desk, produced a registration card.

That didn't suit Cora's purpose. She'd been hoping for a registration *book*.

"Motel almost full?" Cora ventured as she scribbled on the card.

Jerry snorted. "I wish. Only half the units full. At Christmastime, no less."

"Suppose it's the name?" Cora asked.

"What do you mean?"

"Sun. Surf. Not exactly Christmassy."

"I suppose."

"None of my business, but I haven't seen much surf around here. Aren't we kind of landlocked?"

"Had a motel on the Jersey shore. When I moved, I kept the name."

"I see," Cora murmured. She was wondering how to turn the conversation.

Amazingly, Jerry Lynch did it for her. "Funny you staying here, you being an amateur detective and all."

"Why is that?"

"We got another detective staying here. English fellow. Here for the holidays."

"Jonathon Doddsworth?"

"That's him. How do you like that?"

"I'll have to say hello. What unit's he in?"

Jerry's demeanor became disapproving. "You can *call* him if you like. I don't encourage visiting between units."

"Of course. What's his extension number?"

"One-oh-seven. But he isn't in."

"Oh?" In light of Jerry Lynch's strict regulations, Cora wondered what devious surveillance methods allowed him to spy on his guests.

"Car's gone," Jerry said.

Visions of the Bates Motel replaced by a somewhat foolish feeling, Cora smiled, accepted her room key. She was in 12, which she figured to be the last unit.

It was. Cora drove down to the parking space in front of her door. Whoever had plowed the parking lot had piled a mountain of snow up against the walkway, leaving Cora with the option of scaling a glacier or trudging back to a gap about halfway down the row. Cora chose the latter option, and found herself in front of unit 7. There was a light on in the unit. It filtered through the paper-thin curtain.

Cora cast a glance at the front office. It had a side window, through which proprietor Jerry Lynch undoubtedly kept tabs on the comings and goings of his guests. She wasn't sure at that distance, with her frosty breath fogging her glasses, but she thought she could see his face in the window.

Cora frowned. She walked down to unit 12, turned her key in the lock, pushed the door open, switched on the light.

It was your typical motel room. A queen-sized bed with neutral blue-gray coverlet tightly tucked under a row of pillows at the head. Two nightstands, one undoubtedly containing a Gideon Bible. Over a double dresser hung a framed print of dogs playing poker. Cora wondered if it, too, had traveled from the Jersey shore.

At the foot of the bed was the TV Jonathon Doddsworth had mentioned. Cora was glad he had. The Surf & Sun was the only motel in the Bakerhaven phone book advertising cable TV.

The telephone was on the bedside table. Cora checked the number. Her extension was 112.

Cora nodded in satisfaction. If phone extension 112 was unit 12, surely extension 107 was unit 7.

Cora slipped off her coat and pondered her options. With nosy Mr. Lynch watching the unit, the front door wouldn't do.

Cora checked out the bathroom. As she had hoped, there was a window in the back wall. Small, high, and frosted, with a single metal-framed pane that could be cranked open or shut. The window bore out Cora's none-too-glowing opinion of the motel's design. A woman of her stature could hardly reach the crank, let alone turn it.

Under normal circumstances.

These were not normal circumstances.

Cora grabbed a towel off the rack, dried the soles of her boots. Then she stepped up on the toilet seat and climbed to the back of the toilet tank. She stretched her right leg out until her foot reached the rim of the sink. She tested it, found it would support her weight. Straddling the two plumbing fixtures, she was able to get a tentative purchase on the crank. She turned it, was rewarded when the window swung out with a creak.

Cora surveyed the open window with displeasure. It was big enough, but just barely. The buttons of her tweed jacket would surely catch on the sill. Not to mention the buttons on her matching skirt. Was she nuts? Surely she could use the door.

Cora hopped down, went to the front door, opened it, and stepped out boldly, as if she had just forgotten something in her car.

The proprietor's face was definitely in his window.

Cora snapped her fingers, as if she'd suddenly remembered something that negated the need for whatever it was she'd forgotten, and went back inside.

She wriggled out of her tweed jacket, flung it on the bed. Likewise her tweed skirt. Clad only in her blouse, boots, and bloomers, Cora went back in the bathroom. She climbed up on the toilet and the sink, put her hands on the sill of the window, and launched herself through.

As she'd hoped, the snow broke her fall. She'd be sore the next day, but nothing was broken. She pulled herself to her feet and brushed herself off. Then, starting with twelve, she counted the bathroom windows down to seven.

To her delight, Doddsworth's bathroom window was partially open.

To her chagrin, she couldn't possibly reach it.

Cora looked around for something to stand on. Nothing. Any plank, box, or ladder that might exist was buried under snow.

Cora frowned. She reached down, picked up a handful of snow. It was wet, formed a dandy snowball. She could chuck it through

Doddsworth's window. . . . Wouldn't that give the old bore a jolt when he came home?

Instead, Cora dropped the snowball, bent down, pushed it with her hand, rolled it along. She cursed the fact she had no gloves, but they were in her coat, back in her motel room. No way to get them now.

Cora rolled the ball of snow diligently, as if she were building a snowman. When it was big enough, she rolled it over to Doddsworth's window, smushed it up against the motel wall. There. If it would just hold her weight . . .

Cora patted the huge snowball down until it felt solid. Discovered to her chagrin that she had no way to climb up on it.

Cora rolled a smaller snowball to use as a step.

Moments later she was enjoying a view of Jonathon Doddsworth's tiny bathroom.

The toilet seat was down, which was a plus, but the tile floor looked hard. This would not be like falling in the snow.

The shower curtain rod was almost within reach. Cora pushed herself over the windowsill. The more weight she put on it, the more the dull metal edge cut into her stomach. Cora grimaced, leaned out, and . . .

Grabbed the shower rod!

Now, if the damn thing would just hold.

It didn't.

Just as she swung her legs free, the shower rod pulled out of the wall. Cora crashed to the floor. She lay there tangled in the shower curtain, and began to have serious misgivings.

Maybe 107 *wasn't* the phone for unit 7.

Maybe one of the windows she had counted was the housekeeping and maintenance room, and this wasn't unit 7 at all.

Maybe this *was* unit 7, but the proprietor was wrong and Doddsworth was there!

Get a grip, Cora told herself. Doddsworth was at dinner with the TV reporter. And he'd have to be deaf not to have heard her entrance.

Cora pushed the bathroom door open a crack and peered out. There was a light on, but the unit was unoccupied.

Cora heaved a sigh of relief, switched on the bathroom light, and inspected the damage. Not too bad. The shower rod was only slightly bent. Cora straightened it, rethreaded the shower curtain, and hung it back up. She surveyed it critically, hoped the dent wouldn't show.

Cora scrubbed a snowy footprint off the toilet seat, set a razor back on the sink, and hung up a towel. Satisfied everything was more or less the way she'd found it, she switched off the light and went into the bedroom.

The bedside lamp was on, not the overhead, which was too bad. Cora would have loved to switch on the general lighting, but the nosy proprietor would be sure to notice. So she made a hasty inspection without it.

It was Cora's experience that men tended to live out of their suitcases, but Doddsworth was apparently staying long enough to have unpacked. His suitcase was in the closet, along with a suit jacket and two dress shirts. Cora closed the cheap accordion closet door, then turned her attention to the room.

A dresser identical to the one in her room held nothing of interest. Three drawers held clothes. Two drawers were empty. The drawer on the bottom right was stuffed with dirty clothes.

There wasn't much else. The nightstand the light sat on held a Bible. The other nightstand held nothing.

Cora snorted in exasperation. She'd gotten banged up for this?

Then she saw it. On the floor. Leaning up against the dresser. A small leather briefcase.

Jackpot!

Cora snatched it up, discovered it was not a briefcase but a leather-bound notebook. Grinning, she took it over to the bed, unzipped and opened it. It was a binder for three-hole notebook paper. On the first page, she could see jottings in ballpoint pen.

The name *D. Taggart* topped the page.

Underneath were the notations, *Max—10:00–11:00; S. Carter—12:00–1:00.*

The name *S. Carter* was heavily underlined.

On the rest of the page were names and times of the other actors from the tableau.

Cora turned the page, and her face hardened. There was the notation *S. Carter—Visa,* followed by what was obviously Sherry's credit card number and expiration date, and the record of her purchasing Enigmacross.

Cora turned the pages hastily. Doddsworth could be back at any moment. There were copious notes about the dart, the blowgun, and the sandbag, and copies of each of the poems. Everything she would expect to find in a good policeman's notebook.

Only one thing was missing.

Aside from the live Nativity schedule, there was no mention anywhere in the notes of Maxine Doddsworth.

Cora frowned as she read the last written page. She riffled through the rest of the pages, but they were blank.

Next she examined the notebook itself. A slit on the inside back cover caught her eye. She reached in, felt something, pulled it out.

It was a red envelope!

Cora fought to contain her excitement, told herself the envelope didn't necessarily mean anything. After all, Doddsworth had found the envelopes. Maybe he'd hung on to one, just for comparison.

Cora wasn't buying it.

She flipped back to the front of the notebook to see if there was a similar pocket. There was. She reached in, felt another envelope, pulled it out.

This one, however, wasn't red but white. It was addressed to Doddsworth in London, England. This, Cora reasoned, had nothing to do with the crime, and she had no excuse for reading the letter.

Cora examined the envelope, hoping for something to change

that assessment. There was no return address. But the postmark was Bakerhaven, Connecticut. And the date was December 10, presumably just days before Doddsworth had come to America.

Cora pulled out the letter.

It was written on a single sheet of stationery, in a woman's flowery hand.

> My dearest Doddsy,
> I hear you are coming to see Maxine. Do you really think that is wise? I would never stop a Father from seeing his Daughter, but even so . . . It has been many years, but nothing has changed. I still feel the way I did, and so does Horace. If you must come, and I know you will—I was *never* able to talk you out of anything—but if you must, I beg you, stay away from us. For your Daughter's sake, as well as for mine. You cannot fix anything. You can only make it worse. I beg you to be smart.

Cora turned the paper over, read the closing.

> Be smart, Doddsy.
> All My Love,
> Mindy.

Cora's mouth fell open.

A car pulled up to the unit. A motor roared and died.

Cora shoved the letter back in the envelope, thrust the envelope back in the leather case. Zipped the leather case shut. Propped the case up against the dresser where she'd found it. Thanked her lucky stars she hadn't turned on another light.

A key scraped in the lock.

On cat feet, Cora sprinted for the closet, squirmed inside, tugged the accordion door.

Moron! she told herself, her heart hammering. *The first thing that neatnik will do is hang up his coat!*

The door banged open and Jonathon Doddsworth stomped inside, muttering something about American rental cars, which apparently were not up to the highest British standards. Judging from his tone, he and Rick Reed had hoisted a few at the Country Kitchen. Even so, Cora figured, the inspector was probably not drunk enough to fail to notice a woman in her skivvies huddled in his coat closet.

Which he would open any minute.

But he didn't. Through the crack in the door Cora could see Doddsworth's coat land squarely on the bed as the detective himself stomped into the bathroom.

Quick as a wink, Cora slipped out of the closet, closing the accordion door behind her, and sprinted out the front door.

Instantly, Cora could feel the eyes of the proprietor on her. There was no help for that now. She hurried down the walkway, panicked that she didn't have her room key, then remembered she'd left the door unlocked. With a gusty sigh of relief, she let herself in to unit 12, shivering with the cold.

She went in the bathroom, shut the window. Then she checked in the mirror: no obvious scrapes. She pulled on her clothes and coat.

The mound of snow made her walk past unit 7 again. She was sure that just as she reached the door Doddsworth would come popping out to confront her. He didn't. Cora hurried to her car, revved up the engine, and pulled out.

Her headlights illuminated the figure of a man blocking the driveway. Cora slammed on her brakes.

The proprietor walked around to the driver's side, motioned to her to roll down the window.

"Yes?" Cora asked brightly, as if everything were just fine.

Everything clearly wasn't.

Jerry Lynch shook his head. "You checked in with no luggage. I might have said something, but I didn't. Gave you the benefit of the doubt. But when I see you, in your *underwear*, coming out of the room of a gentleman guest, that's something else." He stuck his nose in the air. "I don't run that sort of motel."

Cora grimaced.

And here she'd thought she was compromising *Sherry's* reputation.

39

THE TAGGARTS' SPRAWLING, THREE-STORY COLONIAL WAS SO BIG that Cora expected a butler, but Mindy Taggart answered the door herself. Her face seemed startlingly pale in contrast to her black mourning dress. Her blond hair was tied back. Her eyes were dull. Haunted. "I'm sorry," she said. "My husband isn't seeing anyone."

"I came to see you. May I come in?"

"I'm not seeing anyone either."

"Yet here we stand."

Mindy Taggart took a soft breath. "Miss Felton, I just lost my daughter. Could you have some compassion?"

"My niece has been charged with your daughter's murder. She didn't do it. I mean to find out who did."

"You've come to the wrong place. I know nothing that would help you."

"I think you do."

"Well, you're wrong. And now you're being impertinent, as well as intruding on my grief. I'm going to ask you to leave."

"What about Doddsy?"

Mindy Taggart's pale face froze. "I beg your pardon?"

"I was hoping to discuss your dear Doddsy. But if you're not up to it, I'll just have to ask him. . . ."

Mindy Taggart glanced around in consternation, lowered her voice. "Come into the parlor."

In light of her grief, Cora resisted retorting, "Said the spider to the fly." Instead, she followed Mrs. Taggart into what at one time would have passed for a Victorian sitting room but now was dominated by a big-screen TV.

Mindy Taggart closed the door and turned. Her face had become a mask of anguish, as if her whole world were collapsing. "In the name of heaven, why are you doing this to me?"

"I'm not doing anything to you. I'm trying to solve your daughter's murder. That may bring up things you'd rather forget. But wouldn't you like to know?"

"As if I didn't."

"You're saying you know who did this?"

"No, of course not. Please. My daughter's been taken from me. Haven't I been punished enough?"

"Is that how you see it?"

Mindy said nothing.

"Tell me about Doddsy."

"There's nothing to tell."

"I read the letter."

"What letter?"

"The one you wrote. Just before he came here. *'My dearest Doddsy'* is not exactly ambiguous. So there's no need to pretend."

"Men are such fools!" Mindy sank into a chair by the coffee table, lifted the lid of a ceramic box that proved to contain cigarettes. "Mind if I smoke?"

"Thought you'd never ask." Cora draped her coat over the back of the couch, sat down and dug into her purse. "I prefer my own. Here, let me give you a light."

The two women lit up, sat back smoking.

Mindy Taggart took a deep drag, blew it out, said, "Where were we?"

"We were talking about the stupidity of men. I've married enough of them to agree completely. With regard to Jonathon Doddsworth: I gather you two were an item. I assume by the way you spirited me off at the slightest mention of his name that your husband doesn't know?"

Mindy said nothing, merely glared.

"Oh. Of course he knows. That was the whole point. Your affair with Jonathon Doddsworth was to pay your husband back for his affair with Doddsworth's wife."

"So that's what you think."

"That isn't true?"

"The story holds up after all these years."

"What story?"

"My husband is a powerful man, Miss Felton. A man used to getting what he wants."

"What he wants? As in Pamela Doddsworth?"

"Yes and no."

"What do you mean by that?"

Mindy took another drag on her cigarette, blew it out. "I will tell you. And then you must go away. And leave me in peace. Peace. As if there could ever *be* any peace. But I will tell you. And you will tell no one. Because that's how it works." She laughed ironically. "Fifteen years ago, Jonathon Doddsworth was quite the young man. Thinner, with a mop of curly hair. And that English accent. And those twinkling eyes. Witty. Amusing." Mindy smiled at the memory. A sad, wry smile. "I was a married woman. I wasn't supposed to fall in love. But those things happen."

Cora rolled her eyes. "Tell me about it!"

"All I know is when I was with Jonathon I was happy. It seemed so innocent. Until Horace found out."

"So, it was the other way around. Your husband and Pamela Doddsworth got together to pay *you* two back."

"You still don't get it, do you?" Mindy tapped her cigarette into the ashtray, then looked Cora straight in the eye. "Horace and Pamela *never* got together."

Cora blinked. "I beg your pardon?"

"It didn't happen. That was just a story Horace put around."

"What?"

"Like I say. My husband is a powerful man. Used to buying whatever he wants. In this case, he wanted Doddsy gone. They had been the best of friends. When he found out about us, Horace was hurt, terribly betrayed, and angry. He couldn't bear to see Jonathon anymore."

"So what happened?"

"There were children involved. Dorrie and Maxine were too young to understand, to even know what was going on. We didn't want them hurt. You have to understand that."

"I'm trying to understand. I'm not having much luck."

"Horace's solution was amazingly simple. Jonathon would take his family back to England. The girls would miss each other for a while, but they were young, and they would forget. The problem was Pamela. She refused to uproot her family on some rich man's whim. Doddsy could go if he liked. Her feelings toward him weren't too cordial along about then."

"Imagine that."

"So, they cut a deal, Jonathon and Pam. He would go back to England. Pamela and Max would stay here. Horace would settle a sizable amount on Pamela for child support, as long as she kept quiet about the affair."

"And she agreed to that?"

"Why not? Her husband was leaving Bakerhaven. She and my husband were the aggrieved parties. Why shouldn't they make a pact to help each other through a rough time?"

"But they never had an affair?"

"Horace and Pamela? Don't make me laugh! That was just the story Horace put out to explain Doddsy's leaving. He merely leaked it to a few key sources. It got around soon enough. It wasn't long before the whole town knew.

"Then Doddsy comes back after all these years, and tongues begin to wag. Time has passed, the two girls have grown. Suppose they were to hear? You see why Doddsy's so upset? He thinks she found out. He thinks she did it."

Cora frowned, puzzling out the tangle of human emotions. "Your theory is Maxine Doddsworth found out what your husband did, sending her father away and spreading lies about her mother, and became so enraged she murdered his daughter to make him suffer?"

Mindy looked at her with just a trace of a smug smile.

"Not Maxine. Pamela."

40

PAMELA DODDSWORTH WASN'T OVERJOYED TO SEE CORA ON HER doorstep either. "Why are you here?" she demanded sharply. "Why can't you just let well enough alone?"

"And let your husband solve it?"

"*Ex*-husband."

"I thought you wanted me to beat him to the punch."

"I do. You're wasting your time talking to me."

"I don't think so." Cora, nudged by Pamela, took one of the candy canes off the Doddsworths' Christmas tree, examined it critically. "I just came from Mindy Taggart."

Pamela's nostrils flared. "Oh, is that so?"

"I don't imagine you like her much."

"We're not exactly close. But our daughters were best friends."

"I've heard the story. Mindy came clean. I know what you've been through, and I think I understand what you feel." Cora held the candy cane like a gun. "What I'm trying to figure out is just how vengeful you are."

"What in heaven's name are you talking about?" Pamela seemed genuinely bewildered.

"It had to be a strain to have your husband come back after all those years. Bringing up ugly old memories. Rekindling ugly old resentments. Particularly if your daughter still idolized her dad."

"Certainly it's hard. What's your point?"

"Hard enough to make you kill?"

"What!?"

"Someone killed Dorrie. I'm looking into the very good possibility it was you."

"Are you out of your mind? I wasn't even there."

"No, but your daughter was."

Pamela's face darkened. "What are you saying?"

In the reflection of one of the silver balls on the tree, Cora could see Maxine Doddsworth listening from the stairs. Evidently Pamela wasn't aware of it. That was just fine with Cora.

"I would imagine your daughter still trusts you enough to do what you tell her. Suppose you were to give Maxine a necklace or scarf or choker to slip on Dorrie's neck in the crèche. Suppose whatever it was had a poison pin."

"I don't recall any such object being found on the body. But I suppose you have a *theory*"—Pamela said the word mockingly—"of what became of it."

"I haven't thought it all out yet."

"I'll say you haven't. Why in the world would I kill the child like that, knowing it would directly implicate my daughter?"

"Maybe that was the point," Cora replied. "You are a woman who has suffered a great wrong at the hands of three people. Your husband who betrayed you. The woman he betrayed you with. And her husband, who compounded the injury with lies and deceit. Well, here's revenge on them all. The Taggarts you deprive of their only child. And your husband—the person you hate most—on him you inflict the even worse punishment of thinking his daughter did the deed."

Pamela Doddsworth stared at Cora in growing horror. "Are you insane? Do you think I'm such a fiend? What sort of a twisted mind would it take to come up with something like that?"

Cora had come up with the idea in no time at all. She tried not to take offense. "It would depend on the degree of hatred. I imagine yours runs rather deep."

"You have no idea."

Maxine Doddsworth came scampering down the stairs. "Oh, come on, Mom. You still love Dad, and you know it. Otherwise you wouldn't care so much."

"Max! How long have you been listening?"

"Long enough. But don't worry, Mom. I didn't learn anything I didn't already know. Your secret's safe with me."

"Oh, my God!"

"Yeah, oh, my God. You're not a bad woman, you're just a martyr. Sacrificing your good name for my sake. And for Dad's. Any money you got for doing so is entirely coincidental."

"This was never about money!"

"No, of course not," Maxine said sarcastically.

"How long have you known?"

"Oh, a while." Eyes flashing, Maxine turned to Cora Felton. "Is that what you're here for? To root out scandal? Spread it around? Take the heat off your niece? Is that why you're here?"

"No. I'm trying to find who killed your friend."

"You needn't bother. Daddy's on the case. He's the real deal. He'll prove who did this, no matter what it takes. He'll run rings around you. You're nobody. He's the best."

"Max, don't be rude."

"No, she's right. For experience, your husband has me beat hands down." Cora twirled the candy cane thoughtfully around her finger. "Maxine, can I ask you a question?"

"Depends what it is."

"Are you in *The Seagull*?"

Maxine blinked. Whatever question she'd been expecting, it wasn't that. "Yeah. Why?"

"What do you play?"

"A small part. A walk-on, really."

"What's going to happen with *The Seagull* now? Is it still going on?"

"How the hell should I know? Who cares about some stupid play?"

"I thought you might take over Dorrie's part."

"Yeah. Like that would really happen. I'm no actress."

"Then why were you in the play?"

"Because Dorrie was. She was nuts about that stuff. Me, I could never see the point."

"But Dorrie took it seriously?"

"Worked her tail off." Maxine made a face. "Mr. Winston's such a perfectionist. Everything's gotta be just so. He kept Dorrie late maybe two or three times a week."

"You mean for private lessons?"

"Sure. She was a star. Director's pet. Even in rehearsal, she was the one he worked with most."

"Any of the other actors jealous of the attention?"

"No. Why should they be? He's a real pain, fussing over one thing or another. They just resented the time. Mr. Winston's rehearsals drag on forever."

Cora suppressed a groan. *She* had two days of Rupert Winston's rehearsals left. "Did Dorrie mind?"

"She ate it up. She loved playing that part."

"Uh-huh." A thought occurred to Cora. "Was Lance in the play?"

"Lance? No way. He's a jock."

"Mmm." Feeling her way, Cora ventured, "So, did you stick around for these late rehearsals Dorrie had?"

"Are you kidding? Would you stay after school if you didn't have to?"

"But Dorrie told you about them?"

Maxine frowned.

Cora pounced. "What is it?"

"Nothing," Maxine said irritably. "Dorrie just wasn't herself lately. I wondered why. Now I know."

"You mean her being pregnant?"

"Uh-huh."

"But that had nothing to do with rehearsals. Was there anything about *rehearsal*?"

"Of course not. What could there be?"

Cora was embarrassed to discover that she had absently unwrapped the candy cane. "I don't know. Would she have discussed her pregnancy with Rupert Winston?"

"Get serious!"

Cora shrugged. "If she needed advice. And didn't want to go to her parents."

"She'd tell *me*," Maxine said emphatically. "She sure as hell wouldn't tell Rupert Winston."

"Even if she had something she wasn't sharing with you?"

"Even then. No way she'd talk to him."

Cora stuffed the candy cane in her mouth and thought that over.

41

THERE WAS A LIGHT ON IN THE THEATER, EERILY REMINISCENT OF the night before. That intrigued Cora. The stage was now a crime scene. By rights no one should be there.

Cora pulled in, found Rupert Winston's VW Superbeetle parked by the door. That utterly confused her. Rehearsal had been canceled, and even if Rupert had gotten permission to work with a few select people he deemed needed it most, surely she would be high on the list. Not that she *wanted* to rehearse. Still, the fact that she hadn't been asked intrigued her. Was it possible Rupert *wasn't* rehearsing? And if he wasn't, what was he doing?

Cora tried the gym door. It was unlocked. She eased the double doors open and stepped into the theater.

The basketball court was drenched in shadow. The stage lights were on. Downstage left, a slender young girl stood in a single spotlight. A teenager, with wispy black hair, thin lips, and haunted eyes. Attractive, in an artsy sort of way.

As Cora watched, the girl declared, " 'I'm a seagull.' " She paused, touched her forehead. " 'No, that's not it! I'm an *actress*.' "

Rupert, in slim black pants and turtleneck, catapulted onto the stage from the shadows, as if he were a dancer in an avant-garde ballet performed on a trampoline. "No, no, no!" he cried. "Laura, darling, you are not auditioning for a toothpaste commercial. You are back to see your childhood sweetheart, Konstantine, after your tempestuous affair with the writer, Trigorin. It's been years, and much has happened. You've had and lost a child. You've tried, but failed, as an actress. A seagull is what Konstantine killed and laid at your feet in act one, declaring someday he'd kill himself in the same way. It also happens to be the title of the play. So you cannot say you're a seagull as if you were at a McDonald's window asking, 'You want fries with that?' "

The girl's face twisted in anguish. "I know. . . ."

"See?" Rupert said triumphantly. "Now you're giving me true emotion. Feel that bad about the seagull. Feel that bad about your wasted life, your shattered dreams. Your abandoning Konstantine. Okay, try it again, and—Hello! Who's there?"

"Me," Cora said, coming forward. "I was driving by and saw the light. I didn't expect anyone to be here, it being a crime scene and all."

"The police released it this afternoon. Too late to call people for the pageant, but at least I could work with Laura." When Cora raised her eyebrows, Rupert said, "You find that heartless? *The Seagull* opens two weeks after vacation. Terrible scheduling, but it's not my doing. I just lost my ingenue, which is devastating. If Nina's no good, the play doesn't work. Konstantine's tragedy is tied in to her tragedy. I've only got two weeks. That's Laura's handicap. Everyone else has had six weeks already, and she only gets two. Dorrie's death is tragic, of course, but for me it's a disaster of epic proportions. *The Seagull*'s my first play in Bakerhaven. I want it to be perfect."

"Laura is Dorrie's understudy?"

Rupert snorted. "I *wish.* In this high school they don't *have* understudies. Laura was playing one of the bit parts. At least she's *seen* some of the blocking. Even if she hasn't learned the lines." He glared at the young woman, who visibly wilted under his disapproval.

"So what will happen with Laura's part?"

"I'll have to get someone. One of the other actresses will move up."

"Maxine Taggart?" Cora suggested.

"Good heavens, no. That girl can't act to save her life."

"Then why'd you cast her?"

"I didn't. What's-his-name did. The drama teacher."

"Mr. Erskine," Laura prompted helpfully.

"Yeah, him." Rupert spread his arms theatrically. "Flew off to Colorado to take care of dear old Mommy, who had a stroke. Left me with this play. It was in bad enough shape before. If it goes on now it will be a true miracle. Even if I *do* get to rehearse."

Cora said, "I only stopped by because the last time there was a light in the theater it wasn't good."

Laura shuddered.

Rupert rolled his eyes at Cora, mouthed, "Thanks a lot!"

On her way out, Cora paused in the doorway to watch the actress standing young, and pale, and exquisitely fragile in the pool of light, telling the world she was a seagull.

Judging by Rupert Winston's assessment of her performance, Laura wasn't that good in her new role. Still, she seemed happy enough to be playing it.

Cora couldn't help wondering how much Laura had wanted the part.

42

Sherry Carter was shocked. "You broke into his motel room?"

"Well, if the guy's going to leave his door unlocked . . ."

"Inspector Doddsworth left his door unlocked?"

"No. But if he had, I could have walked right in." Cora surveyed the contents of the refrigerator with displeasure. "Didn't you make dessert?"

"I did. We ate it. So if the door was locked, how did you get in?"

"Bathroom window."

"Aunt Cora!"

"What difference does that make? The point is, I got in and I found the evidence."

"What evidence? You found out Doddsworth had an affair with Taggart's wife umpteen years ago."

"It's why he left town."

"So what?"

"And Mindy's still hot to trot."

"Good lord, Cora. That ice queen, hot to trot?"

Cora pawed through the refrigerator. "That's the problem with you younger generation. You can't imagine the older generation having a sex life."

"I can imagine them having a sex life. I just can't adjust to your vernacular characterization of it."

"Oh, dear. Was I speaking in the vernacular? And I do so try to avoid that." Cora found a cup of custard pudding, held it up critically. "How many weeks old is this?"

"Cora!"

Cora stuck the custard back in the refrigerator.

"If it's too old to eat, throw it out," Sherry said.

"It's too old to eat *now.* Later I may not be so fussy." Cora grabbed a package of cookies from the cupboard, poured a glass of milk, took them to the kitchen table.

Sherry sat opposite her, sighed, then said, "Okay. What is it you think you found?"

"Oreo cookies."

"Aunt Cora."

"I found enough motivation for Jonathon Doddsworth to frame you for murder."

"I thought you already had that."

"Yes. His daughter being a suspect. But now I have the motivation for him *believing* her a suspect."

"You had it before. Dorrie stole Maxine's boyfriend."

Cora waved that suggestion away with a cookie. "Boyfriends are a dime a dozen. I never really liked that motivation. Now, you put together a whole history of family intrigue and betrayal, this thing begins to look a lot better."

"You're saying you think Maxine murdered Dorrie?"

Cora said something, but her mouth was crammed with cookie, and Sherry couldn't understand her. "Was that a yes or a no?"

Cora took a gulp of milk, washed the cookie down. "I'm just saying there's enough reason for her father to be afraid little Maxie might have croaked Dorrie. To the point of framing *you* to take the heat off *her.*"

Sherry frowned. "You want me to try to sell that to Becky Baldwin?"

Cora waved a fresh cookie. "Absolutely not. I don't want you to even *tell* Becky Baldwin. Or Aaron, either. This is some information you and I happen to have. I'd rather not explain how we came by it. I'm also not too keen on spreading gossip."

"Heaven forbid," Sherry said. "Let me be sure I've got this straight. It was Doddsworth and Mrs. *Taggart* who had the affair. But Taggart deliberately led everyone to believe it was he and Pamela Doddsworth?"

"That's it in a nutshell." Cora dipped a cookie in her milk. "You know, they're better when you dunk 'em."

"Aunt Cora. Stick with me here. If you don't think Maxine committed murder, what's the good of all the gossip you just found out?"

"Didn't I tell you it wasn't gossip? Damn!"

"What's the matter?"

"My cookie broke off in my milk." Cora heaved herself to her feet, fetched a teaspoon from the silverware drawer, plopped back down, and began fishing noisily for her cookie.

Sherry got up and poured a glass of milk.

"There you go." Cora nodded approvingly. "You might also want a spoon."

"I'll be careful." Sherry sat down, dipped an Oreo delicately in milk.

"So where'd Becky and Aaron go?" Cora asked.

Sherry grimaced. "Well, aren't you the soul of tact?"

"Sorry. Let's take them one at a time. Where did Jimmy Olsen go?"

"Back to the paper to work on his story."

"Where did Perry Mason go?"

"Home."

"Did they leave at the same time?"

"Damn!"

"What's the matter?"

"My cookie broke."

"I told you to get a spoon."

Sherry fetched a spoon. The two women sat in companionable silence eating cookies and drinking milk.

"Any phone calls?" Cora asked after a while.

"Just your favorite director."

"Rupert? What did he want?"

"We have rehearsal tomorrow afternoon at one o'clock."

"You have got to be kidding."

"Not at all. We lost tonight's rehearsal. We have to make it up."

"You mean we have rehearsal tomorrow afternoon *and* tomorrow night?"

"Tomorrow night's dress rehearsal, in case you've forgotten."

"I'm trying to. Well, how do you like that. The son of a bitch didn't have the nerve to tell me to my face."

Sherry frowned. "What do you mean?"

Cora told her about dropping in on Rupert's *Seagull* rehearsal. "So there's another motivation down the drain. The idea Maxine killed Dorrie to get that part."

"She might have *thought* she'd get the part," Sherry suggested.

"Not unless she's a hell of a better actress than Rupert Winston gives her credit for. I'd swear she wasn't interested."

"Too bad."

"I'm gonna check out the girl who got it, though. Laura something. She claims it's a big surprise, but that may or may not be true. I'd also like to know if she was one of the virgins."

"Why? Even if she was the Virgin Mary, she wasn't there when Dorrie got killed."

"I know. I'm grasping at straws. I have no idea what's up in this case. I can use all the help I can get."

Sherry dunked a cookie, considered. "So what's your present theory? Was the killer trying to kill Dorrie? Or was he or she trying to kill Becky Baldwin?"

"There's evidence to support both."

"Is there any evidence to support the theory that Becky Baldwin was the intended victim that doesn't make me the killer?"

"Not so you could notice," Cora said glumly. "Becky let me look at her client list. She hasn't been practicing long. There's no one likely to hold a grudge."

"Anyone *not* on her client list?"

Cora shrugged, picked up a stack of Oreos. "I suppose Rick Reed could have done it to boost his TV ratings. Or because she's a lousy date."

"Becky as the victim simply makes no sense." Sherry broke off at the sight of her aunt dropping cookies into her glass. "What are you doing?"

"Well, why not?" Cora demanded. "I've got my spoon. These things are great in milk. Why pretend to dunk?"

Cora dropped two more cookies in her glass, mashed them around. "What were you saying?"

Sherry, mesmerized by the cookie milkshake, said, "I forget. Oh, yeah. How there's no reason for anybody to kill Becky."

"Present company excepted, of course. There *is* no reason. The only one pushing that theory is Doddsworth."

"True," Sherry said. "But there is the little matter of the sandbag."

"Yes, indeed." Cora continued to mutilate her cookies.

"The killer's puzzle poems promised the death of the leading lady," Sherry pointed out. "You've got two leading ladies. One is killed. The other is almost killed. Is it open season on leading ladies, or is the killer after one leading lady in particular? If so, which one? If it's the first one, why try for the second? If it's the second one, why the poem about eating for two? And if it's both, why the clue *Wrong girl*?"

Cora nodded judiciously. "You said that very well."

"Do you have any answers?"

"No, but it helps to state the question." Cora gave the glass one last stir, brought up a huge spoonful of cookie glop. "Mmm, would you look at that."

Cora stuck the spoon in her mouth. Her eyes closed, her grin stretched from ear to ear. If she were a cat, she would have been purring.

"Earth to Cora. Remind me. What do I do when you go into sugar shock?"

Cora smiled. Her teeth, plastered with Oreos, made her appear a dental disaster. "In that happy event, you call our Bob Fosse wannabe and tell him I won't be at rehearsal."

43

"THERE'S ANOTHER ONE," JIMMY POTTER SAID.

Rupert Winston flung up his hands in despair. "Jimmy! It's not your entrance yet. When it *is* your entrance, you will know it because the piano will be playing. You will know it because Becky will be singing. You will know it because you will hear the words *'my true love gave to me.'* Did you hear any of those things, Jimmy?"

"No, Mr. Winston."

"Then you should not be onstage. You should be *off*stage, holding your pear tree, waiting to come on. I don't know how many times we have to go over this."

"Yes, Mr. Winston."

"Is your pear tree there?"

"Yes, Mr. Winston."

"Is the partridge in it?"

"Yes, Mr. Winston."

"Then why are you not standing offstage *holding* your pear tree, waiting to go on?"

"There's another letter."

"What?"

"Another red letter."

Rupert Winston looked at Jimmy skeptically, breathing hard. "You mean there's another puzzle in the pear tree, just like before?"

There was a pause while Jimmy digested that query. "No."

"There *isn't* an envelope in the pear tree?"

"Yeah, there is."

"Then why did you say no?" Rupert bellowed in exasperation.

"Not like before. Before, the partridge was gone. Now there's a letter *and* the partridge."

"There's a red envelope in the pear tree?"

"Yes, Mr. Winston."

"Get it! Get it! Before someone takes it!"

Jimmy went offstage, returned immediately bearing the pear tree. The partridge was perched crookedly on one branch. The red envelope nestled between two others.

The actors emerged from the wings, crowded around.

"It's another one," Harvey Beerbaum announced. "If it's a puzzle, I should take charge of it."

Cora Felton, clutching her milking stool, exchanged a glance with Sherry Carter. "That's right," she said emphatically. "Harvey solved the first puzzle. He definitely should get a crack at this one."

Dan Finley, who had been watching dutifully from the back of the audience, pressed forward. "Don't touch it," he warned. "I'm calling Chief Harper. He'll be right over. In the meantime, did anyone see where this envelope came from?"

No one had.

"Jimmy, was it there when you got here?" Dan asked.

"I dunno."

"Why not?"

Jimmy pointed to the basketball court. "Mr. Winston said sit out there. So I sat out there. While he talked. Then I went backstage, and there it was."

"You mean just now?"

"No, before. When I came out onstage."

"Oh, for goodness' sakes," Rupert grumbled. "How long is this going to take? I've got a *rehearsal* to run."

"The chief should be here any minute."

He was. Chief Harper came stomping in from outside, spanking the snow off his coat. He glowered at the pear tree, which Jimmy had set on the apron of the stage. "All right, where did this come from?"

"No one seems to know," Dan Finley told him.

"How is that possible? You're supposed to be keeping an eye on things. This happened under your very nose?"

"No, sir. It was probably here before we got here."

"Uh-huh." Chief Harper eyed the envelope critically but did not pluck it from the tree.

"Well, aren't you going to open it?" Harvey Beerbaum said excitedly.

"I certainly am. But not with an audience."

"You mean you're not going to open it here?" Harvey wailed.

Before Chief Harper could answer, Jonathon Doddsworth burst in from the parking lot. His face was flushed, and his brow was creased in a scowl. "What the deuce is going on? Do I understand correctly there's another red missive?"

"See for yourself." Chief Harper pointed to the pear tree.

"Is it another acrostic?"

"I haven't touched it."

"Who's responsible for this?"

"No one knows."

"Well, someone must have lodged it there." Doddsworth surveyed the group. "I see Miss Carter is onstage. Would *she* have had the opportunity to plant this envelope?"

Chief Harper shrugged. "I just got here myself."

Doddsworth swung on the director. "Winston, you're in charge. Could Miss Carter have placed that envelope in the tree?"

"Any of the actors could have slipped backstage before the rehearsal started."

"I'll consider that an affirmative." Doddsworth shook his head.

"Well, bit of a lark, now, isn't it? I wonder if it might shed any light on the second murder. There was no clue with that."

"We'll soon find out," Chief Harper said grimly. "Mr. Winston, I'm sorry, but we're going to have to borrow Miss Felton again."

"Gee," Cora said. "I'm the one who really needs rehearsing. Why don't you have Harvey do it?"

Harvey Beerbaum eyed Cora suspiciously. "You'd rather *rehearse* than see what the puzzle is?"

"I don't wanna ruin the play. Go on, Harvey. I know you're dying to."

"I'd be happy to do it," Harvey Beerbaum informed Chief Harper.

"I'm sure you would, Harvey, but I want her. Frankly, she's faster than you. I need this solved *now*."

"That was with Sherry helping me write down the answers," Cora reminded him.

"Right. I need her too."

"Well, you can't have her," Rupert snapped irritably. He stabbed his finger at Cora. "And you can't have *her* for long. None of this

	1 S	2 I	3 E	4 O	5 H	6 A	7 J	8 L	9 F		10 I	11 L	12 R		13 N	14 A
15 G		16 B	17 G	18 E	19 I	20 P		21 P	22 C	23 R	24 M	25 B	26 D	27 E	28 I	29 Q
	30 O	31 B	32 D	33 F	34 G	35 L		36 H	37 K	38 P	39 I		40 G	41 B	42 C	
43 J	44 C	45 M	46 F		47 P	48 I	49 H	50 O	51 K	52 D		53 S	54 A	55 E		56 O
57 M		58 E	59 C	60 H	61 A	62 S	63 K		64 G	65 P	66 A	67 O		68 D	69 G	70 Q
71 B	72 R	73 I		74 H	75 C	76 S		77 A	78 Q		79 L	80 B	81 P	82 R	83 N	
84 Q	85 B	86 I		87 A	88 E	89 R		90 B	91 P	92 M	93 K		94 O	95 J	96 N	97 E
	98 L	99 P	100 A	101 I	102 O	103 J		104 K	105 N	106 L		107 N	108 C	109 D		110 I
111 H	112 D	113 J		114 M	115 O	116 C	117 F		118 D	119 S	120 O	121 C		122 H	123 D	124 B
	125 O	126 B	127 H	128 Q		129 K	130 N	131 J	132 G		133 R	134 A	135 O		136 I	137 N
138 E	139 S	140 B		141 E	142 N	143 Q	144 L		145 H	146 B	147 K	148 S		149 B	150 M	151 D
152 P	153 A	154 H		155 F	156 H		157 D	158 P	159 H		160 K	161 D	162 N		163 C	164 O
165 Q		166 G	167 L	168 M		169 H	170 B	171 G		172 O	173 N	174 A	175 R	176 C		

Clue	Letter positions
A. Schwarzenegger flick, e.g. (2 wds.)	54 87 134 6 174 153 66 100 61 77 14
B. Transmission type (4 wds.)	90 80 41 124 170 71 25 31 146 149 16 126 85 140
C. An extra inch in the waist, for instance (3 wds.)	75 116 22 121 42 44 176 59 108 163
D. Psychiatric facility	26 112 52 118 32 68 109 157 151 123 161
E. Hostile environment (2 wds.)	97 55 138 27 141 18 88 3 58
F. Daphne's beloved	33 155 117 46 9
G. Cop treats	166 40 171 34 69 132 17 15 64
H. "One if by land, ___" (5 wds.)	74 127 154 5 36 60 49 122 145 169 156 159 111
I. Real dullards (2 wds.)	48 2 136 19 28 10 101 86 110 39 73
J. Overacts	131 7 95 113 103 43
K. Medieval weapons	93 160 63 51 104 37 129 147
L. Ship's left (2 wds.)	98 11 144 106 35 167 79 8
M. "Let ___ ring"	114 150 57 24 168 92 45
N. Tough gangster (2 wds.)	105 13 137 107 96 142 83 130 162 173
O. Partially decrease impact (3 wds.)	102 120 135 94 4 50 30 164 67 56 125 115 172
P. "___, Mrs. Robinson" (3 wds.)	158 152 38 99 21 47 65 20 91 81
Q. The night ___ (2 wds.)	70 29 84 165 143 78 128
R. Dulling	89 12 23 82 133 175 72
S. Trains	148 76 139 53 119 62 1

whisk-her-off-to-the-police-station stuff. There's no one in the dressing rooms. Open the envelope in one of them. If there isn't a puzzle in that damn envelope you won't even need her."

"Fine," Harper agreed. "We'll use the girls' dressing room. Go on with your rehearsal. We'll get Miss Felton back as soon as we can."

"I'd rather you took Harvey."

"Sorry."

Chief Harper pulled an evidence bag out of his pocket, used a handkerchief to put the envelope in. "Dan. Stay here, watch Miss Baldwin. Miss Felton, you come with me."

Harper and Doddsworth walked Cora to the door. She flashed a look over her shoulder at Sherry as she went out.

"Odds are it's a puzzle poem," Doddsworth said. "We didn't get one with the second victim. In a way, we're sort of owed one."

"On the other hand," Cora said, "it could just be a message like *Wrong girl*."

"That would make your job easier," Harper said. "But I'd bet my pension it's a puzzle."

"I'm afraid you're right," Cora told him glumly.

The girls' dressing room was dark. Chief Harper fumbled on the wall, switched on a light. "Well, no dead bodies."

"Were you expecting one?" Cora asked.

"With this case, I don't know what to expect."

"Come, come, let's have a look," Doddsworth said impatiently.

Chief Harper set the evidence bag on the makeup table. He fished a pair of thin rubber gloves out of his pocket and pulled them on. He slid out the envelope and slit it open with a jackknife.

Inside was a folded piece of paper. As Chief Harper carefully unfolded it, Doddsworth, looking over his shoulder, whistled.

"What is it?" Cora said.

Chief Harper turned the paper around.

"So, it is a puzzle," Cora said. "And it looks complicated. Let's just get Harvey. . . ."

"No. You do it."

"Or at least Sherry to help me . . ."

Chief Harper shook his head. He pointed to the puzzle.

"No. Do it. Now."

44

Cora Felton flopped her drawstring purse down on the makeup table, rummaged through it, finally came out with a pen. She stared at the puzzle judiciously. "You want me to copy this over? I'm not sure I have a sheet of paper."

"Here's one." Doddsworth tore down a page that had been taped to the makeup table mirror. It was a cast list for the upcoming production of *The Seagull,* with handwritten notations next to each actor's name.

"That's the costume lady's measurements," Cora protested. "She'll have a fit."

"She'll live," Chief Harper said. "Go on. Write the answers. And make it snappy. I'm nervous about this. What if this tells us someone is going to be killed?"

"Then you better xerox it. It'll take me forever by hand." Cora stuck the costume list tidily back on the mirror.

"Bloody *hell*!" Doddsworth exclaimed. "Where's the copy machine?"

"Room by the business office."

"Wouldn't that be locked?"

"Jimmy Potter used it."

Doddsworth pulled out a handkerchief, grabbed the puzzle by the corner. "I'll pop upstairs and run this off. Damn sight faster than arguing."

He was back in minutes. "All right, here's a copy you can scribble on. No more stalling. What's it say?"

Cora frowned, then exhaled heavily. "Okay, let me take a look."

Cora peered at the puzzle. She fumbled in her purse, came out with a pack of cigarettes, lit one again.

"*Smoking* in the high school?" Doddsworth could not have sounded more scathing had he accused her of burning the place down.

"I am if you want me to solve this."

"There's a dandy example to set for the students."

"What students? You see any students?"

"If it makes her faster, I don't care," Harper interposed.

"Faster? She hasn't written a bloody thing!"

"I have to find a clue I'm sure of."

"You're not sure of *any* clues? Typical! Let's get Beerbaum."

"Fine with me." Cora blew out a smoke puff. "You want me to go up and send him down?"

"No. I want you to stop stalling and do the puzzle," Harper said irritably. "Leave her alone, Doddsworth, and let her get to work. Come on. Start filling in clues like you did in my office."

"Well," Cora said. "*Trains,* seven letters, is probably *teaches.*"

"Fine."

"Or *subways.*"

"What?"

"As in *subway trains.* See? That's why I have to start with something I'm sure of."

"And that would be . . . ?"

"Hard to find. This isn't very well constructed."

"You had no problem last time."

"I was lucky. Some clues were obvious."

"And they're not here?"

"For the love of Mike!" Doddsworth exploded. "This isn't a debate. Just solve it the best you can."

"Yes, Your Highness." Cora bent her head to the puzzle. "Okay, let's see. *One if by land,* five words, is going to be *and two if by sea.*"

"What?" Chief Harper said.

" 'One if by land, and two if by sea,' " Cora quoted. "And *Blank Mrs. Robinson* is going to be *Here's to you, Mrs. Robinson.* From the Simon and Garfunkel song. Let me fill those in and see what I've got."

Cora began scribbling. For once, the men didn't interrupt her. Doddsworth even held out an old Styrofoam cup for her cigarette ash.

In a matter of minutes, Cora turned the paper around.

"There you go. Pretty interesting, wouldn't you say?"

"No, I wouldn't," Chief Harper said. "Don't make me struggle with this. Just read it out."

"Sure." Cora read from the page. "The author is *A Friend.* The title is *A Helpful Hint.* The poem goes:

"Sometimes you get lucky.
Sometimes things work out.
Some things can be proven.
Some things are in doubt.

"You can fool some people,
But you can't fool them for long."

She paused, then said pointedly to Doddsworth:

"When it's clear your best friend
Is the one who did you wrong."

Doddsworth's face drained of color. For a moment he seemed too stunned to speak. He quickly recovered. " *'Best friend.'* That's the ticket. The dead man's mate. Who was Virdon's best friend?"

■	1 S S	2 I O	3 E M	4 O E	5 H T	6 A I	7 J M	8 L E	9 F S	■	10 I Y	11 L O	12 R U	■	13 N G	14 A E
15 G T	■	16 B L	17 G U	18 E C	19 I K	20 P Y	■	21 P S	22 C O	23 R M	24 M E	25 B T	26 D I	27 E M	28 I E	29 Q S
■	30 O T	31 B H	32 D I	33 F N	34 G G	35 L S	■	36 H W	37 K O	38 P R	39 I K	■	40 G O	41 B U	42 C T	■
43 J S	44 C O	45 M M	46 F E	■	47 P T	48 I H	49 H I	50 O N	51 K G	52 D S	■	53 S C	54 A A	55 E N	■	56 O B
57 M E	■	58 E P	59 C R	60 H O	61 A V	62 S E	63 K N	■	64 G S	65 P O	66 A M	67 O E	■	68 D T	69 G H	70 Q I
71 B N	72 R G	73 I S	■	74 H A	75 C R	76 S E	■	77 A I	78 Q N	■	79 L D	80 B O	81 P U	82 R B	83 N T	■
84 Q Y	85 B O	86 I U	■	87 A C	88 E A	89 R N	■	90 B F	91 P O	92 M O	93 K L	■	94 O S	95 J O	96 N M	97 E E
■	98 L P	99 P E	100 A O	101 I P	102 O L	103 J E	■	104 K B	105 N U	106 L T	■	107 N Y	108 C O	109 D U	■	110 I C
111 H A	112 D N	113 J T	■	114 M F	115 O O	116 C O	117 F L	■	118 D T	119 S H	120 O E	121 C M	■	122 H F	123 D O	124 B R
■	125 O L	126 B O	127 H N	128 Q G	■	129 K W	130 N H	131 J E	132 G N	■	133 R I	134 A T	135 O S	■	136 I C	137 N L
138 E E	139 S A	140 B R	■	141 E Y	142 N O	143 Q U	144 L R	■	145 H B	146 B E	147 K S	148 S T	■	149 B F	150 M R	151 D I
152 P E	153 A N	154 H D	■	155 F I	156 H S	■	157 D T	158 P H	159 H E	■	160 K O	161 D N	162 N E	■	163 C W	164 O H
165 Q O	■	166 G D	167 L I	168 M D	■	169 H Y	170 B O	171 G U	■	172 O W	173 N R	174 A O	175 R N	176 C G	■	■

A. Schwarzenegger flick, e.g. (2 wds.)
A C T I O N M O V I E
54 87 134 6 174 153 66 100 61 77 14

B. Transmission type (4 wds.)
F O U R O N T H E F L O O R
90 80 41 124 170 71 25 31 146 149 16 126 85 140

C. An extra inch in the waist, for instance (3 wds.)
R O O M T O G R O W
75 116 22 121 42 44 176 59 108 163

D. Psychiatric facility
I N S T I T U T I O N
26 112 52 118 32 68 109 157 151 123 161

E. Hostile environment (2 wds.)
E N E M Y C A M P
97 55 138 27 141 18 88 3 58

F. Daphne's beloved
N I L E S
33 155 117 46 9

G. Cop treats
D O U G H N U T S
166 40 171 34 69 132 17 15 64

H. "One if by land, ___" (5 wds.)
A N D T W O I F B Y S E A
74 127 154 5 36 60 49 122 145 169 156 159 111

I. Real dullards (2 wds.)
H O C K E Y P U C K S
48 2 136 19 28 10 101 86 110 39 73

Clue	Answer	Numbers
J. Overacts	E M O T E S	131 7 95 113 103 43
K. Medieval weapons	L O N G B O W S	93 160 63 51 104 37 129 147
L. Ship's left (2 wds.)	P O R T S I D E	98 11 144 106 35 167 79 8
M. "Let ___ ring"	F R E E D O M	114 150 57 24 168 92 45
N. Tough gangster (2 wds.)	U G L Y M O T H E R	105 13 137 107 96 142 83 130 162 173
O. Partially decrease impact (3 wds.)	L E S S E N T H E B L O W	102 120 135 94 4 50 30 164 67 56 125 115 172
P. "___, Mrs. Robinson" (3 wds.)	H E R E S T O Y O U	158 152 38 99 21 47 65 20 91 81
Q. The night ___ (2 wds.)	I S Y O U N G	70 29 84 165 143 78 128
R. Dulling	N U M B I N G	89 12 23 82 133 175 72
S. Trains	T E A C H E S	148 76 139 53 119 62 1

"You think this applies to Jesse Virdon?" Cora asked.

"We had a poem for the first crime. This is the poem for the second."

"Then why wasn't it with the body?"

"It wasn't written then. Which would fit right in. The killer had no plan to kill Jesse Virdon, but the murder became necessary. After the deed, the killer wrote a poem."

"Well, that's fascinating," Cora said. She didn't sound a bit fascinated. "Now, if you boys don't need me anymore, I'm going back to rehearsal."

Cora handed her cigarette to Doddsworth, grabbed her purse, and sailed out the door.

Rupert was working on French hens when Cora returned.

Sherry sidled up to her. "How'd it go?"

"Like clockwork. I had one rough moment when I forgot what a *tough gangster* was, but since I knew the poem I was able to work backwards."

"See, I knew you could do it," Sherry said. "For a minute I actually thought you were going to talk them into using Harvey."

"That would have worked too."

"Yes, but they'd have wondered why. Besides, it isn't often you get a chance to show off your expertise."

"Yeah, great," Cora said. "You manage to plant the letter?"

"No problem. I slipped out while they were doing turtledoves."

"Anyone see you?"

"Cool it," Sherry hissed. "Here comes Harvey."

Harvey Beerbaum pushed his way up. "So, did you solve it? You must have, or you wouldn't be back."

"Can we keep it *down* in the audience!" Rupert Winston screeched from the stage.

"Oh, Harvey," Cora sighed. "Now you blew it for everybody."

"Me? What do you mean, me?"

"Puh-leeze!" Rupert thundered.

"I can't tell you anything." Cora lowered her voice. "You have to ask Chief Harper."

"Where is he?"

Cora shrugged.

Harvey elbowed his way through the crowd, slipped out the gym door.

"Chief Harper left by now?" Sherry asked.

"Oh, yeah. Long gone. Him and Doddsworth."

"Think we'll get some action?"

Cora grinned. "Count on it."

45

"YOU LOOK RAVISHING."

Cora fixed Aaron Grant with an evil eye. It was dress rehearsal, and Cora was clad in her milkmaid outfit. Her white cotton blouse was pushed low to leave her arms and shoulders bare. Her peasant skirt was short enough to require lacy bloomers, a last-minute addition from the costume mistress. Sandals were another added touch, as was the flower in her hair.

Aaron, in a red-and-blue uniform, looked tame by comparison.

"Gee, thanks, soldier boy. What fife-and-drum corps did you escape from?"

"I'm not sure if we're military," Aaron said amicably. "But I'm not really up on the British army. On the other hand, I'm quite sure you're . . . rural."

"What gave it away? My skivvies, or my lack of breeding? Oh, look at the lady dancing!"

Sherry Carter, with her hair up, silver earrings, pearl necklace, and blue satin gown, looked positively gorgeous.

"Oh, dear," Aaron told her, grinning. "This will never do. You'll upstage that girl who gets all the dumb presents."

"Hey, that's my lawyer you're talking about," Sherry said. "She happens to be very good."

"So where is Becky?" Cora demanded.

"It's hard to tell in this crowd," Aaron said. "This place is a zoo."

The dress rehearsal was the first time the cast of *The Twelve Days of Christmas* and the high school chorus had rehearsed together, and it was a bit of a shock. In addition to the choir, each grade from seventh through twelfth had a representative number. So the whole student body was there.

Luckily the singers didn't require costumes, just green pants and red shirts for the boys, and red skirts and green tops for the girls, so the dressing rooms weren't jammed, but the gym floor was so crowded it was almost impossible to move.

Harvey Beerbaum pushed his way toward them in his lords a-leaping costume. His ruffled shirt, purple velvet pantaloons, and golden slippers were vivid, to say the least. Cora found it impossible to look at him with a straight face. "You held out on me," he grumbled. "Chief Harper told me what the poem said. It was even on the evening news."

"I was sure he'd tell you," Cora said modestly, "but it was his place, not mine."

"Well, it's wonderful news for you, Miss Carter. The bit about the best friend doing you wrong, I mean. I gather Miss Baldwin is not your best friend."

Before Sherry could reply, Becky came walking up with Dan Finley in tow. Becky, in pink and white, looked like something out of a children's book, all sweetness and sugary innocence, just the sort of lass to receive mountains of gifts from her hopelessly smitten true love.

Dan Finley, however, looked exactly like a harried cop.

"I still have my shadow," Becky told them. "I swear Finley's gonna go onstage with me, like those gangsters in *Kiss Me Kate.* Really, Dan, these are just high school kids. I doubt I'm in much danger."

"A high school kid got killed," Dan pointed out stubbornly.

In the painful silence that followed that observation, Jimmy Potter hurried up. "There's no puzzle in the pear tree, Miss Felton! Isn't that great news? I just checked. I thought you'd want to know."

"Where's the pear tree now?" Harvey Beerbaum asked.

"On the props table."

"Is anyone watching it?"

"No." Jimmy's eyes widened. "Oh!" He whirled and darted away.

"Was that nice?" Cora Felton asked Harvey.

He shrugged. "These puzzles keep appearing. *Someone* ought to watch the tree."

"That might be a good job for you," Becky told Dan Finley. "As for me, I guess I better warm up."

She sailed off toward the piano with Dan persistently behind.

"Is he the only cop around?" Cora asked.

"The only one I've seen," Aaron said.

"From both sides of the ocean?"

"No sign of Doddsworth either. But his daughter must be here. All the high school kids are."

"That's right, isn't it?" Cora murmured. "If you people will excuse me for a moment . . ."

Cora elbowed her way ruthlessly out onto the gym floor. It was tough going. Red-and-green teenagers were everywhere, looking remarkably similar. Picking one person out in this mob scene was not going to be easy.

Cora completed a circuit of the court. Maxine Doddsworth was nowhere to be seen, but a girl talking to a pimply-faced boy with wire-rimmed glasses and a blond ponytail seemed familiar. The girl was gaping up at him with soulful eyes.

It was the actress Cora had seen working with Rupert Winston. The one who had taken over Dorrie Taggart's part. Laura.

Cora stomped on a foot or two, pushed through the crowd, said, "Hi."

The boy and girl looked at her without a trace of welcome. Clearly she was an annoyance.

"Hi, there," Cora said blithely. "I saw you last night in the theater rehearsing the play."

"Yes. And that's what we're doing now," the girl said. "This is Konstantine."

"Oh. Pleased to meet you, Konstantine."

The boy smiled.

"In the play," the girl said. "I'm Nina. He's Konstantine."

"And Konstantine's your lover?"

She frowned. "Don't you know *The Seagull*?"

"Never saw it."

"He's Nina's childhood friend. He *wants* to be her lover. But she runs off with his *mother's* lover. It's part of his tragedy—the disillusionment that leads him to kill himself."

"Really? He kills himself over you?"

"No," the boy said. "He kills himself for failing to achieve his dreams. He's a minor writer, real minor, manages to get stories published, but fears no one reads them. He compares himself unfavorably to Trigorin—that's the more successful writer Nina has the fling with." He shrugged. "Basically, he kills himself because it's the only way he can achieve the romantic image of himself he's aspired to, having fallen short in his Art."

Cora nodded approvingly. "That's fascinating. Does Rupert agree with that interpretation?"

The boy flushed, and Cora belatedly realized Rupert not only agreed with the view but had probably authored it.

"So," she said, turning her attention to the girl. "When you took over the part you weren't prepared? You hadn't learned the lines?"

"No. That's why we're rehearsing them now."

"Can you learn them in this short a time?"

"Two weeks? Sure. I could learn them in one."

"Laura's going to be good," the boy playing the suicidal Konstantine said.

"As good as Dorrie Taggart?"

"Oh, sure. Laura can act rings around Dorrie."

That had not been Rupert Winston's assessment the night before. Cora figured the girl's presence was at least partly to blame for the boy's gushing praise. "Oh, is that right?" she asked the young actress.

The girl made a face. "Please. Dorrie's dead. But I would certainly *hope* to be better."

"She'll be great," the boy assured Cora passionately.

"Glad to hear it. Tell me, had you learned any of the lines in advance, just in case you had to take over Dorrie's part? Or was your getting the role a complete surprise?"

Laura's eyes flicked.

"Something wrong?" Cora pressed.

"I don't want him to tease me for it."

"Tease you for what?"

"When I heard about what happened to Dorrie, it occurred to me that Mr. Winston might choose me for the part. So I sort of looked the lines over. Before he told me, I mean."

"Well," Cora said approvingly. "That was definitely the right thing to do."

The gym lights blinked out, precipitating a burst of shouts, protests, giggles, and the usual juvenile horseplay.

Onstage, a spotlight came up on Rupert Winston and Mr. Hodges. Rupert, as usual, was self-assured and content to be the center of attention. The music teacher, on the other hand, seemed to have a bad case of stage fright. He looked as if he were on the verge of a nervous breakdown. He kept shuffling his feet, fidgeting, and fumbling with his clipboard. He snuffled, cleared his throat twice, and asked for quiet three times to absolutely no avail. Rupert Winston let him fail two more times before thundering, "QUIET, PLEASE!" in a voice that shook the rafters.

"Thank you," the music teacher said when the room instantly fell silent. "This is the dress rehearsal, so you are dressed."

This got a laugh.

Mr. Hodges waited nervously for the noise to subside. "Tonight we are going to try to get through the whole pageant without stopping. Treat this as a real performance. There are a lot of you here, just getting you on and off the stage will be complicated."

It certainly was. Mr. Hodges had a plan that consisted of everyone waiting downstairs except the singers performing and the singers about to go on, which meant the choir would sing while the seventh-grade chorus went downstairs and the eighth-grade chorus came upstairs, or something to that effect. Cora would have been willing to bet any amount Hodges cared to name it wouldn't work.

"After the senior song is the last choir number," Hodges concluded, "leading into *The Twelve Days of Christmas.*"

Rupert Winston pounced on his cue. "Please pay attention, actors, you have many duties here. There are more of you than anybody else. So your first duty is not to sound like a herd of buffalo. Your second is to get in place on time. There are too many of you to get backstage during the last choral number without thundering up the stairs. So you have to start earlier. You move silently, single file, on tippytoes, without talking, during the senior song. And when I say *silently,* I mean *silently.* The seniors spent a lot of time rehearsing, and they deserve to be heard."

"Thank you," Mr. Hodges said. "Seniors and choir members: as soon as you are done, get downstairs. *The Twelve Days of Christmas* is . . ." He looked at Rupert. "Would the word *chaotic* apply?"

"That will do nicely, thank you. After our song we will all take our bow, and part to the sides while the choir comes forward. Then all the other singers will mob the stage for a huge communal bow."

Everyone cheered.

Rupert put up his hands. "After that, hang in. We'll give you your notes and send you home. All right, people, places, please! Everybody, break a leg!"

From the expressions this benediction produced, it appeared not all Bakerhaven High students were familiar with the theatrical version of "good luck." After some confused general milling, almost everyone headed downstairs.

"I'm not looking forward to this," Cora groused.

"Relax," Sherry said. "It's a dress rehearsal. How awful could it be?"

Actually, as it turned out, it could be pretty awful. The choir was made up of the best singers in the school. That left the worst singers to do the class numbers.

Also, despite Mr. Hodges's explicit instructions, no one got the entrances and exits right. As a result, it was difficult to build up much pace.

The Twelve Days of Christmas wasn't much better. Cues were dropped, entrances were missed, props were misplaced. One turtle-dove jumped her cue, coming in an entire line early, so the song should have gone *"Three French hens and a turtledove; One turtle-dove; and a partridge in a pear tree."* Naturally, nobody sang this.

The lords a-leaping completely missed their entrance, although they managed to be onstage for the first reprise.

The twelve drummers drumming made their entrance minus a prop, although here again no one sang *"Eleven drummers drumming and one drummer pantomiming a drum."*

The maids a-milking, in Cora's humble opinion, were terrific. She was right on beat if not exactly on pitch. Actually, she shouted rather than sang her line. If Rex Harrison could speak entire songs in *My Fair Lady,* why couldn't she be forgiven one phrase?

In fact, Cora decided, *The Twelve Days of Christmas* was a smashing success because they got through it without stopping and nobody died.

Rupert Winston, however, was not so easily pleased. Just as Cora and Sherry and the other actors were all congratulating themselves on the fact that it was over, Rupert leaped up onstage to remind them he had notes.

Did he ever. While Mr. Hodges's notes to his seven singing groups took a total of four minutes, Rupert Winston's notes ran an extremely tedious forty-five.

"There is an old adage in the Theater," he began. "Bad dress rehearsal, good performance. By that yardstick, this will be the best play mankind has ever seen."

After that bit of praise, he got nasty. Before he was done, all the pipers piping were seething, and one of the golden rings had been reduced to tears.

Of Cora's performance, Rupert remarked, "It is rare that one sees an actress demonstrate her deficiencies so openly and utterly."

It was a huge relief when the actors were finally released. Most merely shed their clothes hastily and left, planning to take their makeup off at home. So it was virtually a mass exodus. What with the show running long, and notes running even longer, and everything starting late to begin with, it was nearly a quarter to eleven when the pageant actors gratefully fled the theater.

The tech crew was not so lucky. Naturally, Rupert Winston had notes for them. Missed cues (for which Rupert had just minutes ago vented his spleen on the actors) he now blamed scathingly on the unfortunate Alfred Adams.

Rupert might as well have saved his ire. Alfred was a punching bag, so conditioned to receiving criticism that insults rolled off his back. The teenager listened to Rupert's rant passively, serenely nodding at all the salient points. With no opposition, Rupert eventually wearied of his tirade. He ordered Alfred off to bed, blaming the techie's miscues on sleep deprivation, and followed the poor boy out, reminding him for good measure of every early, late, or errant light. On his way he hit the switch for the house lights, plunging the gym into blackness.

Up in the rafters, Cora Felton let out her breath with a soft sigh. She'd been hiding in the light booth since the end of actors' notes, until Rupert's decision to retry one of the light cues had sent Alfred Adams scrambling obediently into the booth and Cora scrambling desperately into the grid. She had stayed there for the rest of the tech notes, waiting with mounting impatience for a chance to climb down.

But she hadn't expected to climb down in the dark.

The grid over the stage consisted of a series of parallel two-by-twelve beams running upstage and downstage about eighteen inches apart. From Cora's point of view, each beam was a two-inch step in the middle of a three-foot-wide, thirty-foot-deep hole.

Cora's progress across the grid was slow. Only panic had gotten her out on it to begin with, and that had been with the lights on. With them out it was impossible. Even crawling, as she was, on her hands and knees, she'd grope for a beam that wasn't there, tangle herself in a rope that was. Encounter a clamp or a light cord. Or a hole in the grid for lifting scenery through.

Cora slipped, fell flat, clung to a beam. Cursed.

Prayed for a light.

And then, like an answer from heaven, there was one. Cora couldn't see where it came from, but she *could* see the grid. See the rope. See the beams. See the two-by-four nailed across them that had just tripped her.

See the stage below.

Good God, it was worse than in the dark.

Cora fumbled for handholds. Found an upright two-by-four. Clung to it. Pulled herself to her knees.

Looked down toward the source of the light.

The door was open. Light was streaming in from the foyer.

Someone had slipped in through the gym door.

Which was closing again.

Cora looked toward the light booth ladder ten feet away. She had to reach that ladder. On hands and knees, she crawled across the beams. Her drawstring purse hung down, bumped against the grid. She couldn't risk sparing a hand to pull it up.

Just two more beams.

Cora reached the ladder. Grabbed it. Slung her leg over. Reached down, grabbed her purse, slung that over too.

The gym door clicked shut.

The light went out.

In pitch-blackness, Cora backed down the ladder to the loft. So where the heck was the other ladder? She groped along the platform, touched a two-by-four nailed flat along the edge as a handhold. She gripped it, slung her legs over the side, found the second ladder, climbed down.

Cora peered out into the darkness from behind a stage-left flat. She saw nothing, but she was convinced that she could hear a creak on the stage-right stairs leading up from the audience.

She reached into her purse, pulled out her gun, clicked the safety off.

The intruder was coming slowly across the stage, feeling his way cautiously in the dark.

Cora slipped back into the wings, crept downstage. Fumbled on the wall for the light switch. Found it, pushed it on.

The she stepped out onstage and leveled her gun at the intruder, trapped in the blazing, pitiless glare of the lights.

Jonathon Doddsworth.

46

"GREAT SCOTT! WHAT THE DEVIL ARE YOU DOING WITH THAT pistol?"

"I'm aiming it at you."

"I can see that. Would you please put it down?"

"No. I like it fine just like this."

Jonathon Doddsworth gawked at her. "Are you demented? Have you taken utter leave of your senses?"

Cora frowned. "You really need to brush up on your people skills. Perhaps you're out of practice. Here's a hint. Questioning a woman's sanity is *not* the way to her heart."

Doddsworth took a step toward her.

"Stay where you are," Cora told him crisply, in a tone gleaned from TV shows. "Keep those hands where I can see them."

"I don't carry a weapon."

"I do. Don't make me use it."

"You wouldn't shoot me."

"Yes, I would. Although I'd regret it. I regretted shooting Henry. My fourth husband. Cost me a fortune in alimony."

"You shot your husband?"

"In the leg. A double disappointment. I was sorry I shot him and sorry I didn't aim higher."

"Miss Felton—"

"Keep those hands up."

"I assure you, I'm unarmed."

"Maybe so. But I don't want you destroying the evidence."

"What evidence?"

"Why are you here?"

Doddsworth scowled. Took an exasperated breath. "I'm examining the scene of the crime."

"Oh, give me a break. There's nothing to examine. Did you bring the money?"

"Whatever do you mean?"

"Don't play dumb." Cora quoted, " *'You know and I know she did it. Get five hundred dollars in small unmarked bills. Bring it to the theater after rehearsal tonight. Perhaps we can continue to share our secret together.'* "

Doddsworth gawked at her, openmouthed.

"Got the money?" Cora asked sweetly.

"You? That was you?"

"Did you bring the cash?"

"Of course not."

"I think you did. I think you have it on you right now. That's why I'm not going to give you a chance to ditch it before the cops get here."

"The police?"

"You think I want to hold a gun on you all night? The cops are going to take you in for questioning, inventory your possessions. I don't know if you got the blackmail letter on you, but I'm layin' odds you got the five C's. What did you do, pull it out of an ATM? Or did you have to cash traveler's checks?"

Doddsworth was sweating. "It's stifling in here. I'm going to remove my coat."

"Be my guest."

He slipped his overcoat off, let it fall to the stage floor.

"What makes you think your daughter's pregnant?" Cora inquired.

Doddsworth looked as though he might follow his overcoat. He was the picture of consternation. "How much do you know?" he asked Cora.

"I'm learning more every minute. That was a guess. An educated guess, but a pretty easy one. What would it take to make a law-abiding police officer act like a common crook? Obviously a desire to protect his daughter. That only makes sense if the case against her looks particularly black. Do you know Maxine's pregnant, or just suspect it?"

"Damn you."

"Damn *me*? You frame my niece for murder, and then damn me? You're lucky I'm such an old softy, or you'd be dead right now." Cora gestured with the gun. "Grab your coat and let's sit down. I've been hanging in the rafters, and my leg is cramped like you wouldn't believe."

Cora marched Doddsworth down the stairs to the audience. The inspector tripped at the bottom, fell awkwardly in a heap, with his overcoat on top of him. Cora kept the gun trained, in case it was a trick, and watched for any sudden moves. But Doddsworth merely clambered to his feet. He and Cora sat on folding chairs, under the basketball hoop. The stage lights barely reached them, made them shadowy figures on the court.

Cora dropped her purse on the floor, kept her gun in her lap. "Okay, let's talk turkey. I don't think your daughter bumped off her best friend. You don't either, but you're not sure. That's what's killing you. But we're more or less on the same page. The difference is, you'll protect Maxine even if she's guilty. I won't. If she did it, she's goin' down.

"So here's the deal. I'm gonna do some talking. You're gonna shut up and listen. If you're a quick study and pay attention, I won't have to shoot you.

"Here's what I think happened. Dorrie Taggart was killed under circumstances that implicate your daughter. Horace Taggart suspects her. He brought you in not for your help but to hang you out to dry. You know that, but there's nothing you can do about it except try to solve the crime. Only problem is, everything you find only makes things worse. Maxine has the acrostic program on her computer, the red envelopes in her room. You go through her garbage, find a discarded early pregnancy test box. That's when you decide to frame my niece. Only two girls had the opportunity to kill Dorrie. If it wasn't Maxine it must be Sherry. So how can you set Sherry up?"

Cora shrugged. "Right away you catch a break. Sherry has the acrostic computer program too. She bought it the day the first puzzle arrived, so she and I could work on it. No matter. The fact is, she has it. And no one knows your daughter has it yet.

"So, one down, two to go. You call on Sherry, ask her about a pregnancy test. Sherry never *took* a pregnancy test, but that's no matter. You're smart enough to know you can create the story just by asking the question. 'Suspect Sherry Carter today denied accusations that she was pregnant, and refused to take an early pregnancy test.' Damning.

"Two down, one to go. The envelopes. You had every intention of planting them, but, bad luck, Sherry never left you alone in our house long enough. No matter. You're comin' back with your warrant. You'll plant them right under our very noses. Sure enough, Dan Finley downloading computer files keeps me and Sherry occupied. All you have to do is distract Harper, then stick 'em someplace he hasn't already searched."

Cora shook her head. "Now you've got my niece strung up good, but you're not too happy about it, because you know it ain't gonna stick. Bet you a nickel your kid doesn't have an alibi for the second murder, even if you were able to discuss it with her, which you're probably not. So right now you're runnin' around like a British chicken with your noggin chopped off, tryin' to find some way out, when, bang, you're hit with a blackmail demand.

"Well, I got good news and bad news. The good news is, I wrote the blackmail note. The bad news is, I wrote the blackmail note. I happen to have enough ammunition to blow you out of the water. How do you like that, *Doddsy*?"

Doddsworth blinked, set his jaw.

"Not bad," Cora said, nodding approvingly. "Mindy Taggart's reaction was much bigger." His face twisted. "Yeah, like that."

Doddsworth's lip quivered. "Who told you about Mindy?"

"Why, is it a secret? I guess it is. I guess people bought the story Horace put out, how the real lovebirds were him and your wife. That must have been tough for you to swallow. Being estranged from your daughter *and* branded a cuckold. No wonder you stayed away so long."

"My daughter," Doddsworth muttered. He heaved a huge sigh. His eyes glistened with tears. He rubbed his face awkwardly, brushing them away.

Cora's mouth fell open. "Oh, my God!" she murmured.

Doddsworth's head jerked up.

Angrily.

Defensively.

"You were making a deal," he said evenly.

Cora looked at him. Her face softened. Her voice lost its edge. "I couldn't understand why you would go so far. Take such risks. Planting the envelopes on my niece. Writing the message, *Wrong girl.* Even with your daughter in danger, it seemed a little much. After all, you're a cop."

"What do you want?"

"I don't know. A minute ago I wanted to watch you squirm. Now I just don't know."

"What do you mean?"

"The story keeps changing. But some of it's true. You and Mindy Taggart did get together. The only question is when. And the answer is, you got together way before anyone thought. By the time Horace found out about you two, the affair was quite longstanding."

Doddsworth said nothing, set his jaw.

"I should have known. The way you fussed over her at the Grants' Christmas party. The way you fell apart when you saw her dead." Cora smiled softly. "The way you tripped coming down the steps just now. Klutzy, like her."

"I don't know what you're talking about."

"I'm talking about your daughter." Cora paused, said gently, "Dorrie Taggart."

Doddsworth's face drained of color.

Cora shook her head. "It's more than any man could bear. His one daughter killing the other. No wonder you snapped."

Doddsworth's mouth opened. No sound came out.

"So, let's talk turkey," Cora said, giving him time to recover. "There's too many clues in this case. I don't wanna bust my hump on the ones I have you to thank for. And vice versa. So you don't waste your time on the poem about your daughter Max doing her best friend wrong. And I won't waste my time on the *Wrong girl* letter. On the other hand, I didn't plant the blowgun, and I bet you didn't either. And I think I can safely say neither of us had anything to do with the attached note. It being about pregnancy and all."

"Damn it, woman! Can't you hold your tongue!"

Cora nodded. "Of course. The final straw. Both daughters pregnant. By the same man. What would that do to you? What would that do to Taggart? Or to your wives?"

Doddsworth trembled.

Cora said, "Well, it may be small consolation, but I don't think Maxine is pregnant."

"How do you know?"

"Just from talking to her." Cora shrugged. "You wouldn't understand."

Cora raised the gun, looked at it thoughtfully, put it back in her lap. "So here's the deal. You lay off Sherry, I'll lay off Maxine. Whaddya say?"

Doddsworth met her gaze, held it several seconds. Then he sighed deeply. "There's a problem."

"What's that?"

"Taggart's scheduled Dorrie's funeral for the day after tomorrow."

"That's Christmas Eve."

"Horace doesn't care. That's when he wants it. It's inconvenient, but I imagine most people will attend it."

"I'm sure they will. So what's the problem?"

"I'm giving the eulogy."

Cora's mouth fell open. *"What?!"*

Doddsworth nodded. "That's right."

Cora stared at him. "No offense meant, but why in the world would Taggart *want* you to give the eulogy?"

"He wants me to say who killed her."

Cora whistled. "What you gonna do?"

"The only possibilities are your niece and Maxine. I'm most certainly not naming Maxine."

"You're most certainly not naming my niece."

"So what can I do?"

Cora frowned, gnawed her lip.

The gym door banged open and Santa Claus stood framed in the light from the foyer. His curly beard hung around his neck, but otherwise his scarlet-and-fur costume looked fine. His wide black belt held in his padded belly, which shook when he laughed like a bowl full of jelly.

But Chief Harper wasn't laughing. "I don't wanna hear it," he snarled, forestalling any comments on his festive appearance. "I had a Christmas party at the children's hospital. I was on my way home and saw the light." He pulled the red Santa hat off his head, shook out the snowflakes. "What are you two doing here?"

Cora Felton surreptitiously shoved her gun in her purse. She looked over at Doddsworth, who returned her gaze miserably.

"Just checking out the crime scene," Cora told Chief Harper.

47

Becky Baldwin leaned back in her desk chair and frowned at Cora Felton, who was perched on the windowsill smoking a cigarette. "You want me to stop a *eulogy*?"

"Sounds bad when you say it like that."

"Okay, *you* say it so it sounds *good*."

"I want a simple injunction." Cora glanced at Sherry for help. None was forthcoming. "Or restraining order. Or gag order. Or whatever you call it when you don't want someone to do something."

"I don't believe this."

Cora blew smoke out the open window. It came back in her face. "Doddsworth won't hurt us unless he has to. In which case we have to stop him."

"Since blackmailing him didn't work," Becky pointed out sarcastically.

"Heaven forbid," Cora said. "I thought I told you expressly I was *not* blackmailing Doddsworth. I merely asked the question."

"Yes, and what a lovely hypothetical *that* was. 'I'm not blackmailing Doddsworth, but if I *were* blackmailing Doddsworth, what would I do if the situation happened to be this?' "

"I thought you lawyers *liked* hypothetical questions. Ow!" Cora reached down and rubbed her leg. "Burned myself on your radiator. I'd sue you, if I knew a good lawyer."

"Very funny," Becky said. "Well, I hate to disillusion you, Cora, but I am not stopping a eulogy."

"Then Doddsworth is going to stand up and accuse me of murder," Sherry said.

"That's not all bad." Becky nodded slyly. "Tainting the jury pool will probably get us a change of venue."

"Do we *want* a change of venue?"

"It couldn't hurt. The Taggarts own half the town. It's not exactly the ideal place to be tried for murdering their daughter with a poisoned dart."

"Hey, no one's getting tried yet." Cora flipped her cigarette into the snow, heaved herself off the windowsill. "And no one's gonna be. I'm just exploring options."

"Well, stopping a eulogy is a pretty poor option. I would strongly suggest you come up with something else."

"We should have told her," Sherry said as she and Cora drove home ten minutes later.

"Told her what? The Doddsworths and Taggarts may have had their own little Peyton Place, but it doesn't mean they killed anyone."

"Peyton Place?"

"Before your time, sweetie. The point is, why fling mud if it isn't gonna help?"

"You're such a softy. You don't want Maxine to have to know the best friend she lost was also her half sister. Plus, you don't suspect her anymore."

"She's not guilty."

"Well, if it's not her and it's not me, that leaves Lance and the techie."

"It's not Lance."

"Even if he knocked 'em both up?"

"I don't think he did."

Cora roared up their snowy driveway, skidded into a parking space in front of the garage.

"Well," Sherry said. "Who does that leave?"

48

ALFRED ADAMS'S EYES WIDENED. "YOU STAY AWAY FROM ME!"

"Just a couple of questions," Cora said.

Alfred was sitting on the high school stage taking apart a spotlight. He held a screwdriver out in front of him like a weapon. "That's what you said the last time. When Mr. Virdon got killed."

"You think that was my fault?"

"Did you talk to Mr. Virdon?"

"No, I didn't. Obviously I should have."

"Oh, is that right? Someone kills Mr. Virdon so you can't talk to him, so now you think you should have? You're living poison, lady. You're the kiss of death."

"I'm nothing of the kind." But Cora didn't sound too indignant.

"You stay away from me."

"Relax, Alfred. I talked to you before and nothing happened to you. Obviously you don't know anything."

" 'Course I don't know anything. I told you I don't know anything. So why do you want to talk to me?"

"You were in the crèche. You could have killed Dorrie Taggart."

"Why would I do that?"

"And you were in the theater. You could have killed Jesse Virdon."

"Mr. Virdon? I liked Mr. Virdon." Alfred wiped his brow, managed to smear grease on his forehead. "Say, what is this? First you put me in danger, then you accuse me of murder? You're bad news."

"What was your relationship with Dorrie Taggart?"

"I didn't *have* a relationship with Dorrie. I barely knew Dorrie."

"But you knew who she was. You recognized her in the stable. When she came to play Mary."

"No, I didn't. I only saw her from the back. The whole thing's very whatchamacallit—stylized. You're not acting, you're *posing.* I wish I'd never done it."

"I bet you do. Are you claiming you didn't know who Dorrie Taggart was?"

"Of course I knew who she was. She was in the play."

"What play? *The Seagull*?"

"That's right."

"You're working on that?"

"If it's in this theater, I work on it."

"Were you here when Dorrie had her late rehearsals?"

"No. Why should I be?"

"So when did you see Dorrie act?"

"During the regular rehearsals." Alfred snorted. "She was *bad.*"

"Why do you say that?"

"Mr. Winston was always stopping her, telling her she was doing it wrong."

"He does that to everybody."

"Yeah. I suppose."

"You know the girl taking over the part?"

"Laura? Sure, why?"

"Had she wanted that role?"

"Are you kidding? All these girls wanna be the star. Pretty dumb, you ask me. I mean, what's so important about some dumb high school play?"

"I don't know," Cora said. "But someone killed Dorrie Taggart. And someone killed Jesse Virdon. Did it ever occur to you maybe someone was trying awfully hard to stop *The Seagull*?"

Alfred sneered. "That's stupid."

"Why is that stupid?"

"Mr. Virdon wasn't important. He was just the tech director. I'm filling in for him, no problem. And Dorrie stunk. You don't hurt the play by killing her. If you wanted to stop *Seagull,* you'd kill Mr. Winston."

Cora Felton's eyes widened. "Oh, for the love of—"

"What's the matter? Are you sick?"

"You're a lot smarter than you look." Cora thought a moment. "You know where Mr. Winston is now?"

"Downstairs."

"Oh?"

"Yeah. I get a breather while he chews out the costume lady."

Leaving Alfred, Cora went down to the costume shop, where Rupert Winston was complaining about the milkmaids' cleavage.

"Ah, here's one now," Rupert said. "Miss Felton, please get into costume and I'll show you what I mean."

"You want me to alter *eight* costumes?" the costume lady groused.

"It isn't a case of altering. Just wearing the costume *lower.* They can push the elastic down."

"Then let 'em do it. You don't need me."

"They're your costumes. You have to show them how they're worn."

"I think they look just fine."

"I want them lower."

"Then tell them so."

"I can't go around adjusting cleavage. That's why I have a wardrobe mistress."

"Oh? I thought my job was to make costumes."

"It's to make them to be *worn.* They're not being worn right. Miss Felton, if you wouldn't mind."

"I'd rather be shot dead."

"What?"

"I have rather urgent business. Could I talk to you alone?"

"What could you possibly want to talk about?"

"It's a private matter."

"Perhaps you'd rather talk here," the costume mistress said hopefully.

Rupert glared at her, then back at Cora. "All right. But make it snappy."

Rupert followed Cora out of the costume shop and down the hall into one of the music practice rooms. He closed the door, turned to Cora. "All right. What's so all-fired important that you had to pull me out of the costume shop?"

Cora looked the director right in the eye.

"I think your life's in danger."

49

CORA FELTON PEEKED OUT FROM BEHIND THE CURTAIN. THE GYM was packed. Every folding chair on the court was filled, as were the bleachers on the sides. People were even standing in the back. Cora was amazed. She wouldn't have thought there were that many people in all of Bakerhaven.

Dan Finley sat front row center. Becky had put her foot down about having him backstage.

Aaron's parents sat together on folding chairs.

Jonathon and Pamela Doddsworth sat on opposite sides of the court, as far apart as they could get.

The Taggarts were not there.

A hand tapped Cora on the shoulder. She started, spun around.

It was Harvey Beerbaum. "You shouldn't be looking at the audience," Harvey scolded.

"Oh?" Cora said. "And just what are you doing here, Harvey?"

"Checking my props."

"You haven't *got* any props."

"Oh. Well, I guess I haven't." Harvey dropped all pretense. "So, who's out there?"

"Everybody and his darn brother."

"Let me see."

"I thought we weren't supposed to do that."

"Yes, but you did. Wow! Standing room only!"

"I told you."

"I see Dan Finley's right up front."

"I'm not surprised."

Harvey frowned. "Chief Harper's still afraid something's going to happen?"

"Yes, he is."

"What about you? Are you nervous?"

"Yes, I am." Cora sighed, smiled. "But it's just stage fright."

Cora needn't have worried.

The Twelve Days of Christmas was an absolute smash. Whether it was just that after the recent tragedies people needed some comic relief, or whether it was just that good, the song stopped the show.

The standing-room-only audience had been politely enthusiastic during the choral numbers, applauding the efforts of the schoolchildren. But when *The Twelve Days of Christmas* began, the audience went nuts.

Becky wandered out onstage, young, innocent, dewy, bright-eyed, the very picture of eager anticipation, and sang, " *'On the first day of Christmas, my true love gave to me.'* "

Jimmy Potter marched out, singing, " *'A partridge in a pear tree.'* "

He was so proud, gawky, and happy, that it was funny. There were nervous titters in the audience. As if they wanted to laugh, but didn't want to be rude. As Jimmy exited the stage, it was quite clear the audience was holding back.

They stifled guffaws at the turtledoves, borne by plump Mary Cushman and her equally plump cohort. When Jimmy Potter came marching back, they suppressed giggles.

But on the exit, as the turtledoves and partridge scattered into the wings, and it dawned on the audience that this was the format, and all of these items would be constantly vanishing and reappearing, the dam broke.

A rumble of laughter grew and would not stop. It swelled through a delicious confusion of French hens, calling birds, and golden rings, rattled the rafters as geese a-laying gave way to swans a-swimming.

By the time the eight maids a-milking got onstage and Cora sang her solo line, everyone in the place was laughing so loud that no one could hear her. It didn't really matter—everyone knew what she was singing—but her line was lost in the din.

Cora grabbed up her milking stool and dashed offstage, ruefully counting the hours she had spent rehearsing the damn line.

She was certain she had performed it perfectly.

Cora barely had time to think that before the ladies dancing appeared and she had to rush back onstage again. She ran off, ran back on for the pipers piping, collided with an errant goose a-laying and was knocked flat. She scrambled to her feet just in time to avoid being trampled by the lords a-leaping.

Harvey Beerbaum shot her a dirty look as he went by, listening in vain for his cue. He missed it by three notes, which almost synchronized with his jump, which he missed by four.

It didn't matter. The audience was on the floor, chortling and guffawing too hard to notice that the eight maids a-milking, whose cue had been pushed back three measures by Harvey's unintentional retard, were hopelessly offbeat.

Mr. Hodges at the piano ad-libbed valiantly, inventing musical segues the likes of which had never been attempted in the history of musical theater. Fortunately, no one heard them either, because the turtledoves had just tripped the French hens, and the calling birds were having trouble picking their way over them to get offstage.

Becky Baldwin, in the midst of such chaos, began to look like a woman besieged. When the twelve drummers drumming descended on her, her eyes darted desperately in all directions, as if looking for somewhere to hide.

Her acting was so good that Dan Finley stood up, thinking she'd been attacked. He sheepishly sat back down as the lords a-leaping shot back onstage, and he realized it was part of the play.

Within seconds, every calling bird, French hen, and golden ring was in place, and Jimmy Potter, for the twelfth and last time, came stomping up to Becky Baldwin, as the entire chorus warbled, " *'And a partridge in a pear tree.'* "

The actors froze in tableau, all gesturing toward Jimmy Potter, now down on one knee, offering the partridge and pear tree to Becky Baldwin.

Thunderous applause. The audience was on their feet, clapping, whistling, hollering, and yelling. A standing ovation.

The actors bowed just as they'd rehearsed, then gave way to the students, who quickly filled the stage. As the last class filed in, Becky Baldwin slipped into the wings. She was back moments later, carrying an enormous bouquet of flowers. She gestured to the front row, where Rupert Winston sat, for once quiet and inconspicuous amid the din. She motioned to the director, inviting him up onstage. As the audience realized what she was doing, the applause, which had abated somewhat, swelled again, louder, if possible, than before. Now all the actors beckoned with their hands, *Come on, come on,* until the unexpectedly modest director had no choice but to join them. Rupert scampered up the front steps as he had so many times in rehearsal, accepted the flowers and the accolades of his actors, who were all now applauding. He bowed deeply to the audience, then invited the actors to bow with him. He turned, gestured to Mr. Hodges, still valiantly banging out the tune on the piano. Then joined hands with the actors and bowed again, acknowledging the audience's deafening approval.

For once Rupert Winston didn't seem arrogant. He appeared, instead, deeply moved. Touched. Even humble.

As he came up from the bow, he glanced over at the maids a-milking. Just for a second Cora could see the fear in his eyes. Then he was bowing and smiling again, basking in the applause.

50

CORA FELTON SLIPPED OUT OF BED AT THREE A.M. SHE DRESSED IN the dark, then tiptoed down the hall so as not to wake her niece. In the foyer she pulled on her boots and her overcoat and hat, and stealthily let herself out the front door.

The temperature had dropped, and a bitter wind was whipping the freshly fallen snow, leaving patterns on the lawn. Cora tugged her coat around her, hurried to the Toyota. The door was frozen shut—it didn't want to open even after she had popped the lock. Cora put her weight into it and it gave with a low, cracking groan. She slid into the front seat, started the engine. It protested mightily, then caught with an earsplitting roar. Cora eased back on the gas, prayed she wouldn't pop the fan belt. Which, her ex-husband Frank had been fond of telling her, would make the car overheat before she'd gone five miles. Cora had no time for that now. Nor had she time to warm up the engine, another of Frank's many automotive precautions. Cora put the car in gear, pulled down the drive. She didn't turn on the headlights till she reached the road.

She drove quickly through town and out onto Culvert Drive, where she'd scouted Rupert Winston's rental house the day before.

It was a small two-story, white with green shutters, like most of the houses in town, and had a brick chimney, constructed, no doubt, with Santa Claus in mind.

There was a light on in the living room. The rest of the house was dark. Cora tiptoed up the front steps and tried the door. Locked. She tried to peer in the living room window, but the shade was drawn.

Cora went around the house. The moon was almost full. Her boots left footprints in the snow.

The glass storm door on the side of the house swung open. The wooden door to the kitchen proved to be unlocked also. Cora went inside, found a welcome mat on the linoleum floor. She scraped off her boots, stepped in, and pulled the door closed.

The kitchen, she noted, had fluorescent lights. She didn't want to turn them on, but there was no need. Light from the living room spilled into the hallway. Cora followed the light, stepped through the door.

The living room cried Actor. Bookcases were crammed with plays. A poster of Olivier as Hamlet dominated one wall. A framed certificate of nomination for some theatrical award or another—Cora could tell from the masks of comedy and tragedy in the upper right- and left-hand corners—was displayed over the mantelpiece. Next to it hung a framed theater program, no doubt from the show associated with the award.

On the coffee table sat a half-full glass of water. Next to it sat a case of pills. A daily reminder case, with little compartments for each day of the week. Cora noted that the slot for last night's pills was open, and the receptacle was empty.

A faint scent of bitter almonds filled the air.

Rupert Winston sat on his couch. His head lolled back at an impossible angle. His features were contorted. A streak of saliva dribbled down his chin.

He was clearly dead.

51

DORRIE TAGGART LOOKED GORGEOUS. HER GOLDEN HAIR WAS tastefully arranged against the red satin lining of the casket. Her cheeks were rosy. Her lips were ruby red. She might have been Sleeping Beauty, waiting to be awakened by a kiss.

The coffin lay before the altar. The Taggarts sat in the first pew, Horace Taggart stiff as a ramrod, Mindy Taggart weeping and clinging to his arm. Across the aisle from them, Pamela Doddsworth was attempting to console Maxine, who kept batting her hand away.

Students filled the next few pews. Cora Felton noted the boyfriend Lance Ridgewood, the techie Alfred Adams, the young actress Laura, who had taken over the part of Nina in *The Seagull*, and the teenager playing Konstantine, whose name Cora did not know. All seemed properly awed by the occasion.

Becky Baldwin sat with Rick Reed, who had not been allowed to film but was hoping to grab interviews after the service.

Dan Finley sat behind them.

Just in case.

Also on hand were Chief Harper and his wife and daughter,

Jimmy Potter and his mother, wannabe amateur detective Harvey Beerbaum, out-of-favor-since-arraigning-Sherry Judge Hobbs, dapper doctor Barney Nathan, prosecutor Henry Firth, art teacher Charlie Ferric, and Mr. Hodges the music teacher—Cora had never heard his fist name.

Cora and Aaron sat flanking Sherry, for moral support. Cora hoped Sherry wouldn't need it.

Jonathon Doddsworth rose from beside the casket, tears in his eyes. He walked to the pulpit, leaned on it, looked out over the congregation. His voice was husky. "I knew Dorrie. Knew her as a little girl. She used to play with my sweet daughter Max. So long ago. So very long ago."

He sighed heavily, stroked his muttonchops. "I'm not much good at speaking. Not much good at much. I'll give it a go, for Dorrie's sake.

"I'll do the best I can."

Doddsworth took a breath, seemed to organize his thoughts. "Rupert Winston died last night."

This announcement produced only minor rumbling from the congregation. Clearly, everyone had heard the news.

"Apparently by his own hand," Doddsworth continued. "Bit of a stunner. Could it be true? Or something else entirely?" He paused and looked out at the assemblage.

"This all begins with puzzles. Jingly poems promise the death of an actress. *Die, leading lady, die.* Who are these obscene missives from, and to whom are they directed? They appear to be meant for Miss Baldwin. And they sound like the rhymes of a schoolgirl. Appearances can be deceiving. In this case, what is the truth?"

Doddsworth hesitated, looked out over the congregation. His eyes met Cora Felton's. He took in her niece, sitting next to her, then looked to Cora again.

Her face was iron.

Doddsworth took a breath, then blurted out: "In this case, the truth is *exactly* as it seems. The poems were written by Dorrie Taggart, and they were intended for Miss Becky Baldwin, attorney-at-law."

This announcement produced a loud reaction in the church. Mindy Taggart sat up straight, stared at him openmouthed. Doddsworth's daughter, Maxine, twisted away from her mother and glared furiously at her father.

Cora Felton leaned back in the pew and heaved a sigh. It was out of her hands. It was all up to Doddsworth now.

Having taken the plunge, Doddsworth picked up the pace and pressed on rapidly. "I know, I know. You find that hard to fathom. I shall try to explain. Dorrie Taggart was quite mature, but she was in fact a girl. A young girl, in love with a young boy. I think it is safe to say the lad, by some casual remark or other, gave her the impression that he fancied Miss Baldwin.

"Well, Dorrie's jealous reaction to that was purely adolescent. She penned silly, threatening jingles, and sent them to her 'rival.' One she placed in the pear tree presented to Miss Baldwin. The other she pinned to her costume. And that might have been the end of it. Except for one thing.

"Jesse Virdon.

"The tech director.

"Dorrie was the lead in the Bakerhaven High production of *The Seagull.* She had long rehearsals. They sometimes ran quite late. Dorrie would stay, even after the director left, working on her part.

"While the tech director worked on his set.

"Jesse Virdon was an unstable young man with a history of criminal activities, including offenses against women."

This information, having already been released by the police, was no surprise, either, but its use in this context was. There came a low rumble of voices from the congregation.

Doddsworth rode over it. "We can assume Virdon made some advance which poor Dorrie rebuffed. And that he didn't take her rejection well."

There were audible gasps and whispers.

Doddsworth raised his voice. "We don't know what caused Jesse Virdon to snap. Perhaps a lifetime of rebuffs. Perhaps insanity or rage. But snap he did. Jesse Virdon decided that Dorrie Taggart must die."

Mindy Taggart cried out, a choking sob. Horace Taggart hugged her close and gaped at Doddsworth in amazement. Pam and Maxine gawked at him too. Maxine's mouth was open. Her metal braces gleamed.

Doddsworth waited with patience until his audience was quiet enough for him to continue.

"Lo and behold, an opportunity presents itself. Dorrie Taggart is portraying the Virgin Mary in the live Nativity. She swaps places with Becky Baldwin. In light of the poems threatening Miss Baldwin, if Dorrie were to die, it would appear the killer had mistaken one young woman for the other.

"Jesse Virdon is portraying Joseph, but earlier in the morning, before Dorrie arrives. He will have no opportunity to kill her. But this is good. The actors on hand will be the likely suspects. Who would suspect someone who had already left?

"Virdon must pretend to leave, but actually remain. But how? His costume must be returned to town hall. It must be hanging there for the next Joseph. Which it was. So how did he stay?

"The Joseph costume is not elaborate. It's basically a blanket, long hair, and a beard. He need merely find another. Bring it to town hall and put it on. He wears the other costume over his—after all, it's quite cold. He goes to the manger, plays Joseph for an hour, until he is relieved by Alfred Adams. He returns to town hall, hangs the original costume on the hook where it should be.

"He walks out of town hall in his own costume and returns to the crèche. The actors in the stable will not see him, as the path leads to the crèche from behind. The only danger is that someone in the square may notice Joseph arriving twice. But barring that, Jesse is quite safe. The figure of Joseph, walking along the actors' path at approximately a quarter past the hour, is what everyone expects to see.

"He reaches the crèche, wriggles underneath the platform it is mounted on.

"Waits for Dorrie to arrive.

"At eleven she does. Minutes later, Alfred Adams is relieved by Lance Ridgewood. Dorrie's boyfriend. The youth whose advances Dorrie did *not* spurn. The perfect scapegoat. What could be better?

"Jesse Virdon has brought a poison dart. When the coast is clear, he emerges from his hiding place, opens the door in the back of the crèche.

"All of the actors are facing outward, away from him. Directly in front of him, Dorrie kneels on the floor of the stable, leaning against Joseph, her boyfriend, Lance. The Virgin Mary's cowl is *not* hiding her face, as it was when she was found. Dorrie's features are in plain sight.

"As is the side of her neck.

"Jesse Virdon raises the dart and gives it a toss. God knows he should have missed, even at that distance. For an unpracticed hand it could not have been an easy task. But foul luck is with him. The dart strikes Dorrie in the neck. She slumps against Joseph. The hood slips forward, hiding her face. Because she is leaning against Joseph, she doesn't fall down. Jesse Virdon has murdered her, and no one in the tableau has noticed. Jesse Virdon eases the door closed. The deed is done.

"Before leaving the crèche, Jesse searches Dorrie's coat, which is hanging just behind the door. He finds the third puzzle poem. He has no idea how to solve it. He figures it will be like the others. This is perfect for his plan.

"He's already secreted a blowpipe in the organ loft of the church, to baffle the authorities. He sneaks back into the church and affixes the puzzle to the blowgun. Then he returns to town hall, strips off his costume, shoves it in his backpack, and pulls on his clothes. He hops in his auto, motors to the high school, and resumes painting the set. No one has missed him. He has committed the perfect crime."

Doddsworth allowed himself a brief, self-deprecating smile. "Hard cheese for Jesse Virdon. I am on the scene. Horace Taggart brings me in to investigate. And, because of the acrostic poems, the Puzzle Lady becomes involved. As a result, Jesse Virdon has Chief Harper, Miss Felton, and me all nipping at his heels. A most uncomfortable position to be in. How best to throw us off the scent?"

The inspector shrugged. "What could be easier? The poems appear to target Becky Baldwin. Dorrie was substituting for Miss Baldwin. Indeed, the Virgin Mary who relieved Dorrie believed she *was* Becky Baldwin. All Jesse Virdon need do is underline the notion that the killer made a dreadful mistake and murdered the wrong young lass.

"Not a problem for the young technical director. Jesse finds a sandbag in the grid that's not in use, unties it from the pinrail, and ties it off near his stage manager position. Then, when Miss Baldwin is warbling her notes, he drops the bag onstage. He doesn't care where it falls. He isn't trying to cosh her, he's merely trying to create the *illusion* an attempt has been made. To further the illusion, he attaches a note to Miss Baldwin's costume, proclaiming, *Wrong girl.*

"But this note is telling. While Virdon is able to procure a red envelope, he lacks the skill to fashion a puzzle poem. Nonetheless, the police—and, alas, I—take this 'evidence' at face value, and, on the strength of Miss Carter's alleged rivalry with Miss Baldwin, we arrest Miss Carter for the crime.

"Smooth sailing for Jesse Virdon. He has everybody fooled.

"With one exception.

"Rupert Winston was no dolt. He was an artist—sensitive, intuitive, keenly perceptive. He had noticed Mr. Virdon's infatuation with Miss Taggart. He had cause to observe Jesse Virdon after Dorrie's death.

"Rupert Winston did not like what he saw.

"Jesse Virdon appeared to fancy many of the girls in the play. In particular, the actress whom Rupert Winston had tapped as poor Dorrie's successor in the starring role of Nina. If his suspicions were true, that girl would not be safe.

"On the night in question, after everyone else had left the theater, Rupert Winston confronted Jesse Virdon and accused him of the crime."

Doddsworth grimaced. "Not a prudent move. Cornered, Jesse Virdon attacks. Seriously outmatched, and in fear for his life, Rupert Winston snatches up a length of wood and lays him out. Jesse Virdon drops to the stage floor, dead.

"Rupert Winston panics. It is just days before the Christmas pageant. The loss of a few rehearsals could be vital. If he tells his tale to the authorities, even if they believe he acted in self-defense, they will never leave him time to rehearse.

"What can he do?

"He ties a rope around Jesse Virdon's neck and hoists him up into the grid. The idea is to make it look as if the young man hanged himself in a fit of remorse. It is a poor idea, not very well thought out—the wound on Virdon's head will instantly contradict it—but by now Rupert Winston is desperate. He closes up the gymnasium, goes home, and waits to be awakened with the news of Virdon's death.

"So who, you may ask, killed Rupert Winston?"

Doddsworth shook his head. "Irony of ironies, it was Jesse Virdon."

That announcement produced an uproar entirely out of place in a church. The Reverend Kimble strode out in front of the pulpit and held up his arms for quiet. Even so, it was some time before Doddsworth was able to resume.

"Yes," he told the congregation. "You heard me right. Rupert Winston's killer was Jesse Virdon. From the tenor of Mr. Winston's questions earlier in the day, Virdon realized the director had his measure.

"Jesse Virdon had access to poison—soon we shall learn from where. He had the curare that killed Dorrie Taggart, and also the cyanide that would kill Rupert Winston.

"Mr. Winston took a variety of medications. He had one of those weekly pillboxes with a compartment for each day. He carried it in his briefcase. Had it with him during each rehearsal. While Jesse Virdon was working on the set.

"What could be better? The daily pillbox told Jesse Virdon exactly what pills Rupert Winston would be taking, and when. Jesse Virdon had only to remove one and replace it with a similar-looking capsule containing cyanide. Rupert Winston, gulping down four or five pills at a time, would scarcely be likely to detect the substitution. Even less so, if he was slightly tipsy. So Jesse Virdon cleverly chose the night of the Christmas pageant. Rupert Winston was sure to be celebrating, and would never notice.

"He didn't.

"And he died.

"Ironically, by then Jesse Virdon was also dead."

Doddsworth motioned to the casket. "And so we must now lay Dorrie Taggart to rest. I regret that I cannot bring her killer to justice. Someone else has done that for me. But at least it is done: Jesse Virdon has died for his crime. May Dorrie now rest in peace."

With a tear trickling down his cheek, Jonathon Doddsworth said, "I am sorry, Horace. I am truly sorry."

Horace Taggart rose from his seat by the casket. His face was wet with tears. He went up to the Scotland Yard inspector, and the two men embraced.

Mindy Taggart hovered, watching her husband and her former lover. She made no attempt to join in. But beneath the sadness, her face registered enormous relief. She waited there to hug her husband when he was done.

As Horace Taggart turned back to embrace his wife, Maxine Doddsworth hurled herself, sobbing, into her father's arms. He held her close, patted her head. She snuggled on his shoulder, then turned, reached out an arm to her mother.

Pamela Doddsworth choked back a sob. She rose slowly from her seat, her mouth open, her eyes wide, a mass of conflicting emotions. Tears streaming, she stretched out her arms to her daughter.

Maxine grabbed her mother, hugged her.

Doddsworth drew mother and daughter in, held them close.

And as they embraced, Mindy Taggart pulled her husband away, away to the casket, away to Dorrie, their Dorrie, where they belonged.

Leaving the Doddsworths alone, hugging each other, in front of the whole town.

In the back of the church Cora Felton smiled a sad, wry smile.

Aaron Grant leaned across Sherry to whisper, "Brilliant. Absolutely brilliant."

"Yes," Cora agreed. She lowered her voice confidentially.

"And it was all a pack of lies."

52

"What are we doing in the stable?" Aaron Grant asked.

Aaron, Sherry, and Cora were sitting in straw. Across the green from the stable, Rick Reed was conducting interviews with the people streaming out of the church. At the moment he was filming Jonathon Doddsworth, who stood on the church steps with his arms around his ex-wife and daughter.

"It seemed appropriate," Cora said. "And we can grab a few moments alone."

"Great. We're alone. I'm going nuts here. What was that about a pack of lies?"

"This is not for publication."

Aaron threw up his hands. "Everything you give me these days isn't for publication. Some journalist I am."

"It's not for Becky, either," Sherry said. "Just for you."

"You held out on your own attorney?"

"The case is over," Cora said. "Becky's not Sherry's lawyer anymore."

"Yeah, yeah, fine, so I won't tell Becky," Aaron said impatiently. "Come on, what's the scoop? You said Doddsworth's denouement wasn't true."

"Oh, no," Cora said. "I don't mean the whole thing wasn't true. Just a few small details."

"Such as?"

"Jesse Virdon didn't have the hots for the actresses. Jesse Virdon didn't poison Rupert Winston. Jesse Virdon didn't murder Dorrie Taggart. Jesse Virdon didn't drop a sandbag on Becky Baldwin."

" 'A few small *details*'? " Aaron said incredulously.

"Well, he couldn't get *everything* right," Cora said complacently. "The important thing was closure, bringing the Taggarts some peace."

"By lying, concealing facts, and letting a murderer go free?"

"No one went free, Aaron. Like I say, it's only the details that were wrong."

"And just exactly what was *right*?"

"Actually, not much. Wanna know what really happened?"

"You mean the part I can't print?"

Sherry snuggled up against him. "Trust me, Aaron, you won't want to."

"Hey! Are you trying to influence a member of the press?"

Cora shook her head. "Look, Aaron, you're basically a nice guy. Here's what really happened. On the day of Dorrie's murder, Alfred Adams was in the gym doing tech. He got caught up in what he was doing and lost track of time. Rupert pointed out that he was late and drove him into town. Alfred changed into his Joseph costume, went out and took his place in the crèche. An hour later he was relieved, went back to the gym, and resumed hanging lights.

"The Joseph who relieved him was Rupert Winston, disguised in a beard and cloak."

"Wait a minute! Wait a minute!" Aaron protested. "Rupert Winston didn't relieve Alfred. Lance Ridgewood did."

"That's what everyone assumed. They were so positive that no one ever questioned it."

"No one ever questioned it because it's true. Lance Ridgewood *says* he did. Or are you claiming *he* was in on this?"

"Not at all. Lance Ridgewood is telling the simple truth as he knows it. So is Alfred Adams."

"Then where does Rupert Winston come in?"

"Between the two. Rupert relieves Alfred and plays Joseph until he is relieved by Lance. Fifteen minutes before that happens, Maxine Doddsworth is relieved by Dorrie Taggart. Rupert Winston waits until the very last moment. Just before Lance arrives, Rupert Winston injects a hypodermic of curare into Dorrie's neck. He drops the poison dart in her clothing, to make it seem that was the weapon. But in point of fact, the amount of curare she could have received from such a dart probably would not have been enough to kill. But that's not a problem with a hypodermic. Rupert easily injects a lethal dose.

"Dorrie slumps against him, dead. He holds her up until Lance arrives. Rupert props her up against Lance and slips out without Lance realizing anything is wrong.

"Rupert's already hidden the poem and the blowgun in the church. He takes off his costume, leaves it hanging in the town hall. He returns to the gym, and promptly proceeds to get on Alfred Adams's case about the lights."

"Wait a minute. Time out. There's the flaw in your whole theory. *Alfred Adams* played Joseph. *Alfred Adams* went back to the theater then."

"Oh, but he didn't." Cora smiled. "And it's interesting that you say *time out.* Because that's exactly what happened."

Aaron frowned. "What do you mean?"

"When questioned about that morning, Alfred gets confused about time. 'Time,' he says, 'absolutely flew.' Well, it certainly did. Rupert planned it that way. All he had to do was assign Alfred something messy where the boy had to remove his watch. Cleaning paintbrushes, for instance. Rupert took his watch and set it an hour ahead. Then he got Alfred engrossed in some project so the boy wouldn't notice the time. At the right moment, Rupert calls Alfred's attention to the fact that he's late. Alfred is amazed the time passed so quickly, but he looks at his watch and sees that it's true. Rupert whisks him outside and drives him to town hall. Alfred Adams goes in, changes into his Joseph costume. As far as he's concerned, it's ten-fifteen. It's actually *nine*-fifteen. At *ten*-fifteen, Rupert Winston relieves Alfred at the crèche and takes his shift. Alfred returns to the high school and resumes working tech.

"When Rupert is finished, at eleven-fifteen, he returns to the high school and uses some other subterfuge to reset Alfred's watch. Alfred may be somewhat disoriented, and slightly confused as to the time, but he'll be willing to swear he played Joseph in this crèche from ten to eleven."

"I don't understand," Aaron said. "Wasn't someone scheduled to play Joseph from nine to ten?"

"Sure. Jesse Virdon."

Aaron's mouth fell open. "Oh, for goodness' sakes."

Cora nodded. "Yes. *That's* why Jesse Virdon was killed. Not for trying to drop a sandbag on Becky or havin' the hots for high school girls. No, Jesse was killed for something he *didn't* do. Which was play Joseph from nine to ten. Because Rupert called him the night before and told him he'd been rescheduled. To make room for Alfred Adams.

"Ordinarily, that wouldn't have been a problem. The nine-to-ten time slot had nothing to do with Dorrie's murder, was totally irrelevant, who could possibly care?"

Cora shrugged. "Who else but plodding Inspector Doddsworth, an inexorable force painstakingly sifting every tiny clue. He shows up at rehearsal, demands a copy of the crèche schedule. Rupert has to give him one. On that schedule, from nine-fifteen to ten-fifteen, is the name Jesse Virdon. Jonathon Doddsworth will question Jesse Virdon about playing Joseph, and Virdon will say he wasn't there."

"So Jesse Virdon has to go," Aaron concluded grimly.

"Bingo. That's the only part of Doddsworth's fairy tale that was true. Rupert *did* kill Jesse. Though not at all for the reason Doddsworth gave."

"So who wrote the puzzle poems?"

"Which puzzle poems? The first two Rupert Winston wrote. With Dorrie's help. Rupert told her it was a game. An elaborate practical joke on Maxine. The idea was to send a bunch of letters and make it look like Maxine, then watch her try to deny it. So when Rupert told her to, Dorrie hid the red envelopes in Maxine's room. She even installed the acrostic program on Maxine's computer.

"She also planted the first two puzzle poems. The first one she snuck up the back stairs and substituted for the partridge while the actors were all out in the gym. The second she pinned to Becky's costume when no one was in the girls' dressing room.

"The third letter was Dorrie's idea, though Rupert Winston isn't thrilled—the eating-for-two bit isn't really appropriate—not if the victim's supposed to be Becky Baldwin. But Dorrie thinks it's hysterically funny. Of course, she has no idea it matters. And, she doesn't know she's pregnant. So she thinks it's a gas.

"But that's just the first three letters. *Wrong girl* was the work of Johnny Doddsworth, trying to implicate Sherry and clear his daughter. He's found the envelopes in Maxine's room and he's going nuts. He uses a red envelope to send the letter.

"The last poem was back-at-you-in-spades. That's the puzzle I wrote. Or rather, Sherry and I wrote. I wrote the poem, she wrote the puzzle. Anyway, we did it.

"By this time, Rupert Winston has to be freaking out. I mean, first he tries to drop a sandbag on Becky to point out the fact she was the real target, and immediately Doddsworth finds the clue *Wrong girl.* Where the hell did that come from? It's helpful, but it's not his. Things are spinning out of control.

"And then the last puzzle poem arrives. I was watching Rupert's face when it appeared in the pear tree. And he was astounded. How can this be happening? He must have felt like his world was coming apart."

"So, who killed Rupert Winston?"

"He killed himself. See, he stocked up on poison when he was planning to kill Dorrie. He stole curare from a hospital in New York. He used a fake letterhead to order cyanide from a laboratory in California. He had it shipped overnight UPS to an electroplating company in the South Bronx, hung out in front, and signed for it when the truck arrived. He'd used the curare, but he still had the cyanide. He simply put some in his tea."

"Why? Why would he kill himself?"

"I went to him, told him I'd figured it out. Cracked the case. Told him I'd take everything I knew to Harper unless he'd cooperate."

"Cooperate how?"

"Surrender to the police. Turn himself in for the crimes."

"Confess?"

Cora shook her head. "No. Just the opposite. Stand mute, and make no attempt to prove his innocence."

"Why in the world would he do that?"

"We made a deal. He agreed to it in return for something he wanted."

"What was that?"

"His play. *The Twelve Days of Christmas.* I promised to put off going to the police until after the Christmas pageant. He really wanted to see it performed."

"And then he killed himself?"

"He knew the cyanide was quick and easy. Far better than being arrested, tried for murder, and executed, or jailed for life. Far better than living in shame."

"Shame? Are you saying *he* was involved with Dorrie Taggart? *That* was what those late rehearsals were all about? *Rupert* was the secret father? That's why he killed her? That's what he was trying to cover up?"

"Not at all."

Aaron groaned. "Then why? Why did he kill her?"

"Because she couldn't act."

Aaron blinked. "What?"

"She was a rotten actress. She was ruining his play. *The Seagull.* She had the juvenile lead. The part of Nina. It's a key role. She had to start off young and naive, then come back world-weary after having had an affair and giving birth to a child who died. She had the heart-wrenching lines, 'I'm a seagull. No, that's not it. I'm an actress.' And the poor girl couldn't act worth a damn."

"How do you know?"

Cora grimaced. "Everyone told me. And I didn't listen. What finally clued me in was when Alfred Adams said she was terrible."

Aaron frowned. "The techie? He doesn't strike me as a particularly astute drama critic."

"Yeah, that's what made the penny drop. It occurred to me if *Alfred* thought Dorrie was really bad, she must really stink.

"Then there was Rupert himself. He kept going on about what a blow it was to lose Dorrie. How it crippled his beloved play. Why? *Because the exact opposite was true.*"

"He killed Dorrie over her acting?"

"In his mind he had no choice. He was brought in to take over the drama department. And he comes with the baggage of a Broadway background. People expect a lot of him because he's a pro.

"So, he's absolutely obsessed with his first impression. You saw how he was with the pageant. Well, the school play was a thousand times worse. He needs *The Seagull* to be the high school production to end all high school productions. And here's this klutzy young actress playing the romantic lead."

"Why didn't he replace her?"

"Dorrie's parents contribute huge amounts to Bakerhaven High. You don't go bouncin' their brat out of the school play."

"And Rupert really killed himself?"

"Yep. Better than going to jail, and having people know he was so vain, self-centered, and insecure that he would kill rather than put on a bad show."

"But no one knows that now."

"Yes." Cora smiled. "But he didn't know what Doddsworth was going to say at Dorrie's funeral."

"How did Doddsworth ever come up with such an outlandish story?"

"I made it up."

"What?!"

"I told him what to say. He said it."

"But it's a lie."

"So what? It's Christmas. We're used to holiday lies. What's the first thing we teach our kids? Santa Claus. Flying reindeer. Elves."

"It's a little different."

"Not much. Santa Claus is a harmless pleasantry that lets kids get presents. Figure this story is my Christmas present to Bakerhaven. It's what people needed to hear, and what they needed to do. Jonathon Doddsworth needs to be a hero in his daughter's eyes. And his ex-wife's. The Taggarts need to grieve for Dorrie and build a theater in her honor. They can't do that if people know why she really died."

"But the truth—"

"The truth is there's no such thing as Santa Claus. You wanna drop by some nursery school and tell the kids the truth? It's what a responsible journalist would do." Cora sighed. "In a perfect world, Dorrie wouldn't have been in the play. Or Rupert Winston wouldn't have been hired to direct her. But we don't live in a perfect world. We've got to work with what we've got."

Aaron got to his feet. "Well, thanks a bunch. What the hell do I do now? Anything true I can't use. Anything I can use is a lie."

"Would you rather she hadn't told you?" Sherry asked.

"And *you* get to say things like *that.*" Aaron shook his head. "I'm gonna go talk to people who don't *know* anything. Maybe I can get a story out of *them.*"

Aaron jumped down from the stable and hurried off toward the church, where Doddsworth was still being interviewed.

"See?" Cora said to Sherry. "Men just don't like honest women."

"Yeah," Sherry said. "I notice, Miss Honest Woman, that you didn't happen to mention the little matter of Dorrie's paternity."

"Aaron had a lot to take in. No need to bog him down with too many details."

"You don't intend to tell him, do you? And you don't want me to tell him, either."

"Trust me, Sherry, keeping secrets from a man is a very important marital skill. You could use the practice."

"Aunt Cora—"

Sherry broke off at the sight of Harvey Beerbaum trudging through the snow. "Cora!" Harvey called. "Cora! Come on. We need you."

"Me? What for?"

"We're going caroling. The lords a-leaping, the maids a-milking, and anyone else we can get."

"Now?"

"Sure, now. We need to put these things behind us. Like it was any other Christmas. Caroling is just the ticket."

"Harvey, I can't sing."

"It doesn't matter. Just mouth the words. Even if you don't sing a note, we can use your moral support."

"I see." Cora looked over to the road, where the carolers were assembling, bundled in bright coats and scarves and mittens. Several of the Bakerhaven selectmen were among them. "I don't suppose this Christmas fervor has anything to do with the fact the TV people are still filming interviews?"

"Well," Harvey said. "The selectmen felt it would be nice if any news report painted a picture of a plucky town carrying on in the face of adversity. And our carolers are more apt to rate coverage if you're one of them."

"Doddsworth seems to have the news crews pretty well occupied."

"Well, sure. He's a hero. He cracked the case. And he's a human-interest story to boot, reuniting with his wife and daughter. They were even talking like they might go back to England with him."

"You don't say? Well, it's gonna be *mighty* tough competing with *that.*"

Harvey, missing the irony, said, "Yes, it is. Will you come?"

"Duty calls." Cora smiled at Sherry, hopped down from the stable, and set off across the village green, chatting with Harvey Beerbaum. They reached the road and joined the carolers, a hardy, ragtag band led by Mr. Hodges, the music teacher, who was busy instructing them on what to sing. Cora, who had no intention of singing a note, immediately tuned out and looked over at the church, where Jonathon Doddsworth was still holding forth. Pamela and Maxine were looking on, as were Aaron Grant, Becky Baldwin, Chief Harper, Rick Reed and the Channel 8 News team, and about half of Bakerhaven.

The Taggarts were long gone, but not, according to Harvey, before Horace Taggart had made a brief statement, thanking Doddsworth for finding Dorrie's killer.

Cora smiled at the thought.

A nudge in the ribs from Harvey finally brought her back to the present. Mr. Hodges was holding up his hands and humming a starting note. The note meant nothing to her, but Cora snapped to attention just as the carolers launched into "Away in a Manger." It occurred to her the title was the only part of the song she actually knew. It also occurred to her that "Away in a Manger" was a somewhat insensitive choice of song, under the circumstances.

Cora looked over at the crèche.

Sherry sat in the stable, all alone, the last surviving Virgin Mary. Cleared of a murder charge. Freed from her legal representation. Worrying, no doubt, about keeping the truth from her boyfriend. More than likely, Cora figured, she'd tell Aaron. And he'd wind up keeping the secret. Just for her.

Ah, young love. Cora remembered it well.

She remembered all of them well.

The carolers swung around, headed for the church. As the selectmen had hoped, they seemed to be attracting the attention of the TV people.

Cora joined in with great gusto, bluffing the song, just as she always bluffed her puzzle-making expertise. As the cameras rolled, she smiled her trademark Puzzle Lady smile and marched along in the snow, heartily mouthing the words.